"If
wil

"Abyss: The primeval chaos. The bottom-less pit; hell. An unfathomable or immea-surable depth or void."
—*The American Heritage Dictionary*

You're holding in your hands one of the first in a new line of books of dark fiction called Abyss. Abyss is horror unlike any-thing you've ever read before. It's not about haunted houses or evil children or ancient Indian burial grounds. We've all read those books, and we all know their plots by heart.

Abyss is for the seeker of truth, no matter how disturbing or twisted it may be. It's about people, and the darkness we all carry within us. Abyss is the new horror from the dark frontier. And in that place, where we come face-to-face with terror, what we find is ourselves. The darkness illuminates us, revealing our flaws, our se-cret fears, our desires and ambitions long-ing to break free. And we never see our-selves or our world in the same way again.

Tunnelvision

R. PATRICK GATES

A DELL BOOK

Published by
Dell Publishing
a division of
Bantam Doubleday Dell Publishing Group, Inc.
666 Fifth Avenue
New York, New York 10103

ISBN: 0-440-21090-9

Printed in the United States of America

Published simultaneously in Canada

November 1991

10 9 8 7 6 5 4 3 2 1

RAD

This book is dedicated to the grandparents,
Rose and Butch, and Toni and George.
Without them,
this book would not have been done on time.

Acknowledgments and gratitude are due Lieutenant Carbone of the Fitchburg Police Department's detective squad for his straightforward answers to my questions.

Thanks are also due an old friend, John Gianetti, director of the Fitchburg/Leominster Cable Access Television Station, for sharing his knowledge of video equipment.

One fine day in the middle of the night,
Two dead boys got up to fight.
Back to back they faced each other,
Drew their swords and shot each other.
A deaf policeman heard the noise,
And came and killed the two dead boys.
                    —Children's jump rope ditty

There is nothing wrong with your television set. Do not attempt to adjust the picture. We are controlling transmission. . . .

—*The Outer Limits*

WELCOME TO TUNNELVISION!

25 Cable Channels for Your Viewing Pleasure

This is your program guide. All programs are on the air at all times.

Channel 1
This Is Tunnelvision!   *Rappin' with Ivy D.*
Here's Ivy!   *Meet the Gages*
The Brother John Show
. . . .

Channel 2
Graveyard Shift
Barbara & Ivy
. . . .

Channel 3
Weather Report   *The Wilbur Clayton
O! Henry!   Show*
Book Nook   *Bill Gage—K mart Cop*
. . . .

Channel 4
The Return of Dr. Peabody
Toilet Training
Beth Shell—Student Nurse
. . . .

Channel 5
Afterschool Special: The Rescue
. . . .

Channel 6
Dragnet
Bill Gage—Special Investigator
Smokin' in the Boys' Room
America's Most Wanted
The Real James Bond
. . . .

Channel 7
This Is Tunnelvision!—II
007 in "The Trash Bag Affair"
Point Counter Point
. . . .

Channel 8
  Jesus Loves Me
  This Is Tunnelvision!—III
  Police Squad
  Face the Facts
. . . .
Channel 9
  Mr. Ed
  Scenes from a Marriage
  Video Valhalla
  Dream TV
. . . .
Channel 10
  Saturday Afternoon Movie: Against All Odds
. . . .
Channel 11
  Smokin' in the Boys' Room—II
  Vicki Dominatrix
  Real People
  To Catch a Thief
. . . .
Channel 12
  Beth Likes Wilbur
  Bond, James Bond
  The Wilbur Relief Fund
  Scenes from a Marriage—II
. . . .
Channel 13
  Copycat
  Beth Shell—Alias Sadie Hawkins
. . . .
Channel 14
  The Love Connection
  Things Go Better with Coke
  Emergency Broadcast System (Warning!)
. . . .
Channel 15
  Operation Wilbur—Part 1
. . . .
Channel 16
  To Catch a Spy
  The Return of Slice Sanchez
  Off the Air
  The Last Stroke
. . . .

CONTENTS

Channel 17
    Bill Gage—Video Detective
    When Bad Things Happen to Good People . . . .

Channel 18
    Meet the Smiths
    Sonny Ray's Not-so-lucky Day . . . .

Channel 19
    The Best-Laid Plans . . .
    Want Some Candy?
    Break Time
    Leave It to Ivy . . . .

Channel 20
    This Is Tunnelvision!—IV
    Wilbur & Beth . . . .

Channel 21
    Dialing for Death   *The Bogeyman*
    Sassy Sarah   *Damnation Chorus*
    Live Miracles!   *72 Hours* . . . .

Channel 22
    Operation Wilbur—Part 2 . . . .

Channel 23
    Waiting for Sassy   *Wilbur's Hobby*
    To Catch a Killer   *Ivy to the Rescue*
    The Invaders   *Bill Gage—Avenger* . . . . .

Channel 24
    To Tell the Truth   *Complications*
    *Operation Wilbur—   *True Confessions*
    Part 3*   *Ivy's Revenge*
    Obsession!
    A Second Chance at Love . . . .

Channel 25
    *Mini-series: This Is Tunnelvision!—V—The Final
    Chapter*
         . . . .
                              Sign-off

CHANNEL 1

This Is Tunnelvision!
Here's Ivy!
The Brother John Show
Rappin' with Ivy D.
Meet the Gages

 The empty airwaves of the mind.
Channels he knows well.
Deep, dark waves that catch the unwary, or the fearful, the abused, the unbalanced, and drag them down. The first signal feels like succor, but it soon turns rancid. Like falling into an open cesspool and drowning with his mouth open. There is nothing to hold on to—nothing to pull him out of the oily black-and-white pictures that play without commercials, bubbling away on the TV screen deep inside his brain. There is no time to scream.

He stands in total darkness. Even his hands waving in front of him like insect antennae are invisible to his eyes. There is only darkness and the sound of his own frightened breathing.
The air is cold. It feels like the grave: dank, dark,

and heavy with potential rot. He tries to move and can't. His heart is pounding in his ears like a locomotive.

Far off in the darkness to both sides there are dual explosions of light widening, then narrowing. He hears the sound of two doors opening on squeaky hinges like bones creaking, then closing with metallic clicks that echo rhythmically.

The echoes turn into footsteps. From down each corridor the footsteps slice through the darkness. They become louder and louder. They start out slowly, as if the walkers are unsure of their footing in the dark, but gradually they quicken. They become heavy, lumbering steps as though a great deal of exertion is going into the picking up and putting down of each foot. They hit the concrete floor like minor explosions.

He begins to sweat. He tries to shrink back but he is already as close to the wall as he can get. There is no room left. There is nowhere to go.

The footsteps grow louder.

His breath is short. There doesn't seem to be enough air anymore. The minor explosions of the footsteps become major ones. They move the air and bounce it off his eardrums until they ache. He tries to scream to drown out the noise, but there is no air left in his lungs to push past his vocal cords and make them vibrate with the mounting terror he feels.

The footsteps become monstrous. They shake the walls, his very bones.

Dual waves of air flow toward him as whoever, or whatever, approaches down the corridors displaces *it and pushes it on until it washes over him in slimy waves, like a burp that rises uncontrollably through his chest and rushes into his mouth with a sour, vomit taste. The air is sweaty and salty. Overhead a light grows around him, gray and flickering, video light, enclosing him in its circle of illumination. . . .*

SLOW MOTION: THE—BLINKING—OF—HIS—EYES—TAKES—FOREVER—AND—SOUNDS—LIKE—RUSTY—MACHINERY—YAWNING—

HIS—BREATHING—SOUNDS—LIKE—A—DYING—VACUUM—CLEANER—

FROM—THE—EDGE—OF—THE—CONE—OF—LIGHT—LIKE—A—SWIMMER—JUST—PIERCING—THE—WATER—ON—A—DIVE—FINGERTIPS—EMERGE—FROM—THE—DARKNESS—BEYOND—IN—PERFECT—SYMMETRY—

LIGHT—PARTICLES—SPINNING—AROUND—THE—INTRUSIONS—THE—REST—OF—THE—HANDS—APPEAR—

HE—TRIES—TO—CLOSE—HIS—EYES—BUT—THE—RUSTY—MACHINERY—ONLY—HUMS—NOW—LIKE—AN—ELECTRIC—DRILL—CAUGHT—IN—A—MESH—OF—METAL—

LIKE—SYNCHRONIZED—SWIMMERS—RISING—OUT—OF—A—POOL—THE—HANDS—ARE—FOLLOWED—BY—WRISTS—THEN—ARMS—

A—LEG—APPEARS—IN—PERFECT—HARMONY—FROM—EACH—CORRIDOR—FOLLOWED—BY—A—PAIR—OF—BODIES—HEAV-

ING—AND—SPLATTERED—WITH—DARK—
SPOTS—

FAST FORWARD: *And his breath is back in a
rush like getting the wind knocked out of him and
having it return in a flood as the loudest scream ever
to have passed his lips begins to fill his throat and
the rest of the two bodies lunge from the darkness
with hands reaching to throttle him and legs pumping and chests rising and falling and rising and
fallingand risingand fallingandrisingandfall-
ingandrisingandfallingand—*

SLOW MOTION: UNDER—HEADLESS—
SHOULDERS—

THEY—HAVE—NO—HEADS—

THE—TWO—FIGURES—ARE—HEADLESS—
THE—NECKS—ARE—BLOODY—STUMPS—
LIKE—YOUNG—MAPLE—TREES—FELLED—
IN—THE—PRIME—OF—THEIR—SAP—PRO-
DUCING—SEASON—

A—MACABRE—WATER—FOUNTAIN—OF—
RED—BUBBLES—FROM—SHARDS—OF—
BONE—AND—VEINS—SPILLING—OVER—
THE—FLESH—TORN—RIM—OF—EACH—
NECK—IN—EXACTLY—THE—SAME—
AMOUNTS—AND—CONTORTIONS—OF—
DRIPS—UNTIL—

FAST FORWARD: *The blind searching hands
find his neck and clamp shut like vises and the roar
of the heartbeat train is deafening now and his face
is red from the silent scream that builds and builds
and builds and builds—*

Until he wakens, clutching the covers in his fists,
his mouth gaping in mute terror.

* * *

"Lamzy, get away from that railing and come in here and help me."

The small, dark-skinned boy ignored his mother. He always ignored her when she called him "Lamzy." That was a sissy's name, a baby name from a dumb song she used to sing to him when he was little. *"And little lambsy'd Ivy,"* was all he could remember or understand of the words and they made no sense. His name was Ivy, but he wished he had a cool nickname like Fresh Prince, or Ice T, or M. C. Hammer, or some of the other rappers he liked to watch on MTV. His mother, though, was stuck in the past, still calling him baby names and treating him as if he was a kid. He was *eleven years old,* for crying out loud!

There was another reason why Ivy wasn't quick to move away from the third-floor porch railing. He was listening to an argument in the house next door. The voices, two of them, were loud, but distorted by emotion and the house's walls until he could understand only every third or fourth word. Even so, he was sure that one of the voices was on a television talk show turned up louder than any normal TV should be.

Ivy giggled. The guy was arguing with a TV set? He listened, and giggled some more.

"And five, four, three, two, one! You're on!"
"Good morning, ladies and gentlemen, and welcome to the start of our broadcast day. You are watching *Tunnelvision!"*
Channel change.

"What are you doin', dipshit?"

"Washin' tunnelvision, Mummy."

"It's television, stupid, and didn't I tell you never to call me Mummy?"

Slap!

Canned laughter.

"Where'd you get that tunnelvision crap, anyway?"

"Grandma tol' me."

More laughter.

"Figures. Well, forget it. And forget her—she's dead."

"No she's not, Mummy, she's onna tunnelvision."

Slap!

"I said, '*NEVER CALL ME MOTHER!*'"

More slapping.

Laughter peaks.

Cue chuckle-tongued announcer.

We'll be right back after a word from these friendly folks. . . ."

Rosie stands behind the counter. A man and a woman come in and sit on the stools. Their heads roll off their shoulders onto the countertop, spilling coffee and blood everywhere.

"Quick, Rosie! Get a towel!" the heads shout as they roll down the counter.

"Just any paper towel? Who said two heads are better than one?" Rosie quips. She picks up the woman's head and balances it on a paper towel stretched taut between her hands.

"Here's your average paper towel." Blood soaks the towel until it tears. The woman's face wears a look of surprise and distress as her head falls through the bloody rip in the towel and into the sink.

"Now, here's *Bounty,*" Rosie says, putting the man's head on a Bounty towel. The blood soaks it but the towel doesn't tear.

"Wow! Rosie, Bounty *is* better!" the man's head says.

Rosie puts the head back on the counter and leans over to look the man in the eye. "Next time, get a*head* and get *Bounty—the quicker picker-upper!*"

Channel change.

Static.

Monitor on.

Residue of the dream is slick and hot in his mind. It boils behind his eyeballs and fries his brain. The banshee wail of an electric guitar makes the very air vibrate like a living thing.

The laughter of ghosts is never far off.

He can feel the heartbeat of the earth through the floor.

The dream appears on the TV.

Heart—

Smoky black-and-white terror.

Beat—

Only now he's sure it isn't a dream.

Heart—

It's a prophecy.

Beat—

"What did you do?" he screams at Jesus, but the Son of God isn't paying attention.

Brother John, dressed in the all-black suit that gave him his nickname, hosts his own talk show. Fat and bald, he sits in the beanbag chair under the fluorescent black light glow of Hendrix burning his guitar. John's been dead for seven years but doesn't look a day older than the day he died, the day Jesus slit his throat in the bathroom. The slit is still there, blue under the chalk-white skin and dry as an old raisin.

"I'll tell ya what He did, Wilbur," John says, but it's the slit in his neck that moves like a mouth, the ragged edges of the gash working like lips to form the words. "He did to them what they were going to do to you." His voice is watery with bodily fluids and almost gurgles.

"Satan is a many-limbed beast and must be destroyed limb by limb!" Grandma pipes up from her room inside Wilbur's head. She has her TV on, praying to it as always.

"Now, all the others who failed Jesus must pay for their sins," she says, her voice filled with religious fervor. Her head sways on her shoulders in front of the TV screen. "The agents of Satan must be killed head by head, limb by limb."

Jesus is on the TV. He turns up the volume. The Dead are on the stereo. Wilbur's head is full of voices. The Son of God doing a computer commercial. Jerry Garcia singing off key. Brother John doing a beer commercial. (*"Tastes great!"* he dribbles out of his neck wound.) Grandma singing a hymn.

The channel changes and Jesus is a Barbie doll riding a pony. The doll's mouth opens. Like a quiet knife, His flat voice slices through the din, parting the noise as Moses did the Red Sea. *"Vengeance is mine, saith the Lord!"*

On his talk show, Brother John's Cheshire-cat smile continues, but his image crumbles around it.

"What do you mean?" Wilbur asks Jesus, but another commercial is on. "They can't come back, can they?" he implores a woman mooning over her favorite brand of tampon.

She won't answer. Garcia's guitar boogies up and down a scale. The black-light posters adorning the walls shimmer, sending needles of color slicing through his eyes at the slightest movement of his head.

"The others must pay. The special grown-ups."

"No," Wilbur pleads.

"Give yourself over to Jesus, son," Grandma implores from her room. "The Lord's will be done." She's sitting with her hands against the TV screen so she can feel the power of Jesus surging through the greasy televangelist and his wife, who implore the faithful to heed God's word and send money.

"You gotta trust in God, son," Gram says. "Doubt Him and bring pain and suffering upon yourself. Give Jesus whatever He requires, do what He commands, and He shall deliver you."

He listens to Gram. Didn't she rescue him? Didn't she teach him all about Jesus? And when they told him she died and was gone forever, didn't she prove them wrong by moving into his head with her TV set?

"Trust in Jesus," Gram says, her face momentarily on the living-room TV, smiling out from the cover of a cereal box.

* * *

"Lamzy . . . LAMzy . . . LAMZY!" Exasperated sigh. "Ivy?"

"Yeah?" Ivy answered finally, moving away from the railing. The house next door was quieter now anyway. His mother pushed open the screen door and held out a five-dollar bill to him. "There's a small grocery store down at the corner. If you won't help me in here you can make yourself useful and go get me a couple packs of cigarettes."

"Can I get something?" Ivy asked, grabbing the five-dollar bill.

"Yeah, okay," his mother replied reluctantly. "You can spend fifty cents. That's it. Got it? I'm going to count the change when you get back."

"Yep," Ivy answered and was off down the stairs.

"Remember, get me Merit one hundreds," she called through the screen door after him, but Ivy didn't acknowledge. He knew what brand of low-tar and nicotine butts she smoked, as if the low tar would make a difference since she chain-smoked. Hadn't he been running to the nearest store for her cancer sticks ever since his father had died and she'd started smoking?

And her threat to count the change! He hated it when she said stuff like that, showing how little trust she really had in him. He also hated it when she treated him like a dumb kid. Someday he'd love to show her just how smart he was; how he'd taught himself algebra from an old high school textbook he'd found in the cellar of the house they'd just moved from. He'd also found a book on German and had been well on the way to mastering it before Jeff Brink, the neighborhood bully, saw him reading it and tore it up, making him eat some of the pages and calling him a damn nigger Nazi all the while.

Ivy grimaced for a moment at the memory, but quickly smiled again—a hard cruel smile for such a young face. He'd taken care of Jeff Brink, hadn't he? Shaved the back-wheel brake pads off his ten-speed bike so that when Brink reached the bottom of the steep hill he lived on (and always tore down at full speed), only the front brakes worked and he flipped the bike over, sailing head over heels into the middle of Route 12, breaking his left arm and collarbone. Bully Brink had just missed getting squished by a Mack truck, too, which really had an effect on Ivy.

While carrying out his revenge, Ivy had been vaguely aware of, but had never fully acknowledged, the possibility that he might seriously hurt Jeff Brink. When he almost *killed* him, Ivy was at first shaken, but as time went on, he began to relish the memory of his revenge. Eventually, he got to a point where he actually envisioned what would have happened if Brink *had* been killed and came to the conclusion that he would've gotten away with it. He also tried to tell himself that murdering Brink wouldn't have bothered him, but he remained secretly glad that he'd been lucky.

Yeah, he thought, mentally returning to the subject, *I'd love to show Mom I'm not stupid.*

He sighed. It would be no use, he knew. No one would ever believe he was so smart. That had been brutally proven to him in the first grade.

His father, Otis Delacroix, a big, burly, black master sergeant in the army, was still alive then. Ivy, who inherited his father's strong African features and his mother's Caucasian reddish-brown hair, was what his mother called an "army brat." By the time he was old enough to go to school, he'd lived in three different states, all of them in the South. The year he became six, and eligible to attend school, they were living in their fourth home at Fort Devens in Massachusetts. The second week of school—a fun and exciting place he'd thought at first—all first-graders were given a long multiple-choice test where they had to color the answers in little circles on an answer sheet.

Ivy found the test to be no challenge at all and quickly went through it. The next day Ivy discovered what most black people eventually learn: There's just as much racism in the so-called liberal North as in the rebel South.

He was called out of class to a small office where Dr. Peabody, the man who'd administered the test, was waiting for him. The doctor didn't beat around the bush. He immediately began shouting at poor little Ivy, accusing him of guessing at the answers.

"I didn't!" Ivy answered truthfully. This angry, shouting man frightened him. Fright turned to terror when the man grabbed him roughly by the shoulders and shook him.

"Don't lie to me!" the man snarled.

Ivy tried to pull away, as much from the man's reeking tobacco breath as from his reeking hatred.

"Nobody's ever scored this high before. You'd have to be a genius, which you are not, *boy*. Now you tell me or I'll slap it out of you. You guessed, didn't you?"

"No!" Ivy sobbed, tears spilling from his eyes.

The man slapped him. Hard. "Yes, you did, boy. Either you got lucky and guessed all those questions right or you cheated. Now which is it? Did you guess, or are you a cheater?"

"No! I didn't cheat!" Ivy cried.

Dr. Peabody let go of his arm. He seemed suddenly much calmer. "Then you guessed at the answers. It's one or the other."

"No, I didn't!" Ivy repeated, backing away and wiping tears from the red slap mark on his cheek.

"Yes, you did," Dr. Peabody said, smiling, the hatred submerged, replaced by a smug, superior look with just a touch of pity. "It's all right. Admit it. I know the test was difficult. I'd have guessed, too. But don't worry, we won't make you take it over. My advice to you, young man, is not to mention a word of our talk or your deception because you'll only make things worse for yourself." Without waiting for a reply, Dr. Peabody escorted him to the door and sent him back to his class.

Ivy tried to tell his teacher the truth, but after Dr. Peabody came in and spoke with her it became apparent that she preferred to believe the esteemed Dr. Peabody rather than a six-year-old boy, and a black one at that. Ivy then resolved to tell his father what had happened. His father would believe him. Hadn't his father remarked often about how smart Ivy was?

When Ivy got home, he found the house full of his father's friends and other men in uniform. Several of them were attending to his mother, who was crying hysterically. Through a growing haze of pain and paranoia, he learned that his father had been killed only an hour before in a car accident on base. With the egocentric logic of all children, Ivy concluded that his father's death had been his fault because he had tried to tell his teacher the truth about the test. Ivy was so shaken by the day's events that he convinced himself that his father's death had been ordered by Dr. Peabody as a threat to Ivy and to destroy the only other person, his father, who knew how smart Ivy really was. Ivy decided to heed the warning that being smart and showing it was dangerous. He wanted to get Dr. Peabody for what he'd done, but he was just a little kid. He knew there was nothing he could do, *then.* If he didn't want to lose his mother, too, he knew he should play it stupid. From that day on, that's exactly what he did, kept his genius as a secret identity, like Clark Kent and Superman, biding his time until he was old enough to go and punch Dr. Peabody out.

On his way back from the store, munching a handful of Skittles, he noticed that the house next door was quiet now. As he started up the back stairs, he looked over the fence and through a window. He could just make out a dark figure kneeling in the flickering light of a television screen.

This guy argues with the TV, then he prays to it? Ivy wondered. Maybe this new neighborhood wasn't going to be so boring after all, he thought, taking the stairs two at a time to the third floor.

Bill Gage pulled the résumé and letter out of the drawer below the television where he kept his personal papers. He'd sent them to Chief George Albert of the Crocker Police Department, with whom he'd often worked amiably when he was still part of the state police special crimes unit. Of course, that all seemed a million years ago now.

He closed the drawer, stood, his knees popping, and caught his reflection in the heart-shaped mirror on the near wall. His short hair was salt-and-peppered on the sides, thinning and receding on top and in front. He didn't think he'd ever go completely bald up there, but his hairline was certainly going to be at low tide for the rest of his life. Except for his hair, he didn't look forty-eight. His face was still smooth, though not as hairless as it had been in his twenties and thirties. Back then he'd been able to go three days between shaves and barely show a hint of a beard. When he hit forty, though, more hormones must have kicked in, and now he had to shave every day or have a five-o'clock shadow on his chin, neck, and upper lip. His cheeks, always a healthy red, sprouted long curly hairs haphazardly that kept him from having something he'd always wanted—a full beard. The best he could do was a vandyke, which made his round face look gnomish.

He took the papers to the couch and sat next to Cindy, his wife. An avid sports fan, she was watching one of her beloved New England sports teams, the Boston Celtics, who were fifteen games ahead in first place at the end of November after an embarrassing previous season. Bill didn't mind watching the Celtics—loved to watch Larry Bird in action —but hated it when Cindy got baseball fever and began mooning over the hapless Red Sox, no matter how badly they played.

Of course, he could never say that to her without arousing her ire. She loved the Sox, the Celtics, the Bruins, and even the sorry Patriots, always had, and would hear no ill spoken against any of them. Bill liked sports, basketball in particular, but had grown up in the sticks of Pottsville, Pennsylvania, and could never understand the fanatical love/hate relationship New Englanders, especially in Maine and Massachusetts, had for the Boston Red Sox, and, to a lesser extent, the other teams as well. The Sox were surely one of the most accursed teams in the major leagues, repeatedly disappointing their fans at the brink of victory.

Bill smiled, shrugged, and turned his attention back to the letter and résumé. He read them over, as he had almost every night since he'd sent them a month ago. He'd still heard nothing. He knew there were probably no openings at this time, and that not getting an answer was no personal rejection, but it had taken him a long time to get to the point where he'd felt the need to go back to police work. Hearing nothing was hard.

He chastised himself for thinking it was going to be easy; just write a letter to an old friend and *presto!* You've got a badge again. Maybe he'd been out of it for too long. No matter how good he had been—and he knew cops who'd said he was the best investigator in New England, though he'd never have said it of himself—maybe he'd burned too many bridges.

"Why don't you just call him?" Cindy asked, never taking her eyes from the TV screen. She was mesmerized by a replay of a driving no-look-slam-dunk by Dee Brown. "He's supposed to be a friend, isn't he? Call him. It's better than sitting around every night wondering. At least you'll know."

Bill watched the replay for the third time, from the third different angle. "I don't know," he said quietly. "I'm sure if there were anything, or if he was interested, he'd have gotten in touch with me by now."

The truth was that Bill's pride wouldn't let him call. He'd had a hard enough time just writing the letter and résumé and summoning up enough humble pie to send it. He felt as if he was asking favors, begging hat in hand, something he thought he'd never do. George Albert and he *had* been pretty good friends, though their respective jobs had never let them spend too much time together.

Bill had gotten to know him soon after George got his gold badge, making detective, fifteen years ago. Fifteen long, dues-paying years for Bill. When they first met, Bill had been the big shot, the young, new head of the state police special crimes unit. He'd taken an immediate liking to the hardworking, analytical young cop he'd met while assisting the Crocker police with a missing child investigation.

Bill hadn't seen or spoken to George since 1981. Now the proverbial shoe was on the other foot. In direct contrast to Bill, George's life had been fruitful and successful. He was now Crocker police chief, married, and had a daughter. While Bill had been crawling through the depths of alcoholism, George had built a happy family and successful career. It wasn't fair, but then, life never was. At least never to Bill Gage, not until he'd met Cindy Bellamy, anyway.

"I still think you should call him," Cindy said, but was prevented from saying anything further by a shrill cry from upstairs.

"Mo-o-ommy!"

Cindy looked longingly at the television—the Celtics had just come from behind to tie the score—and reluctantly started to get off the couch.

"I'll go," Bill said, patting her leg and placing his papers on the coffee table in front of the couch.

"You sure?" she asked, already sinking back, eyes on Bird rearing up for a three-pointer.

"Yeah. It'll give me something to do."

By the time Bill got to the nursery, little Devin was already back to sleep. He often cried out like that in his sleep. Bill closed the window shade and stood by the side of the crib staring down at his sixteen-month-old son for several minutes.

Five years ago—hell, *three* years ago—Bill Gage would have thought it was impossible that he'd be married with twin stepdaughters and a son of his own. His life then was an overturned jigsaw puzzle and he'd felt like a blind man as far as being able to put the pieces back together. The thought that he would ever be a whole, sober, productive member of society again was a hope that he had given up on.

He'd come a long way since the dark days of alcoholism he'd sunk into. *(Sunk into, Bill?* he reprimanded himself. *How about more like* dived *into*, embraced, welcomed?)

He left the nursery and stopped outside the twins' room, peering in at them. As usual, Missy was sleeping upside down in bed, covers thrown onto the floor. She wore one of Bill's T-shirts, which made a perfect nightshirt for her. In the other twin bed, Sassy slept in the exact middle of the bed, the covers pulled up to the neck of her frilly pajamas so that only her head showed. Even in the hottest weather she had to wear pj's and be covered by at least a sheet. When Bill had asked her why once, she'd expressed, with some embarrassment, a vague belief that nobody (Bill read, *bogeyman*, though Sassy was trying to be too grown-up to say so) could get her while she slept that way.

Bill watched them sleep and reflected on how ironically misnamed the twins were. Sarah had been nicknamed Sassy but was the perfect little miss, while Melissa became Missy but was the sassiest of children, always talking back and as stubborn as all get-out. He felt as much love for them as if they were his own and worried a lot about whether he was a good father to them, or if they accepted him as their father. He wasn't even sure they should. Though their real father had been a royal loser, by Cindy's description, he was still their father. And though she had kicked him out before the girls were born, and Cindy had no idea where he was, he could still show up someday. What then?

Bill shook his head and backed away from the door. He was such a goddamned worrywart, always had been. *"That's your biggest problem,"* his father used to say. Thoughts of his father dragged up a batch of memories that he no longer wanted to deal with. He'd been dealing with them too long and too hard. *"Give yourself a break,"* he could almost hear

Cindy telling him, as she had so many times. He'd found it to be excellent advice. The past was past.

He went down the stairs, carefully avoiding the creaking steps in the old wood as best he could. A brass band going by wouldn't wake Devin, but a creak on the stairs could.

I guess that shows that he's got a keen sense of survival, Bill thought.

"Celts are up by nine!" Cindy said delightedly when he rejoined her on the couch. "Bird hit two three-pointers and Robert Parrish got fouled by that sissy Laimbeer on a slam dunk and made the free throw. Detroit just called a time-out."

While she went to get a diet soda, Bill picked up the résumé and letter again, reading over his job history for the umpteenth time. The date of his last job in governmental law enforcement, 1981, blared out at him.

"I wouldn't hire someone who hadn't worked for ten years, no matter how good they'd been," he muttered glumly. One side of him said to give it up. That part of his life was over, dead and buried, the past was past. He'd come such a long way, why go back? Because the other side was an empty spot that left him feeling unwhole, no matter how far he'd come since the dark days of a few years ago.

He'd tried it, but his well-paying job as chief of security for three K mart stores spread out from Worcester to Vermont couldn't fill the void that being a police detective had once filled, even though the latter had been a contributing factor to his breakdown and alcoholic nosedive.

"Some men drive; others are driven." Another

jewel from his dad. His dad had known about drive, all right, the darkest kind.

All right! Enough already, he told himself. *Get off the subject.*

"Would you just call?" Cindy said when she returned to the living room and saw him staring at the résumé and letter again, his face screwed up tighter than a childproof bottle cap.

"Yeah, yeah," Bill sighed, but put the papers back after a while and cozied with Cindy to watch the Celtics put the hated Detroit Pistons away.

CHANNEL 2

Graveyard Shift
Barbara & Ivy

 "Come on down!"
The voice is a tombstone echo of the announcer on *The Price Is Right*.
"Come on."

It wheedles and sharpens.

"It's so-o-o ni-i-i-c-ce down here."

Wilbur backs against the hard concrete wall, a cold sweat bubbling his forehead.

The sound of his heartbeat reverberates between the concrete floor and ceiling of the stairwell. It's cold enough to create clouds with his breath.

"Come on down! Catch the next train. It's so-o-o dark and n-n-i-i-i-c-ce. Come on." A tick begins beating in his left eyelid. He looks up quickly, thinking he hears footsteps. The stairwell is empty.

He knows where their voices are coming from. He knows because this is a dream that has a TV of its own in his head, and sometimes in dreams he knows everything.

Slowly, summoning every ounce of courage he has, he walks down the stairs to a large, gray metal door with a sign on it that warns: DANGER! TUNNEL UNSAFE! DO NOT USE!

"You're dead!" he whispers. In the darkness beyond the door, he wonders if anything is moving.

"Are we, Wilbur? Come down and see!"

Wilbur moves away from the door. A slow, shuffling sound that may or may not be footsteps comes from the other side.

"We can come up if you won't come down!"

"No!" Wilbur hisses through teeth clenched in terror. He backs away. Grabbing the stair railing, he climbs. Halfway up, he cannot resist the urge to look back.

The doorknob is turning—the door is opening—a foul green odor drifts from the darkness—

"Don't be afraid, honey," the voices call after him. *"It's only us."*

He tries to run, hurrying away from the voices whose words become laughter chasing him, but his feet are melting, sticking to the floor.

They are coming out of the round darkness now —he can hear them behind him—he can sense them reaching—can smell their fetid breath—

He wakes at the desk in the hospital security office. He stands and leans over the desk, taking deep breaths, trying not to hyperventilate from fear. The voices from the dream are gone, but the memory of them remains like an echo.

He's so frightened he wants to scream. The crevices are widening into cracks inside him, their sides slippery and steep and filling with darkness.

The digital clock on the desk flashes the time, 3:06 A.M. Halfway through the graveyard shift, but he doesn't care. When the dizziness of terror passes, he turns and faces the full-length mirror on the back of the office door. The Son of God wears the same security guard's uniform as Wilbur, but on Him it looks crisp and hard, always at attention. On Wilbur it hangs, wrinkled and sloppy.

"They're gone. Can't we let it be?" Wilbur asks Jesus and is surprised at how calm his voice sounds, not at all reflective of the well of anxiety within.

"You know what we have to do," Jesus says.

"But why?" Wilbur asks.

"Because Grandma said to."

Ivy was bored. Though he'd never admit it, he was even more bored than if it had been a school day. Normally at this time of year, with only a month left until Christmas vacation from school, he would have been looking happily toward a week off. Instead he was dreading it.

Tom Pell, his only friend, was way across town in the old neighborhood. Even if it were summertime and he had a bicycle, it would take him over an hour each way to get there and back. Bus fare was fifty cents each way, which was a dollar more than he usually had in his pockets. He could always ask his mother for it, and she'd probably give it to him, a few times, anyway, but first he'd have to listen to her whine about how hard she worked and how lousy the tips were and so on and so on. After a couple of days she'd get real stingy and more complaintive. Of course, she'd never mention the fifteen bucks a week and sometimes more that she spent on cigarettes and Sangria. Seeing Tom during Christmas vacation wasn't worth that kind of aggravation. They hadn't been *that* good friends.

Ivy got up from the cold concrete wall along the inside of the tenement's driveway and began tightrope walking on it. He walked to the end and jumped off, landing on an empty soda can, crushing it under his foot. He stooped, saw that it was a deposit can, and picked it up.

"One way to make some money I guess," he said aloud. He began walking up the street, searching the gutters and bushes along the sidewalk for more refundable booty.

Barbara Wallach saw the colored boy checking the gutter opposite the one she was bent over. Barbara, seventy-eight, widowed, and full of arthritis that some days wouldn't allow her to get out of bed, was conducting her daily ritual, lousy arthritis allowing, of scouring the neighborhood for returnable bottles and cans.

She knew that most of her neighbors figured her for a wino and a bag lady, and it was true that she did use the money for an occasional bottle, but more often than not the money went to buy a bottle of aspirin for the killing pain in her joints that the alcohol couldn't touch, or for a loaf of bread that with the five-pound block of cheese she got from Welfare once a month she would use to make Welsh rarebit.

From a career spent as an elementary schoolteacher, she had a small pension that, combined with the measly sum she got from Social Security, barely covered the rent on her one-room rathole. She watched the boy fish a bottle out of an overgrown hedge across the street and felt her anger boil until it was hissing out her mouth in a stream of epithets.

She eyed him, sizing him up. She figured he was around twelve years old and looked to be about five feet tall. His skin was light brown, what her late husband Henry would have called "having a lot of cream in his coffee." The boy's hair was the typical, tight African coil, but the color was brown, bordering on red.

Barbara didn't care that the boy was black. He could have been green, purple, or polka-dotted for all that it mattered to her. What *did* matter was that the little bugger was moving in on *her* territory; taking food out of *her* mouth; taking *her* pain-killing aspirin and soul-relieving drink away. And what for? Probably to buy candy or soda, or to waste on one of those vidiot games kids liked so much. The key word here was *waste*. The kid would *waste* the money, whereas it was essential to Barbara—a point of survival.

The boy crossed the street, heading for the same alley Barbara was just about to comb, and which in the past had been a faithful source of revenue to the old woman since it ran between Watson's Market and a laundromat with two soda machines. Now her anger not only had her mouth going, it mobilized her body too. She furiously twisted the top of the wrinkled black plastic trash bag she carried everywhere with her and shuffled to the curb to intercept the boy.

"Hey, you! Those're my bottles. You're stealing my bottles!" Barbara didn't wait for the boy to talk back. These days once she let her anger out of its cage, it wouldn't let her stop until it had burned itself out.

"I'm out here every goddamned day collecting bottles! This is *my* neighborhood. You might think I'm just some old bag, but I've got to buy bread and aspirin with this money. If you want to waste your brain on vidiot games, ask your mother for the money! Don't take mine! I need this money to live! So you just clear the hell out of here and leave my property alone!"

Barbara knew she was ranting, which she also knew didn't help dispel the standing impression she gave of being the neighborhood loony. She couldn't help it. She'd always gone a little crazy when her "red-eyed demon" (as Henry had called her temper) took hold of her, but lately she had gotten worse. Her temper always seemed to be waiting just under the surface of late, waiting for the slightest provocation to boil over.

She'd had run-ins with the neighborhood urchins and had learned how foulmouthed and disrespectful they could be even when spoken to kindly. Once she started yelling at the boy, she was reluctant to stop. She fully expected the boy to unleash his own verbal assault, as nasty and as disrespectful of Barbara's age and sex as it could be. Barbara expected the boy to call her things, and to use language that her own husband, who'd been a sailor, would've been embarrassed by, words that made her glad she was no longer a teacher if students knew such things.

Barbara expected the worst, and the black youth seemed about to accommodate, grimacing at her.

He opened his mouth, and then did a funny thing. He paused, mouth open, and looked right into her eyes. What she saw in his was a well of compassion revealed that she'd thought had gone dry in today's youth.

"I'm sorry, ma'am," the black youth stammered politely, lowering his eyes after a moment. "I didn't know. I'm new around here. We just moved in down the street," he explained, pointing to a gray tenement a block away.

Barbara was mute with shock. Her temper spluttered and stuttered. When the boy laid at her feet the several bottles and cans he'd collected, the red-eyed demon fled the old woman as quickly as her voice had. Suddenly Barbara felt very ashamed of herself and what she had let herself become.

"Hey, kid!" Barbara called as the boy walked away. "I, uh, could use some help carrying these. I'll cut you in for ten percent," she said by way of an apology. "What do you say?"

Two hours later, after they'd cleared the neighborhood of two trash bags full of discarded bottles and cans, Ivy helped Barbara carry them into the old woman's tiny apartment.

"Wow!" Ivy exclaimed in spite of himself. He put down the bag he was carrying and stared in awe at the contents of Mrs. Wallach's home. The one-room apartment was crammed with books. They were everywhere—stacked nearly to the ceiling along the walls, covering all the furniture, two armchairs, a dresser in the corner, and a coffee table, even covering half the narrow cot in the corner where the old woman obviously slept. Ivy went to a stack that was small enough for him to reach the top of and began perusing the titles.

"Those aren't comic books, son," Barbara groused in spite of her newfound humility. She didn't like anyone handling Henry's and her books who couldn't appreciate them. "Those are real, live books, the kind they don't teach you about in school anymore. You won't find any comic books in there." Barbara expected the boy to lose interest when he realized that she spoke the truth, but she was again taken aback by this strange, polite boy. Ivy was handling the books with the care of someone who believed he was holding something of immense value. Henry had always handled the books that way, with love.

"You like books, do you?" Barbara asked, removing a pile of books from one of the old overstuffed armchairs and placing them on the floor before settling her weary body into the seat. Though she was tired, she had to admit that because of Ivy's help, she didn't feel as sore or exhausted as she usually did after bottle collecting. *And* they'd hauled in a record load, too.

Ivy gave his usual noncommittal shrug, that had become like a reflex whenever an adult's questions got into an area that might expose his true intelligence. It was a halfhearted shrug, though. This woman was obviously so alone and poor that she was no threat to Ivy. Ivy felt sorry for her, but he also liked her, liked the colorful way she talked, and the things she said.

Ivy pretended to read the first page of a book called *Steppenwolf* while he glanced sideways and saw the old woman was smiling at him. It wasn't a smile of ridicule, or of mushy "isn't he cute" sentiment—it was a knowing smile, and an understanding smile. Ivy hadn't seen one like it directed at him since his father died.

"Yeah," Ivy stammered, his face flushing hot. "They're okay, I guess."

Though he was doing his best to hide it, one look at Ivy's shining eyes and Barbara knew the depth of emotion the boy felt when he said that. They had that same shining intensity Henry's eyes had whenever he read or talked about books. Every book in the apartment was a prized possession. Though they cluttered up the place to the point of being a fire hazard and made the room practically uninhabitable, she couldn't part with them. She and Henry had so loved their books, they'd been almost like children to the barren couple. And having them around still was like having a part of Henry still around, and a very big part at that.

A voracious reader, he'd loved books and spent his life laboring to become a writer, only to have it remain an unfulfilled dream. Over the course of their forty-eight-year marriage they had shared their love of reading the way some couples share their joy of children and then grandchildren. His tastes had covered everything from great literature to pulp novels, and he'd held each in the same high regard. "Doesn't matter what the book is," he used to say. "If it was good enough for someone to publish it, then it's good enough to read. Even the worst book ever written is a world unto itself and can take you places you've never been."

Barbara smiled to herself and settled back into the armchair. The smell of the books—Henry's smell—and the sight of Ivy settling into the other chair, enthralled with a book, gave the normally gloomy apartment a warming glow. Barbara dozed as Ivy, a pile of books on his lap, sat and read. Several times she came half-awake and thought Ivy was Henry sitting there reading. She smiled each time and drifted back into sleep, happy.

CHANNEL 3

Weather Report
O! Henry
Book Nook
*The Wilbur Clayton
Show*
Bill Gage—K mart Cop

"Now here with the weather is Brother John!"

"Thank you. It's a cold one out there tonight. Our first kiss of winter after Indian summer. It's a clear sky with a brilliant full moon, which the farmers in these parts call a 'tunnel' moon this time of year, because the sky is so clear and the moon is so bright, the heavens look like a tunnel with the moon the opening at the other end."

Channel change.

There is a car parked in the rear lot, behind the boiler room. He unholsters his flashlight and approaches it.

"Cool it! It's a cop," he hears a female voice whisper at his approach.

"Nah! It's just a hospital security guard," a male answers.

The driver's window is open. He can smell pot in the air.

"Hi!" the driver of the Corvette, a dark-haired, good-looking kid, says in a friendly voice. "We're just sitting up here talking. You know," the kid explains, giving Wilbur a conspiratorial wink.

Wilbur plays the light over the passenger side and catches a glimpse of open jeans and a sweater pushed up over pale breasts before the light reveals her face.

Jesus appears in an explosion of holy white light, sitting in the cramped backseat. *"Her!"* He says.

Wilbur's entire body trembles. Jesus has reminded him. He knows this girl.

Replay.

She worked in the coffee shop two years ago.

"Yeah, I was a human services major," he overheard her tell a customer one day, "but did you ever see what welfare and social workers make? It's not worth the hassle. I'm switching to business where the money is."

The word *money* echoes out of the past.

Blip.

The girl holds her hands up, shielding her eyes and trying to cover up under his scrutiny. The driver asks him to turn off his light but Wilbur can't hear him. Jesus' face is in the rear door window, up against the glass, screaming, *"Her! She's the first!"*

Wilbur can't speak. The driver swears at him, starts the car, and peels out, nearly running over his feet.

He watches them go, the memory of her face, and the Crocker State sweater she wore, burned into the night air around him.

Barbara Wallach stood peering through the small grimy window that faced the street, looking for any sign of Ivy. She'd already made over a dozen excuses to herself for her repeated window gazing until she finally gave in and admitted that she was waiting anxiously for the boy.

She could imagine what Henry would've had to say about her waiting by the window like a girl before her first date. He'd have called her a doddering old fool, and a senile geezer for the way she was acting over this boy. For the past week Ivy had come over almost every day to help Barbara collect cans or just to sit in her room and read. It had been so long since Barbara had had any companionship she'd quite forgotten how nice it was to share time with someone. But it wasn't just having company—she could go to the Senior Citizens Center or the Y for that—it was the *type* of company that Ivy provided.

The boy was *so* polite and respectful that Barbara found herself doubting her previous conclusion that rock 'n' roll, television, and video games had destroyed the youth of America. Beyond that, Ivy was incredibly bright and inquisitive, with a thirst for knowledge that shone through despite the boy's obvious attempts to hide it. Oh! he was smart— *special* smart—the kind of smart that could take him places if he ever realized its potential power and learned how to harness it. Henry'd had smarts like that, though maybe not as keen as young Ivy's. Henry had never been able to truly realize and harness his, prompting Barbara to often wonder if she had somehow been the cause for his failure. Maybe if she could help Ivy it would somehow make amends.

Though Henry had never complained and had always given the impression that he was happy being a schoolteacher, married to a schoolteacher, Barbara suspected differently. Many a night she'd awakened to find his side of the bed empty. He'd be at the kitchen table, sometimes writing furiously in a spiral-bound notebook, an open bottle of whiskey before him and muttered curses on his lips, but most times he'd just be sitting there drinking, staring into space, a look on his face of one who has realized that he will never achieve his dreams. It was an expression that made his strong, intelligent face sad beyond bearing.

Barbara knew Henry would have liked Ivy immensely, though he would have tried to hide it the way Ivy tried to hide his shining intelligence. Henry had never been a lover of family, or of children under sixteen, which was why he taught high school, but he was greatly appreciative of intelligence and talent, both of which he would have immediately seen in young Ivy. Though he used to warn her about becoming too involved with her students, she thought he would approve of her befriending the boy now.

She and Henry had often talked of the one thing they'd longed for in their teaching careers: a gifted student in whom they could awaken the spark of greatness. They'd both had intelligent, even gifted students over the years, but through some fault of the students' families or character, or more probably, Henry often said, through their own inadequacies, they had never been able to reach them, to open worlds for them. When they'd finally been forced to resign within a year of each other, they'd also had to resign their shared dream. It was ironic how twelve years after leaving the classroom and nine years after Henry's death, Barbara should have that wish come true in Ivy.

Ivy had promised to stop by after school and it was now 3:25 P.M. He was an hour late. Barbara hoped nothing was wrong. Though the boy hadn't as yet revealed much about his home life, Barbara could guess. No one in this neighborhood seemed to have a normal family.

With still no sign of Ivy through the window, Barbara closed the curtain, called herself an old fool, and turned away. Her face was as gloomy as her tiny apartment.

Ivy tucked the books under his arm and hurried down the sidewalk. The day was cold and the books kept slipping so that he had to slow down to keep from dropping them. He didn't know what he would do if he ever damaged one of Mrs. Wallach's books. The old woman had *trusted* him with them. No one had ever trusted him unquestioningly before. When he brought books back to her, she didn't look at them and examine them the way his mother did if he ever borrowed anything of hers, or the way she always counted the change he brought back from the store. By the way Mrs. Wallach handled the books and spoke about them, Ivy knew they were her most prized possessions. That made her trust in him even more special. They were quickly becoming Ivy's most prized possessions, also.

Ivy had no worries now about how he was going to spend his upcoming Christmas vacation. He wasn't going to have to ride across town to see Tommy or sneak into the library for books, hoping he didn't see anyone he knew. Now he had his own *private* library. He'd already made headway in Mrs. Wallach's books, reading ten of them in the past week. There were more than enough left to get him through not only Christmas vacation, but the rest of the school year and summer vacation too. In fact, he doubted that he'd be able to read them all by the start of school next September, but he was going to have fun trying.

Though Barbara Wallach was old and disheveled and a white woman, like his mom, she reminded him more of his father. He'd first thought this when he met her and she yelled at him. She'd used the term "vidiot games" that day. It was a term that had been one of Otis Delacroix's favorites. He'd despised video games and thought they dulled the mind.

There were other things about her, too, more intangible things. Like the way she listened when he talked. He could tell she wasn't thinking of something else or getting ready to butt in the way his mother always did. She respected what he had to say and often admired it the way his father had, even though Ivy had been only six when he died.

And the way she talked to him! She asked his opinion and discussed things with him as if he were her equal. He knew that would sound funny to anyone who saw her because she *did* look like a bag lady, but she wasn't. She told him she and her husband had been teachers. She was smart and funny in a loud way—like his father—and Ivy liked being with her.

He switched the books to the front, hugging them close to his chest, and ran up the dark stairs to Mrs. Wallach's apartment. He'd made the mistake of stopping at home first, and his mom had been there with the afternoon off from the comb factory because the furnace was out and there was no heat in the shop. It had taken him until now to slip away. As usual, at his knock the old woman opened the door only a crack, as far as the three chain locks would allow. She peered out suspiciously, always wary of danger in the rough neighborhood.

When she saw it was Ivy, the fear and apprehension in her face disappeared and was replaced with a look of joy and excitement that made Ivy feel great. That look was more than enough to make Ivy feel special. Except for his father, no one, not even his mother, had ever been so happy to see him. Having access to her wonderful library of books was just an added bonus.

"Hi, Mrs. Wallach," Ivy said as the old woman undid the locks and opened the door. "I finished these," he said as he entered the tiny apartment.

"Already, Ivy? That's amazing. Even my Henry couldn't read as fast as you can." Barbara patted Ivy on the head and went to the little kitchenette, which was to the immediate left of the front door. "You want some hot chocolate? I got a sample package of Ovaltine in the mail."

"Sure." Ivy put the books on a new stack just inside the kitchen. Barbara had started it to keep track of the books he'd read.

"So tell me, what did you think of those?" Barbara asked from the sink where she was filling a teapot with tap water.

Ivy climbed up on the only stool and leaned on the counter. Since his third visit, when Barbara had let him take some books home, they'd begun a sort of ritual where he reviewed each book he'd read while Barbara listened, smiling knowingly, sometimes asking questions, and *really* interested in what he had to say. Ivy had always been a reader, albeit a secret one, but he had never had a chance to talk comfortably about what he'd read.

With every book they discussed, he felt a little more safe in allowing Barbara to see the real Ivy. At first he'd trusted her because she was completely cut off from the rest of the world with no friends or family. She lived like a hermit and most of time gave the impression she wasn't right in the head. No one cared what she had to say and no one would believe her anyway.

Ivy reached over to the stack and picked a book, reading its title aloud. *"The Sound and the Fury.* This was okay, but it was kind of boring and hard to figure out what was going on at first. When I realized the story was mostly being told by a retard, it was easier to understand."

Barbara just smiled and nodded, exerting great

self-control. She knew college professors who hadn't been able to make heads or tails of Faulkner's most famous work. The fact that Ivy, an eleven-year-old, had been able to get through the novel, much less understand it, astounded her.

Ivy read the next title. *"Dr. Jekyll and Mr. Hyde.* I really liked this one."

"Why?" Barbara asked, putting the teapot on the small two-burner gas stove.

"It was kind of scary, but it was sad too. I ended up feeling bad for Dr. Jekyll. He couldn't help what he did. He was like a junkie, 'cept he was hooked on being Hyde, who was cruel and evil. But Jekyll wasn't a bad person, he just couldn't help himself. I liked that his name was Hyde, too. That was cool."

"Do you think a lot of people have this problem?" Barbara asked, inwardly marveling at the boy's insight and understanding.

"You kidding? Read the papers."

The cynicism in Ivy's voice was too much for Barbara and she had to laugh. Ivy looked at her uncertainly for a moment, then figured he must have said something funny and laughed with her.

"What I meant, Ivy," Barbara said, still giggling between the words, "is, do you think everyone has two sides to them, a good and an evil side that battle for control of your body?"

"Oh." Ivy stopped laughing and considered her question. He thought about how close he had come to killing Bully Brink and how he hated it whenever anyone called him "nigger." Did he become another person when he got angry and hateful? "Yeah, I guess they do. It isn't like in the book, though, unless you *are* talking about a junkie. Crazy people might be like that, really bad, you know, not able to control their different sides. But most people wouldn't just drink a formula and become a monster. I think if you hate a lot it's like releasing a monster and you act different. Maybe if you do it enough the hate will take over."

"I guess everyone has moments like that," Barbara said, reflecting on her own frequent outbursts of anger and just plain orneriness that, before meeting Ivy, had threatened to dominate her life of late.

"Of course," Ivy went on, warming to the subject, "if someone was born without one side or the other, they'd really be screwed up. A guy with no good side could be like a killer and a guy with no bad side could be like Jesus Christ."

"That's very perceptive of you, Ivy," Barbara said.

Ivy beamed. "And I bet luck has got a lot to do with it too," he said.

"How?"

"Like, if you're lucky and good things happen to you, you'll probably be a good person. But if you're unlucky and bad things happen to you, then your bad side will be in control. Like, if you're unlucky enough to be born into a poor family where your parents are bad people and beat you, then you've got a better chance of growing up to be a bad person too. Sometimes, if someone you know dies, that can change you too."

Ivy spoke the last sentence with such a pathetic quality to his voice that Barbara felt her heart go out to him. He'd spent every afternoon and all day on the weekend at her apartment for the past week, yet he hadn't let her have any information about his family. Sometimes, when he was interpreting books, he'd come out with a comment that made her certain he was talking about himself and his home life. Over the course of their short relationship, Barbara had come to admire Ivy's ability to internalize completely everything he read, seeing and interpreting it in terms of himself and his own life.

"There are many different sides to everyone," she said, choosing not to confront him with personal questions. When he was ready he would tell her. "You don't act the same here as you do at home, or as you do at school."

Ivy immediately tensed, blushing nervously. He searched Barbara's face for a clue as to what she meant. Did she know that he went out of his way to be average or worse at school and had gotten all C's and D's on his last report card? Had he let his guard down too much? Suddenly all his reasons for trusting her seemed like bad ones. What if she wasn't a lonely old bag lady after all? What if she was working for Dr. Peabody, to keep tabs on him? She *did* say she used to be a teacher.

"What's wrong, Ivy? Are you all right?" Barbara asked, concerned over his flushed face and sudden tenseness.

"Yeah." He got up and went to the window.

"So what about the other three books you read?" Barbara asked, picking the books up. "Hesse's *Narcissus and Goldmund, Steppenwolf,* and *Beneath the Wheel?* What did you think of those?"

"I don't know," Ivy said without turning around.

Barbara opened *Narcissus and Goldmund* and brought it to him at the window. "I thought this one and *Dr. Jekyll and Mr. Hyde* were similar in their themes on the duality of human nature."

Ivy barely glanced at the book and resumed his stare out the window. Barbara sensed he was warring with some inner conflict but didn't know how to help.

"I don't know, Mrs. Wallach. To tell you the truth, I—uh—didn't really finish those books. I just read the first couple of chapters," Ivy blurted out, his eyes averted.

Barbara started to laugh, thinking he was joking, but quickly saw she was mistaken. Eyes down, hands in his pockets, Ivy headed for the door.

"I gotta go now. My mother needs me to help her with some stuff," he said unconvincingly.

Barbara stood mute with shock as he went through the door, closing it quietly behind him.

What did I say? she asked herself.

Blip.

The music comes up slowly, as canned as the applause sprinkled with expectant laughter that accompanies it.

"It's time once again for . . ." an announcer crows in a voice trained to sound like your oldest and best friend about to tell you a juicy secret, *"The Wilbur Clayton Show!"*

He opens his eyes. The lights hit them like raw, poking fingers. Their heat is magnetic, drawing a metallic sweat from his pores. His makeup begins to run. He blinks sweat from his eyes.

Canned giggles, twitters.

The lights are too bright. They bake right through him, leaving him brittle and dry.

This isn't his TV.

I'm okay. I'm okay. He breathes the thought deeply.

He flees the light and looks for a place to hide. A door beckons. He opens it and is swallowed by darkness.

I can wake up any time I want to, he thinks, ill at ease in the all-encompassing blackness.

"Can you?"

A flicker of light and sound giggles out of the darkness ahead.

"Two. Two. Two mints in one!"

Wilbur reaches for the soothing light and finds a remote control in his hand. He looks back. The darkness makes fleeting faces at him.

From thirty feet he hits the remote. Channel Thirteen. By the flicker of cold black-and-white video light he sees himself cringing in the tunnel.

He changes the channel.

Doors open and close. A quick beam of light. Hollow footsteps.

He changes the channel.

Close-up of his face, sweaty with liquid fear.

He changes the channel.

Heart like a train in the darkness.

Changes it again.

Locomotive breath.

Changes it again.

Slow motion. Dust dancing in the shifting light.
Again.
The darkness is pierced. Fingers reaching. Hands clutching.
Again.
Arms searching.
Again.
Chests heaving.
Again.
The bodies lurch out of the black into the white and Wilbur forgets the remote. He gapes at the screen. The bodies are not headless. Their shoulders carry TV sets instead. Each set plays the same scene.

The parking lot. The girl in the Corvette stares out at him from each screen.

He watches himself on TV watching the girl on the TV heads. A shadow looms over her.

He sits up in the darkness.

I'm okay. Just a dream. No harm in a dream. I'm awake now.

He reaches for the covers but can't find them. Instead his hand finds stone, curved and smooth. He isn't sitting anymore. He's standing.

I'm awake, he tells himself. He refuses to look when he hears the dual doors opening.

I'm awake. I want to stop dreaming now.

The dream doesn't hear him. It rolls on relentlessly.

Maybe this isn't a dream. The thought comes to him like a cold chill on his neck.

Maybe it's a replay.

There is a new sound out of the darkness.

Maybe it's for real!

Rewind.

I'm not *awake*.

A rolling sound, drumming toward him. He scrunches against the wall. Somehow he knows what this is. Doesn't want to see it. He dances on tiptoes, wishing he could melt into the wall.

The blood comes first, flinging out of the dark. Liquid balloons sailing past his face in slow motion. He can see his reflection in a droplet. The blood paints a bad abstract on the floor.

Here comes what the first dream was missing.

The heads. Heads like bowling balls thrown for strikes. Heads like bombs, blood hissing from their necks like fuses. Heads ready to explode. He can feel static electricity in his fingertips. There is a bright flash of light.

Channel change.

"It's the *New Dating Game!* Starring Jim Lange!"

Wilbur opens his eyes. He's kneeling in front of the TV. Jesus is the contestant, a well-stacked blond bimbo giggling her way through Jim Lange's innuendo-filled introduction of her.

"Why don't we get started by having each of our bachelors say 'hi' to this pretty lady," Jim says in his honeyed voice. "Ready, guys? Bachelor number one?"

"Hi, Wendy," says Wilbur, bachelor number one.

"Bachelor number two?"

"Hello, Wendy," number two, Wilbur, offers.

"And three?"

"Hi Babe! What's shakin'?" Wilbur gives a bachelor-number-three wink to the camera.

Jesus giggles. "Like, okay. Bachelor number one, how old were you when you lost your virginity, and how did you lose it?"

Moans and applause. Catcalls and wolf whistles. Laughter.

"Are you there, bachelor number one?" Jim Lange asks, a lecherous chuckle in his voice.

"I'm here. But I've got to change the channel for this darling," Wilbur number two says.

Channel change.

His memories are replayed on public television. Stark documentary images with rough, crackling sound.

A party. Long-haired men, beaded, loose-breasted women. A smoke-filled room. Music pounds: the Grateful Dead wandering through "Dark Star."

Brother John grabs him by the shoulder as he toddles through the living room. The stem of a pipe is thrust in his face. A blond-ringleted girl—holy blue eyes rimmed in devil-red—puts her lips over the bowl of a corncob pipe. She blows. Smoke billows out the stem and swallows his face.

Choking. Coughing.

Falling. Crying.

Laughter.

He becomes the entertainment, a source of experiment. How much wine can a four-year-old guzzle? Does he like to get stoned? He is passed expectantly around the room like the water pipe and toyed with like the Rubic's cube they've all become bored with.

A dark girl with a large chest pulls him to her. He can see the outline of her heavy swinging breasts

*under the thin material of her blouse. He can smell
her even now through the TV screen and the years.
She reeks of tuna fish and patchouli oil. Her neck is
dirty. Her eyes are wasted. She has feathers in her
hair. She sticks his face in her chest and rubs her
breasts against him.*

*"How old are you?" She exhales in his face. It
smells of wine and garlic. Her tongue is coated
white.*

"Four." He holds up fingers to prove it.

*The girl looks at her friend, a freckle-faced red-
head. She is tall and smokes long, thin black cigars.
She has a tattoo of a snake nestled in the cleavage of
her breasts.*

*"Ever wonder how big a guy's thing is when he's
only four?" the one who smells of tuna says to the
redhead. Red holds up two fingers an inch apart.*

"Let's see." They pull off his pajamas.

"You're wrong. It's smaller."

"What about when it's hard?"

*The redhead reaches down and fondles him. She
bends over and uses her mouth on him.*

*He is frightened. He's afraid she's going to bite
him. He cries for Grandma, then his mother.
Grandma is dead and hasn't moved into his head
yet, his mother-whom-he-must-never-call-Mother is
a few feet away holding the new toy she'd managed
to shoplift from K mart that day, an 8mm movie
camera. She is training the lens on Wilbur and her
friends investigating his anatomy.*

*He is feeling strange. He shivers all over. He
cringes waiting for the girl to bite his thing off but*

she doesn't. She sends waves of hot tingles through his body instead.

"Oh look! It's bigger than an inch."

The girls laugh, others join in. He is handed on once again and makes the rounds until he passes out naked and drunk on the floor.

The sound of moaning wakes him. The room is unsteady. It sways around him. It dips and stretches. The moaning is coming from the couch. His mother-not-Mother is doing to a man what the redheaded girl did to Wilbur. The man is moaning and Wilbur is afraid for him. Like him, they have no clothes on either.

A loud burp rises out of Wilbur. The man stops moaning and looks at him. Wilbur tries to get to his feet but falls over. Suddenly there is pain in his head. His hair is being pulled. He's being dragged by his hair across the room.

"What's wrong, Mary?" the man on the couch asks.

Wilbur doesn't hear her answer as she drags him into the bathroom.

"Ah, leave him," the man says, looking angry as he stuffs his legs into his pants and zips up. "He'll pass out soon."

"Are you gonna be here to listen to his bawling, Joe, when he wakes up in the middle of the night? The Welfare bitch is coming tomorrow. If he's sick she might stop my checks."

She pushes him to the toilet, her hand on the back of his head. She bends him over.

"She's seen him fucked up before and never said anything."

"I can't risk it; I need that money too much. Throw up," she commands. The water is dark yellow. It stinks of urine. Suds gather around the edges. There is a rusty water stain on the porcelain. Half a Marlboro floats around in circles.

"I can't, Mommy," he says.

She slaps the back of his head, hard. "I told you never to call me that! Now, throw up," she commands again.

"Can't," he whimpers.

She squeezes the back of his neck until he cries out. She jerks his head over the bowl and sticks her fingers down his throat.

He coughs, gags, chokes. Nothing comes up.

She shoves his head down into the bowl. He begins to cry softly.

"Throw up now, dammit!"

She pulls him up only to punch him hard in the stomach. He doubles over. The wind flies out of his gaping mouth. She shoves her fingers back in. This time she is successful. Suddenly everything is coming up at once. He empties his stomach for what seems an eternity before he can breathe again.

There is laughter from the door. The man is standing there, filming them with the movie camera. "How'd you like to get off Welfare and make some serious bucks, Mary?" He lowers the camera and looks from her naked body to Wilbur's, a widening grin on his face.

Wilbur frantically changes channels, but Jesus is on every one of them. On four, He's Geraldo Rivera interviewing Borneo headhunters. On five, He's Brother John with a head cold looking for medicinal relief. On six, He's Elmer Fudd having His shotgun backfire in His face, blowing His head off. On thirteen, He's the girl from the parking lot, staring out at him. "First the head," Jesus says through her mouth.

Wilbur shuts the TV off, but escape is not that easy and he knows it. When he turns away from the set, Jesus is standing by the shelves against the back wall. He reaches to the top shelf and takes down a videocassette tape. He puts it into the VCR and turns it and the TV on. There is a crackling sound and the title comes up. *Toilet Training*—a Tunnelvision Studios Production.

On 8mm transferred to video, he watches himself being fondled at that long-ago party. He doesn't want to watch too long because he knows it gets nasty, but as Mary-not-Mother used to do, Jesus holds his head, forcing him to watch, and remember.

"In the beginning," Jesus says, *"I was born of suffering and My suffering was ignored. The day of reckoning for that suffering and ignorance has been too long coming, but it is here now."*

Bill Gage took a deep breath, held it a few moments, then let it out before entering the house. He'd had a bad day and still felt wound up about it. Three hundred and sixty-four days of the year his job was mundane at best. Shoplifting knows no age nor sex limitations, and K mart, with its mazelike aisles of merchandise, is especially attractive. But shoplifting *is* a mundane crime. He thought he'd seen too much of it for it to ever surprise him again. He was wrong.

Today he'd been called to the Fitchburg K mart where the store detective had caught a seventy-two-year-old man teaching his nine-year-old grandson how to steal. The store dick and the local cops who'd been called in got a good laugh out of the whole thing, but it struck a dissonant chord in Bill. He looked at the old man and was reminded that his own father would have been seventy-two if he were still alive. Bill found himself wanting to take the old man and shake him and tell him what a mistake he was making, what a waste. The grandfather was leaving his grandson a legacy of deceit and shame.

Lately, he'd been having a recurring daydream, an image of life as it could have been, like a clip from an old Frank Capra film: His father came to live with them, playing with the girls and Devin, teasing Cindy about her cooking. At first he had thought the fantasy was progress. Previously, thoughts of his father had brought on guilt-laden questions that he could spend forever trying to answer. On the other hand, fantasizing what it would be like if his father were still alive seemed harmless, and even healthy.

Maybe it was just him, going at everything with tweezers and a microscope, picking it apart until it was ruined. Eventually the fantasy brought on even more disturbing questions. Instead the usual questions about his father's motives or how Bill could have been so blind to them, the questions brought on by his fantasy concerned the future rather than the past. Would his legacy be better than his father's or the shoplifting grandfather's? Would his father's sickness prove to be hereditary, and what would he do if it was? What would he someday tell Devin?

Over the objections of the store manager and the local police who wanted to go easy on the old guy, Bill insisted on pressing full shoplifting and aiding-the-delinquency-of-a-minor charges. In addition, he contacted the DSS and reported the old man and what he'd done as a case of child abuse.

Bill forced himself to smile and opened the door. He took off his overcoat and hung it on the mirrored wall rack above the hall table. He could hear Cindy in the kitchen fixing supper, and the kids' bickering voices competing with the blare of cartoons on the television.

On the hall table was the day's mail, which he routinely picked up on his way in and read while waiting for dinner. The top envelope immediately caught his eye. It was long and white and had the official stamp of the Pennsylvania State Police on it. He recognized the name, Captain Robert Barrel, in the upper left-hand corner and felt the familiar ping of anxiety ricochet off the back of his neck. Captain Robert Barrel was Bill's father's former captain.

The rest of the mail, mostly junk and bills, got tossed back on the hall table. He held the envelope tightly in both hands, steeling himself to open it. He knew it wasn't good news. Ever since that winter's day ten years ago when Captain Barrel had called Bill with the news of his father, the trooper's name had become, in Bill's mind, synonymous with bad news. A touch of the old thirst tickled the back of his throat and he tried to dry swallow it away.

"Hey, you going to stand out there all night, or are you going to come in and get something to eat, not to mention a hug and a kiss?"

He looked up at Cindy and was glad to have her pretty face framed in rich auburn hair and her sexy body to come home to. He tried to smile but his face felt tight and frozen. She saw the envelope in his hands and immediately understood his reaction.

"When I saw that today," she said, coming down the hallway to his side, "I thought about hiding it, or just throwing it away."

"I've tried both those," he replied, letting her lean against his arm. "I couldn't hide from it, and you stopped me from throwing my life away."

"No," Cindy said, looking up at him, "*you* stopped yourself from that."

"Yeah. Well. Whatever. No point in repeating past mistakes." He ripped open the envelope and unfolded the letter inside.

"Daddy!" The twins cheered as they charged out of the living room and attached themselves to each of his legs. Devin toddled behind them, waving a Teenage Mutant Ninja Turtle doll in the air. "Da!" he shrieked happily.

Bill put the letter, unread, back on the hall table and leaned over to wrap his arms around the girls. Devin tossed his turtle doll aside and bulled his way into the middle of the group hug. "Hi, Da!" he said in his squeaky little voice.

"Hey, big guy, how you doin'?"

Devin giggled and pinched Missy, who pinched him back.

"Daddy, want to hear what happened at school today?" Sassy asked, her eight-year-old face bright with excitement. She was a born chatterbox and always had something to tell Bill when he got home.

"Tell him later, sweetie," Cindy interposed. "Supper's almost ready and your father has to go get cleaned up, and so do you three. Do me a big favor and wash Devin's hands and face."

Sassy started to protest but Cindy shushed her, pushing her, Missy, and Devin toward the stairs. When they went up, she gave Bill a quick nip of a kiss on the lips and went into the kitchen.

Bill retrieved the letter from the table, but took it into the living room and sat in the easy chair before reading it. It wasn't a long letter, but it didn't have to be. The news it delivered was short, to the point, and, as expected, bad.

When Cindy came in ten minutes later to tell him supper was ready, she found him pacing in front of the couch, the letter crumpled and clutched in his right hand.

"They're reopening my father's case," Bill said in the same tone he might use to tell her he had terminal cancer.

"What?" Cindy sounded shocked. "After ten years? Why?"

"One of the victims' parents is suing the state police, charging them with a cover-up in the case. Captain Barrel wants me to call him at home after eight tonight so he can give me the whole story. I might have to testify."

He didn't get to sleep until after two that night. After calling Captain Barrel, he paced the living room, craving a drink. If Cindy hadn't come down around one and coaxed him to bed where she seduced him to help him relax, he might have gone out for one, and that would have been the end of everything he'd worked so hard for.

Making love was good, and long. It got his mind off things for a while, but his problems still distracted him just enough to prolong his building to a climax. Cindy didn't mind. She could ride all night if he was game.

He collapsed over her at two-thirty and rolled off, snoring softly. Cindy wrapped herself around his body for warmth, and followed him into sleep.

Snapshot.
Flash.
Photographs. They're all there. Eighty-nine. Girls. Women. Children. Even two very old ladies. Their death faces boxed forever in snapshots lovingly pasted in a leather-bound scrapbook.

He hated this dream most of all. It was a weightless dream, spacious. The snapshots were sometimes large, sometimes small, always crystal clear: gray hair, gray face, nylon like a crease in her neck; below her a young girl, pillow by her head, her mouth open in an eternal gasp for a breath that will never come; next to that is a woman with red hair to match her open red throat, one of the few bloody deaths. If there was one thing his father treasured above all, it was neatness.

Did I know this man? he wondered, as he had so many times before in this dream.

"The child is father to the man."

Where did that come from? When awake, the line would dance teasingly just outside the circle of his memory. When he heard himself saying it in the dream it always gave him hope.

"One day you wake up and you're your father."

He couldn't remember where he'd heard that one either, but it didn't matter. In the dream the words always took on the veracity of shining truth— only the light they shed didn't illuminate, it darkened and swallowed.

Every time, just before he woke up, the photos went by faster and faster as if trying to make him see as many as possible before he escaped. Every time, he woke shivering with sweat. Tonight he woke almost convulsed with trembling.

Tonight his father had been holding the snapshots.

He sat up in bed with a sharp gasp. Cindy moaned softly in sleep beside him. He rubbed his eyes and was visited by a memory so clear he could almost touch it: *His father's Ford Falcon. He's sitting on his dad's lap, steering the car while Dad works the pedals. The steering wheel has a spot of dark purple, sticky stuff on it. He wants to ask his father what it is but he's having too much fun. Or maybe he's afraid to . . .*

In the dark, the memory brought as many tears as it did questions.

CHANNEL 4

*The Return of
Dr. Peabody*
Toilet Training
*Beth Shell—
Student Nurse*

Ivy sat in the lopsided armchair near the window, a cold, half-eaten TV dinner balanced on the windowsill next to the chair. It was his mother's night off. She sat on the couch in her Korean silk bathrobe, butt in her mouth, glass of Sangria in hand, watching some stupid show. She was droopy eyed, and between sips she muttered to herself, a sign to Ivy that she was pretty plastered.

Ivy looked out the dirty window and thought about Barbara. He missed her, her books, and their conversations. For the past couple of days he'd been telling himself that she *had* to be okay and that he was just being paranoid. But then, the other morning at school, he was called out of class to the nurse's office to have a hearing test he'd had only a week ago but that the nurse said he'd missed. He'd immediately become suspicious. He knew many of the rooms in the elementary school had two-way mirrors in them for observation of classes. He'd got the feeling that the large mirror in the nurse's office, on the wall opposite where he sat, was one of those. With a dread certainty, he had looked at that mirror and known that Dr. Peabody was on the other side, watching him. With the same certainty, he knew that the hearing test was not what it seemed; it was some kind of trick, or trap. Or warning. But did that mean Barbara had been sent to check up on him, reporting back that he was reading books at the college level and discussing them openly? Was he just being paranoid?

A light in the yard next door caught Ivy's attention. He leaned over the arm of the chair and looked out and down at the neighbor's driveway. The weirdo next door was putting a TV set and two VCRs in the trunk of a gold, early '70s vintage Bonneville; the kind of gas-guzzling American dinosaur that is rarely seen on the roads these days. He went back into the house and came out a few moments later carrying two large spotlights that he put in the back seat. On his next trip he carried two large boxes stacked on top of each other. A wire hung out of the top one and dragged on the ground behind him. He went into the house again and the light went out. Ivy couldn't see anything until the Bonneville's headlights and taillights went on and the car pulled out of the driveway.

"Where's he going with that stuff at this time of night?" Ivy wondered aloud. His mother snored in answer from the couch.

* * *

Closed circuit.

The darkness is alive with voices and sounds out of a nightmare. Jesus is behind the wheel of the big gold Bonneville *(her* car) following the red Corvette as it leaves the hospital parking lot. In Grandma's room, Wilbur sits at her feet and watches the unfolding miracle on her screen.

The red Corvette leads him to the campus of Crocker State College. It parks by a pathway that leads to the rear entrance of a high-rise dormitory. The girl who'd rather make money than help Jesus is dropped off. The dashboard's digital clock flashes: 1:40 A.M. Still plenty of time to get back to the hospital.

Jesus drives by and parks the car in the lot, waiting until the Corvette pulls away. The girl is walking toward the dorm entrance before He gets out of the car. He can hear the stars overhead humming His praises.

She looks back once as He closes the distance between them, but when she sees His uniform and hat she thinks He's a campus police officer making rounds. She enjoys a short-lived moment of feeling safe.

Jesus glides through the night. She uses her electronic key card on the door, and He is within ten feet. The heavy glass door almost closes and locks before He can get a hand on it and slip in after her.

Her footsteps are dull, enlivened by an occasional squeak of her rubber soles against the linoleum. Jesus creeps through the shadows of the entranceway and peers around the corner.

It's a *tunnel!*

The corridor is dark except for the far end where an exit light marks the fire door. Jesus illuminates the darkness and sees her heading for the elevator doors. Ahead, to her left, is a women's rest room. Jesus silently sprints into the darkness, trying to catch her before she goes past the rest room. There is no need. She goes into the bathroom as though she knew He wanted her there.

The door doesn't make a sound as Jesus pushes it open and slips inside. Through a double archway and to the left, there is a mirrored wall offering three porcelain white sinks. To the right are as many toilet stalls. Just inside the door is a sanitary napkin dispenser. The girl is nowhere to be seen, but a soft fizzing sound leads Him to the stalls. He kneels.

"She's behind door number three, Monty."

She flushes the toilet and the sound is deafening. Before she comes out, Jesus hides in the first stall. He breathes the scent of her deeply. It is musky, smoky, beery. She's a little drunk. All the better.

She doesn't see Jesus step out from behind the stall door as she washes her hands. She doesn't see Him until He's right behind her, reaching for her head. She never has a chance to cry out as He grabs a fistful of her hair and bounces her face off the edge of the sink.

"I'll take door number one, Monty," Jesus says as He drags the dazed and bloody-nosed girl back to the first stall.

Static.

Time passes in fast forward.

Channel change.

Lights!

He can't believe his eyes. He stares at the equipment—the lights, cables, cameras—that fills the large empty room on the third floor of the abandoned East Wing Building of the hospital.

Jesus doesn't have time to explain. He's a god on a mission.

Camera!

Jesus is dragging the naked dead girl to the bare toilet against the wall. The reality of what is going on comes back at Wilbur like spitting into the wind. He wants to hide but Grandma has turned off her set and closed her door. It's just Wilbur and Jesus and the dead girl whose eyes the Lord has taken.

An eye for an eye.

Jesus turns on the cameras. *This is my judgment for those who didn't do anything about what they saw.*

Action!

Most of the time Beth Shell didn't mind the dirty work the student nurses were given to do. Part of her last year of training at the Crocker School of Nursing, which was run by the hospital and was situated directly behind it, was to work all different shifts as a practical nurse. She figured it was good experience. She was no stranger to, nor slacker from, hard work. The only chore she *really* didn't like was having to go to the laundry room on the graveyard shift.

The laundry was situated deep in the rear recesses of the hospital near the abandoned East

Wing Building. What she hated about going there was that she had to go by the morgue on the way.

Foolishly enough, what bothered Beth was the silly stories the girls told about seeing dead people wandering the dark morgue at night, or their stories of a vampire living in the abandoned East Wing Building.

Tonight was no different. The closer she got to the morgue, the more anxious she became. It wouldn't be until she was well past the morgue and the old elevators to the abandoned east wing that she would feel safe. But then she had to go through the whole thing again on her way back.

Beth pushed the laundry cart down the deserted corridor. The ceiling lights passed overhead with the effect of very slow strobe lights. She tried to think of things that made her feel safe and happy. Thoughts of her girlhood dog, Daffy, got her past the morgue. She picked up her pace heading for the elevators and the turn into the corridor to the laundry. A sudden massive thud made her cry out involuntarily.

She couldn't be sure, and she certainly wasn't going to stick around to find out, but she thought the sound had come from the morgue. Using all the strength she could muster, she pushed the laundry cart down the corridor as fast as she could. The cart of soiled linen bounced around, threatening to tip over. If that happened she'd not only have to stop, she'd have to handle all the disgusting laundry while putting it back in. She decided to slow down.

A monstrously deep groan shuddered through the corridor. The sound was coming from in front of her now. The dented elevator doors at the end of the hall started to rattle and shake. The groan was joined by a grinding hum interspersed with shrill screams of metal rubbing against metal. A light stabbed out from between the seams of the elevator doors. The humming, groaning, metallic shrieking peaked, reaching a deafening pitch.

She stopped in the middle of the corridor and clapped her hands over her ears. The elevator doors were shaking as badly as her knees. There was another loud *thud* followed by a wave of cold air washing over her, bringing goose bumps and hard nipples with it.

The warped elevator doors cried out as they slid open. For one fleeting moment, she thought something huge and monstrous, hungry and cruel was waiting just behind the doors, ready to pounce on her. She let out a genuine sigh of relief when she saw it was the security guard.

"Oh! Woo! You *scared* me!" Beth laughed, shaking her head.

"Sorry," the guard said softly but curtly as he went past her. She smiled at him and started to say something else, but he was walking away quickly, shoulders hunched as if under a great weight.

Beth had seen him around on the graveyard shift before and thought he was cute. Getting a closer look at him now convinced her that her first assessment had been correct. He looked young, no older than 18 or 19. He had wavy, dark hair, sad soulful eyes, and soft babyish features. This was the first chance she'd had to talk to him, and she was disappointed when he walked away. Shrugging her shoulders, and laughing at herself for being such a scaredy-cat, she continued on her way to the laundry.

Later in the shift, just before 6:00 A.M., Beth was getting the breakfast trays ready to hand out when she saw the security guard again.

"Do you know him?" she asked the floor nurse who was prepping the med cart.

"Just to say 'hi' to. His name's Wilbur. I don't know his last name. He seems like a nice kid." The nurse looked knowingly at Beth. "He's cute too, huh?"

"Yeah," Beth agreed, then blushed when she saw the nurse smiling.

CHANNEL 5

Afterschool Special: The Rescue

 Barbara Wallach stooped to pick a can from the alley gutter and felt a sharp pain in her lower back. She straightened slowly, gulping air in short swallows as she groused at the curse of getting old.

"Hey! Check out this old bitch!"

The youthful voice, harsh and filled with menace, came from the alley behind her. Barbara didn't have to turn around to see it was Luis Sanchez, nicknamed "Slice" for his reputed ability with a switchblade. With him was his gang of punks. Barbara had had trouble with them before and always tried to stay well out of their way.

"Hey, mama! What'cha got today, huh? Got a bottle of MD in that bag for me, baby?" Though she was shuffling away as fast as she could, his voice was closer, as was the hooting cackle of his friends.

"I got somethin' in my pants for you, baby. Somethin' I bet you ain't had in a lo-ong time!" More meanspirited laughter.

Before Barbara could even get close to the end of the alley, they surrounded her. She pulled the trash bag tight against her chest and cowered into the collar of her oversize coat.

"Come on, mama! Give me your bottle and I'll give you somethin' better to suck on," Slice taunted her. He was a tall, well-built youth with dark hair and features, and eyes that were narrow and merciless. He was almost eighteen but had quit school at sixteen, roaming the streets and spending time in and out of juvey hall since.

"I bet she ain't got no teeth, man. She give you a gum job, Slice. Eh, man?" said a short, dirty youth whose skin complexion had earned him the name "Greasy".

"Yeah. How 'bout that, mama?" Slice said, laughing. Without warning, his left leg shot out and kicked her in the gut. She collapsed on her knees heavily, like a sack of wet cement falling, and the air shot out of her.

"I'm talkin' to you," Slice said loudly, his voice losing all trace of its joking tone. He stepped in front of her and stuck his crotch in her face.

"Do it, man!" Greasy urged, a frightening eagerness to his voice.

"Go for it! . . . Make her go down!" the others, joining in, taunted.

Breathless and near fainting, Barbara knew the situation was out of hand but was powerless to stop it. Usually, her cowering silence at worst brought on a kick in the rear, or got her bag dumped and any money or liquor she had stolen. There had always been the threat of more violence waiting, though, which was why she was not surprised it was happening now. She was just unprepared for it.

"Here. Here," she croaked, panting and gulping her wind back. She pulled out her large brown wal-

let and offered it submissively to Slice. She hoped
that if she groveled enough and played the idiot bag
lady to the hilt she might get out of this without
serious injury. When she heard the sound of Slice's
zipper opening, she knew it wasn't working.

Ivy got off the school bus but headed in the opposite direction from his house. He had made up his
mind that today he was going to confront Barbara
about Dr. Peabody and find out the truth. He went
straight to her house and was about to go in and do
just that when a voice from the nearby alley caught
his attention.

"Don't let her bite you, Slice."

Ivy hadn't lived in the neighborhood long enough
to recognize the voice, but he knew the name. He'd
been warned by a kid at school about Slice Sanchez
and his buddies.

"The old bitch's still got a lot of fight in her," the
voice went on.

Ivy's mouth went dry. He headed for the alley, his
feet feeling as if they had gained fifty pounds each.
At the alley entrance, he had a moment of relief. He
could see five leather-and-jeans-clad teens bunched
at the other end of the alley, but there was no sign
of Barbara. Ivy was about to go back to her house
when one of the youths stepped aside and he saw
Barbara kneeling on the filthy pavement, surrounded by the gang. Her nose was bleeding. Her
glasses lay smashed on the ground in front of her.
She was cringing, hands raised protectively over
her face and head.

Ivy looked around for help. He had to do something. A cheer from the gang brought his attention back to the alley. The one that Ivy assumed was Slice had Barbara by the hair and was forcing her face into his crotch. In his other hand he held a nasty-looking switchblade.

Ivy looked up and down Leighton Street. There was no one around; no traffic. At a time of the afternoon when the street usually had steady traffic, it was unusually quiet. And true to the cliché, now that he needed a cop, there wasn't one around. A high crime area, Leighton street was usually patrolled by at least a cruiser every half hour or so. Suddenly an idea occurred to Ivy: Slice and his buddies didn't *know* there wasn't a cop around. Maybe he could fool them.

"Hey! Leave her alone!" Ivy yelled, immediately getting Slice and company's attention. As Ivy was hoping, Slice let go of Barbara's hair. She took the opportunity to duck away and crawl off.

Ivy turned toward the vacant corner of Leighton and Turner streets. "Hey! Officer! Come here! Hurry! Some kids are hurting a lady!"

Slice, who had started toward Ivy, hesitated. Two of his buddies immediately bolted. Greasy and another kid called JoJo remained, but looked ready to follow the others at any second.

Ivy did his best to picture a cop car at the corner, two cops getting out, running to his aid. He figured the better he imagined it, the more convincing he would seem to Slice.

"Hurry up!" he yelled again. "They're going to get away. They're right here!" He pointed excitedly at Slice, Greasy, and JoJo.

"Let's go, man," JoJo said to Slice, a note of pleading to his voice.

Greasy joined in. "Yeah, man. We're on probation, man. We'll get the little fuck later when they ain't no cops around."

Deep down, Slice knew the little black bastard was bluffing, but Greasy was right. They were all on probation for car theft and couldn't afford to take any chances. He pointed a cocked thumb and finger at Ivy and fired a silent threat before fleeing with his buddies in close formation.

Ivy ran into the alley to where Barbara huddled behind a row of trash cans. Her hair was wild, plastered to the tears and blood on her face, hiding her eyes. Ivy touched her arm and she jumped, letting out a tiny squeak.

"It's me, Mrs. Wallach. It's me, Ivy. They're gone."

Barbara peered out at him from between the tangle of hair covering her face. "Oh," she said softly and began to laugh and cry at the same time.

Slice Sanchez and his gang did a quickstep around the block so that they were approaching the alley from Leighton Street, the opposite end from where they'd exited it. There were no cops in sight, which was making Slice very angry. When he saw the kid helping the bag lady out of the alley, he was ready to *really* take care of both of them, probation or no. The only thing stopping him was the sudden appearance of a real blue-and-white Crocker Police cruiser coming from the other end of Leighton.

Slice watched, furiously helpless, as his prey escaped, going into the bag lady's tenement.

Once the officers in the patrol car saw Slice and his gang, they slowed down and told Slice and his buddies to move on.

"I want that little coon," Slice, walking away, said as much to the air as to the others. "We owe him."

Barbara managed to get her keys out of her pocket and open her apartment door while Ivy supported her. Inside, he got her coat off, helped her to the armchair, and sat her down, covering her with the old knit afghan she kept on her bed. He went to the sink to get a cloth to clean her up, and she began crying, first softly, then gradually louder.

Ivy got a dish towel, wet it, and went back to Barbara. He tried to tell her that she was okay and everything would be all right now, but the words died in his throat before he could say them. They were a lie anyway. Everything wasn't all right. It never was. Realizing that words were useless at a time like this, Ivy gave up and finished cleaning the blood and dirt from her face. When he was done, Barbara reached out and clung to him as if she was afraid he was going to leave her.

Ivy wrapped his arms around her. He knew what it felt like to feel that sad, and it hurt him to see his friend suffering so. He held her and silently cursed Slice Sanchez and his bastard friends.

Ivy remained there holding her until the old woman's well of sorrow ran dry and blessed, forgetful sleep overtook her. He laid her head back against the chair and sat on the floor next to her, holding her hand and watching the late afternoon shadows creep into early evening.

Ivy wished Barbara had a phone so he could call his mother. He knew she was going to have a bird because he wasn't home on time, but he didn't care. He already felt guilty enough for abandoning Barbara. If he hadn't been such a baby and so paranoid about Dr. Peabody, he would have been with her today and maybe Slice and his goons would have left her alone. He had to make up for that. He was going to stay with her as long as she needed him, no matter how much trouble he got in at home.

Barbara woke a little after nine. By then, Ivy knew he was in major trouble with his mom. She left for work at the restaurant by eight. He had *never* stayed out past the time she left for work before. He just hoped she didn't do anything stupid like calling the cops to look for him.

Barbara smiled and blinked owlishly at him. He'd retrieved her glasses from the alley but they were too smashed to wear. "Is that you, Ivy?" She reached up and turned on the reading lamp next to the chair. "Oh, I'm glad you came back," she exclaimed, taking Ivy by surprise. "Where are my glasses?" She searched her pockets and the sides of the chair.

Ivy didn't like this. Barbara had a weird, vacant look on her face that scared him. "Your glasses got broken," Ivy told her. "Don't you remember?"

"Broken? Really? Oh, well. It's all right. I have a spare pair in the top drawer of my dresser." She tried to get up from the chair, but Ivy stopped her.

"I'll get them. You stay there." He jumped up and

went to the bureau almost buried under stacks of books in the corner. He opened the top drawer and was confronted by Barbara's underwear. Ivy blushed and looked away. He put his hand in the drawer, trying not to touch anything soft, and felt around until he found Barbara's glasses case. In the chair, Barbara smiled blankly as she tried to focus on a bleary world.

She doesn't remember what happened, Ivy thought, bringing the glasses to her. *She must be in shock.* Barbara took the case and removed a pair of round, wire-rimmed glasses that made her look like a granny out of a fairy tale when she put them on.

"These are an old prescription, but I still see pretty well with them," she explained, peering up at him. "You know, Ivy, I think I owe you an apology. Here I was trying to ram all that egghead literature down your throat and I forgot the first rule of reading. It should be *fun!*"

"No, Mrs. Wallach," Ivy stammered, but Barbara ignored him. She reached over the side of the chair and, with a great deal of effort, picked up a shoe box filled with paperback books. She placed it on her lap.

"I got these out and put them here, hoping you'd come back." She picked up one of the books and stared wistfully at it. "When Henry was younger he liked nothing better than reading a good spy novel. He always said that Ian Fleming's James Bond series was the best."

"James Bond?" Ivy asked, noticeable doubt in his voice.

"Yes, James Bond. Why?"

"You mean like those stupid movies they show on TV sometimes?" Ivy asked.

Barbara laughed, but Ivy noticed it wasn't her normal laugh. This was weary and strained. "No," she said, shaking her head slowly, with effort, for added emphasis. "Except for some of the early ones with Sean Connery, those movies have never done justice to the books."

Ivy was intrigued. He hadn't known that the dumb 007 movies were based on books. And when Barbara went on to tell him how Ian Fleming had been a real-life wartime spy, Ivy was sold. As Barbara became tired again, and put her head back to rest, Ivy picked up the first book, *Casino Royale*, and began to read.

Ivy stayed until midnight, reading and keeping an eye on Barbara, who would sleep for a while, but then wake, sometimes looking very fearful and disoriented. He got her into the bed and covered her before he left, making sure the door was securely locked. He got home just before his mother and had to stuff the box of spy novels behind the couch when she came in. She bawled him out for over an hour (as if he cared) for not being home earlier. Later, when he was sure she was asleep, he crept into the living room and retrieved the box of books, hiding it in his bedroom closet.

CHANNEL 6

Dragnet
*Bill Gage—
Special Investigator*
*Smokin' in the
Boys' Room*
America's Most Wanted
The Real James Bond

 Crackle.

The screen is breathing. Asthmatic. The wind rushes around him. He clings to the doorjamb, trying not to be sucked deep into the lungs of the tunnelvision.

The telephone's ring brings everything to a halt. Nothing moves.

The phone rings and rings and rings until it is dead. The tape Jesus made plays on the VCR. Wilbur watches the ritualistic death until Jesus stops the tape, removes it from the player, and tells him it's time to go.

Wilbur tries to hide in Grandma's TV, but there

are old cop shows on every channel, and Jesus knows how to use them.

Channel change.

Columbo!

The cruiser is parked at the far end of the Dunkin' Donuts parking lot. Columbo is at the counter.

"Give me the ah, plain. Uh, no, on second thought, let me see, I'll have the ah, cinnamon. Just a second. I'm sorry, I have trouble making up my mind. I'm very sorry. I'll have the chocolate. That's it. No, wait . . ."

The approach is easy.

Channel change.

Car 54, Where Are You?

"Ooh! Ooh! Quick! Put the tape in the cruiser!"

Muldoon panics, opens the door, and tosses it in. The videotape bounces off the seat, hits the underside of the dash, and drops onto the passenger's side floor.

"Ooh! Ooh! Now you've done it! Let's get out of here!"

Channel change.

Dragnet.

"Just the jelly doughnuts, ma'am."

Sergeant Friday puts the box of doughnuts on the dash and shifts the cruiser into reverse. The tape slides under the seat and becomes wedged there.

"Could you turn that down?" Bill asked Cindy, holding his hand over the phone. Cindy hit the mute button on the remote and watched the Bruins' goalie making a diving save.

"Yes, George, I'm fine," Bill said, causing Cindy to

take notice at the name of Bill's old friend, the Crocker police chief. Her initial excitement soon faded though as Bill's face became very solemn. He listened for a long time without saying a word, but his look said enough, and it wasn't good news.

By the time he hung up, Cindy had forgotten all about the Bruins and was waiting with an agonizing mix of anticipation and dread to hear what George Albert had said. She sat on the couch, her hands clasped between her knees, and stared at him expectantly. "Well?"

Bill began to pace, seemingly oblivious to her presence.

"Well?" she repeated loudly.

Bill stopped and looked up sharply, like a man awakened from a dream, or a nightmare. "I'm going to be a detective again," he said in a slow voice.

"That's great!" Cindy said, trying to generate some of the enthusiasm she thought he should be showing at this news.

"Is it?" Bill asked.

"Isn't it?"

Bill examined himself absently in the heart-shaped wall mirror. "It's kind of strange, really. George said he'd been putting off calling me because he didn't have a job for me. The city's really feeling the crunch from all the state budget cuts to local aid. There's even been talk of trimming the police force next year."

"I don't get it. How come he's giving you a job, then?" Cindy asked.

Bill let out a sigh. "Because the daughter of some bigwig local merchant was murdered this weekend.

They found the body this morning. Now all of a sudden the mayor has extra money available for a task force and another detective full-time on the case. The detective bureau has been short a man since one of them retired last month, so George was able to convince the mayor that I would be the best man for the investigation. My official title is to be 'special investigator.'"

"So, what's wrong?"

Bill resumed pacing.

"I mean, it's terrible that a young woman is dead," Cindy said, but that's got nothing to do with you."

"You don't think so?"

"No, I don't. You didn't cause her death. It's not your fault that you're going to get back into police work because of her murder." Bill frowned in response, and Cindy sensed he was somehow connecting this with his father. "But the important question is, what do *you* think? If this is going to open old wounds about the past . . . about your father . . . maybe you should reconsider."

"Kind of hard *not* to think of my father. I didn't expect—or at least I guess I was hoping—that in a small city like Crocker I wouldn't be put on a homicide for a while. Murder's a pretty rare occurence here. Narcotics are a much bigger problem. I thought I'd be better off with a drug bust to start back."

"Sounds like if drugs was all they had to worry about, you wouldn't have a job at all," Cindy pointed out.

Bill opened the TV drawer and retrieved a small,

red leather phone log. He sat in the easy chair by the phone. "George wants me to meet him at the county morgue first thing in the morning. It's a good thing I've accumulated a lot of sick time and vacation time. There shouldn't be any problem. I'll call the regional manager and tell him I'm taking the time and my staff can handle things. Since this probably won't be permanent, I guess I'd better not quit my security job yet, huh?" He smiled halfheartedly at Cindy.

"Bill." Cindy went to his side and laid a hand on his arm. "Really. If you're doing this to somehow get back at your father or to make up for what he did, forget it. Please don't do it."

Bill pulled her face down to his lips and kissed her. "Don't worry. I'll be all right," he told her, smiling. She smiled, too, but didn't like the look in his eyes.

Bill spent the rest of the evening pacing until Cindy coaxed him into making love to her. He tried to comply but was too preoccupied and they ended up having frustrated, distracted sex. He tossed and turned for another couple of hours after that. Eventually he fell into a troubled, twitching sleep filled with dark, menacing, yet vague dreams that flipped through his mind like a thick stack of snapshots rifled to create the illusion of motion.

The next morning, a very tired Bill Gage pulled his car into a space reserved for police vehicles behind the county morgue in the town of Bolton. Though Worcester was the county seat, Bolton was the most centrally located town, so twenty years ago the morgue and other county offices were moved there to allow equal access to everyone in Worcester County.

Bolton was only fifteen minutes from Crocker, but the ride had felt like hours to Bill. Getting out of his car and walking into the building, he felt a strange sense of detachment from reality. He guessed it was because less than a year and a half ago he would've sworn he was washed up as a cop and would never be doing something like this again.

Bill knew his way around the building from his time with the state police. It was a concrete slab of a structure, a homely bunker plunked down in a town of gabled colonials and grand Victorian houses. The actual morgue, consisting of an autopsy lab and a freezer that could hold six bodies comfortably, was in the basement. On the top floor were the registry of deeds and the county clerk's office.

Before going inside, Bill took note of a black sedan with CROCKER, MA, CHIEF OF POLICE embossed on the door around a gold Crocker Police Department badge. Bill hoped he wasn't late. This was going to be hard enough without getting off on the wrong foot.

The inside of the building was no more attractive than the outside. The floors were covered with faded yellow linoleum that might have been white once. Everything else was either institutional gray or tan. Just inside the entrance was another door with a sign: COUNTY MORGUE—AUTHORIZED PERSONNEL ONLY!! He went through it and down a set of metal stairs that rang like bells with every step and set his nerves on edge.

Chief George Albert, dressed in his dark blue chief's uniform with matching tie, was waiting outside the autopsy lab for him with two plainclothes detectives. His hair had grayed but was still thick and wavy. He had more lines on his sharp, angled face, but he looked good, a lot better than Bill.

"Good to see you again, Bill," George said as though he meant it, shaking Bill's hand. "This is Captain Mike Mahoney, the head of our detective bureau, and Lieutenant Frank Starkovski. We can go over this more in detail back in my office. Captain Mahoney and his men will be at your disposal, but you will report directly to me. I've got one patrolman, Fred Larken, a real computer whiz, who is in line for his gold badge and promotion to detective. I can give him to you full-time as a personal assistant, and if you need more help, I can put a few men on overtime."

Bill shook hands with Captain Mahoney, a squat, balding man with piercing blue eyes, and Detective Starkovski, thin, with mean eyes and a big nose. He sensed at once a great deal of hostility from the two, especially Starkovski. He couldn't blame them. Cops, particularly detectives who have been around awhile, are very territorial and they don't like anyone muscling in. Bill knew his hiring stank of politics and big money influence, more than enough reason for Crocker's finest to be hostile.

"You ready to go in, or do you want me to give you the background first?" Chief Albert asked. As far as work went, George hadn't changed a bit. He didn't waste time with amenities such as what've you been up to for the past ten years. That might come later, but right now there was business at hand.

The chief looked chagrined a moment before adding, "There hasn't been an autopsy yet so I don't have a medical examiner's report. Doc Seaver, the old M.E., died a few weeks ago and they haven't got a replacement for him yet. Essex County's going to lend us theirs, but he's away till the end of the week."

"George?" Bill said, the name sounding like a cough from his mouth. "Uh, Chief, can I talk to you alone for a minute?"

"Sure." Chief Albert motioned the two detectives into the lab and closed the door behind them. "What is it, Bill?"

Bill Gage looked at his friend and wasn't sure what it was he really wanted to say. "I'm . . . not sure about this. I was sincere about wanting a job when I wrote to you; I just didn't expect to be working on a homicide right away. And your detectives don't seem too happy about my being around either."

"Don't worry about them. They're all up in arms about the layoff rumors. They'll come around when they see you work," George said. The detectives watched them through the lab window. "As far as you handling a homicide, I'll tell you what I told the mayor when he gave me orders to do whatever's necessary to solve this case. I told him I knew *the* best homicide detective I've ever seen. I was talking about you. I know you've been down and out, had your problems; none of that is important now. At one time you *were* the best homicide detective in this or any other state for that matter. I'm betting that you haven't lost it. I'm betting you can be the best again.

"I wish that I could hire you under normal circumstances and let you work your way back in at your own pace, but I can't even promise that you'll have a job when this investigation is over. In fact, I'd say your chances for a permanent position with the force are slim to none. If you feel you can't cut it, I'll understand, no hard feelings, but this is your *only* shot at *any* police work in Crocker for quite a while, the way the budget is looking."

There it was, right out in the open in front of Bill. With the blunt honesty that Bill best remembered his friend for, George had laid out his options plainly. The funny thing was, until he'd walked into the morgue, Bill had thought he'd made up his mind about this. He hadn't counted on a last-minute attack of cold feet.

"I'm sorry, George. Forget what I just said. I want this very badly."

Chief Albert nodded and slapped his shoulder. "Good. I knew you wouldn't let me down. So, shall I fill you in while you look at the body?"

"That'll be fine," Bill answered heading for the lab door.

"One more thing," George said. "This is pretty gruesome. I hope you still have a strong stomach."

Bill followed the chief into the lab where Mahoney and Starkovski waited. The lab was small with no windows, and most of the floor space was taken up by the metal autopsy table. The victim lay in a body bag on top. The walls were lined with shelves stocked with supplies and empty specimen jars. One shelf near the door held a collection of specimen oddities, such as a brain tumor that resembled Richard Nixon. Under it was a large metal double sink and faucets.

"The body was left in front of what used to be the Saxon Theater, near City Hall. Captain Mahoney's got photographs for you," the chief explained.

Mahoney held up a manila envelope and Bill couldn't help noticing the smirks on his and Starkovski's faces.

Chief Albert unzipped the body bag. "She was killed somewhere else, but I'm more concerned with whether the M.E. can tell us if she was sexually molested or not since the cause of death is pretty obvious."

The open body bag revealed a sight that Bill Gage would never have been prepared for even if he'd been a cop with fifty years under his belt. On the table lay the bloodstained body of a young woman. She was naked. She was also missing her head.

Bill swallowed hard. Mahoney and Starkovski were smirking to beat the band. Bill knew why. He knew his face had registered shock, horror and disgust, but that was okay. Bill had yet to meet a cop who could look at *any* victim of a violent death and not react. The stone-faced cop of the movies, TV, and crime novels was a myth as far as he was concerned. He would have liked to have seen Mahoney's and Starkovski's faces when they first saw the body. He was willing to bet at least one of them, if not both, had tossed their cookies.

What was important was how he carried himself

now, after the initial shock was over. He took a deep breath and found, to his surprise, that he was ready for this. He felt the living embodiment of the old adage about a fish never forgetting how to swim. The condition of the girl's body was automatically filed to be dealt with later, most likely in dreams. With a deep breath he went about the grisly task of inspecting the corpse. And, amazingly enough, it seemed as though he'd done this just yesterday. He was relieved beyond words to find that his special talent was still intact, a little rusty from ten years of disuse but functional. He focused on the body.

"Name: Grace Simonds," the chief read slowly from a piece of paper. He gave the smirking Starkovski a withering look and handed the paper to him. "I forgot my glasses. You read this to Special Investigator Gage, Frank."

It was all Bill could do not to smile as Starkovski's face reddened. Jaw clenched, he took the paper and read the contents in a clipped voice.

"Age: twenty."

Bill was inspecting the girl's severed neck, feeling around the edge of the cut. He became aware that the room had grown so quiet he could hear Mahoney swallow twice.

"Identified by her name engraved in her high school class ring on left hand and a birthmark on right shoulder identified by her father."

Bill lifted the headless body to a sitting position to inspect her back and the pattern of dried blood. He put his ear to her back and tapped on her shoulder blades with the heel of his hand. Starkovski tried to hide his sudden gagging with a coughing fit. His voice wasn't so clipped when he read the next item.

"Her parents have supplied us with several photographs and a complete description. Hair: brown. Eyes: brown. Weight: one hundred forty pounds. Height: five feet six. Bell-shaped birthmark in the middle of her right shoulder. No other distinguishing marks."

Bill laid the body down again and spread her legs. Captain Mahoney and Detective Starkovski were no longer smirking.

"She was last seen, uh . . ." Starkovski lost his place trying to read and watch Bill at the same time. He found it again. "She was last seen by her boyfriend and two other witnesses within a period of thirty minutes around one forty Sunday morning when he dropped her off at the rear entrance to her dormitory. Her body was found Monday morning at six o'clock under the marquee of the old Saxon Theater, now deserted. No one who knew her reported her missing in the approximately twenty-eight hours and twenty minutes between the time she was last seen and when she was found."

Bill returned Grace Simonds's legs to a more dignified position and began examining her hands.

"The body was found by a patrolman on duty, Officer Schultz. It was lying at a forty-five degree angle to the street with her arms folded across her chest. The only blood on the scene was on the victim's body and was dry."

Bill finished with an inspection of her feet and closed the bag.

Outside the lab they got cups of rancid coffee

from a machine around the corner that dispensed its caffeine sludge in cups sporting poker hands. Bill held a straight flush.

"Okay, Bill," the chief said, sipping from two pairs, queens and aces, "what'd you find out?"

"Who does the chief think this guy is, Sherlock Holmes?" Bill heard Starkovski whisper to Mahoney. If Chief Albert heard, he didn't let on.

Bill leaned against the wall, holding his coffee with both hands and staring into it. He looked dazed, or like a man who had a pressing problem on his mind. He was still processing and cataloging information from his scrutiny of the body, and until it was finished he would look and talk like the absentminded professor.

"She wasn't molested," Bill started, his voice soft. "She's been dead for at least twenty-four hours. I'd say she was killed almost immediately after she was last seen. Her head was severed with an ax blade, two clean blows, but that didn't kill her. She was already dead when the decapitation took place. The cause of death was drowning."

Bill wished he had been able to give George his findings privately. He knew he was dropping a bombshell on his new boss; the shock on George's face attested to that. The two detectives showed open scorn for his statement with Mahoney laughing openly and Starkovski exclaiming: "What a joke!"

The chief shot them both a fierce look but Mahoney was undaunted. "Come on, Chief! I've had it. I want to go on record as being against this!" he exploded. "It's bad enough you and the mayor get your old buddy in here on a special payroll when *real* cops might be getting laid off, but to have this— this *has-been* walking around acting like some kind of psychic in a bad movie is too much. If we listen to this guy we are going to waste valuable time and effort in this investigation."

"That's enough," Chief Albert barked.

"But his saying she drowned is ridiculous. All you have to do is look at her to see that, for Christ's sake. You don't have to be Sherlock Holmes to deduce that," Mahoney said. By his side, Starkovski grinned and nodded in total agreement.

The chief turned to Bill, eyebrows raised questioningly.

Bill tossed his coffee cup into a nearby plastic-lined trash barrel. "Come on," he said softly and returned to the lab. Mahoney, Starkovski and the chief followed him, gathering around the autopsy table while he unzipped the body bag.

Bill took an empty, quart-size specimen jar from a shelf. He handed it to Mahoney. "Hold this under her neck," he instructed. Mahoney looked for a moment as if he was going to tell Bill to go to hell, then reconsidered and did what he'd been asked to do. He tipped the jar and held it to the severed neck where Bill showed him, and tried not to grimace.

Bill moved to the side of the table and placed his right hand in a fist, the left one cupped over it, on Grace Simonds's sternum. "I know she drowned because her lungs and stomach are full of water," he said. He pumped her as if performing the Heimlich maneuver on her. Pinkish water gushed from the gooey black mess of exposed neck tissue and muscle. It splashed into the specimen jar, some of it getting on Mahoney's hands. He quickly released the specimen jar, which tottered on the tabletop but didn't fall off. Mahoney ran for the sink. Starkovski didn't look well, neither did the chief.

Bill went on. "Further proof that she was already dead when her head was cut off is the drying pattern of the blood on her body. See here? The blood is too uniform, too evenly dispersed. If her heart had been pumping when the decapitation occurred, we'd see more of an abstract spray pattern, and less blood, too, as more would have spurted away from the body than on it. I'd say the removal of her head was done to satisfy some ritualistic need or to try to mislead us."

No one said a word. Mahoney, drying his hands with a paper towel, wore a look of chagrin. Starkovski still had that look that said he thought Bill was full of it, but it was less sardonic. The chief was grinning slightly, enjoying seeing Mahoney and Starkovski shown up.

"Of course, I'm willing to wait until a medical examiner can verify me, so we better save this for him." He indicated the specimen jar with its small amount of lung water. "I'm not trying to grandstand here or do anything other than my job," he said quietly, giving Mahoney a stare that challenged him to do the same.

"Until we can get an M.E. in here, let's do this," the chief said in a tone of compromise. "Bill will conduct his own investigation, and you'll conduct yours, Mahoney. When the M.E.'s report comes in we'll powwow and compare notes, then team up for a full assault."

The look on Mahoney's face told Bill that they were in agreement that the chief's idea was asinine, but Bill consented to it. Without George on his side he would be lost. Mahoney reluctantly agreed also, and the chief told the two detectives to take his car back to Crocker—he'd ride with Bill.

"I know it's not the best approach to solving this case, but Mahoney and his detectives have to be handled with kid gloves right now," George explained after his men were gone. "They're afraid for their jobs and rightly so. As I told you, there's been a lot of talk on the city council of cutting way back on the force and letting the state police pick up the slack. Crocker's small, more of a town than a city, and with the economy and unemployment the way it is, a lot of people think it's a good idea to scale down to town size in the area of police, fire, and teaching positions."

Bill nodded. George hadn't needed to explain, but Bill felt good that he had. It made him feel that George trusted him and was treating him on equal footing, which gave a tremendous boost to Bill's confidence.

"That was quite a display in there," the chief said with a grin as they went up the stairs together. "You really opened Mahoney's eyes. I think he'll come around. He's a good cop, a good interrogator. I think he'll see that he can learn a lot from you. Starkovski is another matter. He's as thickheaded and stubborn as a mule."

Outside, George turned to Bill. "There's one

more thing I want to tell you, but I wanted to wait until we were alone. I thought it would be best if I got this out of the way first thing." He stared uncomfortably at his feet.

"What is it, George?"

"I just . . . I just wanted to apologize for abandoning you when you started to have trouble. I was too—you know—wrapped up in my career. When you started having family problems, I should have been there for you."

"You were, George." Bill tried to soothe his friend's guilt as they got in the car. "*I was the one who did the abandoning. I remember you trying to help, but I pushed you away. I wouldn't let anyone help. You don't owe me an apology, George. If anything, I owe you, and everyone else who knew me then, an apology.*"

George seemed relieved. "You know, to this day I still don't know what happened to you. I know it was some kind of family tragedy, but you left the state police force and dropped out of sight so fast, no one seemed to know what happened, or they weren't telling." George held up his hand before Bill could answer. "If you don't want to talk about it, fine with me. I just wanted you to know I was sorry. You don't owe me any explanations."

"No. It's okay. I think you deserve to know." Bill pulled the car out of the morgue parking lot and fixed his gaze on the road. He began to speak slowly while his memory clicked off slides of the worst moments of his life on the screen of his mind's eye:

Click: There he was, lecturing students at the State Police Academy about the need to remain im-

partial and unemotionally involved in any case, no matter how heinous the crime, when he was inter-rupted with the news that his father was dead.

Click: There he was, at Pennsylvania State Police headquarters looking at pictures of raped and mur-dered women, eighty-nine of them, and listening to investigators present the evidence that left no doubt that his own father, who was a crime photographer for the Pennsylvania State Troopers, was the perpe-trator.

Click: There he was, standing in the living room of the house he grew up in. At his feet, a lumpy black body bag held what remained of his father, who had put a shotgun in his mouth and removed most of his head when he'd realized he was about to be exposed as a mass murderer.

Click: There he was, reading the journal his fa-ther had kept, complete with photos, detailing and reveling in his murders, which removed any doubt Bill might have been clinging to concerning his father's guilt.

Click: There he was: quitting the force, no expla-nation given and moving back to Pottsville, buying the first of thousands of bottles of Jack Daniels and losing himself in the whiskey's amnesiac embrace.

The chief didn't say anything when Bill finished speaking. They rode in silence for some time. He wanted to apologize again, to express his condo-lences somehow, but he was a man who'd always found words of sympathy hard to say.

"The shock of finding out that my own father had been a rapist and mass murderer for most of my life . . . it was too much," Bill said after a while. "I felt like a fraud. Everything he'd taught me about right and wrong and the honor in being a part of law enforcement became a sham. Here I was, being touted as the best investigative detective the Massachusetts State Police had to offer, and I hadn't even been able to see what was going on right before my eyes for years.

"I flipped. I had a breakdown. I imagined all kinds of crazy things, and tried to escape reality in a bottle. If I hadn't come back to Crocker because I needed money and wanted to sell my condo, I never would have met Cindy, my wife. And if that hadn't happened, I'm quite sure I'd be as dead right now as poor Grace Simonds."

"Your wife must be quite a woman," the chief responded.

"She is," Bill agreed.

"For what it's worth, I, for one, am glad you're back," the chief said with a nod of confidence.

"Thanks, George. I think I am, too."

Off the air.

A voice in a dream.

"I never thought you'd do it, Wilbur."

Hit the power button on the remote.

He opens his eyes. The screen is a low cloud and he's lying outdoors. A blue jay flies by squawking his name: *Wilbur! Wilbur! Wilbur!*

He recognizes the voice, a girl.

"I never thought you had it in you."

It's not a dream voice now.

He sits up in bed. Gray video light streams from his open closet. He feels his head swiveling in that direction, totally unconnected to the rest of his body. Tendrils of flickering fog slip out of the dark doorway like escaping ghosts.

"Who's there?" he asks, unsure if his mouth or his eyes have spoken the words.

"I always knew He had it in Him, but not you."

Channel change.

"All right, panelists, time's up. Does anyone want to take a crack at who our mystery guest might be? Wilbur?"

"Is it . . . Deb?"

"Right you are! Take off your masks, panelists, and greet our mystery guest: Deb, the runaway child porno star!"

Canned applause.

Cue the theme music.

Cut to commercial: "Call one nine hundred-KID-PORN and learn all my *tit*illating secrets," Deb says, lounging on a fur-covered bed. She's a skinny thing of fifteen with large breasts and no hips clad in a leather halter top and G-string studded with brass stars and adorned with chains.

"Call now and learn all about the abuse I suffered at the hands of my stepfather. Learn how I ran away and became a child porno star at age ten. Call now and we'll send you, absolutely free, my last porno movie, *The Big Snuff.*"

A grainy black-and-white video. Deb is tied bare-breasted and spread-eagled over an old bathtub. Her leather G-string is crotchless. People move around her, their faces hidden by black hoods. They whip her. They beat her. She screams. The camera shot changes. Jesus stands in a corner holding a

*long wooden pike with a razor-sharp point. He
points it between Deb's legs and charges.*

"Doesn't that look exciting?" Deb is back on her
fur-covered bed, but now her legs are smeared with
blood. "I'm waiting for your call. Only three ninety-
five for the first minute, five dollars a minute after
that. Call me. I *want* you."

"If you wanted me so badly, you wouldn't have
gone off the air," Wilbur said. "You wouldn't have
left me." Wilbur turns the screen in his head off and
gets out of bed. In the mirror he can see Deb sitting
in a puddle of her own blood on the mattress he has
just vacated.

*"We should have run away, Wilbur. I thought
you were kidding when you told me about Jesus and
the tunnelvision. He won't let you stop now, or ever.
He likes this. You better get used to it.*

"Where do you think he put her head?"

"I'm not doing this!" he shouts. "I don't go with
Him. I stay with Grandma!"

Deb lies back and blood squishes onto the mattress. *"Hey, Wilbur,"* she says softly. Her body is
beginning to look strange, the skin hard and tight.
"Remember what I always say?" Her skin is crystal-
izing, hardening to the gloss of a bloody gem.

"You do what you have to do," he answers. Her
crystal body begins to steam, filling the room with a
sparkling red fog and covering him with a ruby
dew. He closes his eyes. He is in the living room
when he opens them again. Jesus is standing in front
of the shelves lined with black videocassettes.

"These are the scriptures of atonement," Jesus
says, sounding like Oral Roberts.

Wilbur looks over the titles of the cassettes. The first one, *Toilet Training,* is missing.

"As I suffered," Jesus says, *"so have they who failed to think. The first atonement has been made."* Wilbur can feel His breath on his neck. The Son of God reaches for the tapes with Wilbur's arms and hands. The videocassettes come tumbling from the shelf until He reaches the correct one. The first two years and ten films, in which Jesus took Wilbur's place, committing adult acts with other children, lie strewn at his feet.

"Those are unimportant," Jesus says, kicking the tapes aside. *"Those are the venial sins."*

The next tape on the shelf is titled: *Smokin' in the Boys' Room.*

"This must be atoned for." Jesus throws the tape over his shoulder. It somersaults in a series of freeze-frames to the VCR where it glides into the machine with a click and a whisper.

The tape comes on. The Son of God's sad face appears on the screen, looking out at Wilbur.

"I was always there for you and no one saw."

The Savior's eyes bulge. Wilbur feels a tremendous pressure in his head. The TV screen expands. A scream tries to escape Wilbur's mouth, but his clenched teeth won't let it pass.

The TV screen explodes, spilling video all over reality. In a flash he is consumed by the gray light. Trapped. There is no Jesus here, no one to take his place. Wilbur's in the video; he's in the script.

Scene 1: A small black-and-white boy huddles near a dirty sink, slightly out of focus. The color is adjusted, the picture clears.

Cut to:

Scene 2: (Close-up) The boy holds a cigarette in his hand. He can't be any older than four or five but he puts the cigarette to his mouth and puffs on it like an adult. The faint strains of Crosby, Stills, and Nash playing "Teach Your Children" can be heard in the background.

Cut to:

Scene 3: A scantily clad Mary-not-Mother wiping chalk from a blackboard.

Cut to:

Scene 4: Mary-not-Mother finds him hiding near the sink with the butts.

Cut to:

Scene 5: Mary-not-Mother pulls his pants down and spanks him hard with a ruler.

Cut to:

Scene 6: He is tied naked to a bed. Mary-not-Mother lights a cigarette and sits next to him. She teaches first his arms, then his chest, finally his genitals, that smoking in the boys' room is against the rules.

The tape ends. The video recedes. The TV screen sops it up and heals itself, sucking glass back into place and sealing it with crackles of electricity.

The ghost of old pain possesses him. He finds release in the tub filled with cold water. His teeth chatter until they hurt, but it is substantially less pain than he feels if he tries to get out of the water.

Jesus is in the medicine cabinet mirror. *"It is time for the next atonement,"* He says in the hellfire-and-damnation preaching style of Jimmy Swaggart.

* * *

Special investigator Bill Gage drove to the campus of Crocker State College. The college was situated on the site of the first known white settlement in the area, a stockade fort built by Josiah Crocker in 1698. It was nestled under the rising grassy slopes of Hospital Hill to the north and stretched to Coolidge Pond, three miles to the south, with an almost equal east-west diameter. Bill wanted to have a look around Grace Simonds's dormitory. He was also interested in privately looking over the case file of the Simonds homicide. Captain Mahoney had assigned him an office that was the size of a closet and was presently filled with stacks of outdated arrest forms. Mahoney had assured him that the room would be cleared by the end of the day, but Bill doubted a desk would fit in there anyway. He'd take it up with George when he saw him at the end of the day; right now he had more important things to do than waste time playing power games with Mahoney.

The file folder was open on the seat next to him, allowing him to glance through it while he drove around campus, following the signs for Whistler Dormitory where Grace Simonds had lived. He parked his car in front of the high-rise building and pushed his seat back as far as it would go. He crossed his legs as comfortably as possible under the wheel, then picked up the case file.

Most of the basic legwork, fact-finding, interviews with family, friends, the last ones to see her alive, etc., was done already. It gave him a point to focus on to begin.

Grace Simonds was the daughter of Lionel Simonds, owner of Simonds Steel Works. She had been a senior at the college, enrolled in the business program. She had started out as a human services major but had switched in her sophomore year. Friends described her as a stubborn but likable free soul who was friendly and always ready to help anyone, anytime; those were the kinds of qualities any parents would be proud to have instilled in their children unless they knew those qualities would someday invite death.

Her friends said she liked her independence, so much so that she insisted on living in the dorm even though her parents' house was less than five minutes from the college. According to those same friends—her roommate, mostly, and two other girls —she had been cutting loose a lot lately. They said since she'd started dating a new guy, one John Cavant, who had a solid alibi for the time of her death. She'd started drinking a lot more and smoking pot, something she'd rarely done before. She had, in fact, been out partying with her beau the night she disappeared.

On that night—actually, Sunday morning—she was seen at two different times in the company of two different men. One had been positively identified as her boyfriend, who'd been seen dropping her off at the rear entrance to her dorm, and the other remained a mystery man in whose arms she was seen twenty minutes later, just outside the dormitory door.

Her roommate had been in bed asleep at the time, but claimed she always woke up when Grace got in. She didn't that night. That, and Grace's undisturbed bed, seemed to indicate that she had never made it up to her room.

Bill moved a paper aside and uncovered a photo of the dead girl on the pavement in front of the Saxon Theater where she'd been found. She lay with legs straight, arms folded across her chest. He'd been putting off looking at the police pictures.

These were the kinds of pictures his father had taken as crime photographer for the Pennsylvania State Police. They were also the kinds of pictures he had taken of his victims, to be looked at and gloated over in his journal like some old pervert slobbering over an innocent child.

He pushed the thought away. Pictures were useful. Because of what his father had taught him about photography while growing up, Bill had made taking his own photos an integral part of his investigative technique during his years as a trooper detective. The fact that he'd learned it from his father didn't make any difference. It was a useful tool, one he was going to have to use again if he wanted to be as effective as possible, no matter how much it reminded him of his father, or made him *feel* like his father.

The first thing he'd done upon getting back from Bolton was to go to a good old K mart on John Crocker Highway, not too far from the campus, and buy a Polaroid Sunburst camera and three packs of film.

He took the camera out and loaded the film, thinking while he did it about the twenty minutes between the last two times Grace Simonds was seen alive. That gap bothered Bill. If she didn't go up to her room, had she gone to someone else's room? Had she gone into the dorm at all? Maybe she had been making out with the mystery man outside the dorm from the time her boyfriend had dropped her off?

He took out a pencil and jotted a note on the cover of the manila case folder to remind him to have someone talk to *all* dorm residents. It seemed that the initial investigating officer, who was Starkovski, hadn't bothered to check that out. He'd interviewed only those people who had come forth to offer info. Bill made a note on the folder to get the extra men George had promised to help with the interviews and another note to have them talk with all the students in Grace Simonds's classes and to her teachers, too.

The camera ready, Bill got out of the car and stood in front of the building. He took a couple of shots of the front, to try the camera out, sticking the developing pictures in his overcoat pocket. He walked around to the blacktopped path at the side of the building. It led to two rear parking lots that required special stickers for legal parking, and the rear entrance of the dorm.

He snapped a picture of each parking lot and its relationship to the dorm and put them into his pocket, retrieving the first two. They had developed nicely and were good pictures as far as the capabilities of the camera went.

He walked to the path that led from the second parking lot to the dorm door. "Grace Simonds was last seen getting out of her boyfriend's car here at approximately one forty in the morning by someone leaving the dorm," Bill mused aloud. He stood for a long moment looking at the second parking lot, then walked down the path to the dormitory's rear entrance.

"Approximately twenty minutes later she's seen here." He stood at a recess created by protruding concrete columns at the side of the entrance, "She's kissing someone else." No, *kissing* was an assumption that brought to mind the old adage that when you *assume* you make an *ass* out of *u* and *me,* another one of his father's Polonian favorites.

If the mystery man had been lying in wait for Grace, it must have been in the parking lot. Otherwise he would have been seen by the witness leaving the dorm who had seen Grace being let off. There was no place to hide anywhere around the entranceway; it was too open. Even the recessed spot where Grace had been seen necking was too shallow and open to hide anyone. If the mystery man had wanted to observe the rear of the dorm from an unseen position, the only way would be from a car in the second parking lot.

He made a note to check with campus police to see if any cars in that lot had been ticketed for not having proper stickers. According to the file, the campus cops made a vehicle tour of the lots anywhere from every half hour to every two hours, on a varying schedule that was supposed to be patternless. On Sunday morning they had patrolled at 1:00 A.M. and again at 2:25. It was possible that the killer had been in the lot from 1:00 A.M. waiting for her, unless he'd been following her and her boyfriend, a very distinct possibility.

Bill walked back and forth in front of the entrance, taking pictures of the spot where she'd been necking, the doorway, the view of the parking lot from there. Stuffing the snapshots into his pocket, he went inside. He took pictures of the inside foyer and the hallway leading to the elevators. He saw no point in inspecting her room. It had already been gone over by the department's one-man forensic/photo lab. Bill had his report in the case file. He hoped that Lieutenant Hanson, the forensics guy, knew how to do his job better than Frank Starkovski knew how to conduct a background investigation.

He walked a short way down the hall and snapped another couple of pictures before heading outside and back to his car. His suitcoat pockets were bulging with snapshots that he put into the case folder once he got into the car. Now came the hardest part of any homicide investigation: interviewing the victim's parents.

Ivy finished the last page of *The Spy Who Loved Me* and closed the book. He was amazed at how different the book was from the stupid movie with Roger Moore that he had seen on television. He didn't understand why Hollywood would take such a great book and change it until the only thing it and the resulting movie had in common was the title.

The Spy Who Loved Me movie had been a ridiculous, unbelievable, globe-trotting story with even more ridiculous and unbelievable characters, such as Jaws, the killer with metal teeth, who was as indestructible (and about as realistic) as a cartoon character. But the novel was a suspenseful, action-packed story in which everything happened within the confines of a small roadside motel. And, unlike the movie, there was very little mushy stuff in the book, which was just fine with the eleven-year-old Ivy.

Ivy got off his bed and went to the closet, pulling the box of James Bond novels Barbara had given him out from under the pile of his dirty clothes where he'd hidden them. Since one of his many chores around the house was to get the laundry ready for his mom to take to the laundromat, he didn't have to worry about his mother's finding the books there. She had rarely seen him reading a book and might become suspicious if she found these or saw him reading as much as he really did.

Though his mother asked him every night at dinner what he'd done that day, in school and at play, he hadn't told her about his new friend, Barbara Wallach. One reason was that his mother asked purely out of reflex. It was part of her routine. She didn't really care about, or even listen to, his answer, as Ivy discovered one evening when he tested her by saying he'd skipped school and hitchhiked to Hampton Beach. She'd kept her bleary eyes glued to the boob tube, her wine glass clutched firmly in her hand, the ever present butt hanging from her lips, and muttered, "That's nice," between puffs.

As far as Ivy was concerned, her indifference was reason enough not to tell her about Barbara. There was a larger purpose behind his silence, though. His mother was probably already aware that Barbara lived down the street and was considered to be the neighborhood bag lady/wino. If she found out that Ivy was spending every afternoon and most of his weekends with the old woman, he knew she'd put a stop to it. That would be bad enough, but Ivy was afraid his mother wouldn't let it end at that.

On the day that his father had died, Ivy's mother had changed. Since then Ivy had stopped trying to figure out why she treated him the way she did. On the one hand she was generally indifferent to him, too wrapped up in her own problems and continuing sorrow. But sometimes, she could be so caring, so attentive (especially when he was sick, which was rare, or hurt) that it bordered on the overprotective.

Ivy thought it very possible that if he told his mother about Barbara, she would call the cops and have his friend arrested for being a child molester or something. There was no way Ivy could subject Barbara to trouble like that. So, like his extraordinary intelligence, Ivy kept his friendship with Barbara Wallach a secret from his mom.

Ivy carried the box of books to his bed and took each one out, placing them on his fraying quilt in the order in which they'd been published. He'd read them all up to *The Spy Who Loved Me* and was a little sad that there were only a few more books to read in the series.

He was torn; he wanted to take his time with the last books and savor them, but conversely, he wanted to devour them as quickly as possible so he could relive them in play and in his imagination. Needless to say, it was not an unpleasant dilemma.

Ivy opened *On Her Majesty's Secret Service*, the

next book in the series, but didn't start reading. He lay back and held the book up to look at. He thought of Barbara and her enthusiasm for the spy novels, which were every bit as good as she'd said.

He was glad he had changed his mind about Barbara. After their run-in with Slice Sanchez and his goons, Ivy became positive that she was who she appeared to be. And now an ironic new element had been added because of the Slice episode: For the first time in his life, someone needed him, really needed him. His mother had never reached out to him after his father's death, and he'd never had a chance to turn his grief into caring and consoling, which would have led to healing. Instead he'd been forced to deal with his pain alone, and it had turned to rancid bitterness. It felt good to have someone need him, to know that someone counted on him.

He hoped Barbara was okay. Her apparent amnesia about what had happened in the alley had really scared him at first, but later she'd seemed all right, if a bit sleepy. At times since then, he'd been almost able to convince himself that she was just refusing to speak of the incident, ignoring it on purpose to show him by example how unimportant it had been. But then he'd remember Slice Sanchez pointing at him and he knew it wasn't unimportant. Slice Sanchez wouldn't develop amnesia about getting even with Ivy. And whether he admitted it or not, there *was* something different about Barbara since the assault, a vagueness that worried him even more than what Slice Sanchez might do to him.

He laid the Bond novel on his chest and folded his hands over it, closing his eyes. His thoughts turned to his recent nemesis and he began to consider some tricks, a la James Bond, that he might devise to spring on Slice and his pals when they tried to get him, as he knew they would eventually.

Getting a pen and paper from one of his school notebooks, he began jotting down ideas and making plans.

CHANNEL 7

*This Is Tunnelvision!
—II*
*007 in
"The Trash Bag Affair"*
Point Counter Point

 Bill Gage sat up in bed, breath held, heart racing. An echo of the nightmare came to him. He was standing in his father's house looking at that awful photo album and had come upon a picture of Grace Simonds's decapitated corpse.

He lay back and listened to the sounds of the house: the wind blowing outside, the occasional creak and pop of the old house settling, and from the kitchen downstairs the loud hum of the refrigerator, which sounded as if it was on its last legs.

Bill glanced at Cindy sleeping next to him and slid silently out of bed to check the kids. He was certain they were okay—if they weren't, Cindy would have been up and tending to them long before him—but he checked them anyway to get his mind off the dream. The hallway running the length of the second floor to the window at the top of the stairs was alive with strange shadows scratching the walls—dark monsters created by the moonlight.

He checked the girls' room first, since it was on his way to the bathroom. Both girls were asleep. Sassy was all tucked in neat and snug as usual. Missy was lying upside down, her covers in disarray, her pillow on the floor. He closed their door, went to the bathroom, then went down to the nursery, where Devin slept on his stomach, his Ernie doll tucked under his arm.

Bill was wide awake. *I guess nothing's changed*, he thought, remembering the nagging bouts of insomnia that had always plagued him when he was on a case, especially a homicide. Once he got involved, his mind never wanted to let up and give him a break, even to sleep and recharge. Thankfully, he was not a person who needed a lot of sleep. When he got overtired, his body would compensate and start pumping adrenaline to keep him going.

Though he hated not being able to sleep, he didn't mind tonight. Tonight, the insomnia was welcome; it was another piece falling into place, telling him that as far as his being a detective was concerned, he was the same as when he was a Statie.

He'd had his first confirmation of that fact when he inspected Grace Simonds's mutilated corpse. Up until the moment he stepped up to that table and looked at her body up close, he had been deathly afraid that the special talent that had made him such a good detective ten years before would be gone, left at the bottom of a bottle of Jack Daniel's.

Before he'd met Cindy, Bill didn't have a name

for what he did when looking at evidence, or a crime scene. Other cops had called him "methodical, with a good eye for detail," and that was as suitable an explanation for Bill as any. He thought everyone had the same ability he had—they just didn't know how to concentrate enough to be able to use it.

It had been during his third week of sobriety and seventh date with Cindy that he found himself telling her things he'd never told anyone. She had been particularly interested when he described how he had the ability to focus completely on an object or scene, seeing every minute facet of it at once in almost microscopic detail. Cindy had been intrigued and pushed him to describe it farther until she came up with the tag, *tunnelvision.*

"The term can mean someone who refuses to see the forest for the trees, so to speak, and in medical terms it's a vision defect," she'd explained. "It's literally like seeing through a tunnel; only a small circular area is clear. In you, because you can turn it off and on and use it, it's an asset."

Actually, it was nothing like looking through a tunnel, but the image conveyed the general idea. Mentally, he *did* block everything out until he had a small focused spot to work on, but he still *saw* what he was mentally eliminating. If her explanation helped Cindy to understand it and, more importantly, pleased her that she'd been able to give a name to his gift, he didn't care. By then he was falling deeply in love with her and was ready to climb out of the bottle if she would consent to marry him.

He went back to the door of his bedroom and looked at his sleeping wife. The LED on the bedside clock radio read 3:45 A.M. Since there was no use in going back to bed—he'd just toss and turn and wake Cindy—he went downstairs to the buzzing refrigerator for a glass of milk.

The case file for the Simonds homicide was on top of the fridge where he'd put it so the kids couldn't get at it. A few days ago, little Devin had discovered Bill's personal papers drawer under the TV and had torn into the resumé copies, car title, insurance and tax records, and other important documents. Bill took the file down and tucked it under his arm. Sipping the cold milk, he went into the living room.

He placed the glass of milk and the file on top of the television while he cleared magazines and a lace doily off the oval coffee table in front of the couch. He pulled the low table over to the easy chair and retrieved his milk and the file, placing both on the table as he sat down.

The snapshots he'd taken of Grace Simonds's dorm, her parents' house, and her bedroom, spilled out of the file folder when he opened it. He put aside the photos of her house and bedroom—they were taken more to help him create a feel for the girl and what she was like than to be scrutinized—and arranged the ones of her dorm and its immediate environs in the order in which he'd snapped them.

From the back of the file, he took the official police photos of the front of the Saxon Theater and of the body itself and placed them in a neat stack to the side for the time being. Next to those he placed

the family pictures her parents had provided him
with. They showed a much younger Grace Simonds,
a girl still happy being in the company of her family:
at the beach, a water park, standing with her dad in
her first prom dress, posing with a bright smile for
her high school class picture. With the photos, her
parents had also given him a cloudy old waxed paper packet that held a lock of Grace's hair from her
first haircut.

It had been difficult, to say the least, interviewing
Mr. and Mrs. Simonds. Bill had expected Lionel
Simonds to be one of those arrogant captain-of-
industry types who think the government and police are their personal employees, but he was surprised. Simonds's wife, Lea, was more like that, a
big socialite in a small pond. Lionel Simonds was a
very quiet, reserved, unemotional man. While his
wife had shrieked demands at Bill, growing more
shrill with every moment until she exploded into a
hysteria of tears, Lionel Simonds had sat and stared
at the ceiling. When his wife broke down, he calmly
went to her and comforted her.

Bill put the packet of hair with the family photographs and pushed them and the Simondses to the
side of the table and the back of his mind. He felt
the pangs of guilt he'd always felt in this stage of his
preparation to use his tunnelvision. He always felt
so cold and uncaring just pushing the victim's relatives and their grief away, partly because he could
do it so easily and so well. No matter how much
something upset him, he could relegate it to a section of his mind to be dealt with at the appropriate
time. It was all part of his routine of self-discipline

and concentration, not a reflection of his emotional or mental stability, but he was certain that in the old days, a lot of his fellow officers had thought he was as cold as stone.

He turned his attention to the photographs. Immediately he put the police pictures of Grace Simonds's body in the morgue back into the folder. They would tell him nothing that his firsthand inspection of her corpse hadn't already. He spread out the police shots of the front of the Saxon Theater.

He had visited the Saxon Theater after going to the Simonds's place, but by then the police, media hounds, and the gore-hungry public had trodden all over the scene. He was hoping that these pictures, which were taken before anything was touched by anybody, might show him something. It was always better to view a crime scene firsthand before anyone else, but since that was impossible, the photos were the next best thing.

He picked up the first in a series of six. It was an eight-by-ten black-and-white glossy of Grace Simonds's body taken from the sidewalk. The way she had been carefully laid out meant the killer had spent some time there arranging her. It was dumb luck that no one came along and saw. Bill had seen or heard of that same dumb luck working in favor of killers so many times before that it was eerie.

The absence of blood on the pavement around the body clearly indicated that she had not been beheaded there. He picked up the next photo, a lower angle of the previous shot. After a few moments of contemplating it, he put it down and picked up the next one, then the next. He wasn't really looking at the photos yet. He was using them as a focal point while he went through a process of audio elimination, cutting each and every individual sound of the night out.

He cut the wind from outside, the hum of the fridge, the creaks and groans of the house buffeted by the wind and settling for the night, and even his own breathing and heartbeat. A mental silence descended over him and he was ready to begin focusing on details of the picture.

He picked up the first picture again, absorbed its overall features, and mentally dissected it into three sections, each section to be scrutinized individually. The first section was at the top of the photo and included the bottom half of the theater doors and the pavement from the foot of the doors to just above the body. The doors had spiderwebby cracks running through their glass panes, their paint was peeling, their brass handles were tarnished so badly he could barely read PUSH on them. The pavement in front of the doors was dirty with a dried wad of bubble gum and various stains of undetermined origin. Brown grass lay dead in a crack, waiting for spring to reanimate it. Bill doubted very much that the killer had gone anywhere near the theater doors.

The next block was the middle of the photograph that included the body from the knees up and the cracked, waffle-surfaced concrete sidewalk on either side. On the sidewalk, approximately one inch to the right of her left thigh, there was a small roundish dark spot. He focused more closely. It was either a stain that had collected fluff and street dirt, making it appear fuzzy-topped, or it was a spot of blood with hair or fibers stuck to it. If it was the latter, he could be in luck. He made a mental note to check with the forensics guy, Hanson, on it. If it was blood, the fuzz might be hair from the killer or fabric from something the dead girl was wrapped in while being transported. Either one would be helpful, though not a case breaker unless there was something really unusual about the hair or fabric that made it easy to trace.

He checked the spot in each of the pictures in which it appeared but was unable to clarify it further. He returned to the first photo, finished scrutinizing the middle section, which turned up nothing, and moved to the last section, the bottom. It covered the body from the knees down, revealing the bottoms of her feet, and included the sidewalk running out of the picture in each direction. At the very bottom of the picture was the granite curbing.

Almost immediately, he noticed a very small scrap of paper that appeared to be stuck or resting on the curb top. It was a torn, roughly triangular, half-inch bit of what looked like an old movie poster or advertisement. He could make out tiny printing that read, *ELVIS*, and underneath that, *stud*, and lower still, *xXx*.

He recognized the three *x*'s as the symbol for hardcore pornographic movies and had to smile. Did Elvis ever make an X-rated movie? The Saxon Theater had been a porno theater in its last days before the city council closed it down, but the thought of Elvis in a porno movie was too comical for him and he couldn't help laughing softly.

An idea struck him. Of course! An X-rated movie might use an Elvis impersonator as a gimmick. Call the film *Jailhouse Cock,* or *Blow Hawaii,* or something equally subtle. He laughed again. Was it worth checking it out?

He looked at the bit of paper again. He hadn't seen it that afternoon and he had gone over the theater front pretty well. The Saxon Theater had closed over four years ago, yet the bit of torn paper appeared to be unweathered, as though it had recently been dropped. Was it a message from the killer, a telltale clue that said, *Here I am, come and get me if you can figure this out?* From the very start he'd suspected this was the work of a serial killer, and such behavior was a common trait among them.

He decided to check it out with forensics to see if Hanson had picked it up. He'd learned long ago never to overlook anything.

Except your father. The self-tormenting dig came out of nowhere, breaking his concentration and bringing the fire of heartburn to his stomach. He pushed the thought away and went for another glass of milk to settle his stomach, downing it before returning to the coffee table for another try. He put the photos of the theater front away slowly, using them as a focal point to eliminate all the background noise. There was nothing more they could tell him.

He spread the ten instant snapshots he'd taken himself. With barely a glance, he eliminated the two test shots he'd taken of the front of the dorm. He arranged the rest in an order representing the events on the night Grace Simonds was last seen. Unlike the police photos, he didn't expect his instant snapshots to reveal any startling or telling details. Rather than scrutinizing them with his eyes, he used a mental form of tunnelvision to help him focus on what he knew so that he could build a mental scenario in which to recreate the events of that night.

First came the parking lot and the spot where Grace had been let off. The killer could have been waiting for her, parked in his car. Next was the blacktopped pathway to the dorm's rear entrance. The area was wide open, no place to hide. If the killer was in the lot, he'd have a clear view of her progress and could get out and catch her at almost any time if he was fast enough.

He picked up a shot he'd taken of the dorm doors. Did Grace Simonds ever go through them? She obviously made it as far as the entrance because she was seen there twenty minutes later. Did someone she know accost her from behind? Did she leave with that person and come back twenty minutes later? Then what happened? Did she go inside to find the killer waiting for her? Did she fight with her mystery lover, who dragged her off somewhere outside to drown her? In the middle of December? The scenarios ranged from the probable/possible to the unlikely/ridiculous.

He started over, returning to his original view of the killer waiting in the parking lot. He realized that even if the killer had been following Grace and

her boyfriend, he still could have pulled into the lot
without their seeing him, especially if they were
kissing good night, as the boyfriend claimed they
did for about fifteen minutes.

He went through each photo from the parking lot
to the dorm doors. At some point as she approached
the doors, he figured she was overtaken by the
killer. The dorm doors were locked. The residents
used key cards to get in. Once inside, she'd be safe.
But that never happened.

Captain Mahoney was of the conviction she
stopped because she knew her assailant, which was
also why he considered the boyfriend to be the
number one suspect despite a solid alibi that had
him returning to his frat house immediately and
staying there for the rest of the night, witnessed by
a dozen or more people.

Bill had to admit there was a good deal of merit to
the idea that she had known her killer. At one forty
in the morning, would she have heeded a stranger's
calling to her? Maybe. She *was* friendly. She might
stop for a stranger she saw as unthreatening. Another woman wouldn't be threatening, but Bill
doubted that the killer was a woman. Crimes this
bloody and violent were rarely committed by
women. When women murdered, they were much
more controlled and neat about it.

Who else might not appear threatening? An elderly person? A cop? The latter was a possibility,
but according to the campus police none of their
people were in the vicinity at the time. The witness
who had seen her twenty minutes later with the

mystery man, said only that he'd been wearing dark clothing.

Tomorrow he could check if there were any Crocker police walking a beat, or cruising in that neighborhood at the time. He was more than a little angry that there was nothing in the case file about it. Checking to see if there had been any police in the area at the time should have been one of the first things Starkovski did on the initial investigation. Even if there weren't any, he should have noted it in the file. It was no major gaffe; Bill doubted that a city cop was the killer, but it was sloppy police work and Bill was willing to bet Starkovski had let it slide out of laziness.

That Grace Simonds probably knew her killer and planned to meet him was a very likely scenario, but there were problems and unanswered questions with it, too. If she'd known her killer, what did they do between the time she was seen getting out of her beau's Corvette and twenty minutes later when she was seen kissing the mystery man in the entranceway? She didn't go into the dorm, or at least not up to her room. At least one other person went into the dorm during that twenty minutes and she saw and heard nothing of Grace or her mystery man.

So what did Grace and this guy she supposedly knew do during those damned twenty minutes? Was it an arranged meeting? If so, they could have left in his car and come back. But if it was arranged and she knew the guy would be waiting for her, why didn't she just wait until beau number one was out of sight and then go to the other guy's car parked in the lot? Maybe he didn't have a car. But if he didn't, he should've been seen with Grace Simonds on campus that night. Saturday night/Sunday mornings are busy party nights on campus, especially with Christmas so close and finals ending. There were a lot of people out. The only way he could have got her off campus without being seen was in a car.

But if the mystery man planned to kill her, and this had all the earmarks of a very carefully planned murder, why would he leave with her and then go back twenty minutes later? If she had gone to her room, Bill could see that maybe she'd forgotten something or the mystery man required something of hers, but that wasn't the case.

"She didn't go up to her room," he mused softly, picking up the pictures of the inside of the dorm, its hallway, and the elevators, and placing them to the side. He sat back and rubbed his eyes. What happened in those twenty minutes? Where did they go? From the coloration of the body, he figured she was killed right around the time she disappeared. Was she killed right after she was seen kissing the mystery man? That still didn't account for the twenty minutes.

He sat up suddenly and began digging through the file folder for the witnesses' statements, the boyfriend's in particular. He found it and read it silently. According to it, Grace and John had been at a party earlier in the evening at his frat house where they played Quarters, a drinking game. Later, they had taken a bottle of wine and gone parking up near the Audubon Sanctuary on Hospital Hill.

Of course! How could he have missed it? He picked up the pictures of the hallway and elevators inside the dorm. In one, a door clearly marked WOMEN could be seen. If she'd been drinking all night, Grace Simonds had probably had to go to the bathroom.

A thought that felt sharp with truth occurred to him. What if she *hadn't* known her killer; in fact, hadn't *seen* her killer until the last second when he attacked and drowned her? The killer could have followed her and caught the automatically locking door before it closed, or he could have access to a key card. He followed her into the bathroom and then . . .

With a sense of certainty and dread, Bill knew what Grace Simonds had been doing during those twenty minutes. She had been dying. A sickening thought surfaced. If the latter were true, then the second eyewitness had seen the killer holding up and kissing Grace Simonds's dead, wet lips.

5 A.M. found Bill back at Grace Simonds's dormitory. After stopping by the campus police station to get a master key for the building, he went in and headed directly for the women's room. Without thinking, he went right in.

"You gut da wrung bat'room, mistah," a chubby, middle-aged cleaning woman informed him in an accent unfamiliar to Bill. It almost sounded Greek, but her curly gray hair and wide, wrinkled face looked more Scandinavian.

Bill took out the badge and wallet ID he'd been given by the chief, and showed them to the woman. "I'm with the police, ma'am."

"Oh! You here 'bout dat dead gull?" the woman said, more a statement of fact than a question.

"Yes," Bill replied. Finding one of the cleaning ladies there was a stroke of luck and would save him time and a call to the college's maintenance director. "Can I ask you some questions?"

She shrugged and nodded.

"Do you clean this rest room regularly?" he asked.

"No," the woman replied, looking at him like he was a jerk for thinking such a thing.

"Oh," Bill fumbled, taken aback by her response and attitude. "How often *do* you clean it?"

"Nevah!" was the huffy reply.

Bill was confused. "What are you doing now?" he asked, unable to keep a sarcastic tone from his words.

"I em'ty da trash can. I do dis ev'y udder weekday," she snapped.

Today was Wednesday, so that meant she had last emptied the trash on Monday, the day Grace Simonds's body was found in front of the theater. "Did you empty the trash in here Monday morning around this time?"

"Yeah." She looked around secretively. "An' I fine *blood* in da sink!" She pointed to the closest of the three sinks.

"What?" Bill rushed over. There was no blood now. Behind him the woman began laughing.

"Jus' a coupla drops. No murder. No girlie wid her

head cut off!" The woman laughed heartily, from the belly, and Bill couldn't help smiling. Someone on the force had leaked to the press the grisly details of the murder, which had been withheld to help weed out false suspects. Bill didn't know why, but whenever there was an unsolved murder, particularly a bizarre or gruesome one, weirdos came out the proverbial woodwork to claim the act as their own. Still the leak wasn't as bad as it could've been; whoever gave the info to the *Worcester Telegram* left out the detail that the head had not been found with the body.

The leak stank of Mahoney and Starkovski the way the story in the paper had represented Bill and his position in the case. Reference was also made that in spite of the obvious facts, he was clinging to a wild theory that had the seasoned and well-trained members of the Crocker detective squad worried about the validity of Bill's credentials and the fact that he might slow down the investigation.

The story had come out yesterday and George had rushed to make sure Bill knew that the story did not have official sanction, nor did it come from an official, legitimate source. He reassured Bill that an official response would be made and if he said the girl drowned, then that was the official version. George had enough confidence in Bill's abilities to have faith that the medical examiner's report would bear him out. If it did, they still had something to weed out the weirdos with.

Bill hadn't minded really. Publicity always accompanied cases like this, and he had learned that the best way to deal with the media was give them information in a controlled setting like a press conference, and then pay no attention to what was written, because they'd always twist something or get something wrong. It was as if the average journalist, and this included television and radio reporters, was a frustrated writer of fiction who couldn't help putting his or her own little creative twist to what was supposed to be a factual accounting of events.

Bill could imagine the effect the story was having on the people of Crocker. He was sure that, as with the cleaning lady, the news of Grace Simonds's having been decapitated was on everybody's tongues today. The scary part was that he didn't think this was going to die down. He had a feeling, based on the features of the crime, that Grace Simonds wouldn't be the last woman to be murdered in that way. The suspicion had been there from the very beginning and now he was almost certain: a serial killer was at work in Crocker.

Grace Simonds's murder had all the earmarks of a serial killing. It was well planned, methodical, and ritualistic—signified by the two acts (drowning and decapitation) to kill her. Bill had an inkling that the decapitation had been a symbolic act that the killer needed to carry out for some reason. Bill was reasonably certain that Grace had been drowned first in a fit of uncontrolled emotional rage, though it, too, could be symbolic.

"Can I finish dis now? I gotta coffee break in fif'een minutes and twelve more a dese ta empty in four buildin's by den."

Bill nodded and stood aside, watching the short

woman handle the emptying of the large trash can with an ease and dexterity that he doubted he would have been capable of. She dumped the contents of the barrel into her canvas-sided roll cart without losing its plastic liner.

"When you emptied the barrel on Monday, did you notice anything unusual in its contents?" he asked.

She gave him a look of utter contempt. "I jus' empty 'em, I don' pick tru dem. Can I go now?"

"Yes, of course," Bill said, smiling at the woman's outspokenness and stepping aside. She wheeled the trash bag out of the rest room with another glance at him. It was obvious she thought he was strange.

Just because I'm in a women's rest room in a college dorm at five in the morning asking questions about the trash, she thinks I'm strange? Bill thought, chuckling.

He went back to the first sink, which the cleaning woman said had blood spots in it on Monday. Either from use, or because someone had cleaned it, the stain was gone. The woman thought she had been teasing him, but if the murder went down the way he thought it had, there very well could have been blood in the sink on Monday. He bent over and examined the porcelain basin surface and the drain carefully, detecting nothing. He wished he had a wrench so he could check the trap.

He turned and stood, leaning against the sink, and surveyed the rest of the bathroom. There were three stalls against the opposite wall, which was made of lime-green-painted concrete blocks. The floor, made up of black-and-white hexagonal tiles that reminded Bill of the pattern on a soccer ball, was fairly clean. Except for the three stalls, matching number of sinks, the trash barrel, and tampon dispenser, there was nothing else in the room.

Bill went to each stall, pushing open its door and looking inside. They were typical industrial-type toilets with plain chrome handles attached to a flush pipe at the back instead of a tank. The toilet seats were black plastic and scarred by cigarette burns.

Bill went back to the first stall and squatted in front of the bowl as if he were going to call *"Ralph!"* He leaned forward and examined the floor around the toilet. There was a faded water mark running in a jagged line around the porcelain base of the toilet, as though it had overflowed recently and the water was left to evaporate.

Steadying his weight against the bowl, he bent lower. He could just make out the tip of a footprint at the edge of the water mark. His heart hammered faster as he got down on all fours and ducked his head behind the bowl for a closer look. It appeared to be from a rubber-soled shoe with a worn diamond pattern to it. It also appeared to be too wide and rounded to be from a woman's shoe, but with fashions today he couldn't be certain. Awkwardly, he removed his left shoe and fitted it to the shoe print without touching it. They were almost the exact same size and shape.

He slipped his shoe back and stood. Something light and feathery brushed against the back of his hand, making his knuckles itch. He bent over and looked, but could see nothing. He reached down, passing his hand along the rim of the seat and felt it again. Very carefully, he lifted the seat to remove it. It was a very fine strand of brown hair. There were two more stuck to the bottom of the seat. He put them in one of the small plastic evidence bags he'd picked up at the station yesterday.

He gave a quick inspection to the other two stalls, but he was certain the first one was where Grace Simonds had died. He found a pay phone in the lobby and called the station to have a couple of uniforms come over to cordon off the rest room and forensics to go over it for more evidence. He'd also need forensics to check if the hairs he'd found matched the sample Grace Simonds's parents had given him.

Immersed in his latest favorite role-playing game, Ivy slipped quietly down the back stairs, placing his feet with precision on the exact middle of each step. According to James Bond, that was the quietest way to go up or down stairs because that's where the stair joists, or supports, were. The wooden back stairs were so ancient and rotten in spots that they'd creak even if James Bond *himself* were to climb them, in his stocking feet, no less. But for the most part, the technique worked. Ivy thought it was cooler than untied sneakers.

The sound of a car pulling into the driveway next door brought him down the remainder of the stairs in a hurry. He ran to the low picket fence separating the two yards and crouched behind it. He could hear a muffled voice talking and crying at the same time. Another voice, deeper, yet dull of tone and weary, interrupted. Though Ivy couldn't make out what was being said, the words seemed to calm the first voice. Ivy couldn't hear it sobbing anymore.

Imagining enemy agents having a secret rendez-vous, he peered over the top of the fence and watched his next-door neighbor leave his car and go into his house. Ivy looked around for the other person he'd heard in the car, but couldn't see him. He wondered how the other guy could have got into the house so quickly. Ivy had heard only one car door open. What the heck was going on?

Once the coast was clear, Ivy went over the fence gracefully, one arm balancing while he swung his legs and feet over. Remaining low on the other side, he crept toward the neighbor's house. He risked a peek in the first window he came to at the side of the house, but could see nothing beyond the back of a torn curtain.

The sound of kids going by on the street on their way to school reminded Ivy that he was going to miss the bus and be late if he didn't get going. If he was quick, he had time for one fast look in the kitchen windows on the back porch. Rubber-soled sneakers quiet on the frozen ground, he crept to the porch and went up the few stairs silently, success-fully using the Bond method again. On all fours he crawled to the window and peered over the sill.

His next-door neighbor was bawling his eyes out and ripping his policeman's shirt and pants off. He stuffed them deep into a large plastic trash bag that was already overflowing with rubbish and closed the top with a wire twisty.

That was *weird!* Why did he do that? Ivy won-dered. Maybe he had bugs in his clothes? But why cry about it, at his age, no less? *This guy is* really *strange,* Ivy thought, hurrying away so as not to miss his bus. This neighbor rated further investigation by 007. Maybe the plans for the secret doomsday machine were woven into the fabric of the clothes and this was just a clever way of passing the information on to another agent who would no doubt be disguised as a trash man come to make the weekly pickup.

I've got to get those plans to M, Ivy vowed, turning the mystery into his favorite game. He spent the day at school planning and plotting elaborate schemes for retrieving the plans woven into the clothes in the rubbish. As is usually the case, reality was much more simple and mundane than his envisioned scenarios. The target trash bag was sitting in front of the house next door as if waiting for him to get out of school. A quick rip up the side of the bag with a broken stick, and he had the clothes without even spilling too much rubbish. He tucked the shirt and pants up under his heavy winter coat, and walked on with such an air of nonchalance that James Bond would have been proud of him.

By noon, Dave Hanson, Crocker Police's forensics technician, was done in the rest room. He'd found one more hair, a minute scraping of blood cells from under the lip of the drain in the first sink, and a piece of a broken tooth in the same sink's trap. The tooth, he told Bill, might be impossible to identify as having come from Grace Simonds's mouth without her head and the rest of her teeth to match it to, but he'd check with her dental records. He said he'd definitely be able to tell if the blood cells and hair came from Grace.

Hanson took the sample the Simonds's had provided into his lab and by two-thirty had an answer for Bill. The hair and blood were Grace Simonds's.

A short while later, in Chief Albert's office, Bill presented his evidence to the chief and Captain Mahoney. As expected, Mahoney balked at it.

"Just because you found a couple of her hairs and a few blood cells that match her type doesn't mean she was killed in the bathroom, *or* drowned. The blood could have been there because she'd had a bloody nose or she popped a zit or anything. That bit of tooth means nothing unless you can confirm it's hers. And hair falls out all the time. Check your own toilet seat, Gage, and see if you don't find a couple of your own hairs. I'll also bet that footprint was left by the cleaning crew."

Bill didn't argue. He knew that what had been found was inconclusive. He'd already run through every possible scenario to explain the presence of the blood, tooth, hair, and footprint. As far as the physical evidence went, it was nothing to hang a case on, but Bill knew he was right. Now there was only one scenario for her death, as far as he was concerned: The killer had followed her into the bathroom, knocked her unconscious by slamming her face into the first sink, breaking her tooth, and then dragged her to the first stall where she'd been drowned in the bowl, the water overflowing to create the watermark around the toilet and capture the toe print of the killer's left foot.

CHANNEL 8

Jesus Loves Me
*This is Tunnelvision!
—III*
Police Squad
Face the Facts

 "Ladies and gentlemen, it's time once again for . . ."
Cue drum roll.
"Jesus Loves Wilbur!"
Cue applause.
Cue music.
Cue Jesus.
"And here's the star of our show, the Lord Jesus!"
Cue cheers.
Cue Wilbur.
"And here's his faithful sidekick, Wilbur!"
Cue Wilbur.
"Yes, folks, here he is, any minute now, Wilbur!"
Cue Wilbur.
Cue Wilbur.
Wilbur doesn't want to go on. He doesn't want to be on this show anymore. He knows what Jesus has

in the black plastic bag. He knows where Jesus is taking it and he doesn't want to go.

He doesn't have a choice.

He weeps all the way down and back.

Channel change.

The abandoned East Wing Building, used for storage of old hospital equipment, had been a place of solitude and escape for him; now it is a place of fear and dread. He can no longer stand the sight of the lights and the video cameras, the bank of monitors, the VTR control board, and tangles of snakelike cable strewn around what used to be the nursery on the old third-floor maternity. Worse, he can't stand the ropes and chains, knives and other paraphernalia of torture and death that Jesus has blessed as instruments of His work, and he dreads the trips into the round darkness below the building.

The deed done, he flees.

Closed circuit.

An elderly woman wanders the empty corridor near the elevators. "Oh, thank God! I think I'm lost," she says.

A memory like a holy vision comes to him. He sees himself as a child, a teacher staring at the burn scars on Jesus' arms but saying nothing and walking away. Over the years, so many more of her profession will follow her example. As if she just stepped out of the past, Wilbur sees that the old woman is his third-grade teacher, Mrs. Perche, and knows that the Savior has performed another miracle in bringing her here.

"Run!" he tries to scream at her but Jesus' voice comes out instead.

"And now you're found," He says to the woman and anoints her lips with His fist.

"Change the channel, Grandma, please?" He buries his head in her lap. He doesn't want to watch anymore. He just wants to crawl into Grandma's lap and rock.

"You used to love it when I'd rock you," Gram reminisces, stroking his hair. "You were so fragile, so hungry for love. *She* never cared for you—left you day and night in that filthy crib. You'd have died if I hadn't rescued you."

The channel changes. PBS. A documentary: *The Early Years,* black-and-white images complete with pain:

The baby cries for hours in the other room, but none of them seem to notice. They drink their drinks and smoke their joints, the stereo blasting "Tommy," and the baby cries because his diaper is wet and soiled with two days' worth of waste. He has a case of diaper rash so bad it bleeds. The baby is hungry. The bottle propped on a pillow next to his head is empty.

Eventually someone comes in. The baby doesn't know if it's his mother. Lucky boy, he does not yet know his mother. Mostly she ignores him, and the rare times he is cared for, it is by others.

A hand takes away the empty bottle and plants a new one on the pillow, plugging the nipple into his crying mouth. His filthy diaper remains un-

changed. When the bottle is empty, the baby cries again from the pain of the rash.

In the next room, they turn up the stereo and light another joint.

"I saved you," Grandma reminds him as the credits run.

In Grandma's room there are two mirrors, hung on the walls opposite each other, with Grandma in the middle, Wilbur in her arms, as close to the TV and the money-grubbing preacher as she can get. They are reflected a thousand times back and forth, reflections within reflections within reflections. Wilbur watches himself repeating to infinity and each repetition is a day, a month, a year.

A deep, mellow, soothing voice-over assures: "We will return after these important messages."

OBSESSION.

The voice is sultry and dripping with lust.

Grandma flips through the channels until she finds *The 700 Club.*

"Why do you pray to the TV, Gram?"

"Don't blaspheme! I ain't praying to the TV, I'm praying to Jesus."

"Is Jesus in the TV?"

"Sometimes." Her voice is dreamy.

"How?"

"It's like a vision. It's like I'm looking through a window, or into a tunnel that leads to heaven. And sometimes Jesus is at the other end of the tunnel calling to me to crawl through and join Him."

"Is that Jesus?" four-year-old Wilbur asks, pointing at Pat Robertson on the screen.

"Sometimes," Grandma says. "Sometimes He's

Jimmy Swaggart, sometimes He's Jim Bakker, sometimes He's Oral Roberts. But it doesn't matter who He is, He's always there to take away your pain and suffering. Remember that. When things look darkest and you think you can't go on, pray to Jesus and He will save you and protect you."

The screen goes blank. Grandma is asleep. Jesus is dragging the teacher across the floor by her hair. Her body slides easily over the cold tile.

"Is He saving me now, Grandma? Is He?"

There is no answer.

"Is He?"

On the whole, Officer Paul Munney was a good cop. The only thing his sergeant ever got on him about was keeping his patrol car clean. Munney was such a slob that the other officers who had to use his car on weekend shifts complained about the old food, coffee cups, and trash that habitually littered the cruiser. It had got so bad that the sergeant had started conducting weekly inspections of Munney's vehicle to keep him on the ball.

It was during one of those inspections at the end of a shift that the sergeant found a videocassette tape, with the title *Toilet Training* printed on the side label, under the front seat. Thinking that Munney must have stopped to rent a film while on duty made the sergeant very angry. He tried to catch Munney before he left the station, but he was too late. The sergeant took the tape into the squad room and put it on his desk to confront Munney with it tomorrow.

One of the other patrolmen in the room noticed

the tape and asked the sarge about it. When he explained, they begged him to play the tape on the VCR in the break room. They claimed Munney, a bachelor, was a connoisseur of porno films. They wanted to watch it so they could razz him about it the next day. Thinking it might not be a bad idea to embarrass Munney, the sarge consented.

What he and the other patrolmen who had gathered around saw sent several of them racing for the bathroom and the sarge running to the phone to call the chief.

Bill Gage felt sick, but he didn't get out of his seat, nor did he take his eyes from the television screen. He swallowed bile and absentmindedly noted the flashing 12:00 A.M. on the VCR atop the TV. In his peripheral vision he could also see the room full of cops around him, but his focus never wavered from the horror on the twelve-inch screen.

This was the fifth straight time Bill had watched the video since the duty sergeant had discovered what he'd really found in Officer Munney's car. Bill had been just about to go home to supper and an evening of staring at photographs and brooding about possibilities when the call came from the chief.

To Bill's right, Captain Mahoney abruptly stood and left the room. Starkovski and the other two detectives who'd still been on duty had already left the room, their faces sickly pale. Uniformed officers kept wandering in to the break room only to leave hurriedly after a few minutes of viewing.

The tape ended and Bill leaned over and hit the

rewind button. As he hit the play button, a groan
went up from several of the cops behind him. That
was when Chief Albert cleared the room except for
officers working directly on the case, which left Bill,
Mahoney, and Starkovski, who'd returned, and the
young cop, Larken, whom George had assigned to
Bill for the case.

"That guy's a ghoul," one of the uniforms said to
another as they left.

"Move it!" the chief barked. He closed the door
after them. "So, what do you think?" he asked,
crossing to stand behind Bill's chair while trying not
to look at the TV screen. Like everyone else who
had entered the room, he found it sickeningly impossible.

Bill shrugged. He wasn't into high gear yet where
he was examining details, but he had immediately
discovered a few things watching the tape. "This
was all staged just for the camera. She's already
dead at the start of this," he explained, pointing at
the screen.

"What?" Starkovski openly scoffed at Bill's statement.

"It's obvious. Look at the pallor of her skin and
the dried blood on her nose and lip and around her
empty eye sockets. She doesn't thrash or fight when
he holds her head in the bowl. My original scenario
still stands. For whatever reason, she was drowned
in the rest-room toilet of her dorm, and taken else-
where so the killer could reenact the murder and
make a tape of it to send to us."

"She's just unconscious," Starkovski said argu-
mentatively.

"No," Bill countered. "Even unconscious, her body would convulse as her lungs filled with water and she died."

"I think Bill knows what he's talking about," the chief broke in. "After all, he was right about the cause of death, and this video proves it."

"But why would he kill her at the dorm and then take her somewhere else to reenact and film it?" Mahoney asked. "I think Gage is right about her going into the bathroom, which would account for the twenty-minute gap in between the last two times she was seen, but doesn't it make more sense that she then left with the killer, he took her to his place, knocked her out to give himself time to set up the camera and lights, and then filmed drowning her in his toilet bowl? There might even be more than one person involved—one to run the camera, the other to drown her."

There was a knock on the door. The chief opened it and took a clipboard with a sheet of paper attached from the duty sergeant, thanked him, and closed the door again.

"No," Bill countered. "She was already dead when she was seen kissing the mystery man outside her dorm."

Another scoffing laugh erupted from Starkovski. "You're nuts! Where do you get this crap from? What are you, psychic?"

"That's enough!" Mahoney said to his lieutenant. Starkovski looked shocked, as did Bill, who pressed the pause button on the VCR, freezing Grace Simonds's eyeless head in the toilet bowl, and turned to look at the captain. Mahoney was looking at the sheet of paper on the clipboard the chief had given him.

"But, Mike, listen to this guy!" Starkovski protested. "Why the hell would he kill her at the dorm, then drag her body somewhere else—let's not forget his *kissing* the corpse—and reenact it for the camera?"

"Because this guy is a serial killer," Bill said calmly.

Starkovski's sarcastic smile faltered a bit, but he recovered quickly. "Bullshit!"

"Can it, Frank!" Mahoney said angrily this time.

Starkovski gazed openmouthed at his supervisor.

"This is the medical examiner's autopsy report," Mahoney said, holding up the clipboard. "Gage is right. Bits of tissue paper found in Grace Simonds's lungs match the same brand of industrial toilet paper the college uses in all its bathrooms. Also the water in her lungs had the same hard water mineral content as the water in the toilets of the dorm. The college gets their water from Snow Pond, which is their own private reservoir and has a different mineral content than the water from the two reservoirs the city uses."

Starkovski opened and closed his mouth several times but had nothing to say.

"Also," Mahoney said, turning to Bill, "Hanson from forensics went back to the dorm bathroom and was able to lift several good men's fingerprints from the first stall. He wasn't able to get any prints off the tape, though, because it had been handled by too many people. He ran a check on the stall prints through our computer and came up with nothing, so he sent them on to the state police and the FBI."

"He won't be on record," Bill stated. There was no argument from anyone this time. Starkovski sat, head down, like a reprimanded child.

"Hanson also took it on himself to check with the cleaning company that had the contract to clean the dorm bathrooms. They use only women to clean the women's rooms, and men for the men's. The footprint behind the toilet is definitely from a man's shoe—the killer's shoe. Hanson hasn't been able to positively identify the brand, but he said it's a work shoe with a steel toe."

"I know," Bill said quietly. "I called them too."

There were several moments of awkward silence before Mahoney spoke again. "I guess I owe you an apology," he said to Bill, then shot a glance at Starkovski. The lieutenant stalked out of the room.

"He'll come around when his hurt pride heals. He didn't like that you pointed out his shoddy work on the initial investigation this morning. I know you never specifically mentioned him, but he knew we all knew."

"It was nothing personal, even though you guys *have* been giving me a rough time," Bill explained. "It's things like that that slow down an investigation, is all."

"Hey," Mahoney said, raising his hands, "I'm not saying you were wrong. Even if it was personal he still should have been called on it, and if I hadn't been such a jerk lately, you might have brought it to *my* attention and then I could have handled it and he wouldn't have minded so much."

"Maybe it's time he started minding," Bill couldn't help saying.

Mahoney let it slide. "Yeah, well, I just want to apologize about the stuff I said before. I want you to know, too, that I had nothing to do with that news leak and what was said about you. As far as I'm concerned, you're the quarterback on this. Tell me what me and my men can do."

Chief Albert clapped Mahoney on the back. "Thanks, Mike."

Bill stood up and shook Mahoney's hand. "I guess the first thing we need is a loop made of this tape in a six-hour extended mode so we don't have to keep stopping it and rewinding."

"You're going to watch that for six hours?" Mahoney asked incredulously. "The whole thing, *including* the decapitation, is only ten minutes or so . . ." He paused, trying to figure it in his head.

"The length of the video is nine minutes and twenty-two seconds," Bill said. "On a six-hour tape it will play thirty-nine times completely, with the fortieth showing only the first four minutes and fifty seconds."

"Right," Mahoney said as if he'd just come to the same answer himself.

"I'd like stills made of each frame and blown up. Can your photography lab do that, or do we have to send it to the state police?"

"We can do the loop and use the Fitchburg Police Department's photo lab. They have the equipment to do the stills. I'll get someone on it right away," Mahoney said, going to the door. "I'll get another room set up with a TV and VCR so the men can have their break room back," he added with a smile.

"I doubt any of them who saw that will feel like eating in here for a while," the chief commented.

"Couple more things," Bill called to Mahoney. "I want someone to check out all area photographers, especially those who offer video services, and all the area's video equipment stores, local TV stations, and college media classes for people with criminal records. I also want to get ahold of someone who knows video and can look at this and maybe tell us what kind of equipment he's using. Then we can run a trace through the local stores that sell that brand to see if any cameras were bought lately, and then check them out. It's a long shot, but the information will be very important the more we learn about this guy, and especially if we catch him."

"Don't say *if*," Chief Albert warned with a smile. "Say *when*."

"Everything's ready as you requested," Captain Mahoney said, popping his head in the door of Bill's new office the next morning. The office was considerably larger than the one he'd started out with, and even had a window.

Bill got up from the desk and followed Mahoney to an empty interrogation room where a TV and VCR had been set up in front of several metal folding chairs.

"The loop Hanson made of *Toilet Training* is in the machine," Mahoney explained, pointing to the VCR. "He should have the stills from Fitchburg by tomorrow afternoon at the latest."

Bill went in and sat in the chair directly in front of the TV. He turned it and the VCR on, waited while the screen was filled with blank light. He pressed the play button. "Unless it's really important, I don't want to be disturbed for a while," he said to Mahoney. "You can watch with me, but you don't have to. Those three officers the chief assigned me are doing interviews of dorm residents today. I'd feel better if you could oversee them, make sure they ask the right questions and don't miss anything important. The chief says you're an excellent interrogator."

"Thanks," Mahoney said. He took the compliment well, not looking uncomfortable at all, as most people would. "I'll do that then. Dispatch can raise me if you need me. I'll have Larken make sure you're not disturbed."

Mike Mahoney opened the door and paused a moment to turn and look at Bill, who was settling back in his chair. As the snuff film began to play and the title came up, Mahoney thought of the six hours ahead of Bill and regarded him with awe.

Two hours later, Bill hadn't moved from in front of the television. *Toilet Training* was playing for the fourteenth time. The first thirteen had been a waste. He hadn't been able to concentrate and focus; too many personal problems insisted on intruding. He tried dealing with them one at a time, but as soon as he succeeded in blocking one out, another popped up in its place. Staring at the screen and not seeing the gruesome pantomime, he wrangled with his problems: Cindy, his growing self-doubt that he could handle this the way he used to, the disturbing dreams he'd had again last night that tied this homicide to his father's activities. By run number fourteen, Bill hadn't solved any of them, but at least he had faced them and was able to work around them.

He stood a moment to turn his chair around and straddled it backward, resting his chin on hands folded on top of the chair's back support. The screen was showing the first of the video's two scenes, the drowning. It and the second scene, the beheading, were both shot from one stationary position, as if the camera was on a tripod, which made Bill think it was one perpetrator. The removal of Grace Simonds's eyes was curiously, and mercifully, left out. The film was very basic, like a home video, and was in black and white. Its one camera angle was a close-up that showed little other than Grace Simonds's head in the bowl in the first scene, and her neck and the back of her head as the ax did its work in the second.

The drowning sequence was the longest portion of the film, lasting seven and a half minutes, the camera lingering on the back of Grace Simonds's head even after the perp had let go of her hair. He stared at it and began the process of whittling down his focus and blotting out everything else.

An hour and a half later he had worked his focus down to the minutely detailed level, blotting out first the sound of the VCR, then the room, working down to cutting out portions of the screen itself.

He focused on her hair, the killer's fingers entwined there, holding her head down. He noted the killer was left-handed: On that hand he had several circular scars that had the shiny red look of healed burn tissue.

Bill shifted focus to the edges of the screen. At the top and right sides he could see the inside rim of the porcelain bowl. Half-hidden by Grace Simonds's hair, he could see raised letters just under the back rim. *P . . . R . . I . . N . . . C*—that was all he could get. The obvious next letter would be an *E* making the name of the toilet's manufacturer *PRINCE*, which, not surprisingly, didn't ring any bells with him, but he'd have Larken check it out.

The end of the drowning sequence was approaching. Bill grabbed the remote from the top of the VCR and prepared to freeze the frame at the right moment. Just as Grace Simonds's head was coming out, turning toward the camera, mouth half-open, eyes gone, Bill pushed the stop button, focused in, and saw what he already knew. Grace Simonds's top front tooth was chipped in what looked like the exact shape as the piece of tooth Hanson had found in the drain. He noticed something else, too. From this angle he should be able to see the toilet tank, but he couldn't. That meant it must be an industrial toilet with just a flush handle and pipe at the back. He pressed the pause button and wrote Mahoney a note to have someone check out all abandoned industrial sites and factories in the area.

He let the tape play on. The beheading was next. He concentrated on the ax. It was an old one; the back of the steel head was marred and gouged as though it had been used unsuccessfully as a sledge hammer. There were dried dark spots that might be blood on the wooden handle, but it was hard to tell in black and white. Reflexively, his finger hit the pause button again. There, just visible for a second as the ax fell into the shot, was a slightly smudged fingerprint on the handle.

He pressed play and watched the rest of the loop, but didn't come up with anything else. At the end, he shut the VCR and TV off and stood, groaning. His spine popped in several spots and he had the strange, ticklish sensation of having his butt fall asleep. Heading out the door to see if Mahoney was back from the college, Bill hoped the needles and pins didn't make him walk funny.

He saw Larken at his computer and told him about the toilet manufacturer's name and the bit of paper with *Elvis, stud,* and *xXx,* and asked him if he could trace the plumbing company and any porno films with "Elvis" in the title.

"No problem, sir," Larken claimed. "I can do it easily by calling the city library, tapping my computer terminal into their files through a phone modem, and having it look through the entire yellow pages of the United States and list all plumbing manufacturing companies that start with *PRINCE.* I can also tap into the computer files at the video store I go to and check for any similar X-rated titles."

"Let's not swamp ourselves with unnecessary information," Bill cautioned the eager Larken. "Concentrate on the ones in Massachusetts first, then expand to New England, et cetera, working your way out."

"Oh, right." Larken looked embarrassed. "That would make more sense. I should have thought of that."

"It's okay. Don't worry about it," Bill reassured him. "You're doing something with that computer that I could never do. Keep up the good work."

CHANNEL 9

Mr. Ed
*Scenes from
a Marriage*
Video Valhalla
Dream TV

Blip.
Static.
Snow.
"Look at the cowboy-and-Indian movie," Joey used to say of a snowy, blank screen.

He used to look. Joey used to laugh, the same laugh he laughed when he and Mary-not-Mother were hurting him.

No, not him. *Jesus.*

Channel change.

This Old House is on. Jesus is the guest craftsman showing how to wield a portable acetylene torch. There is a series of scenes showing the Savior at work, interspersed with close-ups of Wilbur's teacher's face, eyes mirroring the surgical flame as it operates on her. Nostrils flaring, her mouth screams inaudibly behind the heavy gray tape over it.

Channel change.

Nickelodeon.

Theme music. *"A horse is a horse, of course, of course. . . ."*

Canned applause. Laughter.

Mr. Ed shows his gums when he speaks.

"Hello, Wi-i-ilbur. Two down and how many to go? I'm tired of waiting. When can we ride off into the sunset?"

Wilbur Post enters the frame, but the real Wilbur can see by the eyes that it's Jesus in disguise. "Soon, Ed, soon," Wilbur says, holding up an ax and staring fondly at its gleaming blade.

"So what's next?" the talking horse asks.

Cut to:

Wilbur/Jesus breaking down the colonel's door and taking the ax to him. "Colonel?" Wilbur/Jesus, covered in blood, says. "How come whenever I come over here you're always lying around the house? *All* around the house!"

Canned laughter.

Cut to:

Wilbur/Jesus walking toward the camera. In his cupped palms he holds the colonel's severed hands.

"These are next, Ed," Wilbur/Jesus says to the camera. "They're handy things to have around."

Burst of simultaneous laughter and applause.

Channel change.

"There is nothing wrong with your tunnelvision. Do not attempt to adjust the picture, We are controlling transmission."

Wilbur can't stop crying.

Commercial break.

"ScottTissues are more absorbent!"

"Greater value is what you get when you buy Coronet!" A Clooney tune.

"Kleenex brand tissues, the name people trust."

Grandma has shut off her set and Jesus has taken over his. The Emergency Broadcast System is conducting a test ("This is only a test") and the piercing signal makes his head hurt. He wants to change the channel but the remote is broken. It wouldn't matter anyway. Jesus has them on:

Closed circuit.

Video Valhalla

Dustin Hoffman. Tom Cruise. Cardboard Clint Eastwood. Movie posters. *Total Recall.* He doesn't want to see that one.

Jesus places the body in the mud between two dried-up shrubs at the side of the building and just below a small sign advertising the largest collection of X-rated home videos in Crocker. Smoke rises from the teacher's eyes in the cold darkness. The air is pungent with the odor of burned flesh.

Drive.

Jesus has a package for the police. His latest testament of atonement: the arms of those who would not embrace and protect Jesus. At a mailbox He pulls the car over and makes Wilbur put the package in.

Cindy Gage woke up to the phone ringing and felt every muscle go taut as her entire body clenched like a fist. She opened one eye and read the time from the glowing digital clock on the night table. Four o'clock. She shuddered. She didn't have to know who it was to know it was bad news. When the phone rang that early, it was always bad news, whether it was an old drunk friend calling to reminisce, or word that there had been a death in the family. Even something as trivial as a wrong number was bad news because you still had to get out of bed to answer it. At least, Bill did.

Just as surely as she knew the call was bad news, she knew it was for Bill. That was why he slept on the side of the bed with the phone. He was used to getting bad news phone calls in the middle of the night.

He picked it up immediately, before it had a chance for a second ring.

"Yeah, Gage here," she heard him say, his voice low but alert. Cindy knew he'd probably been lying awake in the dark, unable to sleep, too tired to go downstairs or do anything but lie and wait for the alarm clock to go off. She'd awakened several times in the nights since he'd gone back to police work to find him awake, staring at the ceiling, or downstairs staring at his collection of Polaroids spread out on the living room coffee table.

"Where?" He spoke again. "Okay. I'll meet you there as soon as I can. Yeah, I know where it is." He said something else but Cindy didn't hear it. A shrill cry from the nursery commanded her attention instead.

She got out of bed, slid on her slippers, and padded out of the bedroom, not bothering with her robe. Devin's shrieking increased, going up an octave to that terribly high pitch like fingernails scraping on a chalkboard amplified ten times. It went right through her, set her teeth and nerves on edge, and was sure to wake the twins.

She hurried into the nursery. In the dull, yellow glow from the night-light she could see him standing at the crib bars, his eyes barely open, but his wailing mouth more than making up for them. She stroked his hair and kissed his forehead, cooing soothing words to him, trying to avoid picking him up if possible. Once he was in her arms, it was always difficult to get him back in his crib.

Like a siren with its plug pulled, Devin's crying dropped octave by octave until he was silent. He lay down on his stomach, hugging his Ernie doll and pulling his knees up under him. Sometimes a kiss and a few soft words were all it took. Cindy smiled at him and covered him with a Mickey Mouse blanket.

Bill was up and nearly dressed by the time she got back to the bedroom. "Sorry if the phone woke him," Bill said, sitting on the edge of the bed and tying his shoes.

"What's wrong? Where are you going?" Cindy asked.

"Nothing's wrong," he answered quietly.

She knew he was lying; he wouldn't look at her. "It's four in the morning, Bill. Can't it wait?" She reached for her robe, suddenly chilled.

"No." That was it, nothing else; no explanation— just *no!*

Cindy didn't like this. Since starting on this murder case, Bill had become more and more withdrawn and uncommunicative. It had become nearly as strenuous as giving birth to try to have a conversation with him anymore. She wasn't used to having him act this way. Bill had always been so open with her, so sharing of his thoughts and feelings. He told her everything, even all the dark things about his father. To have him suddenly clam up and shut her out hurt, but even more, it made her angry.

A depressing and scary thought occurred to her: The Bill Gage she knew wasn't a cop. Now that he was again, was she seeing the *real* him?

"Damn it, Bill! Can't you say anything other than that? You get a call at four in the morning. It's nothing, but you have to leave immediately. I want to know what's going on! I have a right to know." She was becoming emotional and she hated it when that happened. It made her voice and lower lip quiver and she sounded whiny.

Bill paused at his dresser, took a deep breath, and turned to her. "That was Captain Mahoney, the detective I'm working with on the Simonds murder case. There's been another murder." He opened the top drawer, took out his revolver and holster, and clipped it to the back of his belt, letting his sport coat fall over it.

He didn't say any more, but now Cindy didn't mind. She didn't want to know about murder, didn't really want to know how much danger he was putting himself in.

"I'm sorry," he said again. She'd noticed he'd taken to saying that a lot lately. He knew things had changed, that *he* had changed, and it annoyed her that he wouldn't address it, wouldn't let her help him with whatever was causing him to pull away from her.

Cindy was the type of woman who needed to be strong for her man. It was one of the major reasons she loved Bill and had fallen in love with him in the first place—he had needed her strength so badly. That need had continued all through his drying-out period and up until he had become obsessed with being a damn cop again. Didn't he care what was happening to them?

Though she knew it was unfair to do so—the situation was a lot more complex—she couldn't help viewing his actions in terms of a value judgment: He valued being a cop more than he valued their relationship, their marriage, their family. She hated herself for having such venal, immature thoughts, especially when she deep down knew them to be untrue, but hated Bill more for forcing her into a state where she could seriously harbor such thoughts.

He leaned over her where she sat at the end of the bed and kissed her quickly, then headed for the door. "I might be late again," he said. Then he was gone. She listened to his footsteps going down the stairs and wanted to run after him and say something that would stop him, that would make him suddenly open up to her and change the deadly direction in which they were headed, but the right words were as much a mystery to her as what was going on inside her husband's head lately.

She listened to the closet door open and close as Bill got his overcoat, then the front door. Seconds later the old Toyota coughed in the driveway, tried to turn over, and after three starts, made it. She lay back on the bed and felt like crying.

Sassy, always alert to anything wrong, appeared in the bedroom doorway. "What's the matter, Mommy? I heard the phone ring and Devin crying. Did Daddy go out?" Her young face wore a look of worry much too old for it.

"It's okay," Cindy said, getting up from the bed. "Bill had to go into work early. Remember what he said about being a cop?" She put her arm around her daughter and steered her back to her room. *"A cop is on duty twenty-four hours a day,"* she said in a deep-voiced impersonation of her husband that made Sassy giggle. "Get back to bed now. You've got school tomorrow."

Sassy looked at her mother for a long moment that told Cindy she hadn't fooled her daughter with her joking around. Sassy said nothing, though, and went to bed, kicking Missy's mattress on the way by in an attempt to stop her twin's snoring.

Sassy got into bed and went through her ritual of fixing the covers and pillows just right and smooth, and blew a kiss to her mother. Cindy caught it, blew one back, and closed the door. She went back to her own bed, which seemed too large, empty, and cold now, and tried to get back to sleep. After a long, silent crying jag, she was successful.

This was bad. Oh, this was *really* bad.

Bill Gage was in a small state of shock. A panic stone had dropped into his gut and was threatening to start rolling all over his body. He felt nauseous, and not only from the sound of several patrolmen puking in the bushes at the side of the Video Valhalla store.

He tried not to breathe through his nose, so as to keep out the awful stench of burnt human flesh, but he swore he could *taste* it when he took air through his mouth. It made him gag, and he had to go for a little walk around the parking lot to keep his stomach under control.

He wasn't ready for this, not by a long shot. The way Grace Simonds had been murdered was bad, but this one made her drowning and decapitation seem inviting by comparison. Even ten years ago, at the height of his career with the special crimes unit of the state police, this would have been tough to handle right away, all at once.

"I have to do this," he muttered to himself. "I can't back out now."

Nearby, the forensics van pulled into the parking lot. He was impressed with Hanson's work so far. He went over to talk to him. "I want a lot of pictures," he told the lab man. "And go over that entire spot with a microscope and tweezers if you have to."

Hanson listened and nodded silently while he unloaded his equipment. Bill watched him cross to the site and go to work, and he tried to steel himself to do the same. He knew he could get away with just looking at the photos Hanson took, but there was no substitute for firsthand observation of a crime scene, especially where his unique talents were concerned.

He felt sick again just thinking about going back and looking at that poor woman with nothing but the burnt stumps of her arms left and the look of torture stamped on her face beneath her charred eye sockets.

Mahoney came over, his face a haggard reflection of Bill's own. "It's got to be the same guy, huh?" he asked. Bill nodded. "Motherfucker is really sick!" Mahoney muttered.

"I expected this," Bill said, "but I thought there'd be more time between killings. Most serial killers blow off steam with a killing and then they're quiet for a while until the need builds up again. This guy is in a bad way if he's killing so quickly."

Mahoney shook his head and stamped his feet against the cold.

"I figure we'll be getting another tape soon," Bill said. Mahoney shuddered. "Make sure all officers using cruisers are aware that one's coming and might be delivered in the same way as the last one."

Mahoney nodded, took out a small notebook and pencil, and made a note.

"Well," Bill said with a deep sigh, "I guess I should get it over with so we can get this cleaned up before too many curious ghouls show up."

Walking across the lot toward the horror that awaited him, Bill prayed that he wouldn't lose control when he examined the body. He added another prayer that if he did lose control, he wouldn't head for the nearest bar or liquor store.

That night in the dead of sleep, the armless, eyeless corpse of the woman outside Video Valhalla came back to haunt him. He began to thrash in bed as the dream unfolded and he found himself once again approaching the body he'd forced himself to examine.

Like a terrible torturous form of déjà vu, he relived every minute of his inspection, seeing again the cauterized flesh and bone and blackened holes where eyes should have been. Just above her head in the window a sign advertising X-rated movies. Another message from the killer.

A flash of light made him break out in a cold sweat and moan in his sleep, but in the dream it was only Hanson taking pictures. Or was it? He turned. Since when did Hanson have gray hair?

Another flash; another picture.

The camera lowered.

"I'm back," his father said, smiling, and took his picture.

He woke in Cindy's arms, breathless and drenched in sweat, unable to tell her of the terror the nightmare had exposed in him.

CHANNEL 10

*Saturday Afternoon Movie:
Against All Odds*

 Ivy wished he had a telescope or a pair of binoculars. He was crouching behind the railing of the third-floor porch, looking down into the second-floor window of the house next door. He could see into the house from his bedroom window also, but from here he had a different angle.

Since finishing the James Bond series of novels that Barbara had given him, his favorite game had become playing spy. And his favorite subject to spy on was his weirdo next-door neighbor, one Wilbur Clayton. He had questioned Barbara about him. She knew his name, but not much else about him. She thought he lived with his parents, and though Ivy hadn't seen either of them around he thought he had heard them. He'd heard *someone* other than Wilbur in the house, that was for sure.

Wilbur was a natural choice for Ivy to spy on. He acted so strangely, talking to himself, to the TV. And after seeing him dump his clothes in the trash the other day, Ivy had become intrigued with why he'd done it. Unfortunately, the shirt and pants revealed nothing more interesting than a couple of large black, oily stains down their fronts. No wonder he had thrown them out. It didn't matter, really. His strange behavior was enough of a reason to spy on him. Ivy's imagination would do the rest.

Ivy straightened his right leg and slid his new watch out of his tight pants pocket. It wasn't *new* new—it had a broken strap and a chipped-glass face cover—but it was new for him. Barbara had given it to him; it had belonged to her late husband, Henry. She had another strap for it, but he'd left it as it was so he could keep it in his pocket and out of sight of his mother's prying eyes.

Three o'clock. He was supposed to meet Barbara at three thirty. At his insistence, she had made a doctor's appointment at the free clinic at Burbank Hospital in Fitchburg. She'd taken the bus and he was going to wait for her at the bus stop. Since their run-in with Slice, Ivy tried to make sure Barbara didn't go out in the neighborhood alone. He did all the bottle and can collecting himself, ever watchful for his nemesis, and went to Watson's Market to buy her measly provisions. Still, she went out alone. She claimed she got claustrophobic staying in her tiny apartment all the time.

So far they'd both been lucky in avoiding Slice Sanchez and his gang. Ivy knew their luck wouldn't hold, though. He just hoped that Barbara wasn't with him when the time came to face Slice. He tried to convince himself that Slice didn't care about Barbara anymore and just wanted him, but he couldn't be sure. Ivy had asked around at school about Slice Sanchez lately and had found out he was a very sick puppy, capable of just about anything. One of his favorite pastimes, Ivy had learned, was to douse cats with gasoline or lighter fluid, torch them, and watch them run themselves to death as they burned.

Someone ought to do that to Slice Sanchez, Ivy thought grimly.

In preparation for Slice, Ivy had been busy. In the basement of his tenement he'd found a dozen large rattraps that he'd confiscated. In the garage behind the house, where the tenants were allowed storage space, he found some other useful things like fishing wire, leather thongs, a Bic lighter that still worked, a broken car antenna, and the top half of a plaster arm cast that had been cut off someone from the elbow to the wrist. It was two inches too long for his arm, but with the other stuff it gave him a great idea.

Using a steak knife from his mother's kitchen, he managed to cut the cast, which was still covered with signatures, down to size for his arm. He secured one of the rattraps to the cast with some of the leather thongs and used the rest of them to secure the cast to his arm. At the wrist end of the cast he attached a small, half-inch-high fork-shaped plastic piece he'd got off one of his old toy dump trucks. He made a slit through the cast and inserted the plastic piece in line with the rattrap's spring bar. Next, he honed the tip of the broken antenna to a point by rubbing it on the top of the stone wall next to the driveway and carved a notch in its end, ruining one of his mother's good steak knives in the process. The notched end rested against the trap's spring bar like an arrow against its string, and the pointed end was supported by the plastic fork piece at the other end. When he released the bar, the antenna arrow would fly.

In theory it was a wonderful idea. In practice, it was something else. The first time he fired it, the cast gun, as he'd named it, fell apart and the point of the antenna went no farther than the knuckles of his hand, gouging them nastily. He added more straps and rubber bands, and even Elmer's Glue to hold the trap straight, and was finally able to fire the antenna arrow a few feet with some force. Though it was too bulky to wear under a shirt, he could conceal it under the old army jacket of his father's that he wore outside to play in. The whole jacket was too big for Ivy, and the sleeves were just roomy enough to accommodate the cast gun. It still needed more work, though; the point got caught on fabric every other time he tried to fire it.

The rest of his arsenal was considerably more simple, and reliable. It consisted of more rattraps, a water pistol filled with chlorine bleach, several old burned-out light bulbs his mother kept in a cabinet for who knew what purpose, and a glass jar filled with an extremely caustic furniture-stripping chemical called *Zip-Strip* he'd found in the garage that had burned like hell when he'd accidently got some on his hand. It was almost as good as acid.

He kept his weapons in an old green book bag/knapsack his mother had bought him at a yard sale a few years ago but he'd never had a reason to use it until now. It held all his things plus his schoolbooks and any books of Barbara's that he happened to be reading at the time. At present he had the John

Gardner versions of 007's adventures that Barbara had given him when he'd finished the Fleming series. Ivy found them to be just as exciting, realistic, and *cool* as the original author's stories.

He glanced at his watch again—three twenty—and carefully put it back. There wasn't much going on over at the neighbor's and it was time to go. He went into the apartment to his room and got his knapsack, which he never went outside without these days. He strapped on the cast gun, more for the *feel* of power it gave him than from any confidence in its working, put his dad's roomy army coat on over it, and set off for Barbara's.

Slice Sanchez, Greasy, JoJo, and the other two gang members—Big, a six-foot muscleman, and Eddy, a quiet, enormously fat kid whose real name was Robert but whom Slice named Eddy because, he claimed, "Every gang has to have someone in it called Eddy" (why he thought that, Slice had never revealed to Robert who became known as Eddy whether he liked it or not)—sat atop the high granite block wall at the corner of Leighton Street and Green Hill Road opposite Watson's Market with a full view of the old bag lady's apartment. The branches of a large weeping willow on the other side of the wall hung over and hid them fairly well from sight.

They'd just come out of Watson's Market, where they had been successful in lifting an assortment of candy bars, comic books, and cans of soda. They had been forced to pay for their butts because Old Lady Watson, tired of being robbed blind on cigarettes, had put in a new locking glass case behind the counter in which she now kept the cigarettes. Since coming out to enjoy their booty, the gang had been discussing how they could break into Watson's some night and wipe out the whole cigarette inventory. Strangely out of character for Slice, he did not join in the discussion.

Today Slice Sanchez was concerned with other things. Slice had picked this spot deliberately, though it was dangerously close to Watson's, what with their enjoying their stolen goods and all, but he didn't care. The spot provided a perfect view of the bag lady's place. Sooner or later, that little black peckerwood that had bluffed him that day in the alley would be along. Today was the day Slice decided he was going to even the score.

Before going into Watson's, Slice and his buddies had gone into her tenement and knocked on her door. Eddy's cousin lived on the third floor and had told him the bag lady lived in a small one-room apartment on the first. It irked Slice that the old bitch wasn't home, fueling the rage he was quietly building to unleash on that black bastard. He had wanted to do a number on her first and then wait for the kid to show up so they could watch each other suffer. Now he'd just have to play the waiting game, which he hated, and see who arrived first, the old bag or the little coon. It didn't really matter. He just hoped someone came soon; his rage was reaching meltdown level.

By three-thirty, an hour later, Slice's goons were getting antsy. They wanted to go down to the video arcade on Fairmont Street and shake quarters out of the nerds and play four-handed *Teenage Mutant Ninja Turtles*. The day, which had started warm with temperatures in the low fifties, was cooling off rapidly. Sitting on the stone wall in the shade didn't make things any warmer.

Slice couldn't understand where the hell they were. He had expected Ivy to get off his bus at two-thirty and head straight for the bag lady's place, which Slice had seen him do a couple of times before the alley incident. Every minute more that he had to wait he planned on taking out of the kid's hide.

"Hey, man! I'm cold! Let's go down to the arcade and play some *Turtles*. They ain't comin'," Greasy complained.

"I wanna be Michelangelo!" JoJo piped up. The others enthusiastically joined in, claiming the turtles they wanted to manipulate in the game.

"Shut up!" Slice snapped at them. "We ain't goin' nowhere til a certain little black turtle comes along. Then you can be real ninjas when we beat the shit out of him."

"He's just a little kid, Slice. You're just gonna scare him, ain't ya?" Big asked, looking up from a *Casper* comic book.

Slice came within a hair of punching Big in the face for being so sentimental, but he held his anger in, wanting to save it for his little buddy. Besides, it wouldn't serve his purpose to get Big and the others mad at him by taking out his frustrations on them.

"Sure, Big," he said, smiling broadly. A new anticipation was added, that of seeing Big's face when he discovered how Slice planned to *scare* Ivy. He took his switchblade stiletto out of his pocket and flicked it to life. When he was through with Little Black Sambo, the kid would be able to sip a straw through the sides of his cheeks and hang baseball cards from his nostrils. Slice chuckled meanly to himself at the image.

"He shoulda been here by now, Slice. Maybe he ain't comin' cuz the old bitch ain't home," Eddy whined.

Slice hated the sound of Eddy's voice, which was still trapped in the tonal fluctuations of puberty, even though Eddy was seventeen and as big as the proverbial house. Listening to him squeak and squawk in normal conversation was bad enough, but when he whined, which he was good at, his voice grated unbearably on Slice's nerves.

"He'll come," Slice growled through clenched teeth. *If he doesn't come I'm going to kick your whining face in,* he thought but said, "If he doesn't come, we'll go looking for him."

As if to prove Slice a prophet, Ivy came strolling down the sidewalk across the street, his knapsack slung over one shoulder, daydreaming of Bondian adventures, unaware that he was about to come as close to one as he would ever get.

Ivy knocked on Barbara's door, waited a few seconds, and knocked again. No answer. She hadn't been on the bus and now she wasn't at home. He pulled his watch from his pocket. She'd said she would catch the three o'clock bus from Fitchburg back to Crocker. It had arrived five minutes ago without her. What if the doctors at the clinic had found something wrong with her? He debated whether to wait in the hallway for her, but the darkness and the odors of cat urine and garbage convinced him he should wait outside, no matter how cold it was getting.

On the street, he headed for the alley next to Watson's Market. He figured he'd look for some depositables and work his way over to Turner Street where, at four, he could see the next bus come up the hill from downtown and hopefully spot Barbara on it.

The alley was uncharacteristically barren of bottles and cans. Usually it yielded at least four or five around the dumpster for Watson's Market, but there were none there, nor around the heavy metal barrels of the laundromat. He figured he had enough time to look through the laundromat's barrels before the bus came, but a mean laugh and a harsh voice fixed him where he stood.

"Hey, nigger!"

Ivy's neck bristled with anger at the sound of that hated word. He turned and faced Slice Sanchez, Greasy, and JoJo. The other two goons in the gang were nowhere to be seen.

"We got some shit to settle, nigger," Slice said. He and his buddies spread out, blocking the Leighton Street end of the alley, and advanced slowly on him. Greasy giggled like an excited kid, but JoJo looked nervous and kept glancing back at the street.

"Thought you were pretty smart with your little bluff, didn't you?" Slice said, coming slowly, never taking his eyes off Ivy. Greasy giggled again.

Ivy held his right arm up and pulled back the

sleeve of his coat, pointing the cast gun at Slice. "Don't come any closer, or I'll skewer your balls!" Ivy threatened.

Slice looked at the cast contraption on Ivy's arm and laughed. "You break your arm, nigger? Maybe I can make the other one match it." He took another step forward.

Ivy slapped the catch that was supposed to release the rattrap's spring bar and launch the antenna arrow. Nothing happened. He hit it again. Nothing. Ivy began retreating while he tried to get the cast gun to fire. He hadn't expected to be able to hit Slice with the cast gun, but he had at least hoped it would fire, taking the punks off guard and giving him a chance to run.

Slice, Greasy, and JoJo were following him but didn't seem to be in any hurry to grab him. Ivy figured on taking advantage of their lethargy and bolted, right into the arms of Big and Eddy, who had circled around to Turner Street to cut off his escape. He should have known!

Big grabbed Ivy's shoulders and tried to laugh menacingly to scare him. It sounded merely goofy to Ivy. Big reached down with the intention of lifting Ivy by his arms and carrying him to Slice. His hand closed on Ivy's right arm and he got a nasty surprise. The pressure of his grip set off the stuck firing catch, and the cast gun went off, driving the sharpened car antenna through Big's jeans and half an inch into his left thigh.

Big let out a screaming *"OW!"* and staggered away from Ivy, clutching his wounded leg. Ivy took the opportunity to run and was afforded several seconds' head start while Slice and the others stared dumbfounded at the antenna dangling from Big's thigh like a dart from a fighting bull. His jeans pant leg was dark with blood to the knee.

"He stabbed me!" Big screamed in an unnaturally high voice.

Slice pulled out his switchblade and snapped it open. "We'll just have to cut him back then, won't we?"

"What about me?" Big squealed at his departing friends. Eddy was the only one to stop and go back. With his weight, he had no desire to go chasing after some little kid who could probably outrun all of them. He didn't like it that Ivy had fought back, either. All of them were unused to having their victims fight back. Eddy was glad to be left behind.

Ivy ran as fast as he could down Turner Street, which ran parallel to Leighton with the alley connecting them. At the end of the street, where it connected to Rollstone Road, which led downtown, a dirt road went off to the left side, running up into the woods cresting Green Hill and leading to the city's sandbank lot where the Crocker Parks Department got the sand to spread on winter roads. He headed for it.

The knapsack kept sliding around on his back and made it very difficult to run. Ivy was pretty sure he was faster than Slice or any of his buddies, especially since they smoked and he didn't, but the knapsack was really slowing him down. He was tempted to dump it in the bushes and come back for it later. Losing it would definitely improve his speed, but if he got caught by Slice or any of the others he'd be defenseless except for his bleach-filled squirt gun, which he could carry in his hand as he ran. He opted for keeping the bag and using his wits to elude his pursuers.

Ivy reached the dirt road and struggled up it. He was glad the temperature was dropping. If it had remained as warm as it had been that morning, the sand on the road would have been soft and slippery. With the lower temps it was freezing and hard enough not to hinder him.

Ivy reached the top of the incline where the road leveled off, narrowed to two tire tracks, and made a right turn along the ridge. He stopped a moment to rest and could hear the footfalls of Slice and his buddies nearing the end of Turner Street and the beginning of the dirt path. Quickly he slung his knapsack off his shoulders and onto one arm. He fished around inside for a moment before finding the old light bulbs. He began pulling them out and throwing them in a high arc toward the bottom of the hill and Turner Street. Just as Slice and his boys reached the dirt road, the bulbs began falling around them and popping like gunshots, making Greasy and JoJo dance and forcing even Slice to cover his eyes from the shattering glass.

The last bulb gone, Ivy hefted the pack again and took off along the road. Ahead, he could see the entrance to the city sandbank between two fender-scarred trees. He hoped his attack had caused Slice and company to think twice about charging head-long after him. If he was lucky, he had bought enough time to get above the sandbank where he could circle around to the other side and hopefully lose his followers.

Behind him, Slice was the only one to react immediately after the last bulb exploded. Greasy and JoJo had backed off a way, their heads ducked, their arms raised protectively over their faces. Slice started up the dirt road and realized Greasy and JoJo weren't following him. He stopped and turned back to them, gesturing wildly with his knife and shouting in a winded voice that lacked strength. "C'mon, you wimps. Let's get that son of a bitch."

Greasy and JoJo looked uncertain, but the dark expression of mounting rage on Slice's face convinced them they'd better follow or he might decide to vent that anger on them instead of the boy. Their hesitation bought Ivy just enough time to get to the sandbank entrance where he was completely out of sight of the three punks.

The road rose slightly, peaking at the entrance to the sandbank, then sloping down until it became lost in the deep soft sand of the large flat lot at the bottom of a fifty-foot-wide and forty-foot-tall cliff of sand. Ivy knew the sandbank better than any other part of his new neighborhood. In the days before he'd met Barbara, and during the time he'd avoided her, he had played there almost every day. Through the bushes to the left of the sandbank entrance a path ran up to and across the top of the cliff of sand. It came down in a small stand of trees on the other side where two rows of large concrete drainpipes were stored, stacked in pyramids atop one another up against the bottom of the cliff face.

He pushed through the bushes to the path and

paused, taking stock of the climb to the top of the cliff along the path in front of him. It was pretty steep for the first twenty yards or so, then became easier, but Ivy didn't think he had the legs to make those first twenty yards right now.

He slipped off the knapsack and crouched low behind the laurel bushes that separated the path from the dirt road as Slice, Greasy, and Jojo came up the road. Ivy realized he was better off hiding where he was; if he had tried to climb the path, they would have easily spotted him. Maybe by hiding, he thought, he could fool them into thinking he was in the sandbank, hiding behind one of the many piles of sand there. If they went in after him, he could slip down the road the way he'd come and escape. But, just in case, he got his bleach-filled water gun and the jar of Zip-Strip out of the pack. He opened the jar and placed it at his feet where he could easily grab it, and clutched his pistol in both hands the way he'd seen them do on TV, ready to fire.

Slice, Greasy, and JoJo came puffing up the road. A steady diet of cigarettes, beer, junk food, and the assorted drugs they took when they could afford them, had rendered the three badly out of shape. By the time they gained the entrance to the sand-bank, they were all sweating profusely, which made them very cold as the sweat dried in the near-freezing temperature. JoJo had to drop to one knee and hang his head, gasping for air.

"Where . . . is . . . he?" Slice puffed, his breath white and heavy with moisture. He moved to wipe sweat from his forehead and found tiny crystals clinging to the hair of his eyebrows.

"Dunno," was all Greasy could manage to say. He was bent over, hands on knees, wheezing for breath as badly as JoJo.

In slightly better shape from weight lifting than the other two, Slice found his wind returning more quickly, and he started into the sandbank in search of Ivy. Greasy and JoJo remained where they were, too out of breath and tired to care about Slice's wrath if they didn't keep up.

In the bushes, not six feet away, Ivy tensed. What was he going to do if Greasy and JoJo didn't follow their fearless leader? He guessed he could jump out and run down the road and they'd be too tired to chase him, but they'd alert Slice. Ivy knew that no matter how out of breath or tired Slice was, he wouldn't give up the chase easily. For the time being, Ivy remained where he was, willing Greasy and JoJo to follow Slice and give him his chance to escape.

"Come on, you guys," Slice called to Greasy and JoJo from the first pile of sand, twenty yards into the sandbank.

Greasy straightened and looked to see if JoJo was going to follow. Something white in the bushes behind his friend caught his eye. It was a sneaker. He looked up, and his eyes met Ivy's through a small leafy opening in the laurel bushes.

"Here he is!" Greasy shouted as loudly as his winded lungs would allow.

JoJo flinched and spun toward the bushes on his knee just in time to see Ivy's hand flinging liquid out of a glass jar at his head. He lost his balance and fell over, which saved his face from the Zip-Strip that splashed over his upraised hands and exposed wrists. He howled with pain as the stuff blistered his ragged cuticles and ran into the winter-chapped cracks of his dry skin. He fell on his stomach in the road, crying like a baby and rubbing his hands in the hard dirt, trying to get the stuff off, but only making the pain worse.

Greasy watched in horror as his friend screamed, cried, and writhed in the dirt. He looked up and Ivy was standing in the bushes, squirt gun aimed at his face, ready to fire.

"I've got a license to kill," Ivy said in what he thought was a James Bond tone of voice. "So if you want some acid in your face, come on."

Greasy looked at JoJo, who had gotten to his feet and was stumbling down the road, crying, his hands cradled close to his body. "No way, man," Greasy mumbled. Backing up, he turned and ran after JoJo.

Slice was charging across the lot. Ivy lifted his pack onto his shoulder and started up the path.

"Come back here, you assholes!" Slice screamed at his departing friends from the entrance to the sandbank. Greasy and JoJo ignored him and kept on going. Slice swore loudly. He was incredulous at the fact that the little coon had beaten *his* gang. It was unbelievable.

Slice turned toward Ivy. The kid was already more than halfway up the path. Slice knew he'd never catch him. The climb up that steep path would take out of him whatever wind and energy he had left. He remembered that the path went along the top of the sand cliff through thick brambles that allowed no other avenue of escape, and came down the other side of the cliff. The only way out for the kid now was to follow the cliff-top path to the other side, or to double back and come down the path he'd just climbed. Which would he do? Slice figured there was an easy way to make the kid decide.

"I'm coming after you, *dead meat!*" Slice called up to Ivy, who had reached the not-so-steep part of the path. He made a show of climbing after Ivy until the kid had scrambled out of sight, then went down the path and cut across the sandbank lot.

I'll cut the son of a bitch off at the pass, Slice thought, grinning.

Ivy stopped at the top of the path to catch his breath. The climb had taken more out of him than he expected. His only consolation was that it would take a lot more out of Slice. It might even take enough out of him to make him give up and wait for another day. Ivy sure hoped so. He was exhausted and cold.

He tucked the squirt gun into his belt, hoisted his pack again, and began walking along the cliff top. The path was narrow with thick brambles encroaching on both sides that prevented him from going to the edge of the cliff and looking down at the lot below. If he had, he would have seen Slice Sanchez racing to intercept him at the other end of the path.

By the time he got to the bottom of the path at the other side of the cliff, there was still no sign of Slice gaining on him from behind. Ivy was beginning to think that maybe the jerk had given up.

Another thought occurred to him. What if Slice had tired quickly of the climb and decided to cut across to the other side to ambush him?

He slowed his walk. The closer the path got to the bottom, the nearer the trees grew. If Slice *had* cut across, he could be hiding behind any of them.

Ivy stopped. What should he do? If he went back, he could be walking right into Slice with no escape. If he went ahead, Slice could be waiting to jump out and grab him.

If he's going to get me, Ivy thought, *I'd rather face him down here. If he traps me on top of the cliff, there's only one direction I can escape in. And if he catches me, he'll probably drag me through the thorns. Down here, at least, I have more options.*

He turned, listening for any sign of Slice behind him. The wind was picking up and he couldn't tell. He had to move soon; he was freezing.

Okay, he thought and took a deep breath. He held up his squirt gun, ready to fire. *Down it is.* He started walking.

"Surprise!" Slice screamed, jumping out from behind a tree and knocking the water pistol from Ivy's hand. "Ain't so smart now, are you, nigger?" Slice said with gleeful menace. He held up his switchblade and smiled, showing his teeth like a dog about to bite.

Ivy took a step backward.

"I was just gonna rough you up before, nigger, but now, you're gonna to have to *pay* for what you did to the others. I am going to *slice* and *dice* you, Sambo." Slice seemed to find his last statement hilarious. His laughter chilled Ivy.

Too tired to go back up the hill, Ivy took the only avenue of escape open to him. He dashed to the right. Slice grabbed at him, but Ivy slipped away, lunging through the tangle of brambles and laurel bushes where they were at their narrowest. They tore at his clothes and backpack and face as he pushed through, and then he was free as he dove, over the edge of the cliff.

Since he was nearly at the bottom of the path, the sand cliff at that point was only eight or nine feet high. Ivy slid down the face on his belly and tumbled to the bottom between two piles of the huge concrete pipes that were stacked in rows at this end of the sandbank.

"Come back here, you little *fuck!*" Slice screamed, his anger that Ivy was escaping *again* distorting his beet-red face into an ugly expression of rage. He turned and ran down the path and around the bottom of the cliff into the lot. The bastard wouldn't get far; he still had the kid trapped. There was no way the brat could get out of the sandbank now without Slice catching him. All he had to do was flush the kid into the open.

Ivy, too, knew he was trapped. The sand in the lot was too deep to freeze despite the dropping temperature. He wouldn't have a firm footing to run fast enough to escape Slice. He had to hide. He was lucky his dive over the cliff edge had landed him amid the large drainpipes; it was the only place in the sandbank that offered a decent hiding place.

"I'm coming, *boy!*" Slice yelled from very close by. For one frightening moment his voice sounded just like Dr. Peabody's. Terror ripped through Ivy and he hid in the first place that offered itself, a nearby drainpipe that was on the low end of a pyramid of pipes that went up more than ten feet, following the rise of the cliff. Ivy scrambled into the pipe backward on all fours and found that he could almost stand up inside if he kept his head down and his shoulders hunched. Walking that way, he backed halfway into the pipe, keeping his eyes on the opening for any sign of Slice Sanchez.

It was dark in the pipe, nearly as dark as night, but Ivy didn't notice immediately, so intent was he on watching the opening for any sign of Slice. Suddenly a pair of jeans-clad legs passed quickly by the end of the pipe.

As quietly as possible, Ivy turned to the other end of the pipe and nearly shrieked. It was dark, with no sign of an opening. He was really trapped now! He took his Bic lighter out and struck it to see. The ten-foot length of pipe he had hidden in was right up against the cliff face. A small pile of sand had collected in the end of the pipe. Bent like an old man, Ivy went to the end of the pipe for a closer look.

The sand against the top of the end opening wasn't very thick, and he found he could create an opening by pulling sand down into the pipe. Ivy realized that if he did that, though, Slice would see the sand shifting and sliding down the cliff face and would know where he was hiding. But if he waited until Slice found him, as he surely would if he searched every pipe in the lot, Ivy doubted he would have enough time to dig his way out of the end before Slice could crawl in and grab him.

He needed something to slow Slice down once he

climbed into the pipe, and he had just the thing. He was glad now that he hadn't left his knapsack behind, though if he was going to escape Slice now, he'd have to leave it in the pipe. He took off the pack, and moving quietly, opened it. Working as quickly, yet as quietly, as possible, he took out the rest of the rat traps, set them, and placed them along the length of the pipe, as close to the other end opening as he could without them being seen by Slice.

With the last trap set and in place, Ivy returned to the end of the pipe and crouched there waiting. It seemed colder in the pipe than outside, making Ivy shiver. His legs were cramping, too, from all the running and the constant crouch he was now forced into. He sat on the floor of the pipe and tried to stretch and massage his legs.

"Where are you?" Slice called in a singsong voice from very close by.

Ivy tensed.

Slice's legs appeared in the pipe opening, then his head, almost upside down, as he peered inside. "Bingo!" he said, and knelt, looking in at Ivy.

"Don't make me come in there after you, nigger. It'll be a lot worse for you if I have to come in there after you." Slice paused a moment. "I might even *kill* you, nigger, if I have to climb in there and drag you out." He saw that Ivy wasn't going to come out. "Okay, it's your funeral."

Slice put his switchblade in his pocket and dropped to all fours to climb into the pipe. "You're going to regret this," Slice grunted.

Ivy started digging.

Slice crawled faster, closer.

Ivy was sure Slice must have reached the area of the traps but none had sprung. If Slice didn't trip one of the rat traps soon, Ivy knew he was finished. He dug wildly.

"Forget it, nig—" The rest of Slice's sentence turned into a shriek. At the same time there was a loud *snap* and crack in the pipe. Slice banged his head as he tried to bolt upright. Another crack followed as Slice lost his balance and reached down to steady himself and found another trap that clamped with a vengeance on his cold fingers. He screamed in pain, the sound followed by another *snap* and another scream, then another and another as Slice, in his frantic attempt to turn and get out of the pipe, hit more and more of the traps.

Ivy was on his feet, digging at the sand at the top of the pipe's opening for all he was worth. The sand was giving way quickly, but poured into the pipe against his stomach and legs, making it hard for him to keep his footing.

Slice was stuck halfway into the pipe. Two fingers on his left hand were broken as was the thumb of his right. A stream of obscenities and threats raged from his mouth, but he was helpless to do anything and he knew it. No matter which way he turned, left or right, frontward or backward, he set off a trap. Not knowing how many there were, he didn't dare move.

Suddenly the sand gave way all at once and the opening Ivy was working at widened enough that he thought he could squeeze through. The only problem was the sand cascading in to the pipe gave him little traction to climb out. He wriggled frantically, digging in with his knees and began to make progress. He squeezed his head and shoulders through and out into the air. Pushing with his hands against the pipe he wriggled the rest of the way out, leaving his knapsack and a blubbering, swearing Slice Sanchez behind.

Seeing that Ivy was escaping, Slice screamed more obscenities. He tried to go back the way he came but promptly put his right hand on another trap that broke his pinky in two places. He screamed and bawled in more pain than he'd ever experienced and rolled onto one side, setting off a couple more traps that bit harmlessly into the shoulder and back of his jacket. He jumped at the sounds and put his left hand into another trap, breaking another finger.

Ivy ran along the top of the pipe and leaped to the ground. Slice's angry, tearful screams and sobs from within the pipe brought a smile to Ivy's face. "Double-Oh-Seven escapes once again," he said boastfully, trotting away. "Cool as ever."

Ivy sat on the front step of Barbara's apartment building, trembling with adrenaline and excitement as he relived his triumphs over Slice Sanchez and his buddies. He knew it wasn't over between him and Slice, not by a long shot. All he'd done by fighting back was raise the ante for next time. A beating wouldn't be enough for Slice now. He'd be out for Ivy's *blood* the next time they met.

He wasn't too worried about the rest of Slice's gang, unless they were with Slice. They had shown themselves all to be cowards at heart, like most bullies, and now that he had beaten them once, they would be leery of tackling him again, even with Slice leading them. When it came time to get down to it, Ivy figured it would be just Slice and himself.

Slice was different from the others. Ivy was certain he was psychotic. Slice wouldn't think twice about killing Ivy, even if it meant he'd spend the rest of his life in prison. The next time they met, Ivy knew it could well be a fight to the death. He had hurt Slice, probably in a way *no one* had ever hurt him. Slice would want payback in triplicate.

Ivy took out his watch and looked at it. After five. Enjoyment of his earlier victories faded as real worry set in. The fear that the doctors at the clinic had found something seriously wrong with Barbara returned. He wondered if they would admit her to a hospital even though she didn't have any money. He could imagine, all too easily, her lying in a hospital bed, in pain, alone.

At five thirty he decided to go home and call the clinic in Fitchburg. The sound of off-key singing stopped him. It was coming from down the street. At first Ivy thought it was some old wino. There were a few living in the neighborhood and over on Turner Street. He started toward home again, and found Barbara slumped against a dented trash can on the sidewalk a few houses away. Her coat was open to the cold and her clothes were a mess. At first, Ivy thought she'd had another run-in with Slice, but he didn't see how she could have after Ivy had left him at the sandbank with at least two broken fingers, if not more. Slice would be at the emergency room of Crocker Hospital, or, if he was too stupid to seek medical help, home licking his wounds.

The fact that she was singing told him she wasn't hurt. If she had run into Slice or any of his buddies, she wouldn't be singing. He crouched in front of her, caught a whiff of her hundred-proof breath, and knew she was feeling no pain at all.

She squinted up at him through her old glasses. She smiled, then looked around. Grunting and moaning, she tried to get to her feet. Ivy reached out a hand to help her.

"No!" she shrieked and tried to crawl away.

"It's okay! It's okay! It's me! Ivy!" He tried to take her hand.

"No, please! Leave me alone!" she moaned, batting at him with her hands.

"Barbara! It's me! It's Ivy!" he shouted at her, trying to cut through her mounting hysteria and make her understand.

"Ivy?" she asked, finally recognizing his voice. "Oh, *Ivy!*" she sobbed, clasping her arms around his neck like a drowning person.

Ivy knelt on the cold pavement and let her hug him close, even though the smell of cheap wine on her was overpowering and sickening. Ivy hated seeing Barbara like this; it reminded him too much of his mother. He fought back feelings of disgust by telling himself her getting drunk was a delayed reaction to the incident with Slice. The thought occurred to him that what he saw as his mother's habitual drinking was similar; an ongoing delayed reaction to his father's death. He felt a pang of guilt at having been so disgusted by her attempts to deal with her grief in the only way that dulled the pain for her. It became obvious to him now that was why she drank. He wondered why he'd never seen it before. For someone so smart, he could be pretty stupid sometimes.

"Come on. Let's get you inside where it's warm," he said, trying unsuccessfully to lift her. A new, more frightening thought occurred to him: What if she had gotten drunk because they had given her terrible news at the clinic, like she had a month to live or something?

Barbara's sobs slowed and Ivy was able to help her to her feet. The sun was gone and the sidewalk was becoming pitched in night shadows. With her right arm over his shoulder, and his left around her waist, he piloted Barbara carefully toward her building.

She nearly fell once, and Ivy thanked God they were near a telephone pole that he could use to help keep her upright. He got her moving again, though it took every ounce of his strength to do so, and continued as her crutch. They walked sideways a few steps, then forward, staggered back, sideways again, and forward until they reached her steps. Together they slowly climbed them, and Ivy helped her into the hall.

At her door, Ivy leaned her against the wall, where she promptly slid to the floor. He had seen her take her keys out of her inside coat pocket on more than one occasion so knew where to look for them.

"Henry? Is that you?" Barbara asked him, her face uplifted, eyes closed as if expecting a kiss.

Ivy blushed and got the keys as fast as he could. He unlocked the door and pushed it open. The pile of books behind the door fell over creating a domino effect, knocking over several other stacks. They made a plopping sound and a soft thudding in the darkness.

"Don't let them get me, Henry," Barbara sobbed. "Where are you, Henry?"

Ivy's heart went out to his friend. At the same time, his intense temper flared at Slice and his gang for doing this to Barbara. Any pain or injury he had caused them that afternoon wasn't enough. Today, he had been playing a defensive game, happy to go his own way if left alone. Now, he desired revenge in the worst way to make them pay for hurting his friend.

"You're okay, Barbara," he said calling her by her first name, something he had never done before this evening. "I'm here now and you're going to be okay. You're home." Straining to support her, he helped her up and got her inside.

"Ivy?" she said drunkenly as he led her to the bed. "You're a good kid. Smart as a whip. I was just telling Henry about you." She turned and pointed at the empty armchair and collapsed half on, half off the narrow bed. Within seconds she was snoring.

Ivy lifted her feet and legs and swung them onto the bed. He didn't bother trying to take her coat off; it was chilly in the apartment. He covered her with the blankets and an old, brown knit afghan he took off the back of one of the armchairs and left quietly, leaving her keys on the kitchenette counter and locking the door.

CHANNEL 11

*Smokin' in the
Boys' Room—II*
Vicki Dominatrix
Real People
To Catch a Thief

 Bill watched with admiration as Larken created a new file on the computer for the latest homicide, seventy-year-old Joan Perche. Her husband, age sixty-eight, had called the police reporting her missing and given a description that matched the woman found outside Video Valhalla. He was asked to come to the station and was taken to the county morgue, where he identified his wife's body with screams and a heart attack. Larken had put in a lot of hours doing the legwork: compiling personal data, tracking her last movements, looking for witnesses.

"I want a copy of that file as soon as you're done," Bill said over Larken's shoulder. "Anything on the plumbing companies or the Elvis porn?"

"No luck yet, sir, but I'm still working on it," Larken replied.

Bill clapped him on the shoulder and went to find

Mahoney. He found the captain at the same time the desk sergeant found Bill. In his hand he held a book-size package wrapped in brown paper that had come in the afternoon mail addressed to Special Investigator Gage.

Larken hurried over with a copy of the file on Joan Perche just in time to see Bill remove the black videocassette tape from its wrappings. A title was printed in laundry marker on a side stick-on label: *Smokin' in the Boys' Room.*

Instead of viewing the tape of the second murder right after the lab had dusted it, Bill let Hanson keep it overnight to make a loop as he'd done with the first one. Mahoney came back with the frame-by-frame blown-up stills of the first video, and Hanson's report on the Saxon Theater front, where Grace Simonds was found, plus his examination of Joan Perche in the Video Valhalla lot where her body was found. He'd found no paper with the words *Elvis* or *stud* or *xXx* on it. The dark fuzzy spot Bill had noticed on the sidewalk next to Grace Simonds's body was indeed a spot of her blood with coarse, gray wool fibers stuck to it. In the mud around Joan Perche's body, he'd found footprints that matched the toe of the print in the dormitory bathroom where Grace Simonds was killed. He also got prints from the tape when it came in, and got a several-point match with the bloody fingerprint on the ax in the first video and with what he lifted from the dormitory stall.

The tape was supposed to be ready by noon today. Bill had stayed up late last night poring over

Hanson's photos of Joan Perche's body, telling himself he was looking for anything he might have missed at the scene, but in reality he was trying to prepare himself for watching the video of her death today. He found himself ghoulishly hoping the second murder would follow the same pattern as the first, with the victim being already dead, or at least unconscious, when her arms were incinerated. He knew it was a false hope. The look of pain and horror on Joan Perche's face when he'd examined her outside Video Valhalla told him she'd been alive and fully conscious during the atrocities performed on her.

Bill didn't think the killer had meant to murder Grace Simonds in the dorm bathroom. He figured the perp had wanted her *actual* death on tape but had got carried away. This time though, he'd kept his murderous desires under control until they could be recorded *live* for posterity, or for whatever reason the perp thought he had to film his murders. Motive was not a question Bill found he could deal with easily. Whenever he tried to think along motive lines, his failure with his father got in the way. He still hadn't been able to figure out why his father killed eighty-nine women, took pictures of each of them, and wrote detailed descriptions of each death in a journal; how was he supposed to figure out why a total stranger had the need to videotape his victims?

Bill left his office and went down to the interrogation room that had been converted into a viewing room. Closing the door behind him, not bothering to turn on the lights, he sat in the dark before the blank TV screen, wondering why they always seemed to have an inner glow of their own, even when turned off.

Chief Albert was supposed to join them for the viewing, but Bill hoped he didn't come down until after he'd had a chance to watch it a couple of times alone. He and Mahoney had already agreed that viewing of the tape would be restricted this time. The other men working on the case didn't need to see the video. Exposing them to the horror that Bill knew the tape held served no constructive purpose in the investigation.

The door opened and the lights came on. "What are you doing sitting in the dark?" Mahoney asked him.

"Thinking," Bill answered, not looking up from the blank screen.

"Well, you can stop thinking and start being sick. I've got the six-hour loop." Mahoney held up the tape. Though his tone was light, Bill could see in his eyes that Mahoney was dreading the video as much as Bill was.

"You don't have to watch this now, if you're not up to it, or you have other things to do," Bill said, offering an out. He was glad when Mahoney shook his head and went about the business of plugging the equipment in and loading the tape in the VCR. Contrary to how he'd felt with the first tape, Bill wanted company during the first viewing of *Smokin' in the Boys' Room*. He thought it ironic how such a short time ago, he and Mahoney had been enemies. Now he counted the captain as a new friend and respected him as a man and as a detective.

"All set," Mahoney said, sitting next to Bill and handing him the VCR remote control. "Ready when you are." Mahoney tried to look as if he meant it.

Bill took a deep breath, looked into the blank video light filling the TV screen, and pressed the play button. The VCR whirred to life, PLAY spelled out in glowing green on its face, next to the forever flashing 12:00 A.M. The screen went dark and faded to gray. The title, *Smokin' in the Boys' Room*, came on. Slowly, the camera focused past the fading title, and in living color the poor old retired teacher, Joan Perche, naked, hands tied crucifixion-style to two shower heads, filled the frame. There was gray duct tape over her mouth. Her eyes showed terror. The wall behind her was beige concrete. The floor was dull gray tile.

The picture cut to an extreme close-up of the brass nozzle of a portable acetylene torch.

Another cut, to a close-up of Joan Perche's fearful eyes.

Cut again. The nozzle, a match held to it this time. A blue flame spouted from the metal and grew to needle sharpness.

Another close-up of the woman's eyes. Where before Bill had thought the look of terror in those eyes was unbearable, now it was worse. The blue pencil flame of the torch was reflected in her glassy pupils. It brought to mind the image of her scorched orb sockets.

The rest of the tape was a stationary shot of the

woman from the waist up. The lighted acetylene torch entered the frame from the left edge first and was applied to her right arm. The old woman's body became a blur of gyrations, her head flopping about as she tried to pull away from the flame. The perp was persistent, though, stopping just long enough for her to calm down before beginning on her left arm. He kept this up, back and forth from arm to arm, drawing out the torture, until Joan Perche's body moved only when it came free of her arms and collapsed to the floor. All the time it was at its gruesome task, only the nozzle and the top part of the torch's gas canister were visible. The killer had been very careful not to get himself in any part of the picture this time.

After only a minute of watching the torture, Mahoney left the room, a white-knuckled fist held to his lips. When he was gone, Bill watched until Joan Perche was dead, then shut the tape off and put his head down, breathing deeply to get his own nausea under control.

The door opened and Chief Albert came in, took one look at Bill's face, and grimaced. "That bad, huh?" Bill didn't have to answer.

"This is starting to attract press attention," the chief said, sitting in Mahoney's vacated chair. "A couple of the Boston stations have called asking for details and wanting to know if this murder and Grace Simonds's are related. We're giving no comment for the time being, but we're going to have to release something soon."

Bill nodded. "Whatever information we do release, I think we should hold back about the videotapes. It'll be a good way to weed out the nuts we're bound to get claiming they did it."

"I agree," the chief replied. "Actually, I was thinking of calling a press conference and letting you handle it." The chief smiled at Bill's groan. "It makes sense, Bill. You're in charge of the investigation. I've informed the mayor that we are dealing with a probable serial killer here, but he'd like that kept quiet until we're certain."

"I'm certain," Bill said. "This tape proves it."

"I know, but the mayor wants to avoid any panic, or vigilantism, so he wants us to sit on that information for as long as we can."

"Sure," Bill said sarcastically. "Let a few more women get killed before we warn the public."

"I think he's hoping we'll nab this guy before it gets out of hand."

"Believe me, George"—Bill stood, his voice angry—"it is already out of hand. Tell *Hizzoner* to come down here and watch this tape if he wants to see how out of hand this is getting. I haven't even begun to get a grip on the brutality involved here. This guy is way out there, George. We may never get him.

"I've been away from this for ten years," Bill continued, beginning to pace, "and this is the worst case I've ever seen. Even at the peak of my former career, this case would have thrown me for a loop. So tell the goddamned mayor not to expect miracles." Bill realized he was almost shouting.

"Don't worry about the mayor," George reassured him. "*You* may not realize it, but you're doing an amazing job. Mike Mahoney's turnaround should convince you of that. He's backing you because he can see that you get results."

Mahoney came back, his face pale, lips moist. He nodded and grinned sheepishly at the chief.

"Well," the chief said, looking uncomfortably at the screen, "I'll leave you to it. I've got a meeting with the mayor in fifteen minutes."

The chief left and Bill pressed play, bringing the vision of hellish torture back to life. He and Mahoney watched in barely breathing silence as the camera cut to a close-up of the flame being applied to Joan Perche's dead eyes. Bill thought he'd never eat fried eggs again when the tape was over. Before it could begin again on the loop, Bill pressed stop. They sat silent, each lost in his own personal revulsion at what they had just seen. The only redeeming factor was that the removal (or in this case, the burning) of her eyes had obviously occurred after Joan Perche was already dead.

"Why is he doing this?" Mahoney said, expressing frustration more than asking a question.

Bill pressed play again and didn't answer.

Vicki Clayton lit another joint, took a deep hit, and passed it to David Shipley. She blew the smoke at the van's windshield, fogging it.

"So where the hell are they?" she asked David. He ignored her, rotating the joint as he toked on it so that it would burn evenly.

"Don't Bogart that, asshole!" she yelled at him a minute later, accompanying the verbal assault with a backslap to David's face, causing a nice bruise on his right cheek just below his heavily made-up eyes with her onyx ring. He whimpered and hurriedly passed her the joint.

"Oh, Christ. You put a friggin' duck's ass on it," Vicki complained grimacing at the lipstick marks smearing the joint end. She was nervous, and when she got nervous she got bitchy, verbally and physically. Not that David minded either under the right conditions. Unfortunately, these weren't the right conditions.

Vicki fidgeted, working the joint and then stamping it out in the ashtray even though it was only half gone. David grimaced at the loss of his joint but knew better than to say anything.

Vicki looked up hopefully at the sound of an engine, then swore loudly when a pickup truck went by. She bit her thumbnail and looked out the passenger window. David, thinking she wasn't paying attention, tried to retrieve the joint.

"Leave it there!" she snapped, freezing his hand over the open ashtray.

"B-b-but . . ." he stammered in his effeminate voice.

"I said, *leave it!*" she snarled. Her hand flashed out like an attacking snake and she dug her long nails into the back of his hand, making him shriek. She left gouges of white skin filling with blood just behind his knuckles. He shoved the back of his hand into his mouth, sucking at the blood and sniffling.

If Joey and her cousin Mary didn't get back soon, Vicki was going to run out of coke. She had only two grams left and that would be gone by tomorrow morning. She wished now that she hadn't let Joey talk her and David into going to St. Martinique to meet with the French distributor of Tunnelvision Studios' videos. Joey would have gone himself, but he and Mary had to go to Boston to meet with some European millionaire who wanted a special, private video made that Joey was hoping would bring in mucho bucks.

Once before, about six or seven years ago, they'd had another request for a special video that had netted Tunnelvision Studios a cool half million. Vicki hadn't been involved with the business then, but from what Mary said when she got messed up and talked too much, Vicki understood that a millionaire had requested a snuff film made, and Mary and Joey had accommodated.

She and David got back from the island two days ago, and she'd been calling Mary's house six and seven times a day since, never getting an answer. She'd made David drive her over to their house a couple times a day, too, but no one was at home. Each time, they ended up sitting out front waiting for them, as they were doing now. Today they'd been waiting since 10:00 A.M., and it was now almost noon.

Vicki took a small, folded paper packet and a straightedge razor from her purse and opened the glove compartment door, which had a small flip-up vanity mirror attached to the inside of it. She opened the packet of paper, dumped its pebbly white contents onto the mirror and proceeded to chop the stuff up into a fine powder with the razor.

"You going to snort the whole half a gram, now?" David asked, his lisping voice muffled by his wounded hand still stuck in his mouth.

"What do you care?" Vicki retorted, holding the razor blade up threateningly.

He did care, though he didn't say anything. If she snorted that half a gram now, that would leave her with one and a half, which wasn't going to last long, the state she was in. And when she ran out, there would be hell to pay, with David picking up the painful check. It wouldn't be *good* pain either; he wouldn't enjoy it.

David was glad he couldn't do coke. His nose had been broken so many times that he could barely breathe through it and, without makeup on, looked like a seasoned boxer. He liked to get wasted as much as Vicki, but his tastes ran more to weed and Valium, speed and downers, and anything else he could get his hands on. Now crack, that was another story. He'd tried that once and loved it, but it was still pretty hard to come by in places like Crocker.

"Go ahead and knock yourself out if you want to. It's no skin off *my* nose," he pouted.

"There will be skin off your nose if you don't shut up," Vicki threatened, brandishing the powder-covered edge of the blade in his face again. She hadn't been planning on doing the whole half gram at once, she was just chopping it up to give herself something to do, but now she divided it into several fat lines and snorted them all rapidly, one right after the other, just to spite Queen David. She shivered and coughed at the intense rush. Afterward, she mentally kicked herself for letting the little drag queen goad her into doing the whole half gram. If she ran out before Mary and Joey got back, she was going to make him pay royally.

An hour later, the long, gold Bonneville Mary and Joey drove when the snow kept their bikes off the roads came up the street and pulled in the driveway. The sight of it was enough to elicit a cheer from Vicki until she saw that Wilbur, only Weirdo Wilbur, was in the car, steering it into the driveway.

"Since when does he drive?" David asked, but Vicki was already getting out of the van, heading for the house. David quickly took the half a joint out of the ashtray and stuffed it in his pocket before getting out and following.

Vicki caught Wilbur as he was crossing the backyard, heading for the porch. "Hey, Wilbur!" she shouted, stopping him in his tracks. "Where's Mary and Joey?"

His mouth opened, but he didn't answer. He looked completely freaked out to see them, but that didn't seem unusual to Vicki. She knew Wilbur was a *very* strange kid, maybe even crazy. She'd caught him talking to the TV—what he had called "tunnelvision" ever since he was little, which was where Joey got the name for the studio. Of course, considering the things that had been done to Wilbur over the years (things that Vicki had watched on occasion but never taken part in, kiddie porn not being her bag), it would be kind of amazing if he *wasn't* crazy.

"Earth to Wilbur? Hello?" she called, cupping her hand over her mouth for a megaphone effect. "Are you in there?"

* * *

Change the channel change the channelchange thechannel changethe channelchangethechannelchangethechannel . . .

Nothing happens. This is no new program beamed from the depths of his mind to torture him. These people are real. He knows them. If he wasn't so frightened, he could remember their names.

He wants to hide, to turn off his set and hide, but he can't. They're talking to him, expecting answers. Why don't they leave him alone? Why don't they just go ask their questions of Joey and Mary-not-Mother? Then he remembers. He's alone now, and the intruders want to know why.

Jesus wants to go on the air and answer them but good. He can even put them in contact with Joey and Mary-not-Mother with a few swings of the ax He keeps in the kitchen closet. Wilbur resists Him and is surprised when he is successful. Jesus recedes and waits, watching, ready to go to closed circuit at a moment's notice.

"They had to go away again," he mumbles in answer to her question of where are Joey and Mary-not-Mother.

"When will they be back?" she asks and her voice hurts his ears, like having a trumpet blasted into it from only inches away. She and the man are following him to the house. He doesn't know how to tell them to go away.

"I don't know," he says feebly.

The woman grabs his keys out of his hand and strides to the door, opening it. The man goes by, following her, and winks and smirks at Wilbur.

"You always leave the tube on when you go out?"

she asks him inside. She goes through the kitchen to the living room and stands looking at Jesus on the screen. Of course, she can't see Him in His guise as a sexy young woman on a soap opera, but Wilbur can, and there is blood lust in the Son of God's eyes. He screams at Wilbur to put Him on the air.

"I said, do you always leave the TV on when you go out?" she asks again when he doesn't answer. It's hard for him to hear with Jesus screaming so loudly.

"Kid's wacky," the man says, circling his right ear with an extended index finger and rolling his eyes. The woman turns off the tunnelvision but Jesus remains, staring balefully out at him.

"Look, Wilbur," she says, her tone a little softer, "I just want to know where they went. Joey's supposed to have an ounce of flake for me and I need it."

Wilbur breathes a sigh of relief. *That's* all they want. They can be gotten rid of easily.

"It's here," he says. He goes into the basement where the studio is. From a secret drawer set in the wall under the stairs, he takes an ounce of coke from Joey and Mary-not-Mother's stash.

The woman takes it greedily upon his return upstairs and goes to the kitchen table to try some. Now that she has what she needs she ignores him, but the man eyes him strangely.

"How come you have the key to Joey's stash? He'd never leave that here with you if they're away," he says to Wilbur. "That's not like him."

Wilbur notices the man is wearing makeup and fingernail polish, like a woman, and remembers who he is. His name is David. His last name is

Thefaggot. He has heard Joey and Mary-not-Mother speak of him often, calling him David Thefaggot. His words bring out a cold sweat in Wilbur. The Emergency Broadcast System is about to kick in. Jesus is about to go to closed circuit. Wilbur is about to let Him.

"Joey must have left it with him to give me my stuff," the woman says from the table where she is chopping coke on a dinner plate with her razor. "Shit-for-brains here probably wouldn't have even remembered if I hadn't asked him about it, ain't that right, Wilbur?"

He nods. "I remember now. Joey said to give you the coke. He left the key. He said you'd be coming with David Thefaggot," he says, indicating the man with a nod of his head.

The woman throws back her head and laughs hysterically but the man looks angry. He crosses to Wilbur and pushes him. "Watch what you call me, asshole!" he says in Wilbur's face.

Jesus is plugging in His camera.

"Don't take it out on him. He's like a kid, just repeating what he heard. You should take it up with Joey if you're mad," the woman taunts, still laughing.

David Thefaggot looks as if he doesn't think much of that idea, and he backs away from Wilbur. At the table, the woman snorts a few lines, pronounces the stuff to be good, and packs it up. She sashays over to Wilbur on her way to the door. She puts her hand on his crotch and squeezes hard, making him wince, while at the same time leaning forward and kissing him, driving her tongue deep into his startled mouth. "Thanks, Wilbur," she says prettily and looks down at her hand gripping his most vulnerable area. In an overly loud voice she adds, "Maybe I'll get rid of David Thefaggot and come back here and ride Mr. Ed."

The man bursts into tears and storms out of the kitchen. The woman gives Wilbur one more painful squeeze and lets go. "But don't hold your breath," she snarls and then she is gone, laughing, out the door, a blast of cold December air rushing in like her exhaust.

Slice Sanchez tried to put his hands in his pockets and winced at the pain in his fingers. They weren't healing properly. He realized now that he should have gone to the hospital right away, but he'd had to be a *macho man!* If he went now, he knew they'd have to break his fingers again to set them. If the fingers were going to have to be rebroken anyway, he'd rather break them himself on Greasy's and JoJo's faces for deserting him, or even better, on the *whole body* of the little nigger bastard who broke them in the first place.

The kid had surprised him, that was for sure. Slice wasn't used to people standing up to him and fighting back. He was going to have to be more careful the next time. One thing was definite: he wasn't going to depend on those losers who had been his former friends to help him.

Slice was hanging out in his favorite spot at the corner of Watson's Market. From there he could check out all of Leighton Street and most of Turner Street. More importantly, he could see directly into

Watson's through the side window of the large, mostly glass, store front. From that spot he could watch for cops and see when Old Lady Watson went into the back room to answer the phone or take a whizz or whatever she did back there. That was when Slice went into action.

He had it down to a science, he thought immodestly. He could slip into the store, nab some magazines, lighters, junk food, and a couple of instant lottery tickets before the old lady came barreling out, yelling at him to buy something or get out of her store. He always made sure he had at least enough money for a pack of gum.

A movement in the corner of his vision caught his attention and he turned, looking into the store. Old Lady Watson was looking right at him. He winked at her, and she turned, going into the rear of the store.

Slice looked up and down Leighton and Turner. No cops in sight. He went to the door of the market and peered through its glass. He could just see the old lady's shadow on the wall in the back room. It looked like she was talking on the telephone.

Slice turned the large brass doorknob as best he could with his bum left hand. Only his thumb and middle finger were unbroken on that hand. His right hand was slightly better off, the thumb, index, and middle fingers were okay. He reached up to silence the little tin bell that rang upon a customer's entrance, and jammed his baby finger into the top of the door. He wanted to scream with the pain that shot down his finger, through his hand, up his arm, and into his head where it began hammering on his skull. Gritting his teeth against the pain, he managed to grab the bell and slip inside quietly.

No sign of the old lady. He could hear her muffled voice from the back room, still on the phone. If she came out at any time, he'd make believe he had just walked in. Slice wasted no time. He helped himself to a couple of bags of Skittles and a package of Twinkies. Old Lady Watson was still yappin' so Slice decided to help himself to a coke and a copy of *MAD* magazine.

The sound of the bell above the door heralding the arrival of another customer kept him from getting the magazine. The old lady would be out pronto at the sound of the bell. He had to get over by the counter so it looked like he'd just come in, too.

He turned and forgot all about Old Lady Watson and everything else. The nigger pygmy that had *hurt* him had just walked in. He hadn't yet seen Slice on the far left side of the store behind the narrow bread aisle. The coon stood at the counter, looking expectantly toward the door to the back room for Old Lady Watson.

Slice ducked his head and slipped behind the short, narrow aisles of food to the first aisle. He crept to the front of the store, coming up behind the soon-to-be-dead nigger.

Slice leaned over and whispered in Ivy's ear. "I'm going to kill you," he said, making Ivy jump and scramble to the end of the counter. He laughed until he saw the smirk on Ivy's face.

"Gee! What happened to your fingers, Slice? Did you sneeze while you were picking your nose?"

The kid was taunting him!

"You think it's funny?" Slice asked, holding up the bent digits of his left hand.

"Well, yeah. I wouldn't say *hilarious* funny, but on a scale of one to ten, I give it an eight."

The kid was laughing. The kid *wasn't scared!*

Slice didn't know what to do. In his mounting rage he fell back on childish threats: "Yeah, well, you won't think it's so funny when I get through with you!"

"Yeah? You and what army? The *Grease* patrol?"

The little dumb fuck didn't know when to quit! Slice knew how to shut him up. Even with his broken fingers, he could bring his knife out and flip the blade erect in one fluid motion, making it appear as if by magic.

"You won't think you're so funny when I cut you open," Slice threatened, holding the blade up for Ivy to have a good look.

"How come you're not smiling anymore, bright boy?" Slice asked, finally beginning to enjoy himself with the look of fear on the kid's face. He feinted a thrust with the knife and giggled when Ivy almost fell over backward.

"I might not be able to get you right now," Slice said, glancing quickly in the direction of the back room, "but I will get you, Sambo. Count on it."

The doorbell jangled. Slice whirled around, trying to close his knife and put it away at the same time. His gimpy fingers couldn't manage, and it flew to the floor at the feet of the two police officers who had just walked in. A second later, the Coke Slice had lifted slipped out of his jacket, hit the floor, and began hissing and foaming like a bomb about to go off. The rest of his stolen booty followed.

"See! See!" Old Lady Watson shouted, charging out of the back room. "I *told* you! Him and his friends are robbing me blind! I got you this time, you—you—punk." She wagged her finger gleefully at him.

"All right, Sanchez. You know the routine. Assume the position," the cop said in a tired voice.

"I was gonna pay for that!" Slice said innocently.

"Oh, I'm sure," the cop mimicked. "I'm taking you in for possession of the pigsticker while on probation."

As he bent over, legs and arms spread against the counter, Slice could see Ivy heading around the cop for the door. The cop saw him, too.

"Hey, kid." The cop's voice stopped Ivy in the doorway. "Don't go anywhere. I want to talk to you."

Ivy looked back but said nothing. As the cop handcuffed Slice, the punk gave Ivy a glowering look. Making believe something was in his eye, Ivy rubbed it with his middle finger, subtly giving Slice the bird. It wasn't too subtle for the fuming Slice to pick up on, though.

CHANNEL 12

Beth Likes Wilbur
Bond, James Bond
*The Wilbur Relief
Fund*
*Scenes from
a Marriage—II*

Beth Shell was uncharacteristically looking forward to her next stint on the
graveyard shift. What had been the
worst part of eleven to seven had recently become the best when she learned it was
considered part of the eleven-to-seven guard's du-
ties to escort nurses through the deserted parts of
the hospital, out to their cars, or to the nursing
school upon request. She'd also learned that Wilbur
was some kind of workhorse, working seven days a
week and sometimes double shifts because the part-
time relief guard had quit. So it didn't matter what
night she worked, she was sure to see him.

The night of her shift approached and Beth experienced bouts of excitement alternating with dips of
nervousness and doubt. She was acting silly, she

knew, like a kid with a crush. She hardly knew the guy and had barely heard him speak one word, yet the thought of him made her feel giddy. If there was such a thing as love at first sight, then this was as close as she had ever come.

After torturous days, hours, minutes, and seconds of waiting, the night arrived. She was assigned to work geriatrics, which virtually assured her of having to make at least one trip to the laundry before the shift was over. She went on duty beaming and full of energy.

Four o'clock crawled around, and still no need to take the soiled linen cart to the laundry. Beth was getting antsy. The shift had been as quiet as the graveyard it was named for and as slow as a funeral march.

She finished a bed check on a ninety-year-old woman who'd awakened thinking she was in Kansas circa 1933, and walked slowly back to the nurses' station. She'd had to change only one patient all night, and then it was only for bed-wetting, definitely not enough to warrant taking the nearly empty cart to the laundry.

She resigned herself to hoping Wilbur would come by the station when he made his rounds with the watch clock. The key was at the end of the north hall, next to the emergency exit door. According to the head nurse, whom Beth had pumped for information, Wilbur usually came onto the floor through the emergency door and walked by the nurses' station on his way to the elevators, but if he had tonight, no one, including Beth, had seen him. The head nurse thought he made a round again at 5:00 A.M., but she wasn't positive.

Beth glanced at the clock. Five minutes past four. She groaned and waited.

Five o'clock was a long time coming. When it did, it arrived with disappointment—Wilbur never came by.

Ivy took out the spare key Barbara had given him and tried to unlock her door. Afraid she'd be asleep when he came and wouldn't hear him knocking, she'd told him to take it, warning that the spare had a tendency to stick in the lock. She'd complained, sort of whimsically, that she slept like the dead lately. Ivy hadn't liked the analogy.

He took the key out and reinserted it, trying again.

Barbara never brought up her night of drunkenness, and neither did Ivy. He did try to find out if she had checked out all right at the clinic, but she said she was fine and would say no more. Since Slice's assault, all she wanted to talk about was the past. Ivy didn't mind. He found her reminiscences as fascinating as a good book, but at times he got the strange feeling that she would be reliving them aloud whether he was there or not.

Ivy was very worried about his friend. She wasn't the same Barbara who had run him off her territory that first time they'd met, or who had introduced him to books he would love for the rest of his life. She slept too much, and she was right—she did sleep so deeply that Ivy couldn't wake her sometimes. She had become forgetful and spacey.

Ivy cursed the key under his breath and wiggled it in the lock.

Just the other day, he had arrived and let himself in with considerably less trouble to find her sleeping slumped in the armchair, her eyes closed, her mouth gaping and drooling, her left hand twitching. He'd tried to wake her and had been unable to. She woke herself while he was searching the room for change to use on the pay phone at Watson's Market to call an ambulance. She had assured him she was all right and had no need for an ambulance, sounding just like the old Barbara. He'd stayed while she went to bed and fell asleep. Before he left, she had cried out and begun trembling like a frightened child. Ivy covered her and sang lullabies he remembered his mother singing until Barbara was still.

On his way over, Ivy had been gloating over Slice Sanchez's getting nabbed for stealing at Watson's Market. As far as he was concerned, though, it still wasn't enough to make up for what Slice had done to Barbara. Every day she got worse. Lately, Ivy was worried that she wasn't eating. He'd taken to cooking supper for her before going home to eat with his mother. It was usually just a can of soup or beef stew, sometimes just a sandwich. Most of the stuff he "borrowed" from home, like the half box of elbow macaroni he planned on boiling up and topping with a small can of spaghetti sauce for her supper tonight.

Ivy's frustration level with the key was reaching its peak, but the sound of the door being unlocked from the inside kept him from blowing his stack.

The door opened and something came huffing and rolling and scratching and squealing out of the apartment's gloom, attacking his ankles with ticklish ferocity. He reached down and felt soft little paws box playfully with his hand and a wet nose nuzzle his fingers.

Ivy was speechless. He dropped to one knee and the puppy attacked his face with its friendly tongue. It was a mutt, but its lineage was apparent in its cocker spaniel ears and fox terrier snout. Its body was short and shaggy like a spaniel's, but the paws were all terrier. The tail belonged to neither breed, but was long and bushy and looked completely out of place on the dog.

Ivy looked up at Barbara, who was holding the door open. Expressions of joy and confusion waged a happy battle on his face, making Barbara feel the best she had in a while. He came in and took off his coat, the dog attacking his shoes, ankles, and legs all the while.

"Where'd he come from?" Ivy asked, dropping to both knees. The puppy promptly leaped at his chest, knocked him over, and licked his face until he was giggling wildly. The harder he laughed, the faster the dog licked his face until he had to push it away.

"The landlord found that little fellow in a trash bag in a dumpster at the factory where he works," Barbara said, after closing and locking the door. "He found some other stuff, too, that he gave me. It's in the box over there. You can have any of it that you want. It was a good thing the bag was torn or that puppy would have suffocated. My landlord, Mr.

Crankshaw, is a nice man. He thought I'd like the dog for company. I thought he was perfect for you."

Ivy looked thrilled, then frowned. "I'd love him," he said, with a longing gaze at the frisky puppy biting his thumb, "but my mother would never let me keep a dog. I've been bugging her for years for a dog and she always says no. I haven't even bothered asking for one this Christmas like I always do cuz I know she won't get me one."

"You can keep him here. Your mother doesn't have to know," Barbara suggested.

Ivy's face immediately brightened. "You mean it?"

Barbara nodded.

"All right!" Ivy cried. He picked up the dog and hugged it, subjecting his face to another tongue bath.

"You're going to have to name it," Barbara said, shuffling to her chair. "It's a male."

The dog's amorous attention didn't keep Ivy from noticing that Barbara seemed very stiff today. He carried the dog to the side of her chair and sat cross-legged with it in his lap. "Are you okay?" he asked, looking up into her face.

She smiled back at him, her eyes bright, dispelling some of his worry. "Oh, sure. Damned arthritis is all. Never mind that, it'll go away shortly. I want to know what you are going to name that little terror."

Ivy held the dog close and thought about it a few moments. "I know," he said with a slow grin. "I'll call him, Bond, James Bond. That way, whenever anyone asks me what his name is I can say"—Ivy assumed an English accent—" 'It's Bond, James Bond.' "

Barbara laughed and clapped her hands gleefully. "I love it!" she crowed.

Ivy beamed proudly.

"And now a word from our sponsor."

Jesus holds a videocassette. On a wall of screens behind him, scenes of starving third-world children appear.

"Won't you give a hand to the Wilbur Relief Fund?" He asks, eyes soulful. The pictures on the screens go off one by one. The same title appears on each TV: *Let's Play.* The film starts and there is Jesus being lured into the garage by Joey. And there is Jesus crying, Jesus screaming. And there is Joey holding up a bloody, fouled fist, grinning for the camera. And there are the men lining up for a ride on the Jesus train.

"A helpful hand is all we ask," Jesus says.

"We now pause a moment for station identification."

"You're watching Jesus TV! Praise the Lord and pass the remote control."

Closed circuit.

The Bonneville is a predator as it sneaks along the damp, dark streets. Jesus is the hunger driving it.

Moonlight jumps from behind a cloud, dappling the surface of Lake Whalom. The light dazzles Wilbur. The light mesmerizes.

A sign: JAY EPSTEIN D.M.D. The office of one of the hospital's on-call dentists. Though it isn't the same grammar school dentist who'd laughed at Jesus' tale

of Mary-not-Mother's pulling his teeth, he will do.
Jesus parks and waits. The dashboard clock reads
5:25 P.M.

Soon.

A bearded man wearing glasses comes out, tightens his collar against the cold. Jesus calls to him. The
man recognizes Wilbur from the hospital emergency room. He comes over. With his holy rubber
blackjack, Jesus blesses the dentist's chin.

*"We will return to our feature presentation
after these important messages."*

"Bill, we need to talk," Cindy said from the living
room doorway. It was three thirty in the morning
and Bill had been up all night with his photographs.

"I'll be up soon," Bill said, not looking up from the
table.

"No, Bill. Listen to me!" Her raised voice got his
attention. "We need to talk *now.*" She went into the
room and sat at the end of the couch. "This isn't
going the way I thought it would," she said with a
sigh of exasperation.

"Nothing ever does." Bill sat back, his face falling
into shadow.

"I don't think this is such a good idea anymore,"
Cindy said hesitantly, stumbling over what to say
and how to say it. She looked to Bill for some help,
or some response, but he remained silent in the
darkness. She had no idea what he was thinking. He
sat forward and the streetlight through the window
caught an intense look on his face. Cindy thought,
At last, he's going to tell me what's going on, but

Bill leaned over the coffee table and picked up one of his photographs.

"Bill!" she shouted, not caring if she woke Devin and the twins, not caring about anything but having it out with him.

He looked up sharply, staring around, looking for the reason she was shouting.

"You don't listen to anything I say anymore!" she said angrily. "You sit there staring at your work and it's like me and the kids don't even exist anymore. I know being a detective is important to you, but is it more important than your family? Can't you see what you're doing to us? When you said a cop is on call twenty-four hours a day, you didn't say that *you* were going to *be* a cop twenty-four hours a day." She paused, emotions rising, and tried to keep them in check. She wanted to say more, to get it all off her chest while she had his attention, but she was afraid that once she got going she wouldn't stop until she said something she'd later regret. Past experience had taught her it was always best to shut up and get control of her emotions before flying off at the mouth.

Bill sat and looked at her. If eyes could speak, his would have said volumes, but nothing came out of his mouth.

Cindy couldn't stand it any longer. "Say something!"

Bill became angry. "Keep your voice down!" he hissed at her.

"Then talk to me," she replied in a calm, low tone of voice.

"About what?" he asked, his voice tired.

That was it—the proverbial camel's straw had just been dropped; she couldn't keep control any longer. "About *what? About WHAT?* My God, Bill! Is it that bad? Are you that far gone? Can you sit there and honestly tell me that you don't know what I'm talking about, that everything with us is just *peachy keen?*" She turned her head away from him and began furiously pounding the back of the couch.

Bill stood over her, stalled in the middle of going to her and putting his arms around her. "It's just . . . this case . . ." he stammered.

"I know! I know! It's this *stupid case!*"

"As soon as it's over, things will get back to normal."

"No, Bill," Cindy said, her face against her arm. "It won't be over. It won't be over until you deal with your father's ghost." She stood and faced him, eyes shining with angry tears, but voice steady. "That's what this is all about, whether you want to admit it or not. You dealt with your drinking problem, but you never dealt with what caused it. I think you need professional help, Bill, otherwise you're never going to be free of the guilt, or shame, or whatever it is that haunts you."

There. She'd done it. If she'd said something that had hurt him (she'd seen him wince at her suggestion he needed professional help) it was his own fault. It had *needed* saying.

"I don't know what to tell you," Bill said softly, hesitantly, looking at the floor.

He looked and sounded so much like a lost little boy that Cindy had to fight the maternal instinct to wrap her arms around him and tell him it was okay; but he wasn't a lost little boy, he was a lost adult man and everything wasn't okay, and she couldn't help make things better if he wouldn't let her.

"I want you to tell me what you're feeling. I want to be close to you again. I want you to leave the case at the police station when you come home," she said, a tone of ultimatum in her words.

"And you want me to see a psychiatrist," he added in a flat voice.

She didn't know what to do. She wanted to say yes, but didn't want to hurt him again. He looked her in the eye and she realized her silence was as good as a yes.

"I don't have time for that, even if I thought I needed it," he said gruffly, returning to the coffee table and picking up his photos. "As soon as this investigation is over, I won't be a cop anymore and things will get back to normal."

"You mean this is it? You're not going to go after any other police jobs?" Cindy asked, hopefully.

Bill let out such a distraught sigh that Cindy thought he was in pain. "I don't think so," he said softly.

CHANNEL 13

Copycat
*Beth Shell—
Alias Sadie Hawkins*

 "I think we've got a copycat," Captain Mike Mahoney said, opening the door to Bill's office just wide enough to stick his head in. "It's weird."

"Just come in?" Bill asked, rising from his chair.

"No, last night. It looked like a train accident when the officers at the scene first reported it. A guy was found on the tracks, fully clothed. Looked like he'd been hit by several trains. His hands were severed and missing and his head was crushed. The officers searched the tracks for his hands last night but couldn't find them. They figured if the guy had been hit by more than one train he might have been dragged a ways, so they went back today and combed the tracks for a mile in either direction. They didn't find them. The medical examiner found one of them."

Bill swallowed hard. "Where?"

"It had been put where the sun don't shine, to put it nicely."

Bill sat down again.

"The M.E. also said the guy had been hit by at

least two trains, which caused the injuries to his head. The hands were cut off and he bled to death before he was put on the tracks. When he examined the head, the M.E. found that the victim's eyes were missing."

"What makes you think it's a copycat?" Bill asked.

"You know as well as I do that serial killers don't generally change their pattern of victims. They stick to the same sex, usually female," Mahoney explained.

"True," Bill agreed. "But maybe killing a man as his third victim *is* part of his pattern."

"I guess we just have to wait and see if we get another tape. That's the one piece of information that the press hasn't got ahold of yet," Mahoney said.

"Speaking of which," Bill said, glancing at his watch, "I've got that damned press conference."

His phone beeped. He picked up the receiver and punched the flashing button. It was the chief reminding him of the conference. "Is it too late to cancel?" Bill asked, half-serious.

"Sorry, Bill. I need you there. Just keep it short and sweet."

Bill didn't like it, but he knew he had no choice. As head of the investigation, he had to deal with the press. And now if this latest death turned out to be the work of the same guy, it meant women weren't the only ones in Crocker who were in danger.

Beth Shell was working three to eleven and it was ten forty-five. Fifteen minutes to go until Wilbur came on duty. Student nurses were allowed to leave ten minutes early on the night shifts, but Beth hung around, making a good pretense of wanting to finish filing the patients' medical charts. At eleven, Beth said good night to the nurses on the floor and headed for the elevators and the Administration Building, where the security office was.

Though she'd never been in that part of the hospital before, she found the security office easily. It was on the second floor, above the president's office, payroll, and personnel. Looking out the hall windows as she walked, she could look directly across to the dark windows of the abandoned East Wing Building. She realized the East Wing couldn't be seen from any other part of the hospital, stuck in the back of all the new construction the way it was. She wondered if the rumors about plans to tear it down were true. The hospital could use another parking lot.

Beth thought of the late-night stories the girls loved to tell about seeing someone stalking the halls of the East Wing Building at night. Several girls swore they had seen something, claiming it was anything from a ghost haunting the place where it had died, to a vampire who'd taken up residence with coffins packed with dirt.

It *was* a perfect place for a vampire to hide, she thought, smiling. *Sleep out of sight during the day when the Administration Building is buzzing, and up and around at night when no one's around to see.*

Not only was it a great place for a vampire, many of the girls thought it would be a great place for a party. Situated where it was, and cut off from the rest of the hospital's newer buildings, it was virtually soundproof. If they could get in through the hospital without being seen, all they'd have to worry about was the security guard making his rounds. Beth knew talk of a party was just that, *talk*. Everyone was too busy with classes and work to plan a party, but it was fun imagining one anyway.

Beth saw the sign on the door of the security office out of the corner of her eye. She stopped in front of it, trying to get up the nerve to knock. She ran over her plan to ask for an escort and then ask Wilbur if he liked movies. If he didn't take the hint, she'd already decided she'd do the liberated thing and ask him to go to the movies with her. She reached to knock on the door and heard a voice.

"Grandma, when will Jesus come to save me?"

A child's voice. Beth was certain it had come from within the security office.

"When you're at your lowest low. When you think there's no hope for you and no one cares about you, Jesus will come and save you."

An old woman's voice now. It *definitely* came from the security office. Beth leaned closer, putting her ear to the wood.

"What if Jesus doesn't come, Gram?"

"Oh, He'll come, boy. Until He does you tell the *special grown-ups* if your momma hurts you, understand?"

"What if the *special grown-ups* won't help me?"

"Then the Lord Jesus will smite them with His swift and terrible vengeance!"

Beth pulled back from the door at the force and emotion in the old woman's voice. The strangeness of what she'd heard left her wondering what the heck was going on and who was in there with Wilbur. Without thinking about what she was doing, Beth knocked on the door.

Instant silence.

The door opened and Beth was surprised to see Wilbur standing there, the small security office seemingly empty behind him.

"Can I help you?" Wilbur asked. He seemed different, not as shy.

"I'm sorry," she gushed after several moments of awkward silence. "I thought I heard . . ." She paused, not sure how to describe what she'd heard. She leaned to the right and looked past him. Wilbur was definitely the only one in the office.

"I had my portable TV on," he said, anticipating and answering her unfinished comment.

Immediately, Beth felt like a fool. She didn't know what she had been thinking there for a minute. "I'm sorry," she said, smiling and shaking her head. "I must be overtired."

Wilbur smiled back, and Beth was completely disarmed by the innocent sweetness of his face. There was something so vulnerable in those dark eyes and gentle features that Beth's heart melted and she wanted to wrap her arms around him and cuddle him the way she would a sad child.

"Can I help you with something?" Wilbur asked, his voice even and smooth, not stammering like the last time they'd talked.

"I was wondering . . . Ms. Rayborn, the nursing supervisor, said it was okay to ask for an escort to the dorm when we got off work at night, what with those murders in town and all," she explained.

"Sure," Wilbur said, stepping back into the office. "Just let me get my hat and coat and lock up."

While he got ready, Beth stood in the doorway, trying to be casual and nonchalant as her eyes wandered around the room, falling more often than not on Wilbur's cute butt or a glimpse of his profile.

"You like movies?" she asked. She was so preoccupied with checking him out that she never consciously noticed there wasn't a television in the security office.

CHANNEL 14

The Love Connection
Things Go Better with Coke
Emergency Broadcast System (Warning!)

 Fireworks.

The screen explodes with sky-popping fire flowers of red, yellow, and green. Theme music comes up, swelling loud and snappy: *Love American Style.*

Channel change.

"And now it's time for *The Love Connection* with your host, Chuck Woolery!"

Volume down.

Such thoughts scare him almost as much as the pretty nurse who asked Jesus out on a date last night.

"Think she's pretty, Wilbur?" Debbie asks. She's in a Summer's Eve vinegar douche commercial where everything is satin and lace and warm billowing breezes. Debbie holds up the bottle with her left hand and pulls open her blouse with her right, revealing her cigarette- and knife-scarred breasts.

"Is she prettier than me?"

"Woof! Woof! Anything's prettier than you, Rin Tin Tin." Brother John is Lorne Green with a slit in his neck. It barks while he speaks.

"Are you in love?" Brother John/Lorne asks, holding up a can of Alpo. Wilbur can see his blood-shot eyes, the broken booze veins in the creases of his nose. He can smell his breath, beer and old blood.

"I don't know," he replies hesitantly.

"You don't know if you're in love?" Debbie asks sarcastically, caressing her douche bottle all the while, *"or you don't know what love is?*

Brother John cackles out of his wound.

"Love is Jesus, Jesus is love," Grandma says adamantly from in front of her set.

Channel change.

Jesus on *The 700 Club.* He calls on the faithful to pray, send money. The camera moves in on Him, the prayer grows louder . . .

O Heavenly Father, deliver a grim and terrible retribution on the Sodomites and Gomorrians that have let Your only begotten Son be sinned against while they refused to see . . .

The Savior's eyes fill the screen, commanding every channel, growing larger, spilling out to consume him. The centers of His pupils recede at the same time the eyes are enlarging and becoming . . .

Twin tunnels.

Breath fails him. He shuts his eyes but the images are brighter behind his eyelids. He whimpers at the inevitable, waiting like a frightened mouse for the doors at the ends of the tunnels in Jesus' eyes to open.

They don't disappoint.

Snap!

A whiplike sound in the darkness.

Crackle!

Sparks. Neon tracers live a nanosecond and die.

Pop!

The smell of wet ozone.

The air is charged. The juice is on.

Snap! Crackle! Pop!

She buzzes out of the darkness. Her hair is on fire.

Rice Krispies!

A puff of smoke drifts from her mouth. Her eyes are full of electricity. Her skin is dark brown and getting browner, crinkling, blistering. Only by her white nurse's uniform can he tell who it is.

"No!" he screams at his god. "She's different!"

Channel change

Test pattern.

"Is she?" Jesus asks, His voice a high-pitched beep. *"Prove it."*

Vicki Clayton drove her Harley by Mary and Joey's place on her way back from trying to cop some flake at a local bar. She'd been unsuccessful. Needless to say, *bitchy* was too nice a euphemism for the way she was feeling. She was down to her last gram on the ounce of coke Wilbur had given her and still no sign nor word from Mary and Joey. She was getting suspicious. This wasn't like them.

She parked her Harley across the street from the cape house on Leighton Street, hoping to see Joey's chopper parked next to the garage, but was again out of luck. Even Mary's Bonneville wasn't around.

Vicki turned the motorcycle off and opened the saddlebag she wore strapped to her waist, fishing around in the bottom for the extra key to the back door her cousin Mary had given her a long time ago. Her fingers were numb even through her leather gloves, and she cursed the cold. She was going to have to put her bike away soon for the winter. She usually waited for the first snow, but it had been so cold lately that riding was becoming impossible.

She found the key in the bottom of the bag, stuck to an old piece of bubble gum. She retrieved it, tugging it free of the wad, got off the bike, and went up the driveway around to the back door.

"What a mess," she commented in disgust at the sight and smell of the kitchen, which was worse than usual. She picked her way through the litter and went through the basement door. She knew where the secret stash drawer was, but not where Joey kept the key. Wilbur had had it last time, but she knew Joey kept one hidden somewhere for emergencies. She took a pocket knife out of her bag. The lock on the stash drawer wasn't very strong.

She knew Joey would be really pissed if she broke in and helped herself to his stash, but she didn't care, she was desperate. Besides, it was his fault for not getting back in time. Anyway, maybe she could blame it on Wilbur somehow; he was always a convenient scapegoat.

"What the hell's going on?" she said aloud at the bottom of the stairs. The basement, which served as the studio for Tunnelvision was empty. All the lights, cameras, video equipment, and heaps of cable and wire that usually crowded the basement were gone.

"Oh, my God!" Vicki cried, suddenly struck with the conviction that Mary and Joey had split and taken everything with them. She had been afraid of this, had been suspicious of it when Joey insisted she and David go to Martinique to meet with the French distributor. She knew something big was going down and had suspected that Joey didn't want to cut her in on it.

She ran to the false wall section under the stairs where the stash drawer was. The phony concrete covering was lying on the floor and the key was in the drawer lock.

"Oh, you bastards!" She cursed Joey and her cousin and put away her knife. Certain that it would be empty, Vicki opened the drawer anyway. Another puzzle—the stash was there. Inside was a quarter pound of grass wrapped in four ounce-size baggies, a large plastic bottle filled with speckled green-and-white dexies and other assorted uppers, and a smaller bottle half-filled with small blue Valiums. Under the pot was a plastic bag filled with folded paper packets that Vicki immediately recognized as grams of coke.

She took the bag out and counted twenty packets, almost an ounce. "All right!" she cheered. She was so happy with her find that she didn't hear the car pull into the driveway or the door upstairs open.

* * *

Static.

The back door is open.

"This is not a test."

Another intruder.

"We repeat, this is not a test. The Emergency Broadcast System instructs you to tune in to this station for further emergency relief information."

"It's the cops." Brother John says from an old black-and-white gangster movie. He plays Jimmy Cagney's dead brother.

"Don't worry about the cops," Debbie says from an exercise program. Her battered body sweats as it does deep knee bends.

"It's not the cops," Wilbur says aloud.

In the kitchen, he stands, listening. Jesus looks out at him from the stainless steel side of the toaster on the counter.

"The basement!" Jesus says.

Closed circuit.

The sound of footsteps coming up the stairs. On the stove, a black, heavy cast-iron frypan caked with the molding residue of month-old eggs announces itself as an instrument of the Lord's. Jesus anoints it and makes it holy as he lifts its lethal weight.

Footsteps at the top of the stairs.

A shadow on the floor.

Commercial break.

"Is your home safe from vandals, burglars, and intruders? It could be with the new ZX 9000 Do-it-yourself Home Security System from Ronco. Not an alarm, not a floodlight, but a completely new way to stop intruders dead . . ."

The frypan whistles through the air. It makes an oriental *gong* on impact with her face.

She sails backward, downward, hitting the stairs only twice before crumpling in an unmoving pile at the bottom.

"This completes our emergency. We now resume our regularly scheduled program."

David Shipley looked out the window, then let the shade fall back into place. Vicki should have been back by now. He trembled and bit his lip. She'd been such a *bitch* lately, and when she got *cold turkey* bitchy she was unbearable to live with.

He fingered the welt on his cheekbone; her good-bye kiss, done with a glass ashtray. It hurt like hell but was not the kind of pain he enjoyed. He hoped she'd cop something soon. He missed the old days, before they hooked up with her cousin Mary and Tunnelvision Studios. To some degree things had been better then, before Vicki found herself making more than enough money to afford a coke habit. They'd had less money and drugs, but they'd been happier. He'd been happier anyway.

He fidgeted with the curtains and stopped only by a tremendous effort of will, something he was low on. Two seconds later he was fidgeting again. He had to do *something*. Putting on makeup was always good for calming his nerves.

He went to the bathroom and got his robe, a wet facecloth, and a towel. On his way to his dressing table, which was complete with a light-trimmed theatrical mirror, he passed the stack of newspapers from the three weeks they'd been away.

He'd been meaning to read them, but with Vicki in such a state lately, he hadn't had time. She wouldn't even let him turn on the TV or play the stereo! He picked up the top two and brought them to his dressing table with him, glancing at them while he opened his makeup kit and laid out his various base creams, foundations, blushes, glosses, eyeliners, shadows, mascaras, eyebrow pencils, and lipsticks with their attendant brushes and applicators.

He propped yesterday's paper against the mirror while he cleaned his face with cold cream and tissues. He was so far behind, not only hadn't he read the papers from vacation, he hadn't read the ones that had come every day since they came back.

He glanced at the headline: VIDEO KILLER STALKS CITY! and stopped wiping cold cream from his face. He picked up the paper and read the story of the killings. Although the mayor was denying it, it had come out at a press conference that videotapes had been sent to the police. The titles of the tapes jumped out at him: *Toilet Training!* and *Smokin' in the Boys' Room!*

"Those are Tunnelvision movies!" he said aloud. He swore under his breath and began to cackle. "Wilbur, Wilbur, weird old Wilbur, what have you been up to?" He laughed. It was cut short by a sobering thought. Vicki would probably go by Wilbur's to see if Joey and Mary were back. David had a feeling they were never coming back. And if that were true, and Wilbur was responsible for the series of murders described in the paper, Vicki . . .

No. He didn't even want to think about it. Vicki

could take care of herself, especially with a wimp like little Wilbur whom everyone kicked around.

"What should I do?" he wondered aloud, biting the polish off his long nails. He considered calling the cops, but if Vicki was holding, she could get busted along with Wilbur.

"I better get over there," he decided, forgoing the makeup and getting dressed.

David parked his van behind Vicki's Harley, across the street from Mary and Joey's. It was just as he feared, she was here. He told himself she was all right. He didn't know what was going on, but the more he thought about it, the harder it was to believe that meek little Wilbur was a killer. There had to be something more to it, and when he showed Vicki the newspaper he'd brought along, she'd make Wilbur tell her what was going on.

He walked up the driveway and around to the back door, smiling at the thought of the fun they were going to have with old Wilbur.

"Heeeeeeeeeeeeeerrrrre's Joey!"

Brother John's gashed throat does a decent impersonation of Ed McMahon. He points out of the screen in the direction of the kitchen.

The back door is opening.

"He's ba-a-ack," Debbie squeaks a la the little girl in *Poltergeist*.

The door swings open as slowly as in a dream.

It can't be!

A shadow. A silhouette rimmed in light.

The room grows dark but for the path between him and the figure in the doorway.

It's not him!

Debbie's in a Coca-Cola commercial: *"It's the real thing!"*

"You're in deep shit, Wilbur," the shadow of Death in the doorway says. Its voice echoes out of the TV.

It's not real!

"Where's Vicki? Wait till I tell her about this," the figure says, coming into the house waving something in its hand.

He smiles. Now he knows it's not real. Vicki already knows everything. She's got her own channel and cable access.

"You're dead meat, Willy," the figure says tauntingly. It comes into the light of the TV.

A cold needle drills into the back of Wilbur's head.

It's *him!*

Joey's back!

His face peers out from the screen.

"No! You're dead!"

Canned laughter.

Closed circuit.

A collection of dirty dishes and silverware moldy with decaying food sprawled on the coffee table. A fat-rancid steak knife is a relic wearing a halo.

Reaching for it, Jesus intones: *"Blessed are thee in the name of the Father!"*

"What drugs are you on, sweetie? And where the hell is Vicki?" The ghost doesn't know whether to laugh at Him or threaten Him.

Commercial break.

"The Amazing Ginsu cuts through anything! Cans! Wood! Nails! Plastic! Flesh! And keeps on cutting right through muscle, tissue, and bone just as sharp as the day it was made! Don't try this with just any knife. It slices through iron nails like nothing and still cuts deep into this chest, piercing the heart like a hot knife through butter! We challenge any other knife you own to stand up to that kind of punishment!"

Blip.

He stands over the convulsing body.

The eyes stare up at him.

It's not Joey.

The blood flows, the life goes. Vicki has company on Channel Nine.

Bill Gage sat at his desk looking at the front page headline accompanying the story about the murders: VIDEO KILLER STALKS CITY. The article referred to the press conference he, the chief, and the mayor had held that had turned into a farce.

It was obvious there was a leak in the department, and the source had become apparent when Bill noticed Starkovski grinning in the back of the room. A reporter from the *Worcester Telegram* had very confidential information and had brought it all up at the press conference, forcing the mayor into some fancy verbal footwork. Bill hadn't minded; it took the pressure off him. Now everything was out in the open about the case, and the people of Crocker knew what they were dealing with.

Bill remembered the dream he'd had last night

and frowned. He was starting to notice a disturbing trend. Whenever he was able to sleep lately, which wasn't often or for very long, he dreamed about events connected with the case, reliving moments like his examination of Joan Perche's body and the press conference.

The disturbing thing was that in each dream his father had played a prominent role. In the recent dream of the press conference, Bill had noticed a man with a video camera next to Starkovski, staring. With a sense of suffocation, he'd realized it was his father. And with a lightning bolt of pure and complete realization, such as can happen only in a dream, he had known that his father was the perp the press had now dubbed the "Video Killer."

Bill folded the newspaper carefully and dropped it into the circular file. He tried to drop the memory of the dream in there with the paper, but it was not so easily disposed of.

CHANNEL 15

Operation Wilbur— Part 1

 Ivy sat at his observation post on the windowsill in his room. He looked through the one good lens of the compact binoculars he'd taken from the box of junk Barbara's landlord, Mr. Crankshaw, had given her, and trained it on the house of the next-door neighbor he'd come to think of as Crazy Wilbur.

Soon after he'd begun spying on Wilbur Clayton, Ivy realized there was something seriously wrong with his next-door neighbor. He talked and prayed to his television. He went into hysterics, like when Ivy saw him rip his clothes off and throw them away just because they were stained. And just the other day, after a man and woman had visited Wilbur for the second time in a few days but never came out of the house again, Ivy had ventured for another look in Crazy Wilbur's kitchen window and had seen him standing in the middle of his living room as if at attention, his eyes wide open and a goofy smile on his face. He had stood that way for an hour at least, maybe longer; Ivy had got cold and tired of timing him and gone home. When he left, Crazy Wilbur was still standing there, as straight and unmoving as a board. And though Ivy had yet to see it, he was sure that Wilbur talked to himself *in different voices!*

Today, Ivy had watched Wilbur load two very heavy trash bags into the trunk of his Bonneville. Ivy was curious as to why Wilbur was putting trash in his trunk instead of out on the street for pickup.

All this made for fun spying and some interesting entries in his spy journal, but it also gave him more than an occasional pang of guilt. He felt sorry for Wilbur and wondered what had made him crazy. The guy wasn't that old—not more than twenty, Ivy figured—and he was bonkers. Why?

That became the question Ivy sought an answer to. Of course, he dressed it up in the spy style, envisioning himself as Bond on a mission to discover the secret identity of a highly placed government mole, but it was the answer to why Wilbur was so weird that Ivy was really after. And he knew the best place to find those answers would be in Wilbur's house.

He'd learned from his observations of Crazy Wilbur that he went out every night in his security guard uniform before eleven and returned the next morning sometime after seven. Ivy assumed he worked the night shift, or else he was a vampire. If Ivy waited until his mother got home from work and passed out, which usually happened by one, he could sneak over and have the whole night to break in and look around.

He decided to go for it tonight.

Ivy quietly got out of bed and went to the door. He put his ear to it and listened. Silence. A moment later the darkness was split by a noise like a distant lawn mower starting. The sound was repeated at steady intervals. His mother was asleep, and once she started snoring, nothing short of an explosion could wake her up.

Having gone to bed fully dressed, Ivy was ready to go. He was wearing his best dark blue sweat suit with his long johns underneath so he wouldn't have to wear a bulky coat. The knapsack, which he'd stashed on the porch, would be enough to worry about. He'd gone back to the sandlot for it the day after his run-in with Slice and retrieved it from the pipe along with the rattraps that remained.

Ivy opened his door and stepped into the nearly pitch-black living room. He crossed it from memory, steering clear of the coffee tables, chairs, and lamp stands. In the kitchen, he crept to the back door and paused, reassuring himself from the sound of her snores that his mother slept on undisturbed.

Carefully he turned the lock with his left hand and the doorknob with his right. Cold air met him as he swung the door open and reached for the handle of the storm door. This was the tricky part: to open the storm door and close the back door tight enough so it locked, but not too loudly. His mother was usually a sound sleeper, but sometimes, like when he was sick, she would wake at the slightest sound.

He managed the doors without too much noise and stood on the porch, looking through the door glass for any sign that his mother had awakened. The apartment remained dark. He dug his watch out of his pocket and tipped its face to the moon to read it. Two o'clock. He had given himself a timetable of an hour to get into Crazy Wilbur's house, and another hour to look around. That would get him home by four, with plenty of time before his mother woke up or Wilbur got home.

Retrieving his knapsack from behind the oxidizing iron chair in the porch's far corner, Ivy opened it and did an inventory check of his spy equipment: flashlight, plastic card he'd cut out of the cover of a school notebook with which he could slip the lock to his own apartment with ease (after much practice), a pair of old rubber dishwashing gloves, a screwdriver, his squirt gun filled with bleach, another jar of Zip-Strip, and a couple of the rattraps just in case he ran into any trouble. The cast gun was dismantled and undergoing modifications.

He slipped the pack onto his back, took one more quick peek in the door, and went down the back stairs via the Bond method of stealth. He was getting quite good at it and produced barely a squeak all the way to the first floor.

Ivy stood in the shadows at the rear of the house for several minutes, observing Crazy Wilbur's house over the fence that separated the place from Ivy's tenement. The house was dark, the driveway empty. He had seen Wilbur leave on time as usual at ten thirty.

He peered around the corner of the tenement, toward the street. The coast was clear. Running bent over, hands holding the straps of the knapsack so it wouldn't bounce around and make noise, Ivy crossed the driveway and crouched behind the fence. He stayed there, breathing hot air on his cold fingertips, and wishing he'd brought his fur-lined gloves instead of the rubber ones in his pack. With the house to shelter him, he hadn't realized how cold it was tonight. Out in the open he could feel it. He tried to keep moving. He slid off the backpack, carefully lifted it over the fence, and let it drop to the frozen ground on the other side, then followed it, returning to a crouch on the other side to retrieve the pack.

He'd asked around and found out that Wilbur supposedly lived with his aunt and uncle or his sister and her husband, or something like that—nobody seemed to know for sure—but Ivy hadn't seen either of them since he'd moved in. He figured they were away, or at least he hoped so. He'd hate to break in and find them home sick with the flu or something, but he didn't think that could be. And though the motorcycle and van were still parked across the street, Ivy didn't think the man and woman he'd seen go in, were still inside either. He'd spied through the windows enough with his one-eyed binoculars to know that, at present anyway, Crazy Wilbur lived alone.

Maybe he wasn't always crazy, Ivy thought, slipping the knapsack onto his back again. Maybe his mother's going away sent him over the edge? Another, more imaginative possibility occurred to him. Maybe Crazy Wilbur was really an enemy agent. Maybe Wilbur was really talking to a submarine submerged off the coast when Ivy thought he was talking to the TV or to himself. Maybe Wilbur's house was the base of operations for a vast spy network.

Ivy grinned, letting his imagination run. *Maybe I should write a book,* he thought. He figured he could do it. He had written a couple of short stories that he thought were pretty good, though he'd never shown them to anyone. Lately he'd been thinking about letting Barbara read them.

Thoughts of Barbara sobered him, and he returned to the task at hand. On the count of three he ran, staying low, across Wilbur's driveway to the corner of the house, where he disappeared into the shadows. He paused and scanned the area, his ears alert to all sounds. While he rested a moment, his mind turned to his recent run-in with Slice.

Ivy had heard from Old Lady Watson that Slice had been sent to juvenile hall for thirty days for breaking his probation with the possession of the switchblade. The police hadn't been able to make the shoplifting charge stick since Slice was inside the store and had had enough money to pay for the things he was planning to steal.

The cops had questioned Ivy, wanting to know why Slice had been threatening him and if Ivy would press charges. At first, Ivy had considered telling the police how Slice and his gang had assaulted Barbara, but he wasn't sure she would admit to it if the cops asked her, and if he told them they'd definitely want to talk to Barbara. No, he'd decided Barbara didn't need the hassle. She wasn't well enough. He told the cop Slice was just asking him where Old Lady Watson was. He knew the cop didn't believe him, but he didn't care.

Sliding along the side of the house, Ivy made his way to the back porch stairs. He went up the concrete steps and crept to the door. Like the back door to his apartment, this door had an outside storm door that still had its summer screen on it. The inside door was a typical wooden kitchen door with nine glass panels in its upper half.

Ivy peered through the screen and the door glass but couldn't see anything inside. It was too dark. Holding his breath, Ivy grabbed the storm door handle and eased its button down until he heard it click. Moving as slowly as possible, trying to feel every contraction of his arm muscles, he pulled the door open an inch. No sound. Five inches, a foot; still quiet.

Yaw-w-w-w-k!

If metal could yawn it would sound like the noise the storm door made. Ivy froze. The door was open almost two feet, still not enough room to slip in and maneuver to pick the inside door's lock.

From across the street, a dog started barking. Ivy tensed. A harsh voice silenced the dog. Ivy waited, his arm aching, his hands freezing. The night was silent except for the faraway rumble of a train passing through town.

Grabbing the storm door's inside handle with his left hand while keeping his right on the outside handle, Ivy lifted the door in its hinges and tried opening it again, ever so slowly. The metallic yawn began ticking off almost immediately, though a little less loudly than before. He lifted the door a little more and the sound softened more. Though it sounded as loud as thunder to him, Ivy doubted if the sound was traveling any further than Wilbur's backyard.

Finally the storm door was open wide enough to give him room to get at the inside door. He was struck with another problem. With the storm door against his back, every time he moved it was going to squeak and squawk. And once he got the inside door open—*if* he got the inside door open—he would have to close the storm door, and he wouldn't be in a very good position to lift it as he did.

The obvious solution was to prop the storm door open somehow; then he wouldn't have to worry about it on his way out either. Using his right knee to keep the door from closing, Ivy took off his knapsack. It felt heavy enough to hold the door. Balancing awkwardly on one leg, he opened the pack and took out his plastic card and a long, heavy rubber flashlight.

Carefully he placed the pack on the floor and leaned it against the storm door. He let the door go, gently. The pack began to give and the door yawned. He was going to have to put the flashlight back in the pack to make it heavy enough. He looked back through the door windows at the dark interior of Crazy Wilbur's house and didn't like the idea of going in there without a light. He had his disposable butane lighter, but it was a poor substitute for the flashlight. Not only did the flashlight provide illumination, it was heavy enough to use as a weapon.

He thought about aborting the mission. He hated to give up now. And why? Because he was afraid of the dark? What would James Bond say about that? No. He had to complete the mission, light or no light. He put the flashlight back in the pack and let the door go. The pack held it this time.

Ivy breathed a sigh of relief. Now came the real challenge, slipping the lock on the inside door. Before he did, he checked his watch and saw that he was right on schedule. According to his timetable, he still had forty-five minutes to get inside.

He fitted the plastic card into the seam of the door and slid it down until it hit the lock, which was in the doorknob. He gripped the knob with his right hand and turned it while working the plastic, trying to catch the edge of the lock latch.

It wasn't working. Ivy took a break and rested his head against the door glass for a moment before trying again. Fifteen minutes later it was still no go. He took his watch out again and checked it. Less than thirty minutes left. He tried again but it was futile.

Frustrated and disappointed, Ivy took his bag from the storm door, letting the latter close slowly and fairly quietly, and turned to leave. He noticed the two kitchen windows overlooking the porch and stopped. He checked the first one, found it locked. He took the flashlight out of the pack and turned it on, shining it through the window so he could look inside.

The kitchen was nothing unusual, a regular kitchen, if a little messy. The sink and its adjacent countertop were stacked with dirty dishes. There was a crumpled bag of Tri-Sum potato chips on the floor. Several small dark things skittered away when the light hit it.

Roaches! Ivy thought in disgust. His apartment had them, too, and he hated them.

Ivy played the light around some more. The kitchen walls were a dirty gray, adorned here and there with small posters embellished with words to live by such as: TODAY IS THE FIRST DAY OF THE REST OF YOUR LIFE and MAKE LOVE NOT WAR. There was a doorway to another room at the far left, but Ivy couldn't see much in there.

He moved to the other window for a better look, forgetting to check the sash lock until he noticed it was turned halfway. Without a screen or storm window on it, he was able to slide his plastic card up through the crack and push the sash lock the rest of the way open.

The excitement was back. It looked as if he wouldn't have to abort the mission or settle for a look through the windows after all. The inside window lifted easily enough, but as he discovered when he tried to leave it open, it was no longer connected to its weights and almost came crashing down on his hands. Again, the long black flashlight came in handy, to prop the window open while he lowered his knapsack inside. He climbed in after it, pushing the window up with his back as he straddled the sill and retrieved the flashlight. He then swung his leg inside while holding the window up with his hand.

Once inside, he let the window down slowly. He stood just inside, the flashlight off, listening to the house and letting his eyes adjust. The place was quiet. Ivy turned on the flashlight and played it low around the room, keeping it away from the windows. The place looked as if it had been ransacked, it was so messy.

There was a pile of envelopes and papers on the kitchen table to his right, on the other side of the back door. Ivy went over for a look. It was the mail, or a couple of weeks' worth of mail, to be exact. Ivy sifted through the assortment of bills and junk mail that didn't tell him anything until he got to the bottom of the pile. The return address logo on an envelope caught his eye.

NAMBLA
P. O. Box 696
Ware, MA 02020

The envelope was addressed to Joseph Dreybeck. Ivy wondered if he was the sister's boyfriend or the uncle or what. Seeing the name made him uneasy. If this Joseph Dreybeck was getting mail here, might he not *be* here? Or, if not here right now, might he not come back at any time? Ivy decided to make this a quick mission.

He wondered what the name NAMBLA on the return address meant. He could go to the library tomorrow and look in the Ware phone book for it. If he could scrounge some change from his mother, he could call and find out what NAMBLA stood for.

Ivy stood the flashlight, lens-side down, on the table and picked up his pack. He took out a small spiral notepad with a ball-point pen clipped to it and copied down the name and address for NAMBLA and Joseph Dreybeck. He returned the pad to the pack, hefted the latter onto his back once more, and picked up the light. Ivy played the beam into the pantry, which was as filthy and messy as the kitchen, and found nothing of interest.

The next room was the living room and it was as much a disaster area as the kitchen. The first thing Ivy noticed was the walls adorned with psychedelic black-light posters. They and the walls were a dirty, streaky brown that when touched left a dark sticky substance on the fingers. He sniffed at it. It reminded him of the stale smell of his mother's butts that permeated her room. That was part of the smell, but there was something else too. He had it— it was the same odor he'd smelled in the boys' room at school that time he'd walked in on a couple of ninth-graders smoking marijuana.

Ivy looked at the resin-coated walls in awe. How much pot had been smoked to coat the walls like that? he wondered. He turned and checked out the rest of the room. Amid the trash, strewn magazines, newspapers, and clothes, he saw that there were four chairs and a couch set in a rough semicircle around a massive old-fashioned television console with a VCR on top. The chairs were each different: an old armchair with a broken leg that reminded Ivy of Barbara's favorite chair; an old, cracking, leather beanbag chair; a black vinyl recliner that had its seat taped in several spots; and a rickety-looking cane chair with a round back like the kind on that old show *The Addams Family*. The couch was long and low, its cushions threadbare and its arms burn-scarred.

The flashlight caught the reflection of glass, and he noticed what looked like a china closet set into the far wall. It had double glass doors and shelves inside that held what looked like rows of books, all with the same shiny black covers and white labels on the spine.

He propped the light on the arm of the recliner so that it shone on the cabinet and opened the doors. They weren't books, as he had hoped. They were videotapes. There had to be at least a hundred, maybe more. Every shelf was full except the top one. It had a couple of tapes missing, causing the others to domino to the left. The titles of the tapes were typed on the white labels on each tape's spine.

Ivy leaned closer and read some of the titles: *Let's Play, Want Some Candy?* and *Reform School* were on the top shelf, and other similar names were on the other shelves. Ivy had never heard of any of them.

At the back of the living room a doorway opened on the front hall and stairs to the second floor. Ivy flashed the light up the stairs, revealing what looked like a continuation of the house's messiness, but decided not to risk going up and getting trapped up there if this Joseph Dreybeck guy came back.

Just inside the front door was another door that Ivy almost passed by, thinking it was a closet. He decided to look inside, hoping there might be a family picture album or something on a shelf that might give him some glimpse of Wilbur's past. What he found was a bedroom not much bigger than a closet, but so clean and neat as to make the rest of the house look even worse than it already did.

Ivy stepped into the room and nearly coughed at

the overpowering smell of ammonia and disinfectant. The room was so spotless it almost gleamed. A small student bed was made with fresh white sheets and a simple brown woolen blanket tucked in with perfect corners. A tall, narrow dresser next to the bed was dust free, as were the picture of a white-haired old woman holding an infant in her arms, and a two-sided, magnifying shaving mirror. An old Zenith television sat on a black wrought iron stand in the corner, a VCR on the shelf underneath. On the other side of the bed was the door to a narrow closet containing two of Wilbur's uniforms, neatly pressed, on hangers. Next to them was a leather policeman's jacket with a badge on it. Ivy pulled it out and looked at it. SECURITY, it said at the top of the badge. There was a picture of a building on a hill embossed in the middle of the badge with CROCKER HOSPITAL stamped across it. At the bottom of the badge it said, CROCKER POLICE AUXILIARY.

So that's where Crazy Wilbur works, Ivy thought, putting the jacket back the way it was. And this was Wilbur's room, an island of neatness in a house that could qualify for dump status. Ivy couldn't even begin to guess at what life was like for Wilbur in such extremes. One thing was for certain: this proved that someone else must live in the house, otherwise Wilbur would have the whole place looking like his room. Neat people were like that, Ivy knew. While his mother was a slob, his father had been neat. Ivy remembered his father had had his own little room, that he'd called his office, in every apartment they'd lived in, and that room had been kept neat as a pin.

Ivy looked around Wilbur's room some more and noticed a tape sticking out of the VCR. Its empty case, with the title *Smokin' in the Boys' Room*, rested on top of the VCR. *What a strange title!* he thought.

Curiosity began to get the better of Ivy. He wanted to know what was on that tape. If he and his mother had owned a VCR, he could have chanced taking it and returning it later, but they didn't. He crouched in front of the VCR, wanting to turn it on but afraid to.

Go for it! the James Bond inside him urged. *You must see what's on the secret videotape or the entire mission will be a failure and M will have your hide!*

Having seen a picture of Henry, Barbara's husband, in her apartment, Ivy imagined him as M, and Barbara as Miss Moneypenny. Her landlord, Mr. Crankshaw, who was a really nice guy and good at fixing things, became the secret weapons inventor, Q.

There was no doubt in Ivy's mind that James Bond wouldn't leave without first seeing what was on that tape. That clinched it. After all, what was the point of going to all this trouble of breaking in if he wasn't going to find out anything? He might as well go all the way, take all the risks.

Ivy turned the TV on. Never having used one, Ivy was unsure of how to run the VCR. Hoping it was all set to run, he pushed the tape in and pressed play. He was rewarded with seeing the screen blip to life. Loud rock music blared from the set, making him jump. He twisted the volume all the way down and tried to calm his jangled nerves.

The TV screen filled with white light and the title, *Smokin' in the Boys' Room*, appeared, followed by A Tunnelvision Studios Production. The screen went dark a moment. Starring Lisa Lick and Wilbur the Wonder Boy appeared next.

Ivy giggled at Wilbur the Wonder Boy. He couldn't imagine Crazy Wilbur as a movie star. As the action began to unfold, Ivy realized that poor Wilbur was a movie star only in the sense that he was billed as the movie's star. To Ivy he seemed more like the movie's victim.

Ivy began to feel funny. He didn't like this. When the woman who played the teacher tied Wilbur, the child, up naked to a grungy old bed and started torturing him with a lighted cigarette, Ivy hit the power button on the VCR and the screen went black. For a moment, optical ghosts of poor Wilbur and that awful woman haunted the screen before fading. Ivy felt hot, then cold. What that woman had done to the young Wilbur on that tape was beyond being horrible. He backed away from the TV and bumped into the bed, almost falling.

He was consumed by a sudden panic—scared to death, scared beyond reason. A thought hit home with ferocious impact: if the people in this house were relatives of Wilbur and they could do *that* to him, what might they do to a strange kid they caught breaking in? He thought of the shelves of videotapes and the pile littering the floor in the living room and shuddered with the certainty that similar horrors were recorded there that didn't all star Wilbur the Wonder Boy.

The urge to run blind, to just get the hell out of

there, became as powerful as his earlier curiosity. He fled Wilbur's room, running into the hall and through the living room. He tripped over the edge of the beanbag chair and tumbled into the kitchen doorjamb with his right shoulder. The watch that Barbara had given him, Henry's watch, fell out of his pocket—he'd failed to push it in far enough. It bounced at the edge of the faded gold-and-green rug. Another inch and it would have hit the wood floor and he'd have heard it. It didn't. He didn't, and the watch remained behind.

His need to get out of the house was nearing hysterical proportions. Ivy couldn't take time for the window, propping it, and climbing through. He went out the back door, pulling it locked behind him, and went through the storm door not caring that its squeaky hinges pierced the night. He let the door bang shut and flew off the porch, across the yard and driveway and over the fence like a hurdler doing record time.

He didn't quite make it. His foot caught the top of the fence and sent him sprawling face first on the blacktopped driveway of his tenement. He banged his chin hard, scraping a quarter-size piece of skin off the point, and driving pebbles and dirt deep into the scrapes on the palms of his hands.

He let out an exhaling *"oomph!"* and a small groan, but no other noise. The cold air stung his wounds but he picked himself up. Fighting back the tears in his eyes, he ran to the house and up the stairs to the apartment. He got inside without waking his mother, and returned to his bedroom where he collapsed on his bed and let the tears come.

Even in the safety of his own bedroom, the feeling of uncontrollable fear and panic wouldn't stop making his body tremble. He wrapped himself in covers until he was sweating, but the panic wouldn't let him go.

CHANNEL 16

To Catch a Spy
*The Return of
Slice Sanchez*
Off the Air
The Last Stroke

 It was rare for Slice Sanchez to be out so early in the morning, but he was on a mission. He walked down Leighton Street looking for the number of the house where he'd find the little black object of his vengeful desires. He'd love to kick down the door to the coon's apartment and beat the crap out of him and his old lady, but the recent business with Watson's Market prevented that. He had to keep cool for a while.

He'd had to serve only five days of his sentence in juvey hall because of the county's Christmas tradition of commuting the sentences of all juveniles who have family to go to and are in for thirty days or less. He was there long enough though for the staff doctor to rebreak his fingers and set them properly. He wore metal splints and tape on most of his fingers now. During every moment of pain, he had envisioned what he would do to Ivy in revenge.

But he had to be careful. The cops were keeping an eye on him. If anything happened to the kid, Slice would be a prime suspect after what had happened in Watson's. What he needed was a patsy, a goon, someone to do the dirty work for him so that he could have an alibi. Certainly none of his former gang members would suffice.

He found the gray, three-decker tenement that was supposed to be where the kid lived. Slice had got the information from a kid who rode Ivy's bus and was only too glad to point out the house to him. It was that or take a punch in the mouth every time he refused.

Slice walked past the house on the opposite side of the street. The place was like all the other dumpy two- and three-story tenements on the street. The house next door was one of only two single-family homes on Leighton Street. Slice had bought drugs from the dude Joey who lived there with his old lady and her brother or nephew or something. The last time he'd bought coke from Joey, the stuff had been crap. He'd gone back, ready to take it out of the guy's hide, but Joey had wisely replaced the stuff with some primo flake. Even so, Slice hadn't gone back after that. He didn't trust or like the guy, or his old lady, or the weirdo who sat in front of the television all the time, talking to it.

He stopped to admire the Harley parked at the curb, using it as an excuse to look at the tenement and try to figure which floor Ivy lived on. The kid from the bus hadn't known; several punches had proved that. Slice crossed the street and went up the front stairs to the small porch where three flat, black tin apartment mailboxes were stacked one over the other. He knew the kid had a French-sounding last name, but none of the mailboxes had names on them.

Slice spit on the door and returned to the Harley across the street. A long gold car came up the street and backed into the driveway of the house next to the tenement. The weird kid who liked to talk to the TV—Slice thought his name was Walter or something like that—was driving. Slice glanced back at the tenement and caught a flash of light from the third floor. He looked up. There was movement at the top window overlooking the single-family house next door.

It was the little black bastard. He was in the window, looking through one lens of a pair of binoculars at the next-door driveway and the weird kid getting out of his car.

"Dumb fuck," Slice scoffed, "doesn't even know how to use binoculars." Slice looked up at Ivy, then back at Walter, or whatever his name was, who disappeared behind his house.

"Why's he spying on him?" Slice wondered aloud. *That kid can't keep his nose out of other people's business!* An idea dawned on Slice and climbed to the zenith of his mind's sky.

Joey and his old lady were drug dealers who did business with the Slaves. Slice had seen the gang's bikes parked over there before. If Slice were to let them know that the nigger next door was spying on them, wouldn't they want to do something about it?

Especially if he embellished the story by telling them he'd overheard Ivy bragging that he was gathering information to get them all busted.

He'd heard tales of the Slaves bumping guys off for ratting on them. Though they might not do that to a kid, they'd sure do something to shut him up. Scaring the coon half to death was the least of possibilities. Maybe he'd get lucky and they *would* want to get rid of the brat. Slice hoped they'd let him watch.

"Oh yeah," Slice breathed with the excitement of anticipation, the frost swirling around his face.

Ivy noted the date and time at the top of the notebook page and wrote: *Suspect arrived at enemy headquarters alone.* He hadn't yet decided what to do about what he'd seen on the tape in Crazy Wilbur's house. He'd been evading questions from his mother about where and how he'd got the scrape on his chin. He didn't want to get the guy in trouble or anything, or embarrass him by revealing what he'd seen, but he knew he should do *something*. What that woman had been doing to little Wilbur on that tape was *wrong*. He'd learned about child abuse in school and knew he should tell someone, like the cops.

He flipped back a few pages and read the entry where he'd noted the woman and man who'd gone into the house. The woman hadn't looked like the one in the video, and he got a good look at her as she was leaving. He flipped the page to the second time she went into Wilbur's. That had been two days ago.

She still hadn't come out. Neither had the guy who'd gone in after her.

Of course, that didn't mean they *hadn't* come out, it just meant Ivy hadn't seen them. There had been no sign of them during his break-in, but the motorcycle the woman had arrived on, and the van the man had been driving, were still parked across the street. The James Bond in him wanted to make another nighttime sortie, if just to look in the kitchen windows up close, but Ivy was too scared after the last time to risk it, especially after losing his watch over there. Crazy Wilbur must have found it, and though he had no way of knowing it belonged to Ivy, he must know someone had been in his house.

Ivy put the notebook and binoculars into his knapsack and took it into the kitchen. It was seven forty-five. If he wanted to stop by Barbara's before school and feed Bond, James Bond and take him for a walk, he'd have to get moving. If she was feeling well, Ivy also wanted to tell Barbara about the video of Wilbur and ask her what he should do. She'd been very lucid the past few days, and he'd enjoyed some of his best talks with her about books and other stuff. At one point he'd found himself telling her all about how his father had died and how he believed it was a conspiracy by Dr. Peabody, when he'd really meant to tell her about poor Wilbur. They had been discussing *The Catcher in the Rye*, and Holden Caulfield had reminded Ivy of Wilbur a little, only Holden wasn't as crazy as Wilbur.

Barbara and he had a really long talk about why bad stuff happens to people and the best way to deal

with it. He'd also told her what he'd done to Slice
Sanchez and his pals, and she had talked about the
dangers of revenge—how it could eat a person up
inside and destroy him. Not once, though, did she
ask why Slice was after him, nor did she mention
the incident in the alley.

Frost patterns on the kitchen window advised
him to put on his heavy quilted parka instead of his
dad's army jacket. He zipped it up, and put the
knapsack on. His mother had already left for her
day job at the plastics factory, which was okay with
Ivy. He liked having mornings to himself and had
no trouble getting his own breakfast, usually toast
with peanut butter dunked in a mug of instant hot
chocolate. He skipped breakfast this morning, hurrying out the door, locking it behind him.

Ivy stopped halfway down the stairs, eyes riveted
on Crazy Wilbur's back porch. Slice Sanchez was
standing there, knocking on the door.

What's he doing there? Ivy wondered. He remained motionless until Wilbur answered the door
and Slice went inside. Ivy descended the rest of the
stairs slowly, trying unsuccessfully to see into the
windows next door. At the bottom, he hesitated,
torn between curiosity and responsibility.

He wished he had more time. He was dying to
find out what Slice Sanchez wanted with Crazy Wilbur, but he was afraid Barbara might have a relapse
at any time, and he knew he should check on her
and take care of Bond.

He opted to do the responsible thing and headed
for the street, regretting the missed opportunity for

some great spying, but secretly proud of himself for doing what he knew was right.

Dead air.

All the channels are off.

Silence, a new sensation.

No commercial interruptions. No station identification. No special bulletins.

Just him.

His own face looks out from the mirror on the wall, from the side of the toaster, from the dark screens in the living room and his bedroom.

She has done this. Beth. She's shorted him out. She's deprogrammed his network. She's caused a blackout.

He took her out last night for two hours before work. Jesus had agreed to the date, but Wilbur had kept it, determined to show that this nurse was different. It looked as if he had been successful.

He hadn't known where they would go. He was afraid to be alone with her should Jesus decide she was flunking the test and go to closed circuit. She suggested a movie and he'd been too shy to argue.

It wasn't what he expected. The only movies he'd ever seen were the ones Mary-not-Mother and Joey made with Jesus and the stream of runaways that passed through the house. He'd been afraid one of *His* films would appear on the giant screen and had been relieved and delighted when Disney's *Fantasia* gave him one of the few pleasurable viewing experiences he had ever known. After that, the evening had passed without incident, without channel interference, without voices.

He looks at the blank screen and remembers how soft and warm she had felt as she'd snuggled up to him in the theater, putting his arm around her and holding his hand. He'd never known physical contact with another person could feel so good—not *nasty* good like Mary-not-Mother and Joey liked, but *good* good, *pure* good, *right* good. Jesus can't deny that. His silence proves it.

A knock on the door interrupts his thoughts. The power remains off, the screen dark.

It's nothing, he thinks, forcing a smile. He goes from the living room to the kitchen, his sense of confidence dwindling with each step.

I can do this, he tells himself. *There are no bright lights, no canned applause, no remote control—just a knock on the door.*

"I can do this," he says aloud.

He opens the door and looks at the tall, long-haired youth standing on the back porch. The youth looks vaguely familiar, but Wilbur can't place him.

"Hey! How you doin'?" the youth says, opening the outside screen door. Wilbur takes a step back.

"Walter, right?"

"Wilbur." He forces the name out of a suddenly dry mouth.

"Right. Is Joey or his old lady around?" the youth asks, trying to see inside.

A warning tingle runs up the back of Wilbur's head.

"You know them?" he hears himself say.

"Yeah. I know something they might be interested in."

The hum of the current coming back on is loud in

his head. Grandma, who has been praying silently in the dark, praises the Lord loudly.

"They're not here," he says, his voice calm, showing nothing of the panic and despair welling inside him.

"Oh," the youth says, disappointed. "They be back soon?"

Go away! he wants to shout. He shakes his head. The current is building. Soon Tunnelvision will be broadcasting again. *Go away!* he thinks, *and maybe I can still turn it off.*

"Well . . ." The youth hesitates. "I guess I can tell you." He glances around as if afraid someone might overhear. "When you tell Joey what I'm gonna tell you, make sure you tell who told you," he adds, giving Wilbur a narrow-eyed stare.

The youth pushes past him, into the kitchen.

"Don't you believe in picking up once in a while?" The youth looks around in disgust.

Wilbur doesn't answer.

"You might not remember me." The youth peers into the living room. "I'm Slice Sanchez. I've done business with Joey and your mother before."

"She's not my mother," Wilbur says reflexively.

"Whatever. Just tell them Slice Sanchez told you about the kid next door."

The current falters, confused.

"What?"

"The kid next door, the little nigger who lives on the third floor? He's been spying on your operation here . . ."

Spying on your operation!

". . . and I heard him tell some kids on the bus

that he was collecting evidence to give the cops . . ."

The cops!

". . . and get you guys busted."

"What evidence?" He can barely hear himself above the hum of the transmitters preparing to broadcast.

"You know, the drugs you guys are dealin'. I've bought flake here before, you don't have to play dumb with me. I'm no cop."

"Yes, he is," Brother John says. His channel is back on. He's a guest on Oprah Winfrey.

"Hey, man! You should take better care of your tapes!" The youth is moving into the living room, toward the pile of videotapes on the floor.

All the channels are on again.

"Don't touch them," Wilbur says, but his voice is small and far away, lost in the swell of prime time programming. His vision blurs, the channels begin to change. Jesus has the remote control. Jesus has the ax out of the closet. Jesus takes him to closed circuit and the blood flies.

Barbara didn't look well. Her face was pale and her lips purplish. Ivy immediately noticed her left eyelid was drooping and the whole left side of her face seemed to be sagging slightly. Her left arm seemed to be bothering her, too, and she kept it close to her stomach, not using it.

She was sitting in the armchair when he got there and looked as if she had been there all night. She didn't respond when he spoke to her from the doorway where he was petting the squealing Bond, James Bond. He carried the puppy to her side.

"Barbara?" he asked.

Only her right eye moved when she looked up at him. The left remained hidden behind its droopy eyelid. There was a hint of recognition in her look.

"What's wrong?" he cried. He put the biting puppy down and knelt by the chair.

The right side of Barbara's lip trembled, and that side of her mouth opened a little as if she was trying to speak but could get no words out.

Ivy grasped her arm, and that stirred her to new efforts. She blinked her right eye and looked at him as though she suddenly remembered who he was. Her lips moved again and he leaned closer to hear, but her voice came out surprisingly strong, though a little slurred.

"Ivy, my best friend." Her right hand grasped his. She sat up a little, but still seemed to be having trouble with her left side.

"I'm going to call an ambulance," Ivy said. Barbara clenched his hand with surprising strength to prevent him from moving.

"No," she rasped, then cleared her throat. "I'm all right. This"—she nodded her head to the left to indicate her arm—"is just my arthritis acting up as usual. I'll be right as rain tomorrow."

Her haggard looks belied the calm assurance of her voice. Ivy was uncertain what to do.

"I think you should take Bond home with you for a little while, though, okay? Can you find a place to keep him safe until I can get around better?" she asked, glancing down at the puppy trying to climb his leg.

Ivy nodded his head, his eyes filling with tears. He was afraid he knew exactly what she meant. This wasn't arthritis; it was worse. That's why she got drunk that day after she went to the clinic. They must have told her then she was going to . . . He couldn't even think the word or he was going to burst out bawling.

"I'll take him back in a few days," she said, hanging her right hand over the floor to coax the puppy.

"Are you sure you're okay?" Ivy stammered, afraid to ask her the question bluntly.

"I'm fine, really," she said, reaching up to caress his face. She certainly didn't look it.

"Let me call a doctor, or take you to the clinic. I can bag school today and go with you," he pleaded.

"Tomorrow," she said. "If I'm not better by tomorrow, you can take me to the clinic. But don't worry about me. Mr. Crankshaw's coming by later to fix the leaky faucet in the bathroom. He'll check up on me. If I need help, I'll ask him. Now you get going and feed Bond and get to school. Come by after to pick him up."

Reluctantly, Ivy gave in to the authority in her voice. *Maybe she's right,* the hopeful part of him wanted to believe.

When he stopped by to pick up Bond after school, his hopeful side got a boost. He found her sleeping peacefully, her color good.

Daring to think that maybe, just once, something was going his way, he gathered up Bond and the dog's box, bedding, and dish, and went home more hopeful than he'd been that morning.

Barbara knew she'd had a stroke. Her father had had one just before he died. She saw the ghost of his half-paralyzed self every time she looked in the mirror, and wondered if his had been caused by a brain tumor too.

Her stroke hadn't been as bad as the one that had felled her father, but it was bad enough. When she experienced periods of clarity and could think and talk straight—as she'd been able to with Ivy (thank God)—she tried to figure out what she should do.

The doctors at the clinic had told her the tumor was operable, and treatable with chemotherapy and radiation, but her age made both very risky. That plus the fact that she had no money seemed to have decided her fate. She was torn between fear and longing for death. The doctors had said that without an operation or treatment, she had six weeks to two months to live. That had been two weeks ago. It looked as if their estimates were a bit exaggerated.

If death came quickly, everything would be okay, but if she lingered, in a paralyzed condition like this or worse for any length of time, she was going to be in trouble. She was going to need constant care if that happened. Where would she get it? Who would pay?

After Ivy left, Barbara dozed in the chair, drifting into a deep dreamless sleep. She woke around one, stiff from sitting up so long. She got up unsteadily and, foggy-minded, staggered to the bed. Her left side felt wet and heavy. She was hungry but had no energy to fix something to eat.

With difficulty, she sat on the bed, then lay back, using her momentum to try to swing her legs up onto the mattress. She struggled with her legs for several minutes, straining up on her elbows, before she was successful. She lay back. A second before her head hit the pillow she had a massive stroke. She continued breathing until 5:00 P.M. when her heart fluttered and stopped, and her last breath sighed out of her.

"This is just a test.

"For the next sixty seconds the Emergency Broadcast System will be conducting a test. We repeat, this is only a test."

The remote control is going beserk. Station after station rolls by, channel after channel. Program after program blipping to life and dying in a fraction of a second. Here and gone. Here and gone. Here and gone.

The Son of God's handiwork appears on the screen. Slice Sanchez neatly packed in plastic that will last a thousand years. The Lord's testament wheels by, dominating the airwaves.

Freeze frame.

"This ends our test. Had this been a real emergency, you would have been instructed to . . ."

Shut up!

The news is on. Channel Four. Liz Walker is speaking to him and projecting pictures of Jesus' terrible retribution onto a small screen hovering in the air next to her head.

Liz: Police in the city of Crocker have called a press conference for tomorrow morning. The small, north central mill city has been the site of two brutal homicides involving mutilation of the victims' bodies. Police have reportedly received videotapes of the murders but have refused comment as yet, saying they have no suspects. . . . And farther north, in New Hampshire . . .

He shuts the sound off.

"Don't worry about the police," Jesus says, looking out at him from the other side of the mirror on the wall. *"The police are just as guilty as the others. They, too, will pay."*

Channel change.

Lights dance. Sounds blur. A circle of white appears center screen, and recedes.

The room is gone. Darkness except for the light at the end of the . . .

Doors open and close.

Sounds out of the blackness. A shuffle. A slip. A roll. A snap. A slither.

"No!"

Glowing faintly like deep-sea creatures that spend their lives wrapped in darkness, the creators of the sounds crawl out of the darkness. A hand scuttling like a spider. A leg wriggling like a snake. A torso dragging itself by the shards of bone jutting from its shoulders where its arms should be. A head rolling like a jack-o'-lantern, *her* eyes looking right into him, and they are a thousand times worse in death than they were in life.

"No!" His scream is weak. He can't find the remote. He can't find the off switch. A hand crawls over his foot. He runs . . .

. . . headfirst into the wall separating the living room from the kitchen. His tube is blown and the only sound in his head is the tinkling of broken glass. He hits the floor with a crumpled *thud*, his head crushing Ivy's watch beneath it as it strikes the edge of the carpet.

CHANNEL 17

*Bill Gage—
Video Detective*
*When Bad Things
Happen to Good People*

Though it went against nearly every textbook case and every expert opinion, Bill Gage was gut-sure that Dr. Jay Epstein, who had been identified as the handless man found on the tracks, was the latest victim of the serial killer. The media had taken to calling him the "Video Killer" since all the details of the case had been leaked by Starkovski. Though they couldn't prove it was Starkovski, the chief and Mahoney knew it was. His shit-eating grin at the press conference had been enough to confirm it for Bill.

The mayor had really been put on the firing line after that conference. He'd started out with denials and lies, got caught in them, and had been backpedaling ever since, doing what any good politician would do: blaming someone else—in this case the chief and Bill.

Bill didn't care. The mayor was a jerk. He could

say what he wanted as long as he didn't interfere with the investigation.

The phone rang and Bill pushed all that garbage aside. It was Mahoney down at the front desk. Another tape had just been found on the front seat of a cruiser parked right in front of the station. Typically, no one had seen anything. Telling Mahoney to meet him in the makeshift viewing room, Bill left his office and ran into Chief Albert who was coming to see him.

"Come on. Another tape just came in. I'm betting it's Dr. Epstein," Bill said, not stopping. Chief Albert fell into step beside him.

"That throws a monkey wrench into standard theory, huh?" the chief said, shaking his head.

"This guy's just got a different plan, a different need, is all. He's following a unique pattern and he's waving it in front of our faces like a red flag, but we just can't see the damned thing." He looked sideways at George, who was puffing a little at Bill's pace. "What were you coming to see me about?"

"Bad news," George answered.

"If it's about the mayor, I don't want to hear it."

"It is. He's released a statement that'll be in tomorrow's paper saying he's going to personally oversee the investigation to be sure that the public is kept properly informed." The chief didn't hide his anger.

"That phony! Who does he think he's fooling?"

"It gets worse," George said. They reached the interrogation room, and Bill paused before going in.

"There's more?" he said in an exaggerated tone of voice.

George rolled his eyes. "The mayor wants me to inform him when anything happens, but especially if we get any more tapes. He wants to watch them with us to make sure we're not holding back vital information."

"Call him," Bill said.

George looked surprised. It wasn't the reaction he had expected.

Bill explained. "If this tape is as bad as I think it's going to be, I want to see that bastard's face turn green when he watches it. He'll be running for the john after five minutes and then he won't be so gung ho to bother us anymore."

Chief Albert laughed and nodded his head in agreement. He went to call the mayor, and Bill turned on the lights in the viewing room. He looked at the TV and VCR and grimaced. He was beginning to hate every boob tube and VCR he saw, but he hated this one in particular. He knew it was irrational to hate an inanimate object, but it was a good way to vent emotion—emotion, that if directed at the killer, might cloud his judgment and cause him to miss something.

Mahoney came in. "As soon as Hanson dusts it for prints, he'll send the tape up." He crossed to the TV. "I just saw the chief. The mayor's coming over to watch this?"

"Yeah," Bill sneered. "Want to wager how long he'll last?"

"I give him two minutes, tops," Mahoney said.

"I'll give him a little more stomach than that, but not more than five." They laughed, but it was strained. Neither of them was looking forward to watching the tape. Five minutes later, Larken brought the tape in, handed it to Mahoney and left.

"Should we run it, or wait for Hizzoner?" Mahoney asked, putting the tape on top of the VCR.

"He's on his way over," the chief said, returning. "I didn't even have to call him. He called me. Someone already let him know we got the tape."

"Let's wait," Bill said.

Mahoney looked relieved.

.The tape was what Bill had been expecting, but the mayor's reaction was not. Hizzoner fooled them and sat through the whole thing. His presence bothered Bill, and he was unable to focus or pay close attention at all. His eyes were constantly drawn back to the mayor's face as he watched Dr. Epstein have his arms trimmed at the wrists with a manual saw and one of his hands inserted proctologically.

The mayor's face retained the same frozen expression throughout the gruesome video, a strange, vacant little smile twisting one corner of his mouth, his eyes glistening—with tears, Bill had thought at first, but realized after more study that it was with excitement. He shuddered. The mayor was getting *turned on* by the murder and mutilation of Dr. Epstein. Bill was sure of it, and the thought made him feel more nauseated than watching any of the other videos had.

Bill was glad when the mayor left, talking it up with one of his flunkies about how to handle the latest homicide so that it would best serve his image. Watching him go and listening to his chatter, Bill found something else on which to vent his angry emotions. Chief Albert departed with a snort of disgust at the mayor's performance, leaving Bill and Mahoney in front of the TV.

"I'll get this back to the lab. You want the same makeup on this one?" Mahoney took the tape out of the VCR when it was done rewinding.

"Yeah," Bill said absentmindedly, not able to get the mayor's face out of his mind. Perhaps that was how his father had looked as he photographed his victims dying. Did that mean the mayor was capable of murder? Bill doubted it. People like the mayor and his father—and maybe the Video Killer —walked a very fine line. Where someone like the mayor would never act on his desires, his father had.

"I'll have Hanson make a single copy right away so we can watch it while he gets the loop made," Mahoney said.

"Okay," Bill replied, not moving from in front of the dark screen. Mahoney left. Bill pushed the mayor to the side and turned his thoughts to the latest video. Its title was *Let's Play*. First *Toilet Training,* then *Smokin' in the Boys' Room,* and now *Let's Play*.

He's trying to tell me something and I'm too dumb to see what it is, Bill thought. Breaking the gender pattern notwithstanding, the Video Killer was a classic case of a serial killer. What masqueraded as arrogance in taping his murders and sending them to the police was really a cry for help and an attempt to tell the police how to catch him. Everything this guy had done so far had been planned and laid out very carefully. It was clear he was trying to say something with it all; Bill just didn't understand the language yet.

He sat musing over the possible meanings of the titles until Mahoney came back with the tape. They played it again, and without the distraction of the mayor's presence, Bill was able to pay better attention.

Like the first two videos, there was a title but no sound. The opening shot was a tight close-up of Dr. Epstein's hands tied together through the back of a wooden chair so that his wrists rested on the wooden seat, providing a good cutting surface. A quick switch to a close-up of Dr. Epstein's face, with gray tape over his mouth, to register the fear and panic—and something else Bill couldn't quite put his finger on—and then it was back to the hands on the chair. The saw entered the picture and began cutting. By its dull shine it appeared to be well used, but it was very sharp.

The rest of the tape was a series of tight shots in living color switching back and forth between three different camera angles of Dr. Epstein's tortured face and the bloody removal of his hands. The disgusting finale of the rectal insertion of one of the severed hands and the removal of Epstein's eyes with what looked like a sharpened spoon brought the tape to its end

Bill realized that each tape so far had been a little more sophisticated than the one before it, in terms of technical style. The first tape had been shot in black and white from one camera angle; the second in color with two camera angles; this third with three angles. Another clue? Another message from the killer?

If only he knew what it meant.

He played the tape again, trying to focus his wandering mind on looking, not thinking. The camera work was so tight, each shot revealing so little, that he doubted he was going to detect anything, but he tried anyway. He was feeling stagnated, frustrated. Everything—from the mayor to the uncomfortable way his father's shadow kept falling over the case to his problems with Cindy—conspired to give him the sense that the killer had laid everything out as plain as day, and he was still too stupid to get it.

He looked at his watch as the tape rewound. In twenty minutes, he and Mahoney were holding a briefing with everyone connected with the case. He decided to forgo looking at the tape again in favor of a cup of coffee and a look at his notes before the meeting. It seemed Mahoney had the same idea, shutting off the TV and VCR without a word.

"Not bad," Bill said, almost a sigh of relief in his voice. The briefing was over and all the detectives and patrolmen had left. Though they had briefings every day, they generally didn't produce much, but today he felt less frustrated after it was over. They'd got some things cleared up, and he felt as if he could see a line of progress in the case again.

Two of Mahoney's detectives, Lieutenant Levy and Corporal Porter, who had been assigned to check out empty industrial sites and factories, reported back on fifteen empty factories in the area, any of which would have been a good place for the

Video Killer's death studio, but none of which showed any evidence of occupation.

Another two, Lieutenant Miller and Lieutenant Lachance, who were assigned to check out photographers, the local cable company, and Channel Twenty-seven personnel in Worcester, came up empty as far as suspects were concerned but did learn a few things about the video-making process that were interesting. A Mr. John Giacomo, who ran the cable company's local access station for the cities of Fitchburg, Leominster, Quarry, and Crocker, had been cleared to view a carefully edited selection of scenes from the first two tapes. He had been able to identify that the perp was using home video cameras, probably top-of-the-line Sonys, though he couldn't be definite, with very sophisticated lighting and editing equipment. Except for the video cameras, Mr. Giacomo believed the perp was using equipment that the average video buff wouldn't have.

Larken reported no luck with his attempts to trace the Elvis porno movie, to quite a few snickers and chuckles from the others. He heard more when he went on to report on his trace of the toilet bowl manufacturer whose name began with *PRINC*. He had boiled it down to a list of seven in New England and the Northeastern Seaboard. He had checked with every company already, but found they couldn't tell him if they had sold plumbing to a factory in Crocker without knowing the factory's name because of the way their records were filed in the computers. Larken correctly pointed out that since they didn't know the age of the building the perp was working in, they could be looking for a company that had gone out of business.

Larken also had an update on Joan Perche. He had tried to trace her to a number of the places where her husband had said she might have been and was able to produce witnesses at each who at least thought they had seen her. The last place her husband expected she would go on the night she disappeared was to the hospital to visit a sick friend. Larken had interviewed the friend and found that Joan Perche never showed up. The nurses on the friend's floor and the hospital information desk receptionist had no recollection of seeing her either. Larken came to the conclusion that Joan Perche had been picked up at the bus stop while waiting for the bus to take her to the hospital.

Bill had known it was a long shot, and though it had proved fruitless, it had given Larken a chance to show his unique flare with computerized investigating. Bill made a mental note to point it out to the chief. Larken had the makings of a very methodical detective.

When the reports were done, Bill filled the men in on what the tapes had revealed so far, then opened the meeting to discussion and/or questions. He was glad to see the detectives and extra patrolmen the chief had assigned talking animatedly about the evidence. Starkovski was the only one who sat silent, alternately sulking and smirking, in the back of the room.

Through questions and discussion they had established that there was a definite pornographic connection to what the perp was doing, as evidenced

by the placement of the bodies in front of the Saxon
Theater, an ex-adult movie house; under the
X-rated movie sign at the Video Valhalla rental
store; and on the train tracks—a connection Bill
hadn't seen until one of the younger detectives had
pointed out the sexual implications of *train*. The
titles of the tapes could also be suggestive of pornography.

By the end of the meeting, they had their first
composite, however skimpy, of the perpetrator: a
young male who had probably been the victim of
abuse, as evidenced by the burn scars on his hand in
the first tape; he had knowledge of video equipment and had worked in television or, more likely,
pornographic movies, probably as a cameraman.

It wasn't a lot, but it helped him get a handle on
thinking about the perpetrator as a person with
reasons for what he was doing. Unfortunately, just
when the meeting got productive and Bill was feeling hopeful again, Starkovski put his two cents'
worth in.

Bill and Mahoney were going over new assign-
ments, and Bill was giving Larken the name of the
FBI's New England agent, telling him to check with
him for more information concerning New England's pornographic film and magazine industry.
That was when Starkovski butted in.

"What New England pornography industry?" he
sneered. An immediate stillness descended over
the room. The men looked at neither Bill nor
Starkovski. They could sense a showdown coming.

Bill answered him, unrattled. "When I was with

the state police, there were three production companies in New England that we *knew* about."

"Ten years ago," Starkovski muttered just loud enough for all to hear. Bill noticed then that Mahoney was getting steamed. Starkovski apparently didn't, or he might not have gone on shooting off his mouth.

"So what's the big bad Video Killer going to do next, *Special Investigator?* Come on, swami, what's his next victim going to look like? Maybe you even know who it's going to be! Why don't you save us all this work and just tell us."

Bill and Mahoney spoke at the same time, but everyone heard Mahoney's shouting over Bill's calm, sarcastic tone. "So you can sell it to the *Telegram?*" Bill asked Starkovski but wasn't heard as Mahoney yelled, "If you've got a problem, Frank, you see me. You still report *to* me and *through* me!"

Starkovski unwisely opened his mouth to speak. Mahoney closed it. "Shut up! If you'd stop being such a dickhead and help out with this investigation, we might accomplish something. We don't have time for wiseass questions, Frank, especially *stupid* wiseass questions. They don't make you look clever, Frank, they just show you up for the ignorant son of a bitch that you are."

The room had grown absolutely quiet. Starkovski's face was bloodred with rage and embarrassment. He flashed angry eyes around the room, and all but Bill and Mahoney looked away.

"I'm filing a harassment grievance with the union steward," Starkovski growled, then got up and left.

Speaking in low voices, the men filed out of the

room, a couple of them giving Mahoney the thumbs-up sign.

"Thanks," Bill said when the room was empty.

Mahoney grinned sheepishly and waved it away. "That bastard has had it coming to him for years." Mahoney laughed. "Actually, I kind of enjoyed that."

Bill laughed with him.

Ivy wept the first tears since his father had died. He stood on the sidewalk outside Barbara's apartment house and watched them take her out on a stretcher, the sheet tucked tightly over her head. He didn't even know what he was thinking at that moment, or whether he had any thoughts at all, but a well of pent-up emotion came bubbling to the surface and gave way.

Mr. Crankshaw, Barbara's landlord, was standing on the steps talking to a young policeman. He was crying too. He looked up, saw Ivy, and motioned him to come over.

The tears and hurt were coming so hard and fast now that Ivy couldn't catch his breath. He fled from Mr. Crankshaw, unable to face anyone with the tremendous pain that was cancerating inside him.

He ran. Everything was an outrage. Everything was grotesque, out of proportion, an assault upon and insult to his senses. Exhaust fumes smelled as thick as L.A. Smog. Sunlight had needles to it that made his eyes burn and water with their brightness. The road beneath his feet was filthy, oily, slimy, coated with the residue of the scum of the earth. Of people like Slice Sanchez.

Ivy stopped in the middle of Leighton Street, two

houses from home. *Slice Sanchez* was the one responsible for Barbara's death as surely as if he'd stabbed her with his infamous switchblade. His friends were just as guilty, but Ivy could deal with them later. His first order of business had to be Slice and how to make him pay.

The tears came again, hot with the conviction for revenge. He walked on, and the tears streamed down his face, warming his cheeks for a moment before the air turned them cold. He didn't notice; he was too busy plotting.

He strode up his driveway, oblivious to everything but his pain, grief, and desire for revenge. Halfway up the first flight of stairs, he remembered Bond in the garage. The little pup must be cold, he thought. The tears grew heavy again at the memory of Barbara's giving him Bond, James Bond. He didn't know if he was going to be able to keep the puppy now.

"I guess I'll have to tell him about Barbara," Ivy said in a faint whisper, a surge of tears squeaking off the last few words. Wiping his eyes, he crossed the yard and went around to the back of the garage.

The back door was supposed to be locked, but Ivy had put a piece of masking tape over the locking mechanism earlier to facilitate his searches for weapons. He opened the door and slipped inside quickly. It wasn't much warmer in the garage, and Ivy felt bad for Bond.

He paused and frowned in the darkness. Earlier, as soon as he had opened the door, Bond had started yipping and whining, and he'd had to hurry blindly through the dark obstacle course of junk to his box in the corner to quiet him before his mother or the landlord heard.

Maybe the dog was sleeping. "Here, Bond," he called softly into the darkness. There was no sound from the darkness, no scuffling of paws, no panting of breath.

He's got to be sleeping, Ivy told himself. His sudden concern for Bond had stopped his tears. He wiped his eyes and started across the garage, being careful not to trip or bang into things.

He became aware of an odor in the garage, a different smell than there had been before. It was sour and bad. His heart began to hammer in his ears and his breathing sounded too loud in the darkness. He continued toward the corner slowly, his feet not wanting to move.

In the gloom he could make out Bond, James Bond's cardboard box. It looked as if the puppy had been chewing at it and tipped it on its side. He could make out the dark form of Bond lying on his blanket next to the upturned box. For a moment, Ivy's heart and hope soared.

"Bond!" he cried, running to the corner. The dog didn't respond. Ivy reached the blanket and discovered Bond, James Bond would never again come when called. He had been gutted like a fish readied for supper. On the bottom of his cardboard box, which, turned up the way it was, resembled a headstone, were written two words in the dog's blood:

YOU'RE NEXT!

"He killed my dog!" Ivy screamed in tears at the policeman's back. The officer, who'd just been about to get into his cruiser after ticketing the motorcycle and van parked across from Wilbur's, jumped and whirled around. Ivy tried to speak again but could manage to babble only sounds of grief.

"Calm down, kid," the officer said, closing his car door. He bent over, took off his gloves, and put a hand on the back of Ivy's neck, massaging it gently. "Just take it easy and tell me what's wrong."

Ivy's voice hitched a few times in his throat before he could speak. "He killed my dog!" Ivy said, and the tears gushed again.

"Who did?" the cop asked.

"Slice Sanchez!" Ivy said, his voice a high-pitched whine as he tried to contain his tears.

The cop, the same one who had talked to him about Slice at Watson's Market, introduced himself as Officer Cote. He followed Ivy up his driveway to the back door of the garage. Officer Cote unclipped a small, black, fire-hydrant-shaped flashlight from his belt that powerfully illuminated the dark interior. Ivy pointed the way and the cop led them to the corner with his light.

The air went out of Ivy's lungs like the time Bully Jeff Brink punched him in the gut. His knees quivered, suddenly unsteady.

Bond was *gone*. Not only Bond, but his box, blanket, and dish, too, were missing. There wasn't even a spot of blood left behind! It was as if nothing had ever been there.

"Okay, kid. What're you tryin' to pull?" Officer Cote asked, flashing the light in Ivy's face. The look of shock and puzzlement on the boy's tear-stained face told him the kid wasn't playing any jokes.

"He was here!" Ivy gasped.

Officer Cote believed him. He knew Slice Sanchez well enough to know something like this would be just his style. As evidenced by the scene in Watson's when they busted him for the knife, Slice had it in for the kid.

Cote put his arm around Ivy's shoulder and turned him away. "Did you see Slice kill your dog, or put it in here?" he asked Ivy, leading him outside.

"No," Ivy said despondently, then fiercely, "but I know it's Slice. He threatened me."

"Okay. Without a body or any evidence, or any witnesses, it's going to be hard to accuse Slice of this, but we can pick him up and question him."

Dazed, Ivy let himself be led away.

CHANNEL 18

Meet the Smiths
Sonny Ray's Not-so-lucky-Day

 No place is safe anymore, Franny Smith thought, pulling her collar up against the fine snow falling, lightly dusting the sidewalk. She used to enjoy walking home at night from the Oyster Bar where she worked as a barmaid. Since this Video Killer was on the loose, though, she'd given it up.

The boys who were regulars at the bar—she thought of them as barflies, which was what they were, sitting there drinking night after night when they ought to be home with their wives and kids—were no help and a sorry excuse for men. You'd think one of them would have the decency to leave his beer some night for five minutes to give her a ride, or even walk her to the end of Elm Street where she could get the bus. Oh, no. Instead, they had to make wisecracks about the bogeyman getting her.

Her husband, Ralph, was just as bad. It had been like pulling teeth to get him to agree to pick her up, and now he was late. She stamped her feet. Why couldn't he do one thing right for a change?

A car approached, its headlights washing over her, and pulled to the curb. She sighed in relief before noticing it wasn't Ralph's beat-up old Ford. It was an equally beat-up gold Bonneville that looked familiar. She understood why when she saw that shy boy, Wilbur, who lived in back of them, on Leighton St., behind the wheel.

He rolled down the window and she went over to the car. "Mrs. Smith, your husband's been taken to the hospital. If you'll get in, I'll take you there."

Oh my God! No!

Not one to handle bad news or emergencies calmly, Franny Smith let panic carry her away. She knew Wilbur worked at the hospital—she had seen him there while visiting a relative once—so didn't question why he would be sent to get her or even how he knew where to pick her up. All she knew was that Ralph, her poor sweet Ralph, was in the hospital and she had to go to him.

She quickly got into the car, tears already streaking her heavy mascara. The car pulled away and she never saw the tire iron that cracked her skull.

Ralph Smith drove by the kitchen entrance to the Oyster Bar for the third time, gripping the wheel tightly in annoyance. It was so like Franny to make him go out of his way for her and then not be on time. It was a regular occurrence with her and he was sick of it. Either she learned to drive the damned car or she'd just have to take the bus.

She still wasn't out there. He hated the thought of parking and getting out of the car into the cold night, especially since the old heater in the car had just got around to making things toasty inside.

One more time around, he thought, *and if she's not out, I'm leaving.*

He came around again. She wasn't there, but he didn't leave. Swearing, he double-parked, leaving the motor running, and got out. Someone called his name. He turned. It looked like a cop running toward him.

"Mr. Smith you'd better come with me."

It was that kid from Leighton Street who lived with those hippies. He remembered Franny's mentioning she'd seen him working as a security guard at the hospital, which explained his uniform. Ralph also remembered one night when Franny was working a few years ago: a screaming Wilbur had banged on his back door yelling for help. Ralph had locked the door and threatened to call the cops.

"What are you talking about?" Ralph asked gruffly.

"Your wife's been injured. She's over here."

"What?" Ralph said, disbelievingly. He closed the car door and followed the kid who'd started backpedaling and motioning for Ralph to follow. The kid broke into a run and Ralph copied, chasing him around the corner and into an alley where a car was parked that Ralph recognized as the one he'd seen the kid's hippie mother driving.

"What the hell's going on?" he puffed, confused and out of breath.

"In here. It was a hit-and-run," the kid said, opening the back door of the car.

Ralph staggered to the door, one hand on his aching chest, the other on the cold fender of the car, steadying himself. At fifty-six, he wasn't used to running any farther than the distance from the TV to the fridge during commercials.

There was a pair of nylon-stockinged legs and feet on the back seat. Next to the right foot, he recognized one of the orthopedic white shoes Franny wore because of her fallen arches. A small groan slipped from his mouth. He leaned over and looked inside.

His wife's bloodied face was the last thing he saw.

Sonny Ray sucked the last drop of MAD DOG 20/20 from the bottle and looked at it longingly. He wished now that he hadn't been such a lush last night; it was cold this morning and he could use something to take the chill off. But then it had been cold last night, too. When it got that cold, the only way to spend the night outside was to drink till you passed out, as he had last night.

Normally, he would have done his drinking under the Fifth Street Bridge, where he and most of Crocker's homeless population had created a small shantytown of cardboard boxes and old plastic trash bags and anything else they could find to jerry-rig a shelter. But last night, all his under-the-bridge buddies had been stone-broke and not a bottle to piss in between them.

Sonny had headed uptown to do some panhandling and had hit the jackpot almost right away. A guy in a business suit and expensive overcoat—the kind of guy that never gave money to a bum like

Sonny—slapped a dollar bill into his outstretched hand even before he'd had a chance to deliver his crock about needing the money to buy oatmeal for his starving grandchildren. Though happy about the money, which would get him a quart of MD 20/20 on special at Shamrock's Liquor for ninety-nine cents, Sonny had been a little disappointed at not being able to spout his sob story. He thought it a very creative and heartrending monologue. At one time, in the dim and distant days of his youth before life had broken him, Sonny Ray had wanted to be an actor.

With his favorite rotgut tucked inside his filthy coat, Sonny Ray had decided it was too far to walk to go back to the bridge. The truth was that when he got a full bottle all to himself he became very greedy. He knew a narrow little alleyway across from the police station parking lot where he could drink in peace and be fairly well sheltered from the wind, if not the cold, and the bottle would take care of that. He'd spent the night in that alley before, and once he had more wine in him than was in the bottle, he'd been pretty comfortable. Now, though, he was stiff-legged, cold, and hungry.

He stumbled out of the alley, shading his eyes against the harsh morning light. It did nothing for his headache. He crossed the street to the police parking lot and began a cruiser-by-cruiser window check for candy bars, crackers, or doughnuts. He'd done this before and it always proved fruitful.

Three rows into the lot, he spied a half-eaten cinnamon cruller in one of the small plastic trash baskets that was under every cruiser's dashboard. As was typical of the cops, the patrol car was unlocked, as though they thought that a police vehicle wouldn't get stolen or broken into. The sound of a car stopped Sonny from opening the door.

He ducked behind the cruiser's fender. A long, brightly colored car that looked orange to Sonny in the blinding morning sunlight pulled up behind the reserved section of the lot where the chief and police captains parked their cars.

A kid got out of the car. He wore dark clothing and an overcoat with a black wool knit watch cap pulled low over his ears. The kid put something under the windshield wiper of one of the cars parked in the reserved section. He looked around, didn't see Sonny, and hurried back to his car, then drove away quickly.

Sonny Ray forgot about breakfast for the moment and went over to the reserved section. The kid had left something on the car with the Chief of Police's seal on the door. Sonny went over and saw that it was a videotape. With plans of selling the tape to the nearest video store dancing in his head, Sonny took it off the car and stuffed it inside his coat.

"Hey! What are you doing there?"

Sonny Ray whirled. Two cops were hurrying toward him. He ran, but they caught him easily.

"I didn't do nuthin'. I saw a kid put this on the chief's car and I wanted to see what it was because . . . because, I thought it might be . . . dangerous! Yeah! That's it. I thought it might be a *bomb!*" Sonny Ray was warming to his fabrication.

The officers looked at the tape and each other. "You'd better come inside with us, Ray."

Then they led him inside, Sonny Ray protesting his innocence vociferously all the way.

CHANNEL 19

The Best-Laid Plans
Want Some Candy?
Break Time
Leave It to Ivy

 Beth put her uniform on quickly, but took her time applying makeup and fixing her hair. She had switched shifts with another student nurse so that she could be on from eleven to seven tonight with Wilbur. They had made plans to take their break together and then go out to breakfast after they got off work tomorrow morning. The girl who had switched shifts with her had called her weird, but she had gladly changed with Beth.

While getting ready, Beth thought about Wilbur and how different he was from most guys. If she had pursued any other guys as aggressively as she had Wilbur, they would have thought she was giving them the green light to take her to bed. Not that she would mind if Wilbur showed a little more interest and aggressiveness, but it was just so nice and *different* that sex wasn't the first and foremost thing on Wilbur's mind.

Though they had only gone out the one time,

Beth was falling for Wilbur in a big way. She couldn't stop thinking about him. Just yesterday in chemistry class, instead of taking notes on Dr. Dillard's lecture, she had covered three pages of her notebook with Wilbur's and her names together as husband and wife, encircled with hearts and flowers and other silly, lovesick doodles before she'd embarrassedly realized what she was doing.

She finished her hair and assessed her looks in front of the full-length mirror on the back of the closet door. She was a modest person but she had to admit she looked good. If all went well, she and Wilbur might just be having more than breakfast together tomorrow morning.

Bill Gage and Mike Mahoney were working late again, looking at the tape Sonny Ray had been caught taking off the chief's car that morning. They'd got several different stories from Sonny as to how he got the tape, along with as many descriptions of the person who'd left it and the type of car he'd been driving. This one was titled: *Want Some Candy?* and besides being the most bloody video yet, it also broke the Video Killer's pattern again. This time he killed two people and, instead of waiting for the bodies to be found and then sending the tape, he had delivered the tape first. The bodies had yet to turn up.

"This one *can't* be by the same guy," Mahoney said, a statement he had repeated at least once a viewing since they'd started watching the tape. Hanson had dusted the tape as soon as it came in, but if there were any of the perp's prints on the case or the tape, Sonny Ray's handling of it had ruined them.

There was a knock on the door. Bill stopped the tape, and Mahoney answered it. Larken mumbled something and handed him a fat file folder filled with computer printouts. Mahoney thanked him, closed the door, and from the top of the file picked out a piece of notepaper with Larken's handwriting on it.

"Listen to this," Mahoney said to Bill. "Since we-both-know-who leaked the facts, we've had an average of over fifty calls a day from people claiming the Video Killer is their brother, or father, or cousin, or next-door neighbor who plays his stereo too loud. We've also fielded at least one call a day from some-one who claims to be the Video Killer and wants to give himself up. One crazy lady from Leominster called to say the Video Killer was sending her sub-liminal messages during *Jeopardy!*"

They both had a good laugh at that until Bill pointed out, "All those callers will have to be checked."

Mahoney groaned, looking at the printout of names and addresses of people who had called. "Some of these have been checked already. It seems like a waste of time, but I know we've got to cover all the bases."

He put the printouts aside and sat next to Bill again. Automatically, Bill reached over and started the tape again. After watching it all day, they both still flinched when the ax entered the tight shot and began hacking to pieces the two bodies tied together in the sixty-nine position on the metal table-top.

"I think this one is definitely a copycat killer," Mahoney half whispered as he watched the body parts fly.

"I don't know," Bill said. He was feeling a little out of it—a combination of overtiredness and self-hypnosis from staring at the screen for so long. Though the film didn't fit the killer's pattern in several ways, it did in many little ways that told Bill it was the same guy.

Mahoney didn't agree and explained why. "First, we get the video and no bodies. Second, this tape has sound, even though it's just a music sound track. None of the others did. Third, the other two murders were carried out slowly, methodically. This one is crazy. Once that ax starts swinging it's clear whoever's wielding it is out of control. And what about their eyes? You can't even see if they've been removed and it isn't on the tape. And last, he was seen leaving the tape on the chief's car this time, but wasn't seen any other time. Maybe he just got unlucky, but to me it looks like he suddenly got very sloppy and careless, which is completely out of character for this guy."

Bill had to admit that Mahoney had a good argument. It didn't change his own convictions, though. "I think this guy really is making a statement. He's telling us something with everything he does. The way he kills each victim, the videotapes, their titles, where he leaves the bodies—it's all for a reason. He wants us to understand what he's trying to say. He wants us to catch him. He broke his pattern last time when he killed a man, so now we don't know *what* his pattern is. All I know is that if he thinks doing something a certain way will help get his message across, then he'll do it."

"Okay, but why send us the tape first this time? What is he trying to tell us with that?" Mahoney asked.

"I'm not sure. I guess if I was, I could solve this like that." Bill snapped his fingers. "But I get the feeling that we got the tape first because he's not going to give us the bodies."

"Why?" Mahoney asked, confused.

"Because of what you said before. This *isn't* like his other murders. I think he did lose control. I think his plan this time was to sever their legs, but when he went overboard like you said, maybe he thought it would be too difficult or too messy to dump the bodies in pieces for us to find. Also, without the bodies, it's going to be tough identifying them, especially since we get no full shot of either of their faces in the video." Bill paused. Something just occurred to him. "Maybe he doesn't want us to ID them."

"Why would that matter to him now?" Mahoney asked doubtfully.

Bill didn't answer right away. He was thinking about the look on Dr. Epstein's face in the previous video. There had been something about his expression when looking at the camera—and so the killer —that had bothered Bill, but he hadn't been able to put his finger on it. Now, he realized it had been a look of *recognition* on the dentist's face. He hadn't been looking at some murderous stranger; the look in his eyes said he knew his killer!

"I think he doesn't want us to ID them because they knew him," Bill said. He shut off the tape and stood. "I think Dr. Epstein knew him too. How's Miller doing with Epstein's patients?"

"I don't know," Mahoney said. "He's supposed to report to me on his progress tomorrow. If the dentist knew him too, then why didn't the perp care if we ID'd Epstein but not these two?"

Bill was already thinking of that, and the answer he came up with excited him. "Maybe because he thinks there's some way we can trace him through these two but not through Epstein, which means the perp's probably not one of his patients. If the two people he killed this time knew each other, and we could establish how they knew each other, or maybe where they lived, that could be the key to tracing the perp. Maybe they were neighbors of his, or co-workers."

"I'm confused," Mahoney said, shaking his head. "I thought you said this guy was leaving us clues to catch him. Now you're saying he's trying to avoid being caught?"

"I know, it is confusing. I don't mean he's consciously trying to get caught. It's a subconscious desire. Consciously, this is a game for him. He probably thinks he's superior and has us running around in circles, which isn't too far from the truth. *Consciously,* he's going to try and keep us from catching him, but *subconsciously,* he's trying to tell us *how* to catch him," Bill explained.

"Maybe he did this one different just to throw us off?" Mahoney considered.

"Maybe," Bill mused, "but I don't think so. Like you said, he has followed a pattern. I think he just screwed up and is trying to cover it. I'm willing to bet he did the eyes like the others, but he did it after. Remember, he didn't include the removal of Grace Simond's eyes either. Everything else about this tape—the look, the title, and especially the ax—looks the same. I want Mr. Giacomo to look at some stills and tell us if it's the same equipment used in the previous videos."

The door opened, and the chief looked in. "What are you guys still doing here at this hour?" he asked.

Bill nodded at the blank TV screen. "What are you still doing here?" he asked.

"I just got away from the mayor's annual Christmas ball," George said, rolling his eyes in disgust. "I dropped Lucille at home and came down to get some paper work out of the way. Any news on the bodies yet?"

Mahoney shook his head.

"I don't think he's going to leave them this time," Bill said and went on to explain why.

"Learn anything new from this one?" the chief asked.

"A little," Bill said. "In a way, this one isn't as bad as it looks." Mahoney and George both gave him strange looks. "What I mean is, I don't think either of the victims was conscious during the taping, and I'm pretty sure the woman on the bottom is already dead. The guy on top has a bad head wound just above the base of his skull. It doesn't look bad enough to have killed him quickly, but he's not conscious during the murder.

"The perp's technique is getting better with every film, too. He shot this one from three different angles, edited them together, added a sound track —the middle section from the Grateful Dead's concert recording of "Dark Star" from the album by the same name—and except for a few glimpses of his fingers, kept himself out of range of the camera."

Bill turned to Mahoney. "Another thing that makes me think you're right about him losing control is that there are a couple of spots in the tape where it's obvious something has been edited out. I think those missing shots probably show the perp in the camera frame."

He turned back to the chief. "The lighting is done just right, so that it's hard to see too much of the victims, another reason why I think he doesn't want us to ID the bodies and why we won't get them until we get him. In the opening shot, though, just before he starts with the ax, you can see that the woman appears to have long hair spread out around her head and partially over her face. A lot of what appears to be hair is actually blood, spreading out from what I believe to be a mortal wound in her skull."

Mahoney gave Bill a look that clearly questioned whether they had been watching the same video. "Where was that?"

"Real short part at the beginning," Bill explained. "What bears this out is that as soon as the ax enters the picture, he starts on their legs, which is his primary objective. He's done the head, arms, and hands in previous videos, so legs is his logical next step—another point in favor of the tape's authenticity, by the way. He starts with the man's legs and flays so wildly that he hacks her head too. But in the first couple of chops on the male victim's legs, he moves a little, but she doesn't react at all."

"Then that might mean he was wild on purpose, to try and cover the fact that she was already dead," Mahoney said.

"Right," Bill answered. "What really makes me think he's hiding their identities is the way the lighting is done to hide her face. Even so, you can tell she's definitely unconscious. The paleness of what can be seen of her forehead suggests loss of blood, and the hint of a bruise starting at the bridge of her nose and spreading downward suggests the site of the wound or the collapse of facial blood vessels from the loss of blood, which would mean she was dead."

"Thank Christ for that," the chief breathed.

"I think if we can identify this man and woman and connect them somehow with one of Dr. Epstein's patients or someone he knew, we'll have our Video Killer. Somehow the perp knew all three, though the three might not have known each other. Maybe he worked with them, or lived near them, which is why I think he doesn't want us to know who they are. It would bring us too close. For whatever reason, he felt comfortable enough allowing us to ID Epstein, so, like I said before, I doubt we'll find anything among his patients."

"If he's so worried about us tracing him through

these two victims, why did he choose them? Why not off someone else?" the chief wanted to know.

"That's where the pattern of his need comes in. I had thought maybe it had something to do with the type of person—their occupation, for instance. We had a college student, a teacher, a dentist. It might be a pattern, but I can't see what it might be. If we can ID the latest two, maybe that will help. He might see people as symbols, focusing on one thing about them that represents something or someone he feels he has to destroy or punish. And I think your assertion, Mike, that he knew Grace Simonds is right after all. I think maybe he knew all of them, and that could mean it's some kind of personal vendetta.

"For some reason, it *has* to be these two, just as, for whatever reason, it *had* to be Grace Simonds for the first one, and Joan Perche the second, and Dr. Epstein the third, and why he has to remove a bodily extremity each time. His next murder will involve the feet, I'm willing to guess. If we get a tape or body that *doesn't* fit the body pattern, then I'll worry about a copycat killer," Bill said.

He showed up!

Beth was elated. She hadn't been at all sure that Wilbur would show at break time. Though they'd had fun on their date, there had been nothing like fireworks going off between them or anything. When she had suggested that the next time she worked eleven to seven they take break together and then go out for breakfast afterward, he'd seemed reluctant to agree, and she'd had to cajole him into it.

He'd tried to tell her he never took a break, and then that he never ate at work, but she had used that to her advantage, making jokes about how bad the hospital food was. She'd coaxed a smile from him with that and had pushed on, describing the submarine sandwich she was going to get at a real deli and how the hospital food would flee in sloppy terror at the sight of such delicious, *real* food. He had laughed in spite of himself, and she had taken that as a confirmation of their date.

Coming on duty tonight, she had seen him in the lobby and reminded him again, but during the first four hours of the shift she convinced herself that she had been too pushy and scared him away. She didn't know why she acted so aggressively around him, but she guessed it was to make up for his ultra-nonaggressiveness. She was amazed at herself for plotting to get Wilbur into bed. When other guys she'd dated had done that to her, she'd dumped them.

Beth wasn't a virgin but had slept with only one boy, her high school steady. They had done it regularly, twice a weekend for the three years of their relationship. He joined the army after graduation and she'd been secretly glad. He'd become boring, and she didn't love him anymore. She doubted whether she ever really had.

Her desire for Wilbur, though, was more than just a reflex reaction to his lack of interest. She *really* wanted him. Sex with her old boyfriend Bobby had always been so mechanical, so unenjoyable. It was something she had done only to please him and to keep him as her boyfriend because she'd foolishly thought she couldn't live without him. When their relationship ended, she hadn't cared if she'd never have sex again. When she thought of Wilbur, though, she could imagine sex that was special, magical; she could imagine sex that was *making love*, a ballet of flesh and the fluids of life.

And now here he was, against the odds, rekindling all her fantasies and hopes at the sight of him. He came into the visitors' waiting room and sat on the blue vinyl couch. All the furniture in the visitors' waiting room was done in the same ugly blue vinyl encased in shiny chrome frames. She clutched the top of the brown paper bag with the submarine sandwich in it, got up from the chair she'd been waiting in, and sat down next to Wilbur.

He stood up like a marionette jerked on its strings, then sat down again when she did. He looked as nervous as she felt, which she guessed was a good sign—if he was nervous, then he must care what she thought of him. Maybe he'd even been anticipating seeing her.

They got sodas from the machine in the corner and Beth laid out some paper napkins as a make-shift tablecloth on the low metal coffee table in front of the couch. She took out the two halves of the sub and placed one in front of Wilbur, the other in front of herself.

They ate in relative silence. Wilbur picked at his sandwich, while she ate hers as if she hadn't tasted food in months. She couldn't help it. She was trying not to talk too much or put her foot in her mouth, and the only way she could do that was to put something else in her mouth, preferably food.

Wilbur insisted she take the rest of his sandwich when she finished hers in record time. He'd taken less than five bites, explaining he couldn't eat late at night. Embarrassed, she took the sandwich and quickly devoured it. Wilbur smiled every time she looked at him but said nothing. With the food and sodas gone, there was nothing else to occupy her mouth, and she gave in to temptation and tried to strike up a conversation. It certainly didn't look as though Wilbur was going to start one.

"Whew! After that, I hope I'm still hungry when we go out for breakfast in the morning," she said. She didn't like the look on his face when she mentioned breakfast. He looked surprised, as though he'd forgotten about their date. He said nothing, though.

"You know, instead of going out for breakfast, why don't we go to your place and I'll cook you a breakfast you won't forget. I make great cinnamon French toast," she suggested.

"We can't," Wilbur said quickly, an almost frightened expression on his face. "My . . . my parents are home," he added hesitantly.

"Oh." Beth understood. She didn't know why, but she had been under the impression that Wilbur lived alone. She wished her parents still worked. Though it was an hour to her home in New Hampshire, her parents would have been gone by eight if they weren't retired, and she and Wilbur could have had the house to themselves all day. Since her parents both quit working last year, they were up at dawn every day so they could spend a few extra hours driving each other crazy with nothing to do.

Wilbur suddenly stood, a look of consternation on his face, and Beth thought he was going to cancel their breakfast date. "I got to go," he said nervously. "It's time for my rounds." He turned to leave.

"Wilbur," Beth called, going to him. "Thanks for taking break with me." She stood very close to him. It was now or never. She leaned up, lips parted, tongue waiting, and kissed him. She stepped back and smiled at him. Though he hadn't exactly responded with unbridled passion, he hadn't pulled away either.

"I'll meet you in the lobby at seven, okay?" she asked, licking the taste of him from her lips.

Wilbur stared at her for several moments, and she thought he was going to return her kiss, but he only nodded. Smiling shyly, he left.

Ivy tried to get out of bed, but his head felt so heavy and hurt so badly that he could only lift it a few inches off the pillow. And when he managed even that, he felt as if he was going to be very sick. He gave up and remained in bed. He didn't care if he went to school today. He didn't care if he *ever* went to school, or *anywhere* ever again. The way he felt, if he just lay there until he died, it couldn't be any worse than what he'd been through lately.

With Barbara to share his thoughts, Ivy had begun to enjoy school and his studies again. The fact that bad things had happened to both Barbara and Bond when he'd stopped hiding his intelligence and started using it did not escape him. He knew it was crazy and babyish, but he couldn't shake that childhood conviction that Dr. Peabody was behind all the bad stuff that had happened lately.

Ivy thought back to one of Barbara's lucid periods a few days before she died. He'd told her about his dad and Dr. Peabody. Barbara had told him about paranoia and explained that what had happened the day his father died was all just coincidence his mind had turned into conspiracy. That had only made him feel worse. He knew that what she said was logical and true, but it left him now with nothing to hold on to, nothing to explain why bad things happened to people he loved.

He realized that his cold, aloof attitude toward his mother was really a defense against something happening to her. That must mean he *really* loved her. He guessed he did, but now he'd be more afraid to show it than ever. Again Barbara's logic came to him and he told himself that loving someone had nothing to do with tempting fate.

Unwilling to give up what it had relied on for so long, his mind grasped again at the Dr. Peabody conspiracy theory, trying to link Slice Sanchez to it this time. He imagined Slice was an agent of Dr. Peabody's, who in Ivy's James Bond state of imagination became the leader of an international organization dedicated to wiping out everyone in the world smarter than Dr. Peabody. He could picture Slice meeting with Peabody, getting instructions and maybe payment to kill Barbara and Bond as a warning to Ivy to go back to playing it stupid or else. The scenario had a bad suspense-novel sort of logic to it and might have been fun to play with under other circumstances, but now the stupidity of it was all too evident.

Conspiracy or no, the one person he could definitely lay blame on for Barbara's and Bond's deaths was Slice Sanchez. Ivy gripped the covers in anger thinking about him. He wanted to get Slice so badly that he would gladly have sold his soul to the devil for a chance to get his hands around the punk's throat and squeeze the life out of him.

Though Officer Cote had been sympathetic, Ivy knew the cops wouldn't be able to do anything. He'd had the first indication of that already when Officer Cote had driven by the bus stop yesterday and stopped to tell Ivy that Slice had disappeared; his mother hadn't seen him in days. She didn't think it was anything strange since he often took off for days and weeks at a time. Though Ivy hadn't paid much attention to it, he knew the cops were too busy with this Video Killer everyone was talking about to care. To Ivy, Slice's disappearance was an indelible stamp of guilt on the punk. It was obvious to Ivy that Slice had left town after killing Bond so he wouldn't get caught. Ivy flattered himself with another guess as to why Slice had split after killing Bond: He was afraid of what Ivy was going to do to him.

Ivy smiled grimly at that. *He'd better be afraid.* If Slice Sanchez was ever stupid enough to come back to Crocker, much less the neighborhood, he'd find out that Ivy Delacroix was no one to mess with. Then Ivy'd make him pay. His imagination burned with fantasies of the tortures to which he'd subject Slice.

His mother stuck her bleary-eyed head into the bedroom. "Ivy? I'm leaving for work now. You'd better get up or you're going to be late for school." She focused on him with effort and sat at his side, taking his hand.

"Are you all right?" she asked, concerned.

"I don't feel good."

She felt his forehead and cheeks with the back of her hand. "You feel a little warm. Where does it hurt?"

"My head, my stomach," Ivy complained, groaning.

"No wonder you've been moping around here the past few days like you just lost your best friend. You've been coming down with something. Stay in bed. I'll get you some aspirin and call in to work. I'll be back to take your temperature." She got up from the bed, taking off her coat as she headed for the phone in the kitchen.

Even his mother had noticed how down he was lately, and he'd thought she didn't notice anything about him anymore. It felt good to have her concerned about him and wanting to take care of him. He was in the right frame of mind for some TLC. She was even going to take the day off from work! Now that was something.

CHANNEL 20

*This Is Tunnelvision!
—IV*
Wilbur & Beth

Bill watched the barren winter landscape along Route 140 slide by. He had told Cindy he'd be home in time for supper tonight, something he'd managed once since the investigation started, but now it didn't look as if he was going to make it. Mahoney was driving, taking him and Larken to the North Central Massachusetts Correctional Institution, locally known as East Gardner Prison, to see an inmate who had told prison officials he had information pertinent to the murders in Crocker. The warden had called Chief Albert, who had passed the information on to Bill and Captain Mahoney.

Bill figured he could call Cindy from the prison, but he didn't think this was going to be anything other than a wild goose chase. Some two-time loser was always trying to bargain his way out of time by claiming to know the perpetrator of some unsolved crime.

In the back seat, Larken was going through his briefcase. He was a trained stenographer and notary public, which was why they'd brought him along to record and legally witness the interview with the inmate.

"Don't fuss too much, Fred," Bill said over his shoulder. He was feeling frustrated with the case lately. The only recent progress had been John Giacomo's confirmation that the last video was made with the same equipment as the others. "We'll probably be in and out of there in no time with the luck this case has been having."

The interview room was small and drab, painted in institutional gray and green. A narrow, rectangular steel table with a dark green cork top dominated the room. With the stiff, round-backed metal chairs, there was only a two- or three-foot space left around the table to maneuver.

Bill sat at the middle of the table, Mahoney at his left, and Larken at his right, unpacking his notepad and pencils before he was even in the chair.

"What's this guy's name again?" Bill asked Mahoney.

"Lydell Winnaker," Larken said, then blushed, realizing Bill hadn't been speaking to him.

"He's doing eight to fifteen for trafficking. Cocaine," Mahoney said with a smile at Larken's eagerness.

A door at the end of the room opened, and a prison guard led the inmate into the room. He was a small, skinny, balding man with pale skin and a scraggly beard and moustache. He wore square wire-rimmed glasses perched on a long, hawkish nose, and his teeth were very bad. The guard stayed until the inmate sat across from them, then left.

Mahoney spoke first. It had been decided beforehand that Mike would handle the interview since he had done this more recently than Bill. "Mr. Winnaker, you have told prison officials that you have information pertaining to a series of unsolved homicides now under investigation by the Crocker Police Department. Is that correct?"

"Yeah," Winnaker mumbled, fidgeting and picking at his scuzzy moustache.

"For the record, Mr. Winnaker, you requested to speak to us and have waived the right of having an attorney present. You have not been promised any deals or special privileges in return for talking to us or for any useful information you might provide. Is that also correct?" Next to Bill, Larken copied in shorthand all that Mahoney was saying.

"Yeah, for now," Winnaker answered, settling down a little as he concentrated on picking dirt from under his fingernails with his bad teeth.

Bill and Mahoney exchanged glances, and Bill shrugged.

"What does that mean, Mr. Winnaker?" Mahoney asked.

"It means I can help you guys, but you gotta help me, too," Winnaker said, his eyes darting back and forth between Bill and Mahoney.

"Sorry. You know the arrangement. It's just like I finished reading to you. The only thing I can promise you is that if your information proves helpful, it will go on your record that you helped us, and we'll sign an affidavit to that effect for your next parole hearing."

"Shit! That ain't for five years yet, man. There's

guys in here that want to kill me!" His voice lowered as he added, "And some guys that want to do worse, you know what I mean? Make you scream in the showers? I need some guarantees, man, cuz I'm going to break your Video Killer case wide open."

Bill kept his face impassive. Out of the corner of his eye, he saw Larken look up sharply, but to the young cop's credit, he recovered immediately and went back to his note-taking. If Lydell Winnaker saw his reaction, he didn't show it.

Bill cleared his throat and spoke up. "The way I see it, Lydell," he said, holding the inmate with his stare, "you're putting the cart before the horse. We don't know if your information is any *case breaker*, as you say. It might not even be pertinent. If you want to insist on deals before you even tell us anything of value, we're out of here and you lose. If you want to cooperate and we can use what you give us, then we'll do everything we legally can to help you out. But that's the only guarantee you get."

Winnaker broke the stare, nervous and fidgeting again, his dirty nails forgotten. He looked at his shoes, then the ceiling, then his knuckles, anywhere but at Bill's piercing eyes.

"Yeah, okay," Winnaker muttered finally.

"Sign this," Mahoney said, pushing a form in triplicate across the table at him. "It says that you agree to everything we just explained."

Winnaker took the pen and paper and scribbled his name illegibly on the indicated line. Larken witnessed and notarized it with the stamp he'd brought along.

"Whenever you're ready," Bill said when the paperwork was out of the way.

"Aren't you guys going to ask me questions?" Lydell asked, puzzled.

"Why don't you just tell us your information and we'll ask questions later," Bill said.

"It's kinda a long story," Lydell said, his eyebrows raised.

"That's okay," Mahoney said. "We've got time and you're not going anywhere."

Yeah, Bill thought, looking at his watch. *I've got plenty of time now; I've missed supper and I forgot to call Cindy.*

"It was ten, maybe twelve years ago when I hooked up with some dealers just over the border in New Hampshire who could deliver some quality flake. They had a growing porno film business, too. I knew a guy who belonged to NAMBLA who introduced me to them. He knew them because they were doing some kiddie porn with little boys for NAMBLA. You know what NAMBLA is?" Lydell asked.

Bill and Mahoney nodded. They both knew of NAMBLA—the North American Man/Boy Love Alliance. On the surface, it was a legal organization made up of mostly professional men—lawyers, doctors, and so forth—who lobbied for sexual freedom between adults and children, but especially men and boys. Beneath its surface, though, NAMBLA was involved in child prostitution, kidnappings, child pornography, and black-market child slavery. Though only a few members had been busted, they were known to run a series of "warehouses" in

which young boys were kept for members' plea-
sures, and where the boys were trained to serve the
men.

"He introduced me to this hippie couple, Joey
and Mary. I never heard no last name. I think they
were married. They had a kid, name of Waldo or
something weird like that. Anyway, this guy Joey
was into all kinds of sex. He'd been a runaway and
had been picked up by NAMBLA. He was raised in
one of their warehouses and worked for the organization when he grew up.

"He and his old lady were getting financial backing for their kiddie porn films from a couple of the
richer members of NAMBLA—couple of European
lawyers with connections in Boston, I think. I guess
kiddie porn's pretty big in Europe. I remember
them saying that's where most of their distribution
was." Lydell paused and grinned, carefully watching the detectives' reactions to what he was about to
say. "And Joey and Mary, they used their kid in the
films. Real abusive stuff, too."

Mahoney's jaw tightened, and Larken's pen
stopped scribbling, but that was it. Bill felt something that was a cross between a twinge of nausea
and a jolt of excitement course through his gut, but
his face remained impassive. Lydell looked disappointed.

"So what's this got to do with the so-called Video
Killer?" Mahoney asked matter-of-factly, as though
he'd heard nothing of interest so far. Bill mentally
congratulated the captain's steadiness.

"Well, I later heard these two had made a snuff
film for some rich European. When I heard about

the Video Killer, I thought maybe they were making some more, though why they'd send them to the police is just plain stupid!" Lydell chuckled to himself.

"And you don't remember their last name?" Mahoney asked.

"Like I said, I never knew it. I remember what they called their film company though, it was Tunnelvision Studios."

Bill paled and straightened. "Did you say Tunnelvision Studios?"

"Yeah." Lydell looked from Bill to Mahoney. "They used runaways and kids they got from NAMBLA to make their movies. Most of the films were of kids playing with each other and screwing around, but they also made a bunch of films special for NAMBLA in which adults abused kids, especially their kid, whatever his name was."

Mahoney gave the pale Bill a questioning look, then returned to the interrogation. "How do you know all this?"

"My friend from NAMBLA told me a lot, and I watched once while they made one of the films with a couple of kids in it." Lydell kept looking uneasily at Bill.

"Do you remember if it had a title?" Bill asked, eyes intense.

Lydell shook his head in the negative.

"You went to their studio?" Mahoney asked.

Lydell looked uneasy, like he had divulged more than he had planned. "Well, yeah, but it was a long time ago and it was in Keene, New Hampshire, before they moved their operation to Crocker.

They lived on a farm outside of Keene. I don't remember the road. It was a big place that had been a dairy farm at one time."

"And where's your friend now, the one from NAMBLA who introduced you to these people?" Mahoney continued.

"He's dead," Lydell answered quietly. "He was a junkie—died of AIDS last year." Lydell looked down at his fingernails again and the room was quiet for a moment.

"Can you provide a description of this couple? Would you recognize them if you saw them again?"

"Aw, man, I told you it was a long time ago. I've done a lot of shit since then, shit that's fried my brain, ya know? The guy had long hair and his old lady had big tits, that's all I remember. The kid was about seven or eight when I knew them."

After a few more questions to try to nail down a name, or address, it was apparent that they had learned all they were going to from Lydell Winnaker. Mahoney called for the guard, who came and took Lydell back to his cell. The three of them drove back to Crocker.

In the car, Bill's mind alternately raced with excitement and was haunted with dread. For reasons he couldn't explain and would rather not examine, he had felt his father's presence in the room when Lydell had been talking about Tunnelvision Studios and the films they made. Again, he felt that overpowering but inexplicable sensation of some connection between this case and his father. He had received quite a shock when the name of the kiddie porn studio had been the same name Cindy had given his special focusing abilities.

Bill was certain that Lydell's information was crucial to the case, and that the couple who ran Tunnelvision Studios and their kid were somehow deeply involved in the Video Killer murders.

On the ride back, Bill explained to Mahoney and Larken (leaving out the part about his talent) why he'd been so excited when he'd learned the name of the studio. The piece of paper he'd seen outside the Saxon Theater in the first photos he'd looked at, the paper with *ELVIS* on it and *Stud* and *xXx* under it, now made sense in light of what Lydell had told them. Where before he had thought it was a porno movie with Elvis or an Elvis impersonator, he now realized the paper hadn't been part of an advertisement for an X-rated Elvis movie. It had been a piece of an advertisement for a film from Tunnelvision Studios. And it was almost certainly left there on purpose by the killer.

Mahoney and Larken matched Bill's excitement. For the first time since the investigation had begun, it felt as though they could get a handle on the perp and begin to understand the killer's unique language. It was too bad that Lydell Winnaker hadn't been able to give them a last name, or an address, or the name of a lead they could talk to. Still, it was more than they'd had before.

"We'll check with the Keene police on any old dairy farms in their area. Maybe we can trace this crew, especially if they were hippie types. The cops might remember them," Mahoney said.

"Good," Bill answered. He turned to Larken in

the back seat. "Fred, have you been in touch with the FBI on the porno angle?"

"Yes, sir, but they haven't gotten back to me yet."

"Well call them again with this new info. Maybe they have something on Tunnelvision Studios. I'm sure you can tap in, or whatever you do, to their computer system."

"Yes, sir," Larken answered, writing furiously in his notebook.

"We're going to get him now," Mahoney said confidently. "I can feel it. It's only a matter of time." He banged the steering wheel with his fist.

The ever-growing shadow his father cast over the case made Bill cautious and quiet.

Later that night, Bill let himself into the house as quietly as possible. It was midnight, yet if it hadn't been for the chief's kicking him and Mahoney out again, he knew he'd still be at the station. Mahoney at least had an excuse to work late. He was divorced with no kids or family to speak of.

Bill knew he should have gone home to his family hours ago, right after he'd got back from the prison. He hadn't been doing anything at the station that couldn't be done tomorrow or that Larken couldn't take care of. He was just letting the case work on him, instead of the other way around. Heck, he could do that just as well at home, couldn't he?

He kept the lights off and hung his coat by touch on the hall rack. He felt his way along the wall, letting his eyes adjust to the dark, and went into the kitchen. The digital time readouts on the microwave oven, coffee maker, and stove gave him a supernatural greenish glow to see by. He went to the refrigerator, took out a bottle of ginger ale and drank from the spout. Putting the bottle back, he noticed a faint flickering light from the living room across the hall. He realized the TV was on with the sound turned down.

Cindy was sitting, huddled, on the couch, her knees drawn up to her chin, her long dark hair mussed and hiding her face. Bill flicked the wall switch, turning on the overhead light. Cindy looked up sharply. He could see the light reflected in glistening tear streaks down her face.

He suddenly felt like the world's biggest jerk.

"What's wrong?" he asked, hating the "I'm innocent" tone his voice reflexively adopted.

"What makes you think something is wrong?" Cindy barked in a raspy, tear-hoarse voice. "The twins had a great birthday party. They sat here for two hours waiting for you. I had to send them to bed. Since then I've been sitting here alone for hours, as I have every night, wondering where my husband is and what the hell has happened to him and us and this family." Fresh tears threatened to flow along with the words, but she wouldn't let them. "Or wondering if he's even alive. You said Crocker's one of the safest cities for a cop to work in, but there is a psychotic killer out there. How do you know he won't come after you? I'm sitting here in the dark, and I'm thinking you could be dead," she said quietly. She wiped her face with the backs of her hands and stared at him.

Bill stood in the doorway looking at the carpet, the walls, his shoes—at anything but Cindy.

"Please, Bill," Cindy said, her voice firm, strong.

"Talk to me. Tell me why you can't come home for Sassy and Missy's birthday party, or why you can't call me and tell me you'll be late. You could at least call and let me know that *you're alive!*" She nearly shouted the last two words.

He said nothing. He felt like a small boy being scolded by his mother.

"What's happening to us, Bill?" she asked softly, not looking at him. "Something's got to change. I know you said it would only be until the end of the case, but I don't like the position you've put me in. I feel like some goddamned cliché cop's wife in a bad movie and I don't like it."

Bill released a long sigh. He wanted to let go and talk to her about everything. He wanted to tell her about the dreams and how the Video Killer case had taken on a strange symbolic connection to what his father had done. But if he kept talking and it *all* came out, would he reveal what he managed to keep hidden even from himself most of the time?

Would he be able to admit that this case had become the ghost of his father's crimes? Would he admit that deep down he was convinced that if he could catch the Video Killer he would also put to rest the ghost and get on with his life again?

He doubted it. It was hard enough for him to face those thoughts; he didn't think he'd be able to express them to her in a way that would seem as logical to her as it inherently did to him. He also knew that if he told her that he had to exorcise his father's ghost alone, without her, and that was the reason for his distance, she'd be hurt. When he'd begun to realize the true personal importance of the case, he'd hoped that he could just remove himself from Cindy and the family while he dealt with the present and the past. He told himself he was doing it for their future, but he hadn't forseen the toll it would take.

His cynical side spoke up. *Are you dealing with the past, or is the past dealing with you?* He couldn't argue, but it didn't change what he had to do. If events controlled him, then so be it. He'd ride them out, but he'd do it alone. The bottom line was, he couldn't tell Cindy that, so he didn't speak.

"If you don't want to clue me in on what's going on, and you can't function as a normal father to the kids, I think it would be better if you stayed somewhere else until this case is over. Then you can decide what you want to do. If you're not here at all, you won't disappoint the kids anymore, and I won't worry and wonder when you'll be back." She got up and brushed past him without a glance. She started upstairs, but paused and spoke without turning around. "Captain Barrel called from Pennsylvania again. There's going to be a grand jury investigation into your father's case. He wants you to call him." She hurried up the stairs.

Bill sat on the couch in the darkness, hating himself, hating the Video Killer, but most of all, hating his father for screwing up his life again.

One o'clock found him driving aimlessly along the streets of Crocker. It began to snow lightly, but he didn't put on the wipers. He let the snow accumulate and melt, blurring his vision of the world.

A bright neon sign shone through the rippling sheet of melted snow on his windshield. The light caught his eye and drew him to it like a mosquito to the smell of blood.

BLUE FOUNTAIN LOUNGE, the aquamarine neon letters flashed at him when he flicked on the wipers to see. Below the words a blue neon fountain erupted from a red neon martini glass.

He pulled the car to the curb across the street from the bar and turned off the motor. The snow turned to rain that dotted the windows until the neon sign was a pointillistic abstraction of color.

A drink.

Oh! a drink would make everything all right. A drink would blur things so much better than a little rainfall. He knew he was imagining it, but he swore he could smell the inside of the Blue Fountain Lounge. He could smell the stale smoke, the pungent scent of beer permeating everything, the tense smell of sweat, the spice of the wooden bar and the leather-topped stools, but most of all he could smell the booze, the heavenly booze.

His nose could zero right in on that black-labeled bottle of whiskey sitting on the top shelf, as it is in every bar in the country. His old friend Jack Daniel's. He could almost hear the liquid calling him in a soft Tennessee drawl.

"What the hell are you doing?" he asked himself loudly, trying to jar himself out of the liquor's siren song. He rubbed his face and rolled down his window to clear his head. The cold air only stabbed into his sinuses and started a slowly spreading headache.

His mouth was dry, his throat sore. If he closed his eyes he could see that bottle of Jack Daniel's being taken down from the shelf and poured neat into a shot glass. He could see its reddish-brown caramel color sparkling with the invitation to blissful oblivion.

Taste me! he could hear it whisper.

One sip.

One gulp is all it takes.

Forget about the Video Killer.

Forget about your father.

Forget about Cindy and the kids.

Taste me!

He rubbed his lips with the back of his hand. Suddenly frantic to get away from there, he reached for the key to start the car but his hand was trembling so badly he couldn't even grasp it, much less turn it.

He hugged his shaking hands to his gut and rested his forehead on the steering wheel, taking long, deep breaths. He could taste whiskey in the air. He could feel its bite on his tongue. A picture of himself standing at the bar raising a glass of whiskey came to him so clearly he thought he was hallucinating. The anticipation, the slight hesitation, the first gentle taste, slow, letting it sting over his tongue and gums, letting it sink in without swallowing.

He could taste it, see it, and *feel* it so strongly it scared him. And with the fright came a scary memory of himself during the deep dark drunk days. He'd just closed out his savings account in Pottsville, where he'd been living since his father's death. He proceeded to buy a case of Jack Daniel's to celebrate the fact that in a little over six years he had managed to drink over $30,000 dollars, made up of his savings plus the proceeds from the sale of his father's house. When the case was gone, so was the last of his money, and the landlord kicked him out of his hovel of an apartment.

He'd spent three lost days on the streets of Pottsville before he'd sobered up enough to remember he owned a condo in Crocker that he could sell. He'd hocked his watch to get a bus ticket. If he hadn't come back to Crocker, he wouldn't have met Cindy. If he hadn't met Cindy, he'd be dead, or nearly dead, by now.

And if he went into that bar, he would destroy the last three years of love and life with Cindy.

A sound drew his attention back to the bar. Singing. A burly, bearded drunk was staggering out of the bar, belching and singing an incomprehensible tune at the top of his lungs. He made it to the edge of the sidewalk and slipped on ice, going down hard and heavy into the gutter. He lay there on his side, his misting breath spouting into the light like the blow of a sperm whale.

The sound of belching came from the drunk. Bill closed his window; the guy was feeling no pain. Another craving for liquor shook him. He closed his eyes and tried hard to remember why it was better for him not to drink, but the reasons were elusive.

A thud jolted him as something hit the car. He opened his eyes. The drunk was no longer in the gutter. He was sprawled across the hood of Bill's car. Bill beeped the horn. The drunk didn't budge. Bill pressed the horn longer. Again. And again.

The drunk's head rose slowly and the bleary eyes squinted in at him. Most of the drunk's face was hidden by his beard, his orange hunting cap, and the dirt and snow from the gutter, but there was something familiar about it.

The drunk belched, and his head made a lurching motion. Bill thought the drunk was going to leave his entire evening's imbibing on the hood of the car. He looked away in disgust, but instead of the sounds of regurgitation, a voice came from the man.

"Destiny, Billy-boy," it said.

Raw fear coursed through Bill, and the shakes returned with a vengeance.

"You can't escape it except through a bottle. I know. I tried."

The voice was his father's. He looked at the drunk. The eyes were his father's. The outstretched hand and blood-crusted fingernails that reached toward the windshield were his father's.

"No!" Bill shouted, and the drunk began to laugh. "NO!" Bill pounded his hand against the steering wheel.

The sound of retching stopped him. He looked back at the drunk, who was just finishing getting sick. The whole front of the hood was covered with the mess. The drunk pushed himself away and staggered down the street.

What the hell is happening to me? Bill wondered. He shivered as the snow again began to fall.

The diner was small and greasy, but it was warm and the coffee was good. Beth sat across from Wilbur in the end booth. While he sipped his coffee, she told him about life as a nursing student, often bringing a smile to his lips, and one outright laugh.

"If I'm talking too much, you can just tell me to shut up," Beth said.

"No. You're not," Wilbur replied, an uneasy expression belying his words. "I like to hear you talk." He added, shyly, a few moments later, "I . . . I just don't talk too much."

Beth wanted to climb over the table and make it with him right there. He was so darn *cute* when he acted shy. "I like that about you," Beth said. "Most guys just want to talk about themselves all the time. They don't know how to listen to someone else."

Their food came: pancakes and bacon for her, cornflakes and toast for him.

"Are you sure that's all you want?" Beth asked him. "They have great omelets here."

"This is what I have for breakfast," Wilbur said matter-of-factly.

Beth shrugged and they ate, listening to golden oldies from the radio over the buzz of the diner's morning crowd.

"Gee! I don't even feel tired. Do you?" Beth asked him as they were leaving the diner. Wilbur shook his head in agreement. "I know a real pretty spot on High Rock Road where you can look out over all the farmland around Crocker. With the snow, it should be beautiful up there. We could talk some more," she offered, wrapping her arms around his arm and looking up at him with what she hoped he thought was a seductive look and not just stupid.

"Okay," Wilbur said softly. "I do have to talk to you."

They got into Wilbur's car, and Beth gave him

directions on how to get to High Rock Road, which was on the border with Quarry.

Beth liked Wilbur's car. It was big. The inside could pass for a living room in some of the apartments she'd been in. The back seat was the roomiest she'd ever seen. She didn't think they'd have any trouble fooling around in it—*if* she could get Wilbur back there.

High Rock Road was a twisting, rising trail that hadn't been plowed very well, but it was passable. The sun was doing a good job of melting the snow, and there were only a couple of slippery spots. Beth pointed out the side road at the top of the hill. It hadn't been plowed at all, and Wilbur was hesitant about taking the car down it. Beth assured him it was level and straight all the way in, which was only twenty yards or so through a small stand of pine.

Wilbur seemed doubtful, but Beth pressed on until he gave in. The muffled sound of the snow flattening under the tires had a deep soothing crunch to it. They listened to it in silence as Wilbur maneuvered under sparkling, snow-laden pine boughs along the frosting-covered road that was clean, as if no human had ever come this way before.

As the pine trees came to an end, Beth told Wilbur to stop the car. From there they looked out on a magnificent winter panorama. Beth slid across the seat and snuggled close to Wilbur.

"Isn't it beautiful?" she asked, resting her head on his shoulder. Wilbur was a little stiff at first, but Beth felt him gradually loosen up. When he actually put his arm around her, she could have cheered.

"We might be more comfortable in the back seat, don't you think?" Beth ventured cautiously.

"Okay," Wilbur said, seeming to think nothing of it.

They climbed into the back seat—Wilbur left the motor running and the heater blowing—and Beth took off her coat once she was in the back. Wilbur hesitated a moment, then followed suit.

"It's warm in here. That's a good heater," Beth said. Wilbur put their coats in the front seat. "What did you want to talk about?" Beth asked, snuggling up to him, and raising her face to be kissed. Unlike last night, he responded this time and kissed her tentatively. It sent thrills through Beth and she kissed him back with passion. Soon they had the Bonneville's windows completely fogged up.

She discovered that Wilbur was a good kisser. He began French-kissing her as if he knew what he was doing. She slipped her leg between his and began rubbing against his thigh. His hand slipped up to her neck and he caressed it, his thumb resting on her Adam's Apple. She reached up, took his wrist, and slid his hand down to her breast. It started drifting up to her neck again.

Suddenly he shoved away from her and shouted, "No!"

Beth didn't know what to do. She sat there, her uniform and hair a mess, and horny enough to be ashamed of herself.

"No!" Wilbur cried again. "I won't let you. I won't let you. I won't let you," he repeated over and over again, loudly at first, then gradually diminishing to a mumble.

"It's okay. It's okay." Beth tried to soothe him, but he seemed oblivious to her. She didn't know what to make of it.

She fixed herself up, got her coat from the front seat, and put it on. She retrieved Wilbur's also and put it over his trembling body. She had to face it. There was something seriously wrong with Wilbur. She was becoming frightened by his withdrawal. The motor was still running. She decided to take him back to the hospital and get him some help. She just hoped she didn't slide into a pine tree or get the car stuck trying to back it out. It was a long walk before she'd come to a house.

She opened the back door and Wilbur's eyes flew open and he sat up straight. He looked at her for a moment like someone who sees a familiar face in a crowd and can't quite place it.

"Are you all right?" Beth asked timidly. He didn't look well. His face was pale, his eyes wild.

He shook his head as if to clear it. "I'm sorry," he answered, exhaling loudly as though he had been holding his breath. He opened his mouth, shut it, opened it again. "It . . . It's . . . not you. Really. It's . . . me," he stammered. "I'm really sorry." He put on his coat and climbed into the front seat.

For a moment Beth considered staying in the back. Wilbur's little breakdown and recovery had been too weird for her. But on the other hand, he looked so pitifully miserable as he apologized, that her fright mellowed to pity, and she felt pity was the sister to love. She climbed over the seat and squeezed his arm. He flinched.

"I understand," she said, though she really didn't.

He didn't look at her, but she could feel the muscles in his arm relax. He put the car in reverse and backed it out. During the ride back to her dorm, Beth tried to think of a way to broach the subject of his behavior on High Rock, but she couldn't find one that felt comfortable. They rode in silence.

CHANNEL 21

Dialing for Death
Sassy Sarah
Live Miracles!
The Bogeyman
Damnation Chorus
72 Hours

 Volume up.

The news is on. Liz Walker again. The words CROCKER VIDEO KILLER appear in the air next to her head.

"Special Investigator William Gage, shown here refusing reporter's questions, said today there were no suspects as yet—"

"Him," Jesus says.

"What?"

"The policeman. He will pay for those who failed to serve and protect."

Channel change.

"Okay, we're ready to take calls from our viewing audience, so let's open up those phone lines. Hello? You're on the air!"

"Crocker Police Department, Sergeant Grinds

speaking. Your call is being automatically recorded."

"Is Detective Gage there?" Jesus asks.

"Hold on."

Silence. Clicking.

"Nope, he's left."

"Did he go home?"

"Probably. Can I have your name and number, and I'll see that he gets it."

"Sorry, caller, time's up. We've got to go. See you next time!"

Music up. Cue applause.

Jesus is heading for the door.

"You can't kill a cop," Wilbur pleads. "They'll take you off the air."

"We can. We will." Jesus holds the phone book open to the page where the names CINDY & WM. GAGE appear with an address and number.

"Call," says the Son of God.

The phone rang and Cindy let it ring through to the answering machine. It clicked on and gave her spiel about this being the home (what a laugh) of Bill and Cindy Gage, please leave a name and number, and so forth. The caller hung up at the end of the recording.

She had her hands full tonight. Sassy was sick, some kind of stomach virus that had her running to the bathroom every fifteen minutes or so. On the last dash the poor kid hadn't made it to the toilet and the antique, hand-embroidered hall rug that had belonged to Cindy's grandmother had taken most of the spill.

Uncharacteristically for her, Cindy had lost her temper and blown up at poor Sassy. Cindy had left a bucket by Sassy's bed for her to use instead of having to run to the bathroom, but the girl was so neat and finicky that she wouldn't use it. Seeing her favorite rug ruined on top of having fought it out with Bill last night, Cindy had lit into her daughter for everything from messing the rug to being so neat that she didn't like the way Cindy ironed her clothes.

To her daughter's credit, Sassy hadn't taken it lying down. Sick as she was, she stood right up to a surprised Cindy, acting more like her sister Missy than herself. She apologized very formally, and very icily, for ruining the rug. She offered to pay to have it cleaned, the money to come out of her share of the paper route she shared with Missy.

Sassy knew what she was doing, and Cindy knew it, too, but that didn't keep her from feeling about two feet tall. After all, the poor kid hadn't *meant* to mess the rug.

"And as for my neatness," Sassy had gone on to say, her face pale, her lower lip quivering, "I bet a lot of parents would like a kid with my problem. I suppose you'd be happier if I was more 'normal' and did drugs or something."

Cindy had never seen Sassy so sarcastic. It was the first time she'd ever lived up to her nickname. After having her say, Sassy went back to bed. A few minutes later, Cindy heard her getting sick in the bucket.

"Oh! Gross!" Sassy exclaimed, her voice on the edge of tears, and got sick again.

Cindy went in, bringing her a cold facecloth like a flag of truce. Sassy wiped her lips, face, and hands carefully, then lay back with an arm across her forehead. Cindy washed out the bucket and replaced it by the bed.

Cindy was glad her single sister Evelyn had planned on taking the kids this evening to help her decorate her tree. Sassy was disappointed in not being able to go, of course, and Cindy was, too. Despite her problems with Bill, which left her in something less than the holiday spirit, she still had to do some Christmas shopping. At least not having Devin and Missy there made taking care of Sassy a lot easier. If there was a merciful God, Devin and Missy wouldn't catch the bug, but she knew that was too much to hope for. The one thing she could realistically wish for was that the kids all got it and got over it before she got it, which was also inevitable.

The phone rang again. What if it was her sister calling because Devin or Missy was sick now, also?

"All right," she grunted, getting off her knees. She dashed the few steps to the phone and answered it.

It was Bill. His voice sounded shaky.

"I can't talk right now," she said, her voice edgy. "I've got to try and clean the mess out of the hall rug where Sassy got sick."

"Sassy's sick? What's wrong?" he asked, his voice full of concern.

"Some kind of stomach virus," Cindy said, her voice a touch softer.

"Do you want me to come over?"

Was that a note of hope in his voice or fear?

"No. I can handle it. If you came over you might catch it, then you wouldn't be able to *devote* yourself full-time to your investigation." She didn't know where her attitude had suddenly come from. The words just came out, hostile and angry. She heard his breath catch and hold. She could imagine him tensing up and clutching the phone in a white-knuckled fist. She could also sense his withdrawal as he let his breath out slowly.

"Okay," he said tightly. The proof was in his voice.

She hung up and felt the hot tumult of conflicting emotions that had kept her up all night. Not surprisingly, no tears came with the hurt and anger anymore. Her eyes felt hot and dry. The hurt was numbing, the anger burning out. Cindy wasn't one to pine away, sobbing and carrying on, and she knew that if things went on this way much longer, she wouldn't feel anything toward Bill, and then their break would be complete. Was that what he wanted?

She went back to the rug and finished as best she could. She checked on Sassy and was relieved to see her daughter sleeping. Even though the kid felt miserable, her pillows and blankets were all neatly arranged.

Cindy pulled Sassy's door half-closed and inspected the rug again. She was tempted to wash it some more, but she was afraid of just working the stain deeper into the fabric. She decided to leave it and call a professional cleaner in the morning.

It was nice not having to cook supper for a

change, though if things were normal with Bill she wouldn't have minded at all. Devin and Missy were getting pizza at Evelyn's, so all she had to worry about was herself. After listening to Sassy be sick, not to mention having to clean the rug, Cindy had little desire for food. Talking to Bill hadn't helped either. Their short conversation had left her stomach tight.

She needed a nice hot bath. If Sassy slept long enough, and the damned phone didn't ring again, she might just be able to take one and enjoy it the way she rarely had time for these days.

The 700 Club.
The PTL.
Jimmy Swaggart.
Hour of Power.
Jim and Tammy walk hand in hand with Jimmy and Oral. A miracle is about to take place live on the air.

Grandma would climb into the screen if she could. She caresses it with her hands, repeating the Hail Mary until the words become blurred and nonsensical. At her feet, Wilbur cowers, trying not to look at the screen. He can no sooner will his heart to stop beating.

Tammy Faye is crying, mascara streaking clown tears down her face. The agent of those who failed to serve and protect dwells within the house before which they all stand. "I can feel his evil presence in my very bones!" Tammy cries.

Jimmy Swaggart calls on hellfire and damnation to open the door to the small Dutch colonial. Jim

Bakker implores the faithful to send money and God will open the door.

Wilbur can imagine little old ladies and cripples all over the nation stuffing dollar bills and Social Security checks into envelopes to send to God. And it's working, too. Jesus appears in a radiant beam of light and the televangelists fall prostrate before him.

"Jesus can open all doors!" Grandma shouts, breaking her Hail Mary chant.

Jesus proves her right. The door to the house where the policeman Gage lives opens without a sound.

Closed circuit.

A hallway.

A kitchen.

A living room.

Empty.

A sound.

Water running.

Stairs.

A splash.

Getting close.

Bathroom door. Soft humming behind it. A woman's voice.

An empty bedroom.

An empty nursery.

A little girl sleeping in a room with twin beds.

No Gage. Just a splash and a snatch of song.

A warning then. The woman and child.

Nausea roiling up through her stomach brought Sassy half out of sleep. Her mother's voice crying,

"No!" brought her all the way out. "No!" she cried again, followed by the sound of a loud splash.

Giving Devin a bath, Sassy thought sleepily, wondering why he was home so early from Auntie Ev's. The nausea floated back. Determined to get a head start on the inevitable so she wouldn't have to use the yucky bucket, she got out of bed and headed for the bathroom. It was just too bad if Mom and Devin were in there. She was *sick*. Just *once* she should have priority and she was going to get it.

She rounded the corner of the open bathroom door and stopped. She saw her mother's head bob up out of the tub for a moment. Her wet hair was plastered to her face and tangled around the fingers of the man who was pushing her head back under the water.

Even if she hadn't seen her mother being drowned, Sassy would have reached the peak of nausea at that moment due to being ill. Savage, cruel guilt at having deserted her mother chased her back to her bedroom where she was sick in the bucket. She knocked it over with trembling hands. She righted it, but not before she'd made another stinking mess.

Tears blotted out the room. She wanted to scream and cry and somehow help her mother, but fear had its talons deep into her.

He's coming! The bogeyman!

The sound of splashing from the bathroom had stopped. In the hallway a floorboard creaked.

Hide!

Mommy! Mommy! Mommy! Oh, hide me!

Don't be such a baby. Move!

The closet door was nearest. For once she didn't mind that Missy the slob had left it open. Sassy ducked in, turning and pulling the door shut behind her.

Footsteps in the room.

She heard the bureau being jostled as if someone had just bumped it. The footsteps came closer. She held her breath. She could see the shadow of a pair of feet under the bottom of the door. His heavy breathing, ragged from struggling with her mother, sounded right outside.

No, God! Please! No, no, no, no . . .

The doorknob turned.

Mommy, help me!

The latch clicked.

No!

The door opened.

She screamed.

Evelyn didn't like the looks of the open front door. Her sister was too much of a conservation nut to do that in the dead of winter and waste all the heat. Evelyn carried Devin inside, Missy following, and closed the door.

"Help your brother take off his coat and hat," she told Missy. She went to check the kitchen and living room for her sister. At a younger age, Evelyn had done a lot of reading, especially mysteries. She'd never understood the standard description of a scream as "bloodcurdling." The scream that came from upstairs, while she was in the living room, cleared up that long-standing confusion. If a scream *could* curdle blood, this was surely one of those. It went through her like an electric current.

She dashed to the stairs, her mind racing as fast as her feet. Another scream, and another, and she realized it wasn't her sister screaming; it sounded like Sassy.

"Cindy?" Evelyn called, charging up the stairs. "Sassy?"

The screaming went on with barely a pause for a breath. Evelyn reached the second floor and headed for the twins' room. Behind her she could hear Missy and Devin coming up the stairs. She passed the bathroom, noting with her peripheral vision the open door and wet floor.

A blast of cold air met Evelyn at the door to the girls' room. The window was wide open, the curtain blowing in the icy wind. The screaming was coming from the closet.

Sassy was sitting on the closet floor, hugging her legs to her chest and rocking, her head thrown back as she screamed. Her mouth was wide, her eyes were closed, and her entire body trembled.

"Sassy! *Sassy!* What is it?" Evelyn tried to shout over her niece's screams. She got only more screaming in answer. She reached out to the child, trying to embrace and calm her, but as soon as she touched Sassy, her screaming went up in pitch, her eyes flew open, and she started frantically slapping and kicking at her aunt.

Seeing that her actions were only making Sassy worse, Evelyn backed off, ran to the window, and closed it. She noticed footprints in the snow on the roof of the back porch, just below the window. They led to the edge, where it looked as if someone had slid off the roof to the ground below.

Oh, my God! thought Evelyn. *Sassy must have been frightened by a burglar.* But then, where was Cindy?

"MAMA!" Another scream from the hallway joined Sassy's.

Evelyn ran out of the room. Devin stood in the hallway outside the bathroom. His little face was pale and screwed up tight, ready to release a wailing torrent of tears as only infants can.

Missy backed out of the bathroom her face pale. Short, panting shrieks came from her gaping mouth.

Evelyn ran to the bathroom. She slipped on the wet floor and grabbed at the edge of the tub to catch herself. She landed on one knee as behind her Missy's shrieks lengthened into one long scream sounding in unison with her sister's. At the same moment, Cindy's face floated to the soapy surface of the bathwater, open eyes and mouth filled with suds. It parted the froth for a moment and sank again.

Evelyn's screams joined those of her two nieces. Together with the wailing shrieks of Devin's crying, they made a chorus of such horror and anguish it was worthy of hell's damned.

Mahoney brought the news to Bill. He laid it out straight but gently, the way he'd always thought he'd like to receive such news.

For Bill, the next seventy-two hours became an array of moments frozen in a series of photographs

—records of anguish—he imagined taken by his father. The pictures were stapled to his memory with spikes: picking out a dress for Cindy to wear at the wake and funeral; Sassy, in a deep, comalike shock, hooked up to feeding tubes to keep her alive; Cindy in her coffin at the wake surrounded by a wall of flowers that in life would have had her sneezing and puffy-eyed in seconds; the fearful, sad, forever-changed faces of Missy and Devin.

At times during those three days, events seemed to speed up, everything moving with the jerky pace of old silent slapstick movies: lines of people he didn't know shuffling their condolences and sympathies by him; the mayor pressing the flesh of every mourner in the funeral home in hopes of getting their votes in the upcoming election year; the priest, obviously soused, reading the funeral service at the graveside.

These scenes were out-of-control-comic intervals that made him afraid he would laugh out loud like a madman at the most inappropriate times.

He experienced one of those ridiculous yet horrifying moments in the funeral home men's room the second day of the wake. He was in one of the stalls, just sitting, wanting to be alone for a while, when he heard two men come in and start talking while they went about their business.

"Son of a bitchin' thing to happen, huh?" The first voice was nasal and high-pitched. It was followed by the sound of water running.

"She was a nice-lookin' babe." The second voice was heavier and gravelly.

"Captain Mahoney's ordered a detail round the

clock to protect the kids and the one down at UMASS Medical in Worcester," the first voice said. "You gotta feel for the guy. It's bad enough dealing with being in danger yourself without having to worry about your family. That's too much."

Bill realized he was listening to two cops, probably from the full-dress detachment the chief had sent over.

"I don't gotta feel nuthin' for the bastard," the second voice sneered. "I think he offed his wife himself."

"What?" The first was shocked.

"Starkovski said that last night. I saw him at the Ale Horse. He thinks Gage might even be the Video Killer. You should've heard the stuff Starkovski was telling me. Gage knew stuff no one else but the killer would know."

"I don't know about that," the first voice countered. "I've heard the guy is some kind of methodical and can see stuff other people would need a magnifying glass to see."

"Yeah, right. And when he goes off duty he assumes the disguise of Clark Kent, mild-mannered reporter," the second voice scoffed.

The two left, but Bill remained in the stall. It had been all he could do while listening to the policemen not to laugh hysterically, and he didn't know why. He giggled now, bending over the bowl on wobbly legs, and felt as though he was falling out of himself, headfirst, right into the toilet.

The Grace Simonds perspective, he thought and giggled louder.

He felt dizzy and dropped to one knee, resting his

head on an arm slung over the seat. He had an image of the bowl as the opening of a huge bottle of whiskey that he could dive into and drown. The next instant, he imagined it was a giant camera lens. He knew who was behind it.

"Who are you?" he croaked.

The next thing he knew, he was being helped off the bathroom floor by Mahoney and the chief.

That night, the incident returned to him in his dreams. Again he was leaning over the bowl, questioning his own reflection's identity. A black-and-white photograph floated on the surface of the water. It was a picture of his father.

A hand shot up from out of the drain and clutched the photo, crumpling it. The forearm was scarred with many circular, shiny burn scars. The hand slowly drew back toward the drain.

The hand was getting away with the photograph. Bill shoved his hand into the water and grasped the disappearing fingers. He pulled against the arm, fighting to drag the Video Killer out and reveal him once and for all. He pulled harder. A shoulder appeared, squeezing through. An ear came through. The arm was out of the water up to the elbow. He grabbed the forearm with two hands, braced his foot on the rim of the bowl and pulled with all his might. A clump of wet gray hair showed at the drain opening. It grew thicker. A forehead came into view. Eyebrows. Eyes, looking back at him.

With the sound of an inflated balloon being twisted, the head squeaked through and he looked into his father's eyes. Laughing bubbles rose from his dad's mouth to break on the surface, releasing watery echoes of his mirth.

Bill woke, sweating in the dark, tears streaming down his face. The dream gripped him like a revelation. His building fears had been valid all along. The Video Killer wasn't just a person, or even a group of people; he was the embodiment of his father, and of the part of Bill that had blindly allowed his father to go on killing.

The trauma of the last few days, lack of sleep, and the terror of the nightmare made him latch on to the idea as a secret salvation. It led him to a decision of what he had to do if things were ever going to be set right.

In the middle of the night, in the dark carnival of emotions his mind had become, Bill Gage paid for a ride on the Tunnel of Revenge.

CHANNEL 22

Operation Wilbur— Part 2

 Ivy spent over a week in bed and out of school, his mother doting on him, bringing him tea and juice and putting the TV in his room. Ivy loved every minute of it. He napped in the afternoons and felt well enough by the fifth day, two days before Christmas, to eat some canned chicken soup and toast for supper.

His mother was going to call in sick for work every day and night, too, but Ivy assured her that he would be okay while she went to work. She reluctantly gave in each day and night and went, but called him every hour to see how he was. She hugged and kissed him, more rarities, and fussed over him, fixing his pillows, making sure he had enough juice, before she could go each time.

He went through the routine with her again tonight. After she was gone, he got out of bed and pulled his box of books out of the closet. He *was* feeling much better and he had to admit it was because of his mother's attentions. He had thought he was too old for a little loving care to make him feel so good, but now he thought maybe a person never got too old for that.

He thought about the video he had seen of little

Wilbur and the nasty woman. With everything else that had happened, he hadn't done anything further about it. For the first time it occurred to him that the woman might be Wilbur's mother. He was so young in the video, not more than six or seven; his mother had to have known what was going on.

Ivy felt a pang of guilt, remembering how he'd condemned his mother as a bad parent. Compared to a lot of others, he guessed she could win Mother of the Year. He saw now that her distant attitude was really weariness. After all, she worked two jobs to support them because she refused to go on Welfare. The pang of guilt sharpened when he thought of her slaving away at two jobs to support him while he went around thinking bad thoughts about her and feeling sorry for himself.

He took the series of James Bond novels out of the box and placed them in order from first to last, beginning with *Casino Royale* and ending with *The Man with the Golden Gun*. Since his dog Bond had died and Ivy had lost Henry's watch, these books and the pair of one-eyed binoculars were the only things he had to remember Barbara by.

Thoughts of his lost watch sent him to the window where he looked down at Crazy Wilbur's house. From here, Ivy could see into the second floor and the living room windows on this side of the house. Crazy Wilbur's house was dark. He wondered if Wilbur had found the watch yet. Ivy had looked around Wilbur's yard the day after he broke in, hoping he'd dropped the watch outside, but didn't find it. Knowing that if Wilbur *had* found

Ivy's watch he'd be wary of burglars, Ivy had been too scared to risk breaking in again.

Ivy remembered that the last time he'd seen Slice Sanchez had been the day before Barbara and Bond died. The punk had been going into Crazy Wilbur's. *That's right!* He had almost forgotten that with all that had gone on lately.

Operation Wilbur had been forgotten when Barbara and Bond died. He hadn't bothered going to the library to search for the phone number and address of NAMBLA, the name he had found in Wilbur's. He hadn't cared about anything since then. Now, remembering he'd seen Slice go into Crazy Wilbur's, Ivy thought it was time to resume spying on his neighbor. Hopefully, he might discover a clue as to the whereabouts of Sanchez. He'd heard nothing from Officer Cote, who'd promised to be in touch if and when Slice turned up.

He went out to the living room and checked the ugly Felix the Cat clock on the wall. Eight forty-five. His mother wouldn't be home until after midnight, and Wilbur usually left for work at ten thirty. That would give him almost two hours between the time Wilbur left and Ivy's mom got home to break into Wilbur's and have another look around. He didn't relish the idea of going into that house again, but if it was his only lead to finding Slice and exacting revenge, he'd just have to buck up and be brave like 007 and get the job done no matter what.

Tonight, he resumed *Operation Wilbur*.

Ivy put on his long johns and the dark sweat suit he'd worn last time, so that he wouldn't have to wear a bulky coat. He put on his sneakers, grabbed his fur-lined gloves, and left, locking the door behind him and slipping the key deep into his sock.

The night sky was a milky, gray-white color. The news had predicted the winter's first big blizzard, a nor'easter, by morning. Ivy hoped school would be cancelled tomorrow.

Ivy was traveling light, carrying only his plastic card and flashlight and wearing his chlorine bleach squirt gun stuck in the back of his pants. Ivy figured he could pick the kitchen window lock like last time, or if Wilbur had secured it, he could try the door again. At worst he could look in the window.

He didn't waste time with applying the Bond stairway-stealth-walk tonight. Not having to worry about his mother, who was at work, he knew no one else in the tenement would pay any attention to his leaving. And since he only had about an hour and a half before his mom came home, he had to move.

He dashed across the driveway and vaulted the low fence, holding the plastic card in his teeth. He didn't stop on the other side but kept going, racing to the porch. Only then did he stop, dropping to a crouch while he caught his breath and listened for sounds of pursuit.

He counted to sixty very slowly, then went up the stairs to the kitchen door. The whitish sky reflected the city's lights, providing a glowing ethereal illumination.

Ivy checked the first window. It had been nailed shut! Crazy Wilbur *definitely* knew someone had been in his house. The second window was also nailed shut. He went to the door, remembering to be cautious with the squeaky storm door. He grabbed the handle, picked the door up on its hinges, and pulled it open with one quick continuous motion. The door emitted only a tiny creak. He slid his backside against the inside of the storm door to hold it open and went to work on the inside door, trying not to jiggle the storm door and make it squeak.

After twenty minutes of trying, the plastic card was bent and useless. Ivy was frustrated and angry. "I suck as a secret agent," he breathed, fogging up the kitchen door glass. Careless of the noise, he let the storm door close and stared at the house. He went back to the windows, shining the light around inside, but could see nothing that might tell him about Slice Sanchez.

Ivy shut off the flashlight and stood in the darkness, thinking. There had to be another way for him to get into the house. He left the porch and walked to the side of the house facing his tenement, remaining in the shadows, checking the other first-floor windows. The ones on the side of the house were too high for him even to see if they were locked, much less climb through. He looked for something to stand on, but found nothing.

He noticed a cellar window and crouched on the hard, crusty snow for a closer look. The window was dark. Cupping his hand over the lens of the flashlight, Ivy turned it on and shone it in the window. Nothing but the light's reflection shone back. He leaned closer. The window was painted black! He shut off the light and duck-walked to the next cellar window. It too was painted black.

Weird, Ivy thought. *Why not just hang curtains? What are they trying to hide?* He tried to push the window open. It was either locked or stuck solid. He went back to the first one and tried it, also without any luck. The basement windows facing the back-yard were no more yielding, but one of the cellar windows on the far side of the house gave a little when he pushed on it. He pushed again, but it was stuck. Ivy put down the flashlight and sat in front of the window, placing a foot on each end of the wooden frame. He pushed with his legs. A splintering shriek split the night and the window gave a little more. He paused, listening tensely but hearing nothing, and pushed again. Another shriek; the window moved another few inches.

One more should do it, Ivy thought. He waited, listening again. A car was coming down Leighton Street. He watched for its headlights and timed his next push with the car's passage. The sound of the engine helped to mask the final scream from the wood as the window sprang free and swung inward, and his feet thrust into the dark emptiness of the basement.

He pulled his feet back quickly. *Geez,* he thought mentally chastising himself, *you'd think something was going to grab you and pull you in.* He peered into the dark, felt a draft of warm, slightly musty air rising to his face.

Ivy cupped the flashlight and turned it on again. He could see a concrete floor and a portion of smooth concrete wall, but not much else. He leaned forward and shone the light straight down. Boxes were stacked to within a foot of the window. With a deep breath to steel his nerves, Ivy clicked off the flashlight and slipped it into the back of his sweat pants. Lying on his stomach and pushing himself back over the hard snow, he lowered his legs into the cellar until he felt his foot brush the top box.

The boxes he tried to climb in on were cardboard and not packed solidly full, thus providing little stable footing. If he'd been any heavier, they would not have supported him and he would have been sent sprawling head first onto the concrete floor.

He weathered a couple of unsteady moments and made it down. Ivy took out the flashlight and turned it on. He was in a small storage room. Against the left-hand wall were boxes labeled LOWEL SOFT LIGHTS—1500. Against another wall were boxes labeled FUSES and CABLES.

There was no door on the frame opening into more darkness. Ivy let the flashlight's illumination lead him through, into a large open room that contained a narrow bed with a stained mattress and a couple of chairs on a braided rug in the middle of the floor. Over the area, track lighting, sporting many thick black canister lights, was attached to the ceiling. He flashed the light around some more, not worrying about it's being seen from outside now that he was away from the open window and with all the other basement windows blackened.

In the far right corner, a tub was set up on a small square tile section of the floor. On the ceiling above it was more track lighting. Running like metal veins along the floor were thin, round, wiring casings, like pipes, which led to several four-socket electric boxes.

Ivy continued around the room with the light, trying to figure out why they needed all the track lighting and extra electrical boxes in their basement, and why they had painted the windows black.

His eyes were drawn back to the narrow bed. It looked familiar somehow. It dawned on him that it might be the bed from the video. Wilbur had been tied to a bed like this when the woman did nasty things to him and burned him with her cigarette.

This is where they made that film, Ivy surmised. He went over to the bed and examined it. Though there were no distinguishing features, it looked like the same bed. The mattress was old and badly stained. Some of the spots were blackish-maroon, nasty-looking things. Remembering the things the woman had done to Wilbur in the video, Ivy didn't care to investigate those stains more closely. He looked at the extra electric boxes and figured those had been used to plug in the lights and cameras and sound equipment needed to make a movie.

"This is a movie studio," he said softly to himself. He wondered what kind of sicko would make movies like the one he had seen, and worse, what kind of pervert would like to watch those movies, even paying to see them. Ivy shuddered at the thought of ever meeting such a person and backed away from the bed. He remembered one of the first books Barbara had given him to read, *The Strange Case of Dr. Jekyll and Mr. Hyde.* That was the type of person who would make and watch movies like that, Ivy thought. On the surface, they'd appear as normal as anyone, but underneath, they were sick and full of dark crawly thoughts.

Ivy went over to the tub in the corner. It was the deep, old-fashioned kind with stubby, ornate legs. There was a deeply ingrained rust stain/bathtub ring around the inside of the tub, about halfway up. The drain was plugged with a rubber stopper but where the faucets and water spout should have been there were holes in the porcelain. As far as Ivy could see, the tub wasn't hooked up to any plumbing at all.

He leaned forward, seeing something in the corner behind the tub. He put the light on the floor and got down on all fours, reaching under the end of the tub and pulling the object out. It was a fleece-lined dungaree jacket, exactly the same kind Slice Sanchez wore and had been wearing the day Ivy saw him go into Wilbur's house.

Ivy held the jacket up, turning it in the flashlight beam. It had a dark stain down the back and on the shoulders. Whatever the substance was that had stained the jacket, there had been a lot of it. It crumbled and flaked off as he turned it. The flaky residue looked like rust under the flashlight.

If it was Slice's jacket, why had he left it here? Was it because of the stain? Did that happen here and then he couldn't wear it home? Maybe Crazy Wilbur had offered to have it cleaned? Another, more plausible, image came to Ivy: Slice beating up on poor Wilbur for spilling something on his jacket. He could see Slice threatening Wilbur with his broken fingers (Ivy *had* to throw that in with a grin) to have the jacket cleaned. Maybe Wilbur had tried to clean it in the tub?

Ivy put the jacket back where he'd found it. His imagined scenario was plausible enough to explain the presence of Slice's jacket.

Ivy felt bad thinking of Wilbur at the mercy of Slice Sanchez. The fact that he was crazy had probably made the experience ten times worse for poor Wilbur. He'd probably never even understood why Slice was picking on him. Ivy's thirst for revenge burned brighter, thinking of such things. Slice certainly had a lot to pay for.

Ivy had seen enough of the basement. It was time to have a look upstairs. He went to the stairs at the front left corner of the basement and went up slowly, stopping for a few seconds whenever a step creaked.

The upstairs door opened on the kitchen. Ivy searched for his watch among the litter but had no luck. He went into the living room to do the same and to look for any clues that might lead him to Slice's whereabouts. He checked the floor and carpet, noticing a fresh dark stain in front of the cabinet that held the videotapes.

He turned, and the light played around the walls, away from the windows, flashing over something on the back wall that he couldn't see. It fell in the long shadow of an armchair. He stepped to the side and pointed the beam at the wall again. His skin went cold, then hot, then cold again all over his body. A keening, high-pitched moan came from between his clenched teeth.

On the back wall, hung by the neck with the

leather strap of the watch Barbara had given him, was the gutted, bloody corpse of Bond, James Bond.

Ivy's mother found him shivering in his bed under a pile of blankets when she got home from work at 12:20 A.M.

"I knew I should have stayed home," she lamented, her face worried. She felt his forehead. "Your temp is up again. Did you get out of bed while I was gone?"

Ivy shook his head no, and tried to stop his teeth from chattering. Since fleeing from Crazy Wilbur's, Ivy had barfed three times. Every time he thought of Bond, James Bond's body hung on the wall, his stomach folded in on itself and sent its contents up his throat.

He was glad when his mother got home. He couldn't tell her anything, of course, but her attention and concern helped. She gave him aspirin, then lay on the bed next to him, spooning her body next to his to warm him, and sang "Hey Jude" softly. His shivering soon stopped and his eyes grew heavy. His body felt numb, dead. He slipped into the deep dreamless sleep of emotional shock with one last clear thought: He had to *kill Wilbur Clayton.*

CHANNEL 23

Waiting for Sassy
To Catch a Killer
The Invaders
Wilbur's Hobby
Ivy to the Rescue
Bill Gage—Avenger

Bill Gage sat in the shadows at the side of Sassy's hospital bed and held her limp left hand in both of his. Since Cindy's funeral, this was the fourth straight day of his vigil by Sassy's bedside. Missy and Devin were staying with Evelyn. At least he didn't have to worry about them for the time being.

He'd moved back into the house against the advice of everyone he knew, but he was there so little anyway it wasn't having any effect on him. His routine had become simple: get up at 4:00 A.M.—if he'd been able to sleep at all—and drive to Worcester, twenty-five miles to the south of Crocker, to spend the day with his stepdaughter. Sassy had been flown to the UMASS Medical Center, which boasted the best neurologists and the latest technology for treating coma. On his way home at night, he stopped in to see Missy and Devin at Ev's.

This was Sassy's ninth day in a coma.

During the day Bill kept in frequent telephone contact with Mahoney on the Video Killer case. They were stalled, with nothing to link Cindy's death to the Video Killer. Yet Bill knew—and he thought Mahoney felt the same way—that it had been he.

Bill looked at Sassy, hating the sight of the tubes running from her nose and mouth. He knew she had seen the Video Killer up close. She could identify him. From what Evelyn had told him and from Mahoney's report, after killing Cindy the bastard had gone to do Sassy, too, but she started screaming and then Evelyn came in. The perp jumped out Sassy's window onto the porch roof and to the ground, as evidenced by the open window and the footprints on the roof and ground. The footprints led to the street and disappeared.

If Sassy hadn't been sick, she would have been at Evelyn's and Cindy would have been Christmas shopping and this never would have happened. As he sat there waiting and praying for Sassy to come out of it so she could identify the killer, it was easy to torture himself with such thoughts and more self-incriminating ones—like if he'd had the sense to have an unlisted number the perp wouldn't have found out where he and Cindy lived so easily.

He told himself he was concerned with Sassy's health, but he didn't deny that his foremost objective was to get the information she had, no matter how cold that might seem. As far as he was concerned, he could do nothing better for Cindy or Sassy than to catch the killer.

He had a feeling the killer had been after him. Mahoney thought he meant to kill Cindy and Sassy as a warning to Bill. Bill thought that might be true, but the perp's primary objective had been to get him; he was sure of it.

Why? his cynical side asked. *Because you think he's possessed by your father's ghost?*

Though it was nothing that melodramatic or supernatural, essentially that was the truth. Somehow the perp wanted a confrontation with him, and that confrontation was going to be Bill's last chance to deal with the past, whether the perp knew it or not.

Of course, if Sassy remained in a coma, they might never catch the Video Killer. Even if she came out of it, there was a good chance she wouldn't remember anything. Her doctors had warned him that she might come out of the coma— which was really more a state of shock—with complete amnesia concerning the events surrounding her mother's death.

Bill was praying against that. He sat by the bed hour after hour until eight, sometimes nine o'clock at night, holding her hand and willing her to wake up and tell him who killed her mother.

Last night he'd dreamed it had finally happened. It was one of those dreams that starts out so ordinary and familiar and *real* that you have no idea you are dreaming. Soon, though, the dream takes a left turn into nightmareville and you jolt awake with the cold sweats.

In the dream, he was going to the hospital to be

with Sassy. As he approached her room a doctor came running out proclaiming a breakthrough. Sassy was out of the coma, the doctor exclaimed. Bill rushed into the room and found her awake, sitting up and smiling.

He asked her if she remembered the man she saw. She began describing the killer—gray hair, blue eyes, blue shirt, dark blue pants, black shoes— and it began to dawn on Bill whom she was describing.

"And he had a camera and took my picture," was the last thing Sassy said in the dream. That's when sleep had fled and the shakes had taken over.

Bill's eyes wandered over the cards, stuffed animals, and flowers that filled the room. His eyes fell on a hospital calendar tacked to a corkboard. He realized it was Christmas Eve and felt like crying.

He bolted up straight. Had he just felt pressure on his fingers from Sassy's hand?

"Sassy?" he said softly.

She didn't move. She remained as she had since her screams had stopped in the ambulance on her way to the emergency room.

He had felt it. He was sure of it. His first instinct was to jump up and get a doctor, but the possibility that what he'd felt had been a muscle twitch kept him in his chair. The doctors had said that could happen.

"Sassy? If you can hear me, squeeze my hand again."

He waited. Seconds stretched to half a minute and seemed like hours before he felt her squeeze, oh so weakly. He realized he had been holding his breath and let it out.

" 'S okay, baby." He panted like a winded runner. "Take your time. Gain your strength. I'll be right here."

He sat and waited. Where before he'd gone through near-constant bouts of anxiety and frustration, now he was relaxed. He had become more and more resolute that no matter how long it took, he was going to finish this thing himself, personally. He was going to put away the bastard—an image of his father flashed in his mind—who had killed Cindy and done this to Sassy.

Ivy swore to his mother that he was all right, but she insisted he stay home from school one more day. She reasoned that it was Christmas Eve, the last day of school and a half day at that. She made up the couch in the living room for him, gave him toast and tea, turned on the TV and the lights of the tabletop artificial Christmas tree, and went to work.

Ivy didn't really mind having another day off from school—that was always a welcome thing—but he'd be stuck in the house for the whole day and evening. Even with his mother at work, he knew she'd call ten times to check on him, so he'd better be there when she did. And later when she got home, she wouldn't let him go out because she was an adamant believer that if you were too sick to go to school you were too sick to go out and play after school, even if staying home had been her idea.

Ivy had been hoping to see Officer Cote today to tell him he'd found the real killer of Bond, James

Bond. He'd awakened several times during the night, dreaming that he was in Crazy Wilbur's house again looking at Bond hung from the wall. He lay awake after each time, wondering why Wilbur would want to kill his dog. The answer came to him without reason, but with a cold hard feeling of truth: *Slice Sanchez!*

At some point during the restless night, Ivy had figured it out. Slice must have seen him spying on Wilbur—*probably while stalking me,* he realized. The day Slice went into Crazy Wilbur's, he must have been going to tell Wilbur what Ivy was up to, probably with the hope of enlisting his aid in getting Ivy.

It was the only thing Ivy could think of. Either that, or Slice had killed Bond and nailed the dog there himself. That could mean Slice was hiding out in Wilbur's house, though Ivy had seen no sign of him. It didn't matter really whether Wilbur had done it alone or in cahoots with Slice; he'd make them both pay. He spent the night's sleepless moments plotting revenge until he drifted off to slumber again.

He woke in the early gray light from a different dream, a dream of Barbara. In it, Ivy was standing outside Wilbur's house, holding a gun, waiting for the two puppy-killing bastards to come out. A voice called to him from across the street. It was Barbara, standing in her old bathrobe.

"Don't waste your life on sour, bitter revenge. Don't kill your potential. Everyone gets what's coming to them in the end," she said to him.

The memory of the dream brought tears, and he cried himself back to sleep. In the morning he vowed to turn Wilbur over to the cops and let them take care of it.

When his mother made him stay in, he considered calling the police station and asking for Officer Cote, or even reporting Wilbur to whoever answered. He realized that if he did that—even if he reported it directly to Cote—the cops would come up to the apartment and his mother would find out about Bond and Barbara and his breaking into Wilbur's.

That was another thing. How was he going to tell the cops about what he saw in Wilbur's without getting in trouble for breaking and entering? He figured he could tell the cops about seeing Bond on the wall by saying he'd been cutting through Clayton's yard and had seen him through the living room window. He'd have to hope none of the cops would realize he was too short to see in those windows.

That wouldn't work. Another idea occurred to him. He could make an anonymous phone call. But what would he say? If he told them about Wilbur killing his dog, Officer Cote would probably be sent out to investigate, since the neighborhood was his beat. He'd know right away that the anonymous call had come from Ivy. He had to have something else to turn Wilbur in for.

The videotapes! But Wilbur had been a victim in the one Ivy had seen. So what? They were still illegal. The fact that Wilbur still had them must mean he liked them. But how could Ivy tell the cops about them? He wanted this phone call to be quick so it couldn't be traced.

I'll tell them Wilbur's trying to molest kids in the

neighborhood, Ivy decided. *They'll check it out and find Bond and maybe even Slice Sanchez hiding out. When they find the videotapes, they'll think the call about child molesting was legit, and old Crazy Wilbur will be in a heap of trouble.*

Ivy got off the couch and went into his mother's room to look out her windows at Leighton Street. A school bus went by, but there was no sign of Officer Cote. He went into his room and looked over at Wilbur's. The car still wasn't in the driveway, even though it was after eight o'clock. Ivy decided to wait until Wilbur came home before calling the cops.

Wilbur's car backed into his driveway an hour later, and he got out and went into his house. A terrible thought occurred to Ivy. *He'd forgotten to close the basement window last night!* In his desire to get out of that house, he'd forgotten all about leaving the cellar window open. He hurried to the phone and dialed the police department from the emergency list stuck on the back of the receiver.

I hope they go over before Wilbur finds that window, Ivy thought, *because now, Wilbur will* know it was me that broke in. If he could kill Bond, what would he do if he caught me? Ivy thought about what had been written in blood on Bond's box, the words almost hovering before his eyes:

YOU'RE NEXT!

Sergeant Grinds hit the disconnect button and sat staring at the switchboard for a long moment.

"What's up?" the dispatcher next to him asked.

"Anonymous call. Some kid claiming his next-door neighbor is trying to molest kids in the neighborhood. The kid didn't sound like he was playing a prank, but I don't know."

"He give you a name and an address of the suspect?" the dispatcher asked.

"Yeah, seventy Leighton Street." Grinds answered.

The dispatcher looked at the duty roster on the wall. "That's a rough part of town. I think we've got a cruiser patrolling that neighborhood at night. Here it is. Cote's got it tonight, four to midnight. He can check it out then."

Ivy tried to keep a vigilant watch out the window for the cops, but if they'd shown up by three-thirty when his mother came home, he must have missed them. It didn't really matter if he saw them arrest Wilbur, but it would help quench the thirst for revenge that he still had.

When his mother got home she immediately went to him, checking to see if he still felt well. She made hot chocolate for them and produced a package of Oreos, his favorite cookie.

"I thought we'd splurge a little, seeing as how it's Christmas Eve and all," she said, putting the cookies out on the table with the cocoa mugs. A few moments later there was a knock on the back door.

"I've got another surprise," she said, getting up and going to the door. It was Ronny, the delivery boy for Watson's Market. He had two big boxes of groceries that he brought in and placed on the counter. He waved and winked at Ivy before leaving.

Ivy's eyes were wide with wonder. His mother had *never* bought so many groceries. He got up from the table, a cookie in hand and one in his mouth, and looked in the boxes. There were canned sweet potatoes, real Maine potatoes, cranberry sauce, a couple of different kinds of stuffing mixes, cans of corn and green beans, packaged biscuits to warm in the oven, a cake mix and a can of prepared frosting, and a box of *chocolates!* Ivy couldn't believe it.

"Tomorrow, we are going to have a Christmas feast!" his mother said proudly as he "oohed" at all the food.

"But aren't you working at the restaurant tomorrow?" Ivy asked. With the plastic factory closed on Christmas Day, his mother usually signed on to work the holiday at the restaurant where she worked nights. Since his father had died, Ivy'd had Christmas dinner each year in the kitchen of the restaurant while his mother worked. He'd then taken the bus home to play with the few toys his mother had bought him for Christmas. She'd bring leftovers home around seven, and they'd have supper before his mother drank herself to sleep with a bottle of wine and Christmas specials on TV for company.

"I'm taking the day off!" Her smile was so genuinely happy that Ivy had to smile too. "I'm going to go in at five tonight, though," she added, glancing at the clock.

Ivy helped her put the groceries away, marveling at all the goodies she'd bought, like mince pie, and Christmas-tree-shaped sugar cookies, and chocolate doughnuts for breakfast. The real surprise, though, was the ten-pound turkey she pulled from the box.

"Wow!" Ivy cheered. "We'll be eating turkey for weeks!" They laughed together.

Ivy felt something had changed between him and his mother in the week he'd been home sick. Something had opened up, or maybe something had healed. She really seemed to be in the Christmas spirit, looking forward to a real *family* holiday for the first time since his father's death six years ago.

Ivy could sense an opportunity for some real change in their lives if he could keep this special feeling with his mother going beyond the holidays. He wasn't exactly sure how to do that. He considered starting now, by telling her about Barbara and Bond in the hopes that they'd *really* start talking, but he was leery still.

They sat and finished their cocoa, and then his mother got up to make him something for supper, but he told her not to worry about it. It was after four and she had to get ready to go to the restaurant early. While she went into the bathroom for a quick shower, Ivy lounged at the table, enjoying his cookies and his newfound feeling of warmth.

He couldn't help thinking how strange it was that while in the depths of depression over the loss of Barbara and Bond, he and his mother had rediscovered each other. He guessed a lot of it had to do with Christmas, but there was more to it than that. It was as if his mother was coming out of hibernation.

Though Ivy had been very close to his dad, or maybe because of that, his emotional wounds had healed more quickly than hers, though they were scarred over with desire for revenge against Dr. Peabody. His mother hadn't been able to latch on to a driving emotion like revenge, so it had taken her five years to get over it.

Barbara's words about silver linings and good things coming out of bad certainly seemed to be true. If he and his mother came together and remained close, wasn't it because of all the bad things that had happened to him lately? Hadn't his mother sensed those things when she said he'd been moping around? But was the price he'd paid for getting his mother back worth it? He couldn't help wondering if it was worth Barbara's and Bond's dying, and all that had happened with Slice.

He decided *worth it* wasn't quite right. *Worth* had nothing to do with it. You couldn't put worth, or value, on a life, human or otherwise, or on his relationship with his mother. It had more to do with . . . *fairness.* That was it. It wasn't *fair* that he should lose two loved friends so that he could get his mother back, whom he never should have lost in the first place. There was no sense at all to it, no logic, but Barbara had said that was just the way things were and you couldn't change them, so don't worry about it.

Ivy's mother came out of her bedroom wearing the white blouse and black skirt that was her waitress's uniform. He was washing out the cocoa mugs at the sink.

"Thanks for doing those," she said, surprising Ivy with another first. "It's snowing pretty heavy out there. It looks like the roads are getting slippery. If the buses aren't running when I get off, I might have to call a cab. I could be late so don't worry and don't wait up. You want to be in bed before Santa comes."

Ivy looked at her quickly, the old reflex to denounce such baby stuff on the tip of his tongue until he saw his mother's mischievous grin and knew she was kidding. He immediately relaxed and smiled too. She hugged him, put on her coat, and left, promising to call later from the restaurant.

From the windows in her room Ivy watched her go. His eyes wandered over to Wilbur's house. Still no sign of the cops. It was 4:35 P.M. and as far as he could tell they hadn't shown up yet. They must have thought he was making a prank call.

I guess I'll have to talk to Cote in person after all, Ivy thought. That was going to be tough with tomorrow being Christmas. He doubted Cote would be around tomorrow. He hated to let it wait, but it would be only until the day after Christmas. Then he would find Officer Cote and tell him.

Ivy went into the living room and turned on the TV, watching *How the Grinch Stole Christmas* for a while. A little before eight, he went into his mother's room to look out at the building storm. The ringing phone—his mother calling—pulled him away from the window a moment before a police cruiser pulled up in front of Crazy Wilbur's house.

The Invaders.
Starring Roy Thinnes.
Pinkie raised, Jesus stands in the cellar doorway. He can feel the cold air. It leads Him down. He finds

the open window. He smiles in the darkness. *It's time to deal with the spy*.

Upstairs, Wilbur weeps and takes the dead dog from the wall. Mumbling Grandma's ritualistic *Hail Mary* chant, he wraps the puppy in a plastic bag and ties off the top.

The doorbell rings.

Carrying the bag with the dead dog in it, he goes to the front door. Through the large oval glass in the door, he can see a policeman standing on the front porch.

Static.

"We interrupt this broadcast with a special bulletin from the Emergency Broadcast System. This is not a test. We repeat, this is not a test. Turn off your tunnelvision now and hide. Turn off your tunnelvision now and—"

Closed circuit.

The officer grins with recognition when Jesus opens the door. Wilbur stands very still, hoping the cop won't see him.

"Wilbur! I didn't know you lived here."

The cop is friendly, sincere. He knows Wilbur from seeing him at the hospital emergency room.

"Hi, Jim." Wilbur swears he's never seen the cop before, but Jesus knows his name.

"How have you been? I haven't seen you much since they put me on four to twelve."

"Not bad," Jesus replies smoothly. "Is there something I can help you with?"

The cop looks embarrassed. "Yeah, well there is. We got a call today, from one of your neighbors, I

think, who claims you're molesting neighborhood
kids."

The cop mistakes the look of shock on Wilbur's
face as outrage at the suggestion. "I'm sorry, Wilbur. It must be a prank. If you don't mind, though,
can I come in and look around? That way I can tell
my sergeant I checked you out good and he'll be
sure the call was a fake."

"Sure," Jesus says. This fits His plans perfectly.
"We can kill two birds with one stone."

Wilbur wants to scream a warning at the cop but
Jesus strikes him dumb.

Ivy hung up and went back to the couch, shutting
the TV off. His mother wasn't able to talk long since
the restaurant was exceptionally busy despite the
storm. She was looking forward to making some
good tips.

She'd said another strange thing on the phone
that Ivy sat on the couch puzzling about for some
time. She had mentioned again his getting to bed
early before Santa came. This time she added, "My
mama used to tell me: Santa brings to good kids who
are in bed early the one gift they want the most and
think they'll never get."

What did she mean by that? The thing he wanted
most—for Barbara and Bond to be alive again—no
one could bring him, not even the mythical magical
Santa Claus.

Officer Cote suspected absolutely nothing going
into Wilbur's house. He liked Wilbur. The kid was
quiet and polite. He was sure the call had been a

prank. As he walked through the front hallway, the first thing that registered as unusual—but not so much so that it set off alarm bells—was the smell. The house was a myriad of smells, all of them bad. He couldn't even begin, nor did he want, to separate and identify their sources.

The second thing that struck him was the condition of the living room. It looked like something out of a disaster film. "What happened here?" he asked Wilbur.

"Nice, huh?" Wilbur answered, looking around. "I was renting out rooms to some college kids and they had a party and trashed the place last night while I was working."

"No shit." Cote could believe it. The kids at Crocker State, especially those in the fraternities, had given the police a lot of trouble this year. "You should press charges, Wilbur," Cote told him, sounding stuffed up from trying not to breathe through his nose.

"What is that smell?" he asked Wilbur.

"Oh, they broke the toilets, left garbage all over, burned food, you name it."

Cote felt bad for the kid. He had a nice setup with his own house to rent rooms out and some college jerks had to mess it up. He wondered how Wilbur had been able to afford the house and figured it must have been left to him by his parents or someone. He was going to try to broach the subject, more out of personal curiosity than any suspicion of Wilbur, but he noticed an unusual, dark stain that had dried in drips down the back wall of the living room.

"What did they do here?" He stepped closer to the wall.

"Oh, that? That's my hobby," Wilbur answered.

"Hobby?" Cote asked. He didn't get it.

Wilbur held out the black plastic trash bag and opened the top. "Here. Look," he said, handing the bag to Cote and going to the closet next to the stain on the wall.

Taking the trash bag, Cote looked at the spot on the wall again. "You know, it almost looks like"—he opened the bag and looked inside—*"blood."* His throat went dry, choking off the word.

The last thing that struck Officer Cote as unusual was the ax that he saw Wilbur swinging at him as he looked up from the dead puppy in the bag.

The next time Bill Gage consciously looked at his watch, he saw that it was almost 8:00 P.M., and nearly five hours had passed since Sassy's first signs of revival. She was definitely coming out of it now; it was official. The doctors had been in to check her and her heart rate was up, her breathing had increased, and brain activity appeared normal.

During the past five hours, he'd been running the case over in his mind, looking at photos and case files he'd brought with him. His eyes were sore, he had a headache, and he'd made no progress. He stretched in the chair and noticed a stack of schoolbooks on the table near the bathroom door. Missy had insisted that Bill bring Sassy's books and schoolwork with him faithfully to the hospital every other day since Cindy's funeral.

Bill stood and picked up the top one entitled *Your*

Body, a health and hygiene textbook for kids. He started flipping through it and stopped on the chapter titled: *Don't be afraid to tell!*

He brought it back to the chair and read through the chapter, which instructed children on what to do if they were molested or abused in any way. One sentence in particular caught his eye: *If you can't turn to your parents, tell some other adult, like your teacher, the bus driver, a doctor, the school nurse, a policeman, your dentist, or even a next-door neighbor. They'll help you.*

A big piece of the puzzle fell into place in Bill's mind with a resounding *click!* Two of the victims so far had been a teacher and a dentist. With growing excitement, Bill remembered that Grace Simonds had once been a human services major. If the killer knew her, as Bill suspected, he'd know that. And the latest victims, the unidentified couple, could be the perp's neighbors as he'd theorized.

That was it! That was why the perp was killing! That was the elusive pattern!

He put down the book, stood to go and call Mahoney, and saw Sassy's eyes open and close.

"Sassy!" He leaned over the bed, his hands pushing into the mattress next to his stepdaughter's body.

Her eyes fluttered open again and remained so. Eventually they focused on him. "Daddy," she whispered in a dry cackle.

Relief and pain pierced his heart and brought a lump of emotion to his throat. "I'm right here, honey."

She smiled and so did he. She closed her eyes and

opened them again a moment later. They were full of fear.

"Daddy, the cop . . ." she began, but her throat was too dry. Bill poured her a glass from the plastic water pitcher on the bed table.

After a couple of sips, she spoke again in a dreamy voice. "Did the cop get Mommy?" Her eyes looked as if they were having trouble staying focused.

Bill swallowed hard. "No, honey. The cops didn't get there in time. I'm sorry."

"Mommy's dead?" Her voice was a drifting whisper.

Tears rolled down Bill's cheeks as he fought to keep his voice under control. "Yes, honey," he barely managed to whisper.

"Then the cop got her," Sassy said, her voice barely audible. She seemed to be asleep in a second.

Bill leaned over her, wanting to wake her to ask if she remembered the killer. What she'd just said didn't sink in right away. When it did, he realized she had already answered his question.

He immediately thought of Frank Starkovski.

Sassy came awake, startled, her eyes staring frightfully at him. "Don't leave me," she rasped.

"It was a *cop* that killed Mommy?" Bill asked, eager to confirm it.

Sassy barely nodded. She began trembling. "Don't leave me," she pleaded again to his back as he grabbed his coat and headed for the door. His mind was so full of cold rage and deadly intent he didn't hear her. He strode out of the room, leaving Sassy to cry and call weakly after him.

* * *

Ivy got off the couch and wandered aimlessly around the apartment. He didn't feel like reading and there was nothing but sappy Christmas specials on TV. He'd already watched the Grinch, which was the only special worth watching year after year in his opinion.

Try as he might, he couldn't get his mind off Crazy Wilbur. He found himself wondering what kind of Christmas Wilbur would have. He felt sorry for the guy, especially since viewing that video, and the more he thought of it, the more he became certain that Slice Sanchez was still responsible for Bond's death, whether he put Wilbur up to it or just used Wilbur's house as a hideout.

But why nail Bond to the wall?

Because that was just the sort of nasty thing Slice would do.

He went into his room and looked out the window at the house next door. The storm was a raging blizzard now, a real nor'easter. He watched the flakes swirl and fantasized about Slice caught out in the wilderness in a storm like this. Lost. Freezing. Ivy grinned.

The back porch light came on at Wilbur's. A second later the kitchen door opened and Wilbur came out. He went to his car and opened the back door. Wilbur looked up sharply at Ivy's window, but Ivy ducked back, glad that he didn't have his bedroom light on.

Wilbur went into the house again and came out with someone who was having trouble walking. Wilbur had his arm under the other person's shoulder and was helping him to the open backseat door.

Wilbur leaned the unsteady person into the back-seat, then it looked as if he shoved him, but Ivy couldn't be sure. Wilbur went back into his house.

Who is that with Wilbur? Ivy wondered. There were no other cars in the driveway. He went into his mother's room to check the street. The van was still parked across the street, buried in snow. Parked directly in front of Wilbur's, with less snow covering it, was a patrol car.

The cops are there? Then who was that with Wilbur? Whoever it was had looked hurt. The cop? *Officer Cote?*

Ivy rushed back to his room, where he grabbed his knapsack from under his bed. He sprinted into the kitchen, ripping his coat from the wooden pegs by the bathroom door and ran out the back door, not stopping to check if it had locked.

He went down the back stairs two and three at a time, trying not to slip on the snow that was accumulating on the open stairway while at the same time keeping an eye out for Wilbur coming out of his house. Near the bottom, the odds, and his worn, smooth-bottomed sneakers, caught up with him and Ivy went sprawling on his butt, bumping down five steps to the bottom of the stairs.

He got to his knees, wincing at the pain and cold, but took advantage of his position hidden behind the first-floor porch railing to put on his coat and sling his knapsack onto his shoulders. On all fours he crawled to the short flight of cement stairs leading to the driveway.

The back porch light was still on at Wilbur's, but he was nowhere in sight. Ivy leaped from the porch and ran to the base of the picket fence. On the silent count of three, he jumped over the fence and scurried to the car as soon as he hit the ground.

He crouched behind the rear wheel and brushed snow off him. He took a couple of deep breaths and stuck his head up to peer over the fender. No sign of Crazy Wilbur. Ivy moved to the backseat window. He looked in.

It *was* a cop! He was lying on his stomach, one arm crumpled on the floor, the other twisted at an unnatural angle against the backseat. His head was turned toward the front seat, but Ivy couldn't tell if it was Officer Cote from all the blood covering the face.

Ivy dropped to a crouch and slid behind the rear wheel and fender again. He was having trouble facing the reality of what he had just seen. He had to look again, to convince himself that he wasn't wrong.

This was worse than he thought. He remembered the Video Killer everyone was talking about. He hadn't paid a lot of attention. If Wilbur would kill a cop, wasn't that pretty good proof that he might be the Video Killer? And didn't it confirm that the bastard had killed Bond, too? Ivy thought of Slice's rust-stained jacket in Wilbur's basement and realized it hadn't been rust but blood on the punk's jacket. And it must have been blood on the clothes he'd retrieved from Wilbur's trash.

I've got to call the cops, he thought. Even if they didn't believe him, he had to try. He started to stand and heard Wilbur come out of the house. Ivy crouched and peeked over the edge of the fender.

Wilbur was going around the front of the car to the driver's side, looking up at Ivy's window all the while.

Probably planning on how to get me, Ivy thought as he silently scrambled to the rear of the car. Wilbur got in and started the engine. Ivy caught a face full of exhaust and had to hold his hand over his mouth to keep from coughing.

Ivy didn't know what to do. Should he go back to the apartment and call the cops? Or should he follow Wilbur? With the storm there was enough snow on the roads for him to ski behind Wilbur's car while holding on to the rear fender. As his slip on the stairs had already shown, the soles of his sneakers were worn enough to allow it.

Wilbur put the car lights on and Ivy was bathed in red from the taillights. He had to make a decision quickly. If that was Officer Cote in the back seat, he might still be alive. If Wilbur was the Video Killer, he probably planned to murder him and film it as Ivy'd heard he did. Thoughts of Wilbur being raped on film flashed in Ivy's mind, and he wondered why he hadn't seen a connection before this. If Ivy went to call the cops and they didn't believe him, Officer Cote would die. But if Ivy followed Wilbur, he might get a chance to rescue the cop or at least distract Wilbur until the cops at the station figured out that one of their guys was missing.

The Bonneville began to pull away. Ivy made up his mind and grabbed hold of the bumper.

CHANNEL 24

To Tell the Truth
*Operation Wilbur—
Part 3*
Obsession!
*A Second Chance
at Love*
Complications
True Confessions
Ivy's Revenge

 Bill Gage got back to Crocker at 8:45 P.M. He drove the highway as fast as he dared in the storm, but that still wasn't as fast as the double-nickel limit. He headed straight for the station after taking the Crocker/ Fitchburg exit from Route 2. All the time he was driving, one thought repeated in his mind: Frank Starkovski was the Video Killer.

It had to be. If the killer was a cop, as Sassy had said, it had to be Starkovski. Irrationally, he mentally threw out all the other evidence that'd been compiled so far, including his recent revelation about the perp's motives. None of it pointed to Starkovski as the killer, but in his state, Bill didn't want to be told he was wrong. He just wanted blood.

Sassy had ID'd a *cop*. If it wasn't Starkovski, he was as good a place to start as any. But Bill had a very strong gut feeling about this. He *knew* it was Starkovski.

Mike Mahoney was still at the station when Bill arrived. Bill charged into his office, breathless.

"We've got him," Mahoney said, stunning Bill.

"What? You know it's Starkovski?" Bill cried.

It was Mahoney's turn to be stunned. "Starkovski? No. The perp's name is Wilbur Clayton. Someone called him in for child molesting, but the dispatcher thought it was a crank and didn't send the call up to me. He sent an Officer Cote to check it out. When the officer missed his check-in time, another car was sent out and found Cote's car in front of this Clayton's house. The officer went in and found the place a mess except for one very neat room. There were copies of videotapes in the house with the same titles as the Video Killer's tapes. There was also some literature and mail with the Tunnelvision Studios and NAMBLA logos on them. Hanson's got a team of uniforms over there now helping him tear the place apart. Also, Larken got a report from the FBI on Tunnelvision Studios, run by one Joseph Dreybeck, last known address, Keene, NH. They sent a list of confiscated films, and one of them is titled *Smokin' in the Boys' Room.*

According to a synopsis the feds attached, the film shows a small naked boy being tortured with a lit cigarette end. A report of a missing couple, the Smiths, came in a little while ago too, made by Mrs. Smith's sister. She's coming in to look at photos, but the interesting thing is that the Smiths live right behind Wilbur Clayton. Ten to one they're the unlucky couple in the last tape."

Bill refused to believe, even in the face of such evidence. "It's not him!" he stated adamantly. "Sassy came out of her coma and I talked to her. She saw the killer. She said it was a *cop!* It has to be Starkovski! That's why he's been leaking info—to feed his twisted ego and toy with us. It all fits!" Bill said, his voice tense.

"Bill," Mahoney replied calmly, slowly, "it's not Starkovski."

"But Sassy saw a cop—"

"I know. I know." Mahoney held up his hand to stop Bill. "Wilbur Clayton works as a security guard at Crocker Hospital on the eleven-to-seven shift."

Bill started to protest again, then stopped. *A security guard at Crocker Hospital!* Their uniforms were exactly the same as the Crocker Police Department's. In fact, their badges identified them as Crocker Police Auxiliary, but Sassy wouldn't know the difference.

"Ah, shit," Bill groaned. He felt like an idiot.

"It's okay," Mahoney said. "You've got a right to jump to conclusions. I would have done the same thing under the circumstances. Officer Cote hasn't turned up or reported in yet."

"He wants a cop," Bill said softly. "That's why he came after me."

"I called the hospital security chief, who checked with his three-to-eleven guard. Clayton's car is parked behind the East Wing Building, which is abandoned. Levi was supposed to check out the building before when he was checking empty industrial sites, but because the hospital uses it for storage, he didn't think it was a plausible place for the perp's studio.

"Clayton is due to go on duty at eleven, so I don't think he'll be going anywhere, especially in this storm. The security chief and a maintenance engineer are going to meet us at the hospital with floor plans for the East Wing Building. I've got cruisers already on the way, so we'd better get going too."

On the way to the hospital, a chagrined Bill apologized for flying off the handle, but Mahoney brushed it aside. Bill went on to explain what he'd figured out earlier: The killer was getting revenge against professional people, social workers, teachers, dentists, and so on, who didn't see that he was being abused. While he talked, he remembered that Grace Simonds and her beau had been parking near the hospital on the night she was killed. It fitted with everything Mike had told him, and the attack on Cote reinforced it.

Ivy crouched behind the Bonneville as the car came to a stop behind Crocker Hospital. At first, skiing behind Wilbur's car had been fun. Soon, though, the cold snow in his face and eyes made it excruciating. He'd forgotten his gloves and was forced to grip the freezing chrome bumper with his bare hands. Once, when the car speeded up, he lost his balance and was dragged on his belly for a few blocks, getting the front of his coat and pants wet. Finally the car had stopped at a stop sign and he was able to right himself. He'd almost lost it coming up Hospital Hill, too.

Wilbur shut off the lights and the engine. Ivy pried his cramped and frozen fingers from the bumper, unable to straighten them right away. Wilbur opened his car door and got out. There was nowhere nearby for Ivy to hide. He had no choice. He grabbed the bumper again with his aching hands and pulled himself under the rear end of the car. He held his breath watching Wilbur's feet move around the back of the car to the rear door on the other side. Wilbur got the unconscious or (Ivy hoped not) dead policeman out of the backseat with great difficulty. Supporting him as he had before, Wilbur carried the cop to a solid metal fire door and went into the hospital.

Exhausted, Ivy remained sheltered under the car, blowing warm air on his frozen fingers, and counted out five minutes silently before following. The fire door was propped open with a wedge of wood. He opened it and went through into a dark stairwell. Wide concrete steps with a tiered iron railing went up into the darkness. Ivy could just make out a shadowy landing about a dozen steps up. More steps went up from there. On the wall of the landing he could make out shadowy words stenciled in orange. EAST WING I, they read. An arrow beneath pointed to the next flight of stairs.

He eased the door closed and listened. Far above, he heard heavy steps, a door closing, then nothing. Cautiously, he went up the stairs to the first landing and around to the next flight of steps. He stood at the bottom of these and peered up into the shadowy gloom.

Half expecting Wilbur to leap out of the darkness at him at any moment, Ivy crept up the second flight of stairs to the next landing. This one had a large red metal door with a small window in it. Like the halfway landing, this one had EAST WING I stenciled in orange on the wall, and also in gray on the door. He tried the door. It was locked.

It was cold in the stairwell, and Ivy leaned against the door to breathe on his numb fingers to try to warm them. He figured he'd be lucky if he didn't have frostbite. His feet, too, were numb from slushing through the snowy streets. The moisture had soaked his sneakers right through to his socks.

Opposite the door the stairs continued. His teeth chattering, Ivy climbed them to another half landing, then up another flight to the second floor, marked EAST WING II. This door, too, was locked.

There were more steps going up, to EAST WING III, he assumed. Ivy went to the halfway landing between the second and third floors and had to stop and rest. His legs were still wobbly from car skiing and the stairs were taking what little strength they had left. His pack didn't help any either. It felt as if it had taken on twenty pounds of extra weight. Though slightly warmer in the stairwell than outside, the temperature was still much too cold to help his frozen hands and feet.

Ivy slipped the knapsack off for a moment and knelt on the cold cement landing. It looked as if there was only one more flight to go. The third floor was the top. He peered into the gloom and ducked, flattening out on the floor. The emergency exit door to the third floor was propped open with a piece of wood like the one at the bottom door. Through the crack, he could make out Wilbur walking down the corridor, carrying the cop on his shoulders, fireman-style.

Ivy crawled on his belly to the bottom step. On all fours, Ivy went up the last dozen steps, stopping a step short of the top where he could lie against the edge of the steps and look up to floor level. Wilbur was carrying the cop into a dark room far down the hallway. A moment later the room and the corridor became brightly lit before the door closed.

Ivy stood and took the last step. Slightly warmer air blew out at him through the door's opening. Keeping his chest and cheek to the chilling concrete wall, he slipped to the door and looked through. The corridor was long and dimly lit by the light leaking out from the room. The rest of the corridor and the rooms lining it seemed empty, dark, and deserted.

Ivy pulled the heavy door open wide enough for him to step through and let it close against its stopper again. The corridor was suddenly flooded with bright light, and Ivy heard a door open. He flung himself to the right, ducking into a recess in the wall next to the door, where a glass cabinet held a fire extinguisher. A moment later darkness returned with the click of the door closing and he heard footsteps receding down the hall.

Ivy stuck his head out. He could barely make out Wilbur's silhouette moving down the corridor. About half the distance to Wilbur, Ivy could see light shining out from under the door that Wilbur had come out of. There was a set of large windows along the wall next to the door, with venetian blinds drawn closed but also showing light around their edges. A loud metallic, shuddering noise made him duck his head back. It stopped and he looked out again. Wilbur was at the elevator. Light washed over him as the elevator doors opened. He stepped in and the doors closed behind him, returning the corridor to semidarkness.

Ivy saw his chance. Wilbur must have left the policeman in the lighted room. He ran down the hall to the door and stood, his ear to the wood, listening. He could hear nothing. He moved to the edge of the first large window looking in on the room, but could see little other than blinding light. He moved back to the door, grabbed the knob, and opened it.

The light was so intense it made his eyes water. There was a spotlight on a tripod stand in the corner facing the doorway. Ivy moved into the room, out of line of the light. Green and orange spots floated in front of his eyes for several moments. His eyesight recovered slowly, and he saw that there were brilliant spotlights on in each corner of the room. The room had no windows facing outside, only those looking out on the corridor and into a small attached room at the head wall, that had a

brass plaque on the door identifying it as the
NURSES' STATION.

*It's an old baby nursery like the one at the Army
hospital,* Ivy realized, remembering a visit to a
neighbor who'd had a baby when they were still
living at Fort Devens. The room was full of stuff that
was covered over with canvas tarps and white
sheets. At the back of the room was a metal table
with what looked like a body under a sheet.

Ivy ran to the table, trying not to trip on all the
wiring and heavy black cable that was strewn over
the floor. He bit his lip and pulled back the sheet.
He couldn't help the shriek that escaped from his
mouth.

It was Officer Cote. Ivy could see the rest of the
face that he hadn't been able to see when the body
was in Wilbur's backseat. The shriek from Ivy was at
the sight of the wound that ran from Officer Cote's
forehead down through his right eye to the middle
of his right cheek.

OBSESSION!
Calvin Klein!
A phallic perfume bottle.
Subtle perversions, suggested taboos. Not like on
the Atonement Club. There, it is talk of bound naked skin and violent, slashing steel—the atonement
of those who failed to *serve and protect.* 1-800-JESUS
running along the bottom of the screen is the number for donations and healing prayers. Jesus per-
forms a miracle while He talks of letting the cop's
blood. The red stuff begins to fly from his mouth,
splattering against the inside of the glass.

"Going to need Bounty on those spills, Rosie!"

Jesus is Jimmy Swaggart before his downfall, when he used to touch Grandma with the hands of the Savior through the tunnelvision. *"The testament of atonement is nearly done."* Jimmy/Jesus says. *A cop. A nurse. A doctor.*

Wilbur wants to turn the volume down. The voice of Jesus is full of moaning that is irritating. He doesn't care. He sits and endures without protest, without comment. Everyone is watching, everyone in close-up.

"The nurse is next," Jesus says.

Everyone waits for him to break. He won't.

"No. She's not like the others."

"She's just like them. She's worse. All she wants is to do the dirty things. She doesn't understand. She won't help."

"Yes, she will. She's different. I'll show her and you'll see."

"Everything. Show her everything."

"I will," he says again, less forcefully.

"And if she cannot help, we'll show her more than everything."

Beth Shell finished dinner in the hospital cafeteria and, gathering up her coat and pocketbook, headed for the dormitory to pack a bag for the holidays. She'd just put in a fourteen-hour day, covering half a shift for another girl in addition to working seven to three herself. Her father was coming to pick her up at nine, but when she saw the raging storm outside, she wondered if he'd be able to get through. She didn't think she'd really mind if he couldn't. Though it was a drag to think of spending Christmas alone in the dorm, it was equally if not more depressing to think about spending a *week* at her parents' house listening to them bitch at each other.

She buttoned up her coat and wrapped her scarf tightly around her neck before braving the storm. The path to the dorm was under at least three feet of snow already, with predictions of seven more inches to come, but she followed the general direction of it as well as she could. She trudged along, shoulders huddled, gloved hands in pockets, lulled by the swish of her boots through the deep snow until she heard her name being called.

The area between the hospital, the school of nursing, and the dormitory was well lighted with halogen spotlights, but Beth couldn't see anyone around, and the storm made it hard to tell from which direction the voice had come.

"Beth! Over here!"

She whirled to the left, scanning the parking lots in that direction, then to the right where the Administration Building jutted out from behind the newer, main section of the hospital. Beyond it spread the dark pines of the Audubon Sanctuary that covered the rest of Hospital Hill. There was someone at the corner of the Administration Building stepping into the light.

It was Wilbur. He beckoned to her and abruptly disappeared into the shadows. For a second she thought he had left or that she had imagined seeing him, but then his face and arm were back in the light again, calling and beckoning to her.

She wasn't sure what to do. God knew she had run their next meeting over in her mind at least a million times—nearly as many times as she had gone over what had happened in his car that morning—but she had expected that if there was even to *be* another get-together, she would have to be the one to initiate it because she didn't think Wilbur ever would. That he was doing so now amazed her.

His strange behavior and rejection of her at High Rock Road last week was still a very sore spot. Every time she thought of it, she felt so embarrassed she wanted to flee to a desolate mountaintop somewhere and live out her days as a hermit.

Her first reaction other than lasting embarrassment had been anger. The anger had simmered into outrage that he should embarrass her and that he should think he was better than she. These were nothing but defensive reactions, her ego trying to repair the damage his rebuff had caused. When the anger and outrage burned out, she was finally able to look at the incident objectively.

The truth of the matter was, Beth didn't think his outburst had necessarily been directed at her. Wilbur had said as much himself, though he wouldn't explain what had happened. She almost wished he was one of those macho jerks who liked to play mind games; then it would be easy to hate him and forget him. Instead she felt sorry for him. Wilbur obviously had deep-rooted sexual problems.

She hesitated on the path, mentally debating whether or not she wanted to try to continue their relationship. The urge to walk on and make believe she hadn't heard him was great. She could sense the danger of her suffering real emotional damage if she became involved with Wilbur. If she walked away now, she knew she'd be effectively destroying any chance at a relationship they had.

Knowing how shy Wilbur was, Beth knew it must have taken a great deal of effort for him to seek her out. It was too early for him even to be on duty. He must have come in early just to talk to her. If she ignored him now (and wouldn't that really just be petty revenge for his rejection?), he'd be crushed and would never attempt contact with her again.

The thing was, did she really want that? Wilbur was *so* cute, and nice, and quiet, but his actions in the car had proved there was something wrong mentally and emotionally. So what did she want to do? She stood in the storm, in danger of turning into a snow sculpture if she remained unmoving much longer, and tried to make up her mind.

The part of her that was afraid of being hurt was joined by the part that doubted Wilbur's mental stability and told her to keep walking; she was better off forgetting him. The lonely part of her and the part that was infatuated with Wilbur's sad good looks and haunted eyes told her to go to him.

What decided her was the fact that she knew deep down Wilbur hadn't intentionally meant to hurt her. With that came the realization that he *needed* her.

She went to him.

"I have to talk to you," Wilbur said to her as soon as they were inside the Administration Building's emergency exit stairwell.

"That's okay, Wilbur," she answered. "You don't have to explain anything to me if you don't want to."

"Yes, I do!" Wilbur shot back harshly. "It's important that I make you understand."

"I understand, Wilbur. It's okay, really."

"NO! You *don't* understand. Please. Just come with me. I have to explain . . . something. I have to . . . sh-show you s-something." He became more and more distraught as he spoke and began to stumble over his words.

"Okay, it's okay," Beth said, taking his arm. "I'll come with you."

Wilbur led her under the stairs and through another door and down a short narrow corridor lined with asbestos-wrapped heating pipes and thick, tangled coils of wiring held together periodically by metal collars. At the end he took her through a small door and down a short flight of stairs to a long, dimly lighted corridor. Beth knew where she was now. This corridor led to the morgue, the elevators to the old East Wing Building, and the hospital laundry.

For one terrifying moment, Beth thought Wilbur was going to take her into the morgue and reveal that he was a necrophiliac or something equally weird and perverted. She released a small sigh when he led her past the morgue and continued on to the elevators to the East Wing Building. She was surprised that he stopped and rang for the elevator. She gave him a questioning look, but he didn't answer. The noisy elevator came and he motioned for her to step in. He followed, pushing the button for the third floor.

"Why are we going up there?" Beth asked, indicating the third-floor button.

"I have to explain things to you. It's a matter of life and death that you understand . . ." Wilbur answered, his voice trailing off vaguely while he stared at the first-floor indicator lighting, then the second, as the elevator went up.

"A matter of life and death?" Beth asked, noticing a dark wet stain for the first time on Wilbur's black overcoat. "For whom?"

Wilbur didn't answer.

He had to be dead, Ivy thought through the cold fog of shock that was oozing into his mind. Nobody could have a gash like that in his head and live. Ivy could see the whiteness of bone deep in the wound. It made him dizzy to look at and his stomach did flip-flops. He let the sheet fall back over Cote's face and backed away from the table. He had to call the cops! He tripped on a cable and fell hard on his rump, cracking his teeth together and seeing stars for a moment.

A horrible, rusty shrieking noise made him jump up in terror, looking for escape. He realized it was the elevator at the end of the hall coming back up. That meant Crazy Wilbur was coming back. He had to hide. He ran to the inside door to the nurses' station and slipped through into the small, dark room, closing the door behind him. He crept to the first window looking into the nursery, peeked through the edge of the closed venetian blind, and waited.

He could hear the elevator doors opening, then closing. More than one pair of footsteps, echoing in the hall, followed. They were coming closer. Ivy pressed himself against the wall, trying to see more through the slit at the edge of the blinds. He listened with growing anticipation to the hollow clop of the approaching footsteps.

Ivy wondered who was with Wilbur. Did he have an accomplice? The footsteps reached the nursery and the door opened. He heard a female voice exclaim in surprise at the brightness of the lights. A second later he saw Wilbur lead a pretty blonde in a long navy-blue overcoat into the nursery. Wilbur placed a folding chair in the middle of the room for her and told her to sit.

A case of the shivers, brought on by the dual effects of cold and shock, seized Ivy and he had to back away from the window for fear of making the blinds shake. Officer Cote's face flashed before his eyes and he felt like crying. He had to get out of there and get the police, he thought again. But what about the girl? Why had Wilbur brought the girl up there? Was she his accomplice or his next victim?

Ivy couldn't leave her there with Crazy Wilbur until he knew.

Beth blinked her watering eyes, trying to let them adjust to the incredibly bright light in the room. There were four powerful spotlights on tripod stands set in each corner of the room, providing way too much light for the normal eye. She was getting nervous. Looking at the lights and all the large sheet-covered objects in the room revived and enhanced her earlier doubts about Wilbur's sanity.

She told herself she was being paranoid and foolish. Wilbur must have a very good reason for bringing her here and for having these lights set up like this. He'd explain and she'd see that she'd been unduly frightened.

She sat in the metal folding chair he placed in the middle of the room for her, noticing for the first time all the cables and wires on the floor. Her eyes adjusted to the abnormal light, as she removed and shook the melted snow from her hat, gloves, and scarf and looked around the room. She wondered what all the covered objects were, but not for long as Wilbur began moving around the room uncovering them.

To her left, he pulled a sheet off a video camera on a tripod stand. He turned the camera on and removed a sheet from a similar camera to her right. Behind her, he uncovered two more cameras and removed a canvas tarp from a large bumpy object to reveal two photographer's umbrella reflectors. A nearly seven-foot-tall, square-shaped object when uncovered turned out to be nine television sets stacked in three rows of three on top of one another against the end wall. In front of the televisions another uncovered object appeared to be some kind of master electric board or control panel for the equipment in the room, since everything was hooked up to it.

With the bright lights, and now the umbrella reflectors behind her, it was becoming increasingly warmer in the room. She unbuttoned her coat, looking at Wilbur questioningly concerning all the equipment, but he avoided her eyes and uncovered a small table upon which were laid out an ax, a hacksaw, a portable acetylene torch, and several knives. There was only one thing left covered in the room and Beth definitely did not like the look of it. It looked like a gurney. The outline of the sheet looked suspiciously like a body. She told herself she was crazy, that she'd seen too many weird movies, but she wondered why Wilbur didn't uncover the table too.

"Wilbur, I want to go now," Beth said, standing and putting on her hat, trying not to let Wilbur hear the fear in her voice.

"Please, Beth. Please," Wilbur said, his voice soft. "Stay and let me explain."

He seemed so calm, so sincere, yet so troubled, so *in need* of her. She gave in. "All right." She sat again.

Wilbur began pacing in front of the stacked televisions. He seemed to be wrestling with how to say what he wanted so badly for her to hear. Beth's heart went out to him in spite of her nervousness and fear.

"My mother . . ." he said tentatively, his voice almost a groan, and stopped. He looked at her, then away, his face red and getting redder. He trembled and closed his eyes. When he spoke again, a child's voice came out of his mouth.

With a chill, Beth recognized it as the voice she'd

overheard outside the security office that night when Wilbur said he'd been watching TV. It struck her now that she thought of it that there *had been no TV* in the security office that night.

"My mother's-not-my-mother and she hurts me," the child's voice said from Wilbur's mouth. "She and Joey make me do things. Bad things. They make Jesus *come.*"

Wilbur was weeping and Beth didn't know what to do. She was torn between wanting to hug him and wanting to run away because there was no doubt about it now, Wilbur was really, really, *really* bonkers.

Wilbur looked at her, and the terror and hurt in his face were so intense that she almost couldn't bear it.

"Please," he said in his heart-wrenching little-boy voice. "Will you make them stop?" Tears were streaming down his face. His eyes were pleading.

Beth was completely flustered. Conflicting emotions threatened to spill out all at once. She felt such deep empathy for Wilbur that she wanted to cry with him and hug and console him, even though she didn't understand what he was talking about. At the same time, he was scaring the hell out of her. She felt a growing sense of dread. The cameras, lights, televisions, and his weird changes of voice were keeping her off-balance and in a state of utter confusion.

There was something about all the video equipment that she knew she should fear, but in her confused state, she couldn't remember what it was.

"I don't . . . I don't know . . . what you're talking about, Wilbur," she said.

Wilbur's next change of voice was so sudden and drastic it made Beth jump out of the chair.

"I told you she's no different than all the others!" he screamed, his eyes glaring, his mouth a sneer.

"No." Wilbur answered himself, looking at her with renewed fear in his eyes. "I haven't told her everything. *You said* to tell her *everything!"*

"Wilbur?" Beth said, her voice trembling.

Wilbur rushed to the control panel. He flicked some switches and the screens of the televisions filled with flickering blank light. He flicked another switch and his image, standing in front of the wall of screens, came on each TV. With the camera filming him standing in front of the televisions, the resulting picture on each screen was an infinite number of Wilburs standing in front of an infinite number of TV screens. The effect started the throb of a headache between Beth's eyes.

Wilbur pointed at the image of himself on the first screen in the bottom row. "This is Brother John. Jesus murdered him in the bathroom," Wilbur said. "He has his own channel and talk show, but I don't like to watch it."

Beth stared at the screen, and her mouth went dry. She wished she could believe he was playing some kind of weird joke, but he wasn't.

"This is Debbie. She's on Tunnelvision now, too. Jesus murdered her in a snuff film five years ago. That's what Mary-not-Mother and Joey wanted to do to me and Jesus, but He snuffed them first," Wilbur explained as though it all made sense, all the while pointing at himself pointing at himself pointing at himself, et cetera, on the infinite second screen.

Beth shivered. She felt light-headed.

Wilbur was pointing at another multiple image of himself.

Get out! an urgent voice in Beth screamed. She tried to back away but stumbled against the chair and almost fell.

"This is my grandma. She took care of me. She taught me about tunnelvision and Jesus. Mary-not-Mother said she died but she didn't. She got her own channel on my tunnelvision and became a tunnel-vangelist. Before she died she told me to go to the *special grown-ups* and tell them if Mary-not-Mother and Joey didn't take good care of me. I tried to tell but they wouldn't listen. They didn't help Jesus. Now they must be murdered to make atonement for their sins of omission."

The word *murder* struck her like a slap in the face. He *had* said *murdered*. It was no mistake. She'd heard correctly, she knew she had. The alarm voice in her head shouted louder to get out *now!*

Her eyes wandered to the covered surgical gurney. She noticed something that hadn't been there before—a spreading, dark red stain on the sheet over something shaped like a head.

Her confusion suddenly cleared, and she experienced a moment of absolute clarity as all elements fell neatly into place. The sense of dread she'd had about the equipment, the spreading stain, and Wilbur's talk about murder and snuff films, clicked together in that calm to bring her to a terrifying

realization that drained the blood from her face and
made her legs feel like accordions.

Wilbur is the Video Killer!

Ivy watched through the gap at the edge of the
blinds, becoming more certain by the moment that
the blonde in there with Wilbur was *not* an accomplice. She looked scared to death at Crazy Wilbur's
freaking out the way he was.

If it wasn't so terrifying, Ivy would have thought
Wilbur's display hilarious, the way he kept chang-
ing voices and pointing to himself on the TV
screens. Though Ivy couldn't hear everything Wilbur was saying, he heard enough to confirm his
earlier suspicion that Wilbur was the serial murderer known as the Video Killer.

It looked as if the blonde had just come to the
same conclusion. She was out of the chair, glancing
toward the door like a cornered animal.

She won't get very far before Wilbur catches her,
Ivy thought, *unless I can help her.* He quickly
slipped off his knapsack and jacket. The pieces of
the cast gun lay at the bottom of the pack, but he
didn't bother with them. He'd tried to modify the
gun to make it work better, but hadn't met with
much success. What he was after was the glass jar of
Zip-Strip and his squirt gun filled with bleach.

Ivy went back to the blind and peeked through.
The blonde had managed to slide behind the chair,
a little closer to the door. She stood, nervously
clutching her hat and gloves and casting furtive
glances at escape.

She's going to make a break for it any second

now, Ivy thought. He looked at his coat and pack on the floor, and debated whether to put them on again or not. When the blonde tried to escape, Ivy thought he could surprise and distract, maybe even *injure,* Wilbur enough for her to get away. But then Wilbur was going to come after him and the bulky coat and backpack would only slow him down. After all, he only had to elude Crazy Wilbur until the blonde got away and called the cops, right? That shouldn't be too long. He hoped.

He left the coat and pack on the floor and moved to the corridor door. He opened it all the way. Ivy put the bleach pistol in his belt and unscrewed the top of the jar of Zip-Strip. He quietly placed the top of the jar on the floor to the side and braced himself just inside the door, out of sight.

He was pumped up. He had to tell himself to be careful and wait until the blonde was out and running to the elevators before throwing the furniture-stripping liquid at Wilbur. He hoped Wilbur wasn't too close. He didn't want to get overzealous and accidentally douse her with the stuff.

Come on, make a break for it, he silently urged the blonde, his right leg jiggling with keyed-up nervous energy. With every second he had to wait he could feel his adrenaline level rising.

Come on! Come on!

Suddenly Ivy heard shouting. It was Wilbur. Ivy caught part of it, hearing: "I told you she's like all the others. She has to pay like the rest." Wilbur's voice went on, but Ivy wasn't paying attention anymore. He heard the girl shriek from within the room, and the next moment the door was flung open. Light fairly exploded into the hall. The blonde ran into the corridor, heading past Ivy, in the opposite direction from the elevators.

"Stop her!" Wilbur screamed. He was only a short distance behind.

As soon as she was by him, Ivy went into action. Hanging onto the doorjamb with his sore left hand, and holding the open jar stiff-armed in his right, Ivy swung out of the doorway, flinging the Zip-Strip in a wide arc at Wilbur.

The gelatinous fluid caught the bright light from the room behind Wilbur and shimmered purple for a moment, seeming to hang suspended in air, before splattering across Wilbur's shoulders, neck, face, and chest.

The shout that came from Wilbur was initially one of shock and surprise. His head jerked back, his hands flew to cover his face, and he staggered off-balance. His forward motion was thrown into reverse and he crashed to the floor. As the caustic fluid began to sink in and do its work, Wilbur started screaming in pain. His screams sent a shock of fear through Ivy at first, but there was also an intense and satisfying *thrill* of vengeance.

"That's for Bond, James Bond, you bastard!" Ivy screamed.

Wilbur was writhing on the floor, arms over his face, voice vacillating between screams and moans. Down the corridor, the blonde had stopped at the shouting.

Ivy looked at her, motioning with both his arms for her to keep going. He almost didn't look back at Wilbur in time to see that he was struggling to get

Officer Cote's gun out of his belt. Ivy whipped the jar at Wilbur's head—missed—and bolted.

"Run!" he screamed, heading toward the blonde. She looked confused until a deafening, echoing explosion occurred in the corridor. Ivy heard something whine above his head but he didn't slow down.

"Run!" he screamed again at the blonde, but she was already moving.

"The red door," Ivy yelled. "To the left!" The light from the nursery provided more than enough illumination for her to see. She headed straight for it.

"Call the cops!" Ivy added just before she went through the door.

Ivy reached the door and stopped. He could hear the blonde's footsteps echoing in the stairwell.

That's it, sweetheart, he thought. *Run and call the cops.*

Ivy looked back. Wilbur had fired his first shot wildly from his knees. Now he was getting to his feet, still screaming, with one hand held to his face, the other clutching the pistol.

If the blonde was going to have the best chance to get away and call the police, he couldn't follow her down the stairwell or let Wilbur go after her. He had to find another way out, and he had to make Wilbur chase *him.*

He stepped away from the door, into the middle of the corridor, and faced Wilbur. He didn't know what he was going to do or say until the words came out of his mouth. "Hey! You *scud!*" he cried.

The gun started to come up.

"Your mother rides shotgun on the garbage truck!" Ivy yelled, beginning to giggle halfway through it. He didn't know why he said such a corny thing, but he was just frightened enough and emotionally pumped up enough to find it hysterical, and he brayed wild laughter at the approaching Wilbur.

The gun was up.

"She's *not my mother!*" Wilbur screamed and fired. The gun jerked wildly in his hand. There was a loud explosion and the bullet plowed into the floor five feet ahead of Ivy.

Ivy laughed louder at Wilbur's rebuff and his terrible aim, but the shot got him moving. He ran down the corridor away from the fire door, Wilbur, and the elevator, and saw that the hallway ended in a large room with big windows overlooking the woods and a pathway through the pine trees to the nursing school. To the right he saw a red EXIT light.

Wilbur fired two more wild shots at Ivy. He seemed to have forgotten about the blonde and was hell-bent on chasing Ivy. Ivy was pretty sure he'd gotten Wilbur in the eyes with the Zip-Strip, ruining his aim, but if Wilbur got any closer, it might improve.

Ivy ran to the exit door. It had a round push handle with a red-and-white sign attached to it warning: EMERGENCY DOOR! ALARM WILL SOUND!

Ivy punched the handle and ran outside onto a slippery metal fire escape running down the side of the building. It was banked high with over a foot of drifted snow and as he tried to stop his smooth sneakers slipped out from under him. He saved himself from crashing down the stairs at the last second only by grabbing the freezing-cold railing. A loud bell began to ring in the building. Hanging on to the railing despite the coldness of the metal, Ivy started down. Within seconds of being out in the blizzard, the blinding, blowing snow finished the job of soaking him, and he cursed his stupidity at leaving his coat behind.

CHANNEL 25

* * *

Sign-off

The chief of hospital security, the three-to-eleven security guard, the head maintenance engineer, and the three-to-eleven nursing supervisor were waiting for Mahoney and Bill in the main lobby of the hospital. As requested, the maintenance engineer had brought building plans for the east wing that showed all its exits, ventilation shafts, plumbing, and electrical wiring.

Mahoney briefed them on the situation and instructed the nursing super that there shouldn't be any interference with the normal routine of the hospital, especially since it was past visiting hours and it appeared the suspect was in the abandoned section. He advised her to get an emergency trauma team over to the east wing area in case of any injuries. She went off to take care of that while the others looked at the building plans spread on the round magazine table in the middle of the lobby.

While the security chief and the maintenance engineer pointed out the possible exits from the East Wing Building to Bill, Mahoney radioed his men to take up positions cutting off road access to the rear of the hospital and the East Wing Building in particular.

According to the engineer and the security chief, there were five exits from each floor of the East Wing Building, except for the first floor, of course, whose windows were close to the ground. Each floor had an inside fire escape leading to an outside door on the north side of the building, and an outside fire escape running down the rear southern side. Each floor had access to the elevators that still worked, plus a stairway that ran alongside the elevator shaft and came out opposite the hospital laundry. Each floor also had a door and stairs leading down to a tunnel running from the East Wing Building to the School of Nursing.

"What tunnel?" Bill and Mahoney asked almost simultaneously. They could both feel another piece of the puzzle click into place.

The engineer explained that the tunnel had been built when the hospital was primarily a teaching clinic. Harsh winters atop the exposed hill had prompted the building of the tunnel to allow the students to pass from dorm to school to hospital without venturing into the elements. It also connected to the boiler room.

A crackling voice over Mahoney's portable radio interrupted them. "Levy here, sir. There's activity on the third floor of the East Wing Building. A light, and sounds like gunshots."

"I'll get men over to the School of Nursing, the dorm, and down to the boiler room to cover the tunnel exits there," Mahoney told Bill.

"Tell the other units not to close in unless Clayton comes outside. I want him," Bill said. Mahoney nodded, barking orders into his radio. He didn't have to be told why.

Bill turned to the chief of security. "Take us to the east wing, third floor, by the fastest route."

With the maintenance engineer and a couple of shotgun-armed uniforms in tow, the hospital security chief led Bill and Mahoney out of the lobby.

Between the cold, the fear, and the physical exertion of running down three flights of stairs, Beth was gasping for breath by the time she reached the ground-level door. She ran out into the snow-swirling night and right into the arms of a police officer.

Beth saw only the uniform up close and in the blinding storm and darkness thought Wilbur had her. She began screaming and struggling. It took three more policemen to subdue her before she realized she was safe.

When pain gets this bad you need . . .
Snow.

His face is burning. His right eye feels as if it's melting. He can see only a blood red blur through it, but if he tries to close it the burning increases a hundredfold, sending fireballs of pain through his skull.

He falls to his knees on the top landing of the fire escape, dropping the gun and scooping the lovely cold snow over his searing face with both hands.

It's the coolness of mint with just the hint of retsyn!

Where is he? The Son of God's wrath is world destructive.

"Please bear with us. We are experiencing visual difficulties."

His bad eye turns the blizzard red. The holy pain is diminished by the freezing snow, but as He starts down the slippery fire escape, gun once again in hand, He screams again, tearing at His shirt where the caustic fluid has taken this long to eat through to His shoulders and chest.

He stumbles to the bottom of the stairs and throws himself bare-chested into a snowdrift, screaming His rage into the night and the storm.

Ivy had no idea where he was. He had crossed the road and started down a path through a thinly wooded area. The path had led toward the light from a building beyond the trees. As he'd gone deeper into the woods, though, the path had quickly disappeared, and he was soon up to his hips in snow. The one light he'd been heading for went out, and he could no longer tell for sure in which direction he was going.

His clothes were soaked through. The snow clung to his eyebrows and eyelashes and stung his cheeks. He had lost nearly all feeling in his extremities, and he couldn't feel his ears any longer. He tried running with his hands stuck under his armpits to warm them, but he lost his balance and plunged face first into snow, disappearing beneath it completely.

Ivy struggled to his feet as fast as he could, his breath sucked in with a shriek at the cold that engulfed him. He sputtered snow and tried to shake the stuff off while he staggered on.

He was brushing the snow from his arms and clothes, not watching where he was going—not that he could see in the swirling snow anyway—and walked into something round and hard that caught him low in the gut and in the knees. He tumbled again into the snow.

Ivy started to cry. He couldn't help it. Hitting whatever it was had hurt, especially since he was so cold. He ached all over from the cold—a deep, throbbing, bone-chilling ache. He blubbered through numbing lips, swearing incoherently at the obstacle, but grabbed it to climb to his feet. The force of his collision had knocked most of the snow off. The thing was a bubble-shaped hump of metal with a four-spoke wheel on top. It reminded Ivy of a hatch on a submarine.

There was a popping sound behind him. Ivy could just see Wilbur's shadowy form struggling through the snow after him, gun raised. There was a flash of light and another popping noise. The shots were not as loud in the blizzard as they had sounded in the empty East Wing Building.

Too cold and tired to go any farther, Ivy grabbed the metal wheel and tried to turn it. His fingers were too numb to grasp it firmly. There was another flash of light and Ivy heard a soft *hiss* as the bullet struck somewhere nearby in the snow.

Ivy grabbed the freezing metal again, forcing his unfeeling fingers to grasp it tightly. He screamed as sensation returned to his frozen hands in the form of excruciating pain. Ivy screamed against the torture, finding a surge of adrenaline in the hurt, and put an extra lunge into the turn of the wheel. It gave. Tears streaming down his frozen cheeks, he laughed and cried hysterically, his voice lost in the storm, and opened the hatch.

There was a metallic *clunk* and the hatch popped up a few inches, causing the snow piled against it to fall into the dark opening that appeared around the hatch's rim.

Ivy knew he might be climbing into a trap with no escape, but he couldn't run anymore. He was so cold, his tears were freezing on his face. His struggle with the hatch and his last bout of hysteria had taken what little energy he had left. He could barely lift the hatch, and couldn't stop it from falling all the way open with a rusty groan. There was nowhere else to go and he *had* to get out of the cold.

Ivy didn't like the look or the smell of the hole. There was a narrow metal ladder running down the inside rim into the darkness below. He was out of choices. Wilbur was close. Raising his stiff, pant-soaked legs, and holding on to the rim of the opening with his hurting hands, he lowered himself to the ladder. He reached back for the inside handle of the hatch door and couldn't reach it; the door had fallen open too far. Ivy gave up on it, shot a last look at Wilbur, and climbed down into the stinking darkness.

Bill stared at the floor-indicator lights and mentally cursed the old elevator's infuriating slowness. The crackle of Mahoney's radio broke the tension of Bill's thoughts.

"Levy here again, sir. We've recovered a young woman who says she's just escaped from the suspect. She says he's now pursuing a young black boy who helped her escape. They're on the third floor. Over."

Bill took out his gun.

Mahoney did the same and gestured to one of the shotgun-toting uniforms with them. "You stay in the elevator with these two," he said, indicating the two hospital personnel with a nod of his head. "Push the stop button when we get out and hold the elevator here for us." He pointed his chin at the other patrolman. "You follow us and don't get trigger-happy with that thing. Don't fire unless I tell you to. Got it?" The cop nodded, his eyes shiny with either excitement or fear.

The elevator doors opened onto a dark hallway. Suddenly a loud bell began to ring.

"What's that?" Bill asked the maintenance man.

"Emergency door alarm. They sound if opened," the engineer explained.

"Where?" Mahoney asked.

"And where do they go?" Bill added.

"The only one with an alarm is the one at the end of the hall, on the sun porch. It leads to the outside fire escape."

"Let's go," Bill said. He moved into the hallway, staying low, and crossed to the opposite corridor wall. Mahoney and the uniform took the near wall.

Ahead, about halfway down the corridor, they could see an open doorway with bright light pouring forth. Moving alternately, covering each other, they made their way down the hall to the open door. Mahoney planted himself to the left of the jamb. Bill ducked into the room. Mahoney followed. Scanning the room quickly, they thought it was empty before Mahoney noticed the sheet-covered figure on the table.

Mahoney rushed to the table and uncovered Officer Cote. He immediately took a neck pulse and raised his radio to his lips. "Mahoney to Larken! We have a downed officer on the third floor of the east wing. Tell that nursing super to get that trauma team up here on the double. Over," he barked into the walkie-talkie.

"Yes, sir! Over," Larken answered. He was immediately followed by another voice.

"Levy to Mahoney! The suspect is outside. We gave chase but he disappeared down some kind of hatchway next to the path leading to the nursing school. He's secured the hatch door from the inside somehow. I believe the youth is down there too. Over."

Bill yelled for the other patrolman to bring the maintenance engineer. "What's this about a hatchway in the ground between here and the School of Nursing?" Bill shouted at the man.

The engineer seemed flustered for a moment by

Bill's intensity, but recovered. "That's an emergency exit from the tunnel."

"What's the quickest way into the tunnel from here?" Bill shot back.

"Down there." The engineer pointed to a narrow door on the other side of the hall, behind the partitioned area where the expectant fathers' waiting room used to be. "That door leads down to the tunnel."

Bill turned to the patrolman. "Give me your flashlight and come with me. You take care of your man," Bill called to Mahoney. "I'm going down after him."

"I'll have my men enter the other end of the tunnel, and I'll follow you as soon as a doctor gets here," Mahoney called.

Bill didn't acknowledge but charged across the hall to the door, going through it with the patrolman right behind him.

Technical difficulties.

The remote control is out of control. The remote control is broken. Everything is either fast-forward or slow-motion advance. The volume is too loud, the color is way off—the picture is tainted a blurry bloody red.

The channels change automatically. Nothing but dead air. Video snow. A cowboy-and-Indian movie in swarming specks. One by one the channels are going off the air. The broadcast day is ending.

The snow melts on his skin, reddening it, but the raging heat of his body keeps it from refreezing and it runs in rivulets down his blistered face, neck, and chest. He follows the child through the storm, looking like a man just emerged from a swim.

He moans as he walks. The snow blowing in his face and eye feel good, but only because they make the pain unbearable instead of please-put-a-bullet-in-my-head-and-kill-me bad. Snow is everywhere. In the sky. In his eyes. On the screen in his mind.

Cowboys and Indians. Indians and Cowboys.

Fading laughter.

He looks into the hole.

"What's it remind you of, Wilbur?"

A new voice, yet an old voice.

Where is it coming from? Every channel is off the air.

"Jesus?"

No answer.

The snow is drifting into the hole. That's where the scwewy wabbit went, hah-ah-ah-ah-ah.

Lights.

Blinding.

"Action!"

"No!" he screams. He climbs onto the ladder. Silhouettes caught in the backglow of headlight eyes rush through the storm at him. He descends the ladder, pulling the hatch closed over him. He quickly takes off his belt and loops one end through the inside hatch door handle and fastens the other to the top rung of the ladder.

Round darkness.

"What's it remind you of, Wilbur?"

"Don't listen," he whispers. "Jesus will be back, right, Grandma?" Grandma's gone, her channel dark.

He doesn't like the growing foul odor the closer to the bottom of the ladder he gets.

"What's it remind you of, Wilbur?"

"Jesus? Come back," Wilbur moans, whispering into the darkness. His feet touch a wet surface. He faces a large circular darkness in either direction. It and the stench of death as thick as fog in the black air tell him what he doesn't want to know: Where he is.

"No!" he whimpers. "It can't be!"

Ivy stumbled through the wet darkness, water dripping and trickling ahead and behind him. He kept his hand over his nose to keep from smelling that awful odor.

Twice Ivy tripped over something in the dark, almost falling into what was at least an inch of freezing water covering the floor of the tunnel in spots. The only thing he could see in the pitch-blackness was the glow of lighter darkness from the area of the hatch and the occasional sparkle of a snowflake coming down through the opening. A dozen feet or so into the tunnel, even that light disappeared.

He stopped and hugged himself to try to warm up a little. He listened for any sign of Wilbur following. Unless Ivy'd got Wilbur's eyes with the Zip-Strip better than he thought, the loon had surely seen him go through the hatch. He couldn't hear anything from behind except the steady trickle and drip-drip of water.

In his pocket, Ivy had his Bic lighter. He dug it out of his wet, tight dungarees with difficulty. He crouched in the darkness and flicked the lighter, cupping his hand around it as much to warm it as to shield the light.

The fire flickered eerily, wavering in a steady draft. He kept his hand around the flame as he looked around the tunnel. The floor, walls and ceiling were all concrete. The flame's orange glow painted the rounded walls of the tunnel and cast Ivy's shadow long.

Ivy pointed the flame ahead in the tunnel. A black plastic trash bag sat in the water a few feet away. Ivy moved closer, the bag becoming more familiar with each step. It looked like one of those he'd seen Wilbur putting into his trunk. He leaned down, extended the light with one trembling hand while opening the top of the bag with the other. He nearly dropped the lighter at the sight it illuminated, and had to stifle an erupting scream.

It was Slice Sanchez's head looking out at him with fear frozen on his bloody face. From what Ivy could see of the rest of him, it looked as if Slice had been put through a meat cutter. His body was in pieces. In the depths of the grief and anger he had experienced when he found Bond dead and thought that Slice had done it, Ivy would have been happy to see the good-for-nothing Slice come to such a bad end, but now the sight terrified him. It was one thing to imagine such violent atrocities against a hated enemy, another to see them in reality, up close. The strangest and most surprising thing for Ivy, though, was that he discovered he felt pity for Slice.

Looking at the bag, Ivy fought back a sudden rush of nausea. He stepped carefully around it. Now he knew what that smell was in the tunnel. What bothered him was that the smell was way too strong, and wasn't all coming from Slice Sanchez.

Once past the body, Ivy let the flame go out and walked on in darkness until his foot hit something that sounded like another trash bag. Steeling his nerve, he struck the lighter ablaze. It was just as he feared. At his feet, propped against the tunnel wall, side by side, were two bags, their tops partially open. A rat jumped from one, making Ivy jump in turn, and ran from his light. At the top of the bags were the severed, bloody heads of the man and woman he'd seen going into Wilbur's house on two different occasions. The rest of their bodies looked to have been packed in pieces beneath them the same as Slice Sanchez's. The guy had been driving the van that was still parked across from Wilbur's place, and the woman, on the second visit, had ridden the motorcycle that had either been towed away or stolen. He had thought before that maybe she had driven it off when he wasn't around to see, but now he knew the truth.

Ivy made his way by them. Their eyes seemed to peek out and follow him. Just before he let the light go out again, he noticed arrows and oblong words painted on the round tunnel wall. He stepped closer for a look. The top arrow pointed back the way he'd come and read SCHOOL OF NURSING AND DORMITORY/EMERGENCY TUNNEL EXIT. Ivy guessed the latter was the hatchway he'd come through. The bottom one pointed in the direction he was going and said EAST WING BUILDING AND BOILER ROOM.

That's where I just came from, Ivy thought. *Maybe I can get my coat back and call the cops.*

From behind him came a crash of metal and a loud, rusty squeaking. Ivy let the lighter flame go out. He figured it was Wilbur closing the hatchway, but why? There was no way Ivy was going back that way or outside again unless he absolutely had to.

Ivy's foot kicked something that splashed away. He didn't want to know what it was. He heard Wilbur climbing down the ladder. Ivy stopped and listened. Wilbur's feet splashed into the water. A moment later there was another sound that frightened Ivy more than the sounds of Wilbur's pursuit. The new sound came from up ahead of him. A click in the darkness. Then a light.

About twenty feet ahead of Ivy, a door opened and began to swing shut. A shadowy figure stepped through before the door closed and the darkness returned. Ivy was confused. He was sure that Wilbur was behind him, so who was this in front of him? Was it the cops? Had the blonde got through?

The tunnel, even without the litter of Wilbur's victims, looked as if it hadn't been used for a while. Ivy crept to the left wall and crouched there, listening to the sound of wet footsteps approaching.

Blackness. And realization.
Jesus is gone. He's not coming back.
The screen is black.
The power is ebbing.
The empty airwaves of the mind.
There is no time to scream.
Channels he has known well.

He stands in total darkness. Even his hands waving in front of him like insect antennae are invisible to his eyes.

Where's the off switch?

It's not a replay.

Stop the dream!

It's not a dream.

Far off in the darkness to both sides there are dual explosions of light, widening, then narrowing. There are dual sounds of doors opening on squeaky hinges like bones creaking, then closing with a metallic click that echoes rhythmically.

This is not a program.

This is real. The water soaking into his feet and the smell in the air tell him so.

This is nothing he'll wake up from.

The echoes turn into footsteps. From down each corridor the footsteps slice through the darkness. They become louder and louder. They start slowly, as if the walkers are unsure of their footing in the dark, but gradually they quicken.

This is live. This is no preview of coming attractions. This is a special bulletin, live on the scene, except that all the channels are off.

This is reality, with a club, and no matter how much he can't believe it's true, it is.

He begins to sweat despite the cold. He tries to shrink back but he is already as close to the wall as he can get. There is no room left. There is nowhere to go.

The footsteps grow louder . . . a light grows around him.

And they are there!

Mary-not-Mother stares up at him from the floor near his feet. Her arms are over on the other side of him, her legs farther on, her torso stacked with the trash bags that hold the Smiths near the other end of the tunnel.

Her mouth opens and his screams come from it. She changes his screaming to laughter.

"Wilbur Clayton!"

Joey's head is speaking. It sits by Mary-not-Mother's arms. The rest of him is scattered throughout the tunnel in bits and pieces, none bigger than a bread box.

Joey's mouth opens. "Please, Wilbur. It's all over," he says. More laughter spills from Mary-not-Mother's mouth. A low shadow moves in front of the light. A cellophane sound issues from it. It's Vicki of the dented face. David Thefaggot and Slice Sanchez follow her. They squirm toward him in their bloody *Hefty! Hefty! Hefty!* bags like unnatural slugs. Mutilated pieces of flesh reaching. Scattered body parts keep pace: arms and legs writhing, heads rolling, and hands slithering along the floor, reanimating in one direction, toward one goal, *him.*

"Noooooooooooo!" he screams, his voice rising higher and higher.

He begins to tremble.

He prays for Grandma, for Jesus—for *anyone* to help him pull the plug.

Bill Gage made his way through the tunnel, straining to see into the blackness ahead, not wanting to chance a light that would make him an easy target. "Wilbur Clayton!" he called. "It's the police, Wilbur. It's all over."

Strange sounds came out of the darkness. A shriek. Laughter. Splashing. And a small whispered voice: "Don't shoot! I'm just a kid!" Bill reached out and felt a small hand grab his.

"Okay, kid," Bill said, pulling the boy to him. "Is Wilbur Clayton up there?" he asked.

"Yeah," the boy whispered.

"All right. Get going that way. A police officer's just through the door down there." Bill pushed Ivy toward the east wing door he'd just come through. "And don't stop. Move!"

Bill listened to the kid walk away, then resumed his progress toward Wilbur. He didn't hear as the kid stopped, then began to follow him. He was too preoccupied with a new sound from the darkness ahead.

It was weeping—pitiful, gut-wrenching, lost-soul weeping, the kind of crying Bill had known something of during the depths of his bottle days. He decided to risk a light. From the sound of it, Wilbur was no longer a danger.

Bill turned on the flashlight the patrolman had given him and shone it down the tunnel ahead. From far down at the other end, another beam of light answered as policemen coming from the School of Nursing let him know they were there, too.

Bill played his light along the tunnel floor, picking out body parts and trash bags filled with chopped corpses. He let the light linger on each for not more than a second, coming finally to rest on Wilbur's huddled form, ten feet ahead.

Bill kept the light on him and moved closer. Five feet from the sobbing, bare-chested Wilbur, Bill crouched and picked up Officer Cote's revolver. It was empty. He stuck it into his back pocket.

"Sir?" one of the patrolmen called from the other end of the tunnel. Some obstruction was partially blocking their flashlight. Bill heard one of the officers gagging and retching. "We've got some structural damage and a number of bodies in plastic trash bags at this end preventing us getting through."

"It's okay!" Bill shouted back. "I've got him. I'll bring him out this end. Radio and tell Captain Mahoney."

The policemen readily agreed, eager to get out of the tunnel, and Bill watched their light recede until the far door opened and closed.

At last. Bill had jammed his wallet in the hinge of the tunnel door he'd entered through, thus sealing it. He realized, at that moment, the kid was trapped in there with him. But he was so close. He couldn't worry about that now. Bill returned his focus to the killer in front of him. Now Bill was alone with him. He had him. But *whom* did he have?

"Who are you?" Bill asked, stepping closer to Wilbur. The youth alternately sobbed and giggled. Blistering scars covered Wilbur's face and chest, and a nasty chemical burn had turned his right eye red and weepy. Bill didn't see that. He saw his father's steel-blue eyes instead.

"Why did you do it?" Bill asked. He wasn't hallucinating. He *saw* Wilbur huddled against the wall at his feet, but he *knew* it was his father.

"Tell me why."

Silence.

Wasn't that just like his old man? Ignoring him, secretly laughing at him.

The image of Sassy in a coma flashed in his memory, followed by one of Cindy in her coffin.

"It's time to put an end to the past," Bill muttered. He flashed the light down the tunnel. Empty but for him, his father, and the dead. He didn't care that Ivy had followed him and was not too far back, watching.

"I wish I could have done this long ago when it would have mattered," Bill said to his father's ghost. He raised his pistol to Wilbur's head.

Not really understanding if he was seeking revenge or redemption, Bill pulled the trigger.

Sign-off

 Ivy had a cold that his mother was sure would turn into pneumonia. And though she'd been at the hospital and police station most of the night, she was up early Christmas morning getting the turkey dressed and in the oven.

She wouldn't let Ivy get out of bed until she had made up the couch with pillows and a mountain of covers. She helped him to it, though his legs were just fine—it was his fingers that were bandaged with minor frostbite—and tucked him in snugly.

"I know you're anxious to open gifts," she said, giving him a quick peck on the forehead, "but as soon as we're done I want you to promise to tell me about everything leading up to and including last night. Okay?" Ivy smiled, nodded, and she began handing presents to him.

He liked the M. C. Hammer tape she'd bought him and the few clothes for school. She liked the charm bracelet he'd gotten her with money he'd collected from depositables with Barbara.

"Okay," Ivy said when all the gifts were opened. "I guess you want to know how I got in this mess."

"Oh! Wait a minute," she said, getting up. "There's one more thing I'm forgetting." She went into her room and came out with his father's old USMC gym bag. She placed it carefully on his lap.

"What's this?" he asked. The gym bag moved by itself.

"Open it and find out," she replied. "Remember what I said about Santa giving good boys what they most want and least expect? Well, Santa gave me that to give to you."

A whining sound came from the gym bag. Ivy held his breath in excitement and disbelief. He unzipped the bag and was attacked by a little black fur ball that was all tongue, paws, and cold, wet nose.

"Merry Christmas, Ivy," his mother said, tears of joy streaming down her face to match her son's, and hugged him and the squealing puppy together.

Bill Gage sat in the darkness of the living room staring at the unopened bottle of Jack Daniels on the coffee table in front of him.

He'd bought it on his way home from the Internal Affairs inquiry into the death of Wilbur Clayton. Bill had planned on opening the bottle and downing its contents in record time the second he got home, but once in the house, *Cindy's* house with the feel of her everywhere, he no longer had the overwhelming urge to lose himself in it.

He thought it was funny, the things that could make a person want to get drunk and stay drunk. When Cindy was murdered, he hadn't thought about diving into a bottle at all. He'd been too consumed with paranoia about his father and the desire for revenge. Even the prospect of testifying at the grand jury investigation into his father's case hadn't, surprisingly, made him want a drink. And today, the official hearing into his conduct in the death of Wilbur Clayton hadn't been what had made him want to drink—though he could have one in celebration since the board had determined that Bill shot in self-defense. As far as celebrating went, he could also have one to toast Sassy's getting out of the hospital. She was staying with her sister and Devin at Evelyn's.

The self-defense had been George Albert's idea. Bill hadn't tried to hide anything. He'd told the chief straight out that he'd killed Wilbur Clayton in cold blood. His explanation as to why he did it, however, wasn't as straightforward or as coherent as he would've liked. George had brushed it all aside, convincing Bill that it was self-defense. Bill didn't care and went along. Since Christmas Eve in the tunnel two weeks ago, he hadn't cared about much.

But what had made Bill want to start bumming around with his old buddy JD again was the memory of the look on the face of that black kid, Ivy Delacroix, that night in the tunnel after Bill had shot Wilbur Clayton. After he'd pulled the trigger, he had sensed someone nearby, watching. He'd turned the flashlight to see the kid looking up at him with fear and some other emotion that Bill hadn't figured out until today.

Ivy Delacroix had been called to testify at the inquiry and had sat up there and lied through his teeth, corroborating the official story without anyone's influence or coaching. Describing how Wilbur had lunged for Bill's gun, Ivy had stared at Bill—not with anger, not with fear, but with pity: the same look he'd had in the tunnel. And *that* was what had just about broken Bill.

Outside, after the hearing, Bill got Ivy alone and asked him why he'd lied. The kid had looked at him with eyes so old it was sad. "I know what it's like to want revenge that bad."

Bill blinked the tears from his eyes and looked at the phone, then back at the bottle. Back and forth. They came to rest with decision on the bottle. He picked it up, stood, and held it up for inspection. Sighing, he carried it to the entertainment center and put it into the drawer under the TV. He went to the phone, looked at it for a long moment, then picked it up, calling Evelyn to ask her to bring his kids home.

We now return control of your television set to you. . . .

—*The Outer Limits*